PRAISE for GREG KEYES

THE REIGN
"Keyes is a master of world ... ers who grow into their relatio ... ns of his Age of Unreason and his Kingdoms of Thorn and Bone fantasy series will want to get in on the ground floor of the High and Faraway series." — *Booklist*

"I liked a lot of what Keyes was doing in the novel, in terms of the story itself, the characters, and laying the groundwork for a multi-book narrative. The world where Errol awakens in his new body has a lived-in feel, a world with history and mythology of its own. . . . the story reminded me of Kate Elliott's Crown of Stars." — *SFFWorld*

"Starts in the realm of normalcy and quickly descends into the favorably bizarre and surprising . . . there was not one character that was uninteresting. The world building is epic. A magical realm that mirrors earth while residing under a curse was not only inventive but enthralling."
— *Koeur's Book Reviews*, 4.4/5 stars

THE BRIAR KING
"A wonderful tale . . . It crackles with suspense and excitement from start to finish." — Terry Brooks

"The characters in *The Briar King* absolutely brim with life . . . Keyes hooked me from the first page and I'll now be eagerly anticipating sitting down with each future volume of The Kingdoms of Thorn and Bone series."
— Charles de Lint

THE
REALM OF THE
DEATHLESS

THE HIGH AND FARAWAY BOOK THREE

THE REALM OF THE DEATHLESS

THE HIGH AND FARAWAY BOOK THREE

GREG KEYES

NIGHT SHADE BOOKS
NEW YORK

Cover illustration by Micah Epstein
Cover design by Claudia Noble

For Joyce Bowen

PART ONE:

THE BUTCHERED GIANT

ONE

THE SORCERER'S TOWER

Her father's handwriting appeared on the page as if he were writing it just now, each letter curling into existence in his distinctive style. Neither hand nor pen were present, but Aster smelled the wet ink.

Her vision blurred with tears as she remembered watching him write when she was little. How he had taught her to form the letters of the ancient script, so different from the one she was learning at school. How carefully she had tried to copy him. The smile when she got something right, the frown he gave her when her mind wandered, and the figures were ill-formed. In those days, he had been all there. Body, soul, and mind. Her father.

But then he had diminished. His memory failed, and he could not learn new things. She grew older and older, became a young woman, but he only remembered her as a little girl. She had to explain to him each day who she was. And eventually, each fifteen minutes. He had cursed the universe, and the curse caught up with him.

And now he was gone completely, and she was left with this, what was less than his ghost.

The books in her father's ancient library were all like this, blank until she opened them. There was much of interest in them: Whimsies and Adjurations, Utterances and Names. The everyday habits of unspeakable terrors, the language of flowers, poems written by no human versifier.

But none of it was what she was looking for. None of it would help her set the wrongs of a cursed world right. And nothing here told her how to bring her father back from the dead.

She sighed, rubbed her weary eyes and stood. She walked across the floor of dark, crystal-seamed stone, passed through an arch and onto a terrace. Her father's ancient dwelling was a true sorcerer's tower, a corkscrew spire thrust into the sky, and she stood near its summit.

Above the stars blazed, brightest among them the sun. But only just. It still showed a sphere, and left spots upon her eye when she looked upon it. The sky near it was deep blue, but the horizons were black. Whether the sun was shrinking or getting farther away, Aster did not know. Only that its light was steadily dwindling.

The High and Faraway was running down, like a clock with no one to wind it. And she did not know how to fix it.

She had hoped here, in her father's ancient demesne, she would discover some answers. A cure for the curse. But this had been his dwelling before he cast the fateful spell, before he met her mother, before her birth. Maybe there were no answers to be found here. But she didn't know where else to go, or who else to ask.

The only person who might have shown her the next step was her father, and he was gone, struck down by his own dark magic.

She stood there for a while, feeling the night breeze raise bumps on her arms, listening to the calls of the elder beasts that roamed the wilder lands around the castle, watching the dying sun. Everything was damp from a shower earlier, and the scents of moss and pine and granite surrounded her.

Then she turned back to the study and its books. Billy sat sleeping in one of the chairs; he'd been trying to stay up with her and failed. She didn't disturb him but retired to the little room in the corner and lay on the bed there. She would close her eyes for a few moments, she thought, and then continue her search.

She woke to someone stroking her hair. It felt familiar, and for the beat of a heart she believed it was her father before remembering it couldn't be. She cracked her eyes open, but she did not move for fear that it was some enemy in disguise. Better to let them think she was still asleep.

A woman sat on the bed next to her; with a start she realized it was Ms. Fincher, who had once been her school guidance counselor and later her father's lover. Her chin was down, and her long bangs covered her eyes.

"It's not here," Ms. Fincher whispered. "It's not here, Streya. It's in the house, back in the Reign of the Departed."

"What?" Aster said. "Ms. Fincher?"

"The Moon," she whispered. "The Sun. The Morning Star. To guide you."

Fincher's hand raised and rested on Aster's cheek. She lifted her head and looked into Aster's eyes. "Streya," she said. Only it was her father's voice.

Aster jerked awake again, sweating despite the chill in the air. It had been a dream, nothing more.

But was she awake yet? Ms. Fincher was still there.

"Ms. Fincher?" she gasped.

"Aster?" The older woman turned slowly; she lifted her head, so Aster could see her brow was furrowed. Then she quickly stood up, nearly stumbling.

"Where are we?" she asked.

"My father's demesne," Aster replied. "His castle. Remember? We came here in the silver ship?"

"Of course," Ms. Fincher said. "I was asleep . . ."

"Do you remember saying anything to me?" Aster asked. "About something not being here?"

The woman's frown deepened. "I don't think so," she said. "But it isn't, here, is it? No." She backed away a few steps. "What's happening?" she asked, her voice trembling a little.

"I don't know," Aster said. But she knew something was. Only her father called her Streya.

***

E rrol had the last watch, so when it was over, he went straight to the tower's refectory for breakfast. The sun and heavens were no longer keeping time, but something in the ancient building was. It delivered three meals a day; a breakfast, which was usually an assortment of things, a lunch of roasted meat or heavy stew, and a usually some sort of soup for supper. As with the silver ship, they never knew exactly what would appear on the long stone table. That "morning" it was a soft cheese, black bread, honey, plums, and figs. Errol thought it was improvement over the day before, which had featured small, oily fish complete with heads and tails, something like a cross between butter and blue cheese, some sort of pickle that had not started life as a cucumber, and a curiously spongy flatbread.

They had been in this place for five breakfasts; he didn't know how long it took them to get here, but it hadn't seemed like it had been that long since Haydevil had arrived with the silver ship to rescue them from the Island of the Othersun. He and his sisters had left soon after, not interested in more adventures with Errol and his friends. Errol couldn't say he blamed them.

He sat in his usual spot and picked up the goblet furnished there. He sipped it tentatively and found it to be some sort of fruit juice with a slight flavor of licorice. That wasn't too bad.

He was hungry, but decided to wait until someone joined him before digging in. Dusk had had the watch before him, so she would probably sleep for a little longer, but usually someone else was down by now.

A few minutes later, Aster arrived, alone.

"Morning," he said.

She nodded, took a seat. She looked at the food but didn't seem in a hurry to eat anything. He decided he had been polite enough and reached for some bread and cheese.

"Find anything yet?" he asked, before taking a bite. The bread tasted peppery, and the cheese was pungent but decent. He dribbled a little honey on it using the little wooden spoon in the jar, which improved it considerably.

"Maybe," she said.

"That's good."

The plums were good, but the figs were pure heaven; they took him back to when he was five, eating them off of his grandfather's tree, everything still wet with morning dew, the cicadas just starting to churr as he climbed, barefoot, into the higher branches searching for more.

"What we're looking for isn't here," she said. "It's back at my house. In Sowashee."

"Seriously?"

"I should have considered that first," she said. "It was stupid of me to seek out this place. He lived here *before* the curse. I thought I might find whatever spell he used to do it here, but now I think he made it up on the spot. Any thoughts he might have had about ending it would be back home, where we landed *after* the curse."

"Yeah," Errol said. "That does make sense. Too bad. It's comfortable here."

"You can stay if you want," she said.

"You know better than that."

Her lips turned up in that minimal little smile of hers. "Yes," she said.

"When do we go?"

"We eat," she said. "We pack, and we go."

***

T hey kept watches from an abundance of caution, but once the tower recognized Aster as being Kostye's daughter, it had been a safe enough place, so Errol hadn't put on his armor in days. The same couldn't be said of the forest outside, so after breakfast he took a basin bath and then donned his gear. It was amazing stuff; Dusk had had it made for him from the remains of the automaton his soul had once inhabited, and when he placed a piece of it against him in the appropriate place, it sort of fused to his skin. When he'd first put it on, he didn't think he could take it off, but Dusk eventually got around to telling him how to do it. The armor came with a sword made of the same stuff. He didn't know much about sword fighting, but fortunately the sword knew plenty.

"Are you clothed in there, Errol?"

None of the rooms had doors on them, but when he glanced over, he couldn't see Dusk.

"You can come in," he said. "I'm decent."

"That's not what I asked," she said.

Oh, God, she's flirting, he thought. *What do I do?* Then he realized she really might not have understood him.

"I mean yes, I'm dressed," he clarified.

"Very well," she said, stepping around the corner. Grinning. So she *had* been flirting.

She was also armored, head-to-toe except for her helmet. It was a look she pulled off exceptionally well.

"Back to the whale-roads, I guess," she said.

"Looks like it," he replied.

"It's just as well," she said. "It doesn't sit well with me to do nothing for any length of time."

"Yeah, I kind of gathered that about you," he said. "Are we ready to go?"

"I'm ready," she said. "Are you?"

"Ah," he said. "Yes, I think so. I didn't bring much in with me that I'm not wearing."

***

Delia had found the garden within hours of their arrival at the tower. It was almost as if she had known it was there, and when she saw it, she had a powerful sense of déjà vu. From what she could tell, the tower had been carved from a natural spire of rock, and though it generally grew narrower as it grew taller — like any good tower — it wasn't entirely regular or uniform. The garden jutted out from the main structure. It dropped down in three tiers connected by stairways and by a little stream; the final tier had a balcony overlooking the forest below. The stream passed through an opening in the balcony and became a water-fall. Bromeliads clung to the stone walls, and blooming vines clambered everywhere. Pines and hemlock twisted from cracks in the stone, resembling bonsai. The top terrace was mostly moss and fern, the next a meadow theme with a weeping willow shading the creek and wildflowers underfoot. The third was a small orchard with apples, pears, and peaches. It was clear to her that someone or something tended it, but she never saw anyone, and she'd spent much of her time in it since they had arrived at the castle. She thought she felt Kostye's presence her, or at least the Kostye she knew. The rest of the tower felt — well, evil.

She was surprised to find Aster already there, at the balcony.

"Aster?" she said.

"Hello Delia," she said. "I thought you would come here."

"To say goodbye," she said. "I have enjoyed this place."

"It's beautiful," Aster said. "And I know you like gardens."

"That's true."

Aster turned toward her; the little star on her forehead flickered with light.

"Do you remember anything, Delia?" she asked. "Anything from when you spoke to me last night?"

"I thought it was a dream," Delia said. "I was speaking a language I couldn't understand. The only thing I can remember now is that we're supposed to go home. Back to Sowashee."

"My father used to call me 'Streya', sometimes. Did he ever say that to you?"

"I don't think so," she said.

"But you said it," Aster pressed.

"I don't know what to tell you," Delia said. "But . . . but I have been dreaming about him."

"What kind of dreams?"

"I'll be doing something ordinary," she said. "Gardening or doing dishes —something like that. And then I'll turn and just see him. And in my dreams, it isn't strange. I don't remember that he's not supposed to be there."

"You never said anything about this," Aster said.

"Because It's normal, Aster. It's part of the grieving process. I was trained in this, you know."

"I know," Aster said. "But whatever happened two nights ago—that was more than a dream. I think he's found some way to talk to us, through you. He's trying to help us. So if . . . if he says something to you in your dreams, would you please tell me?"

"Absolutely," Delia said.

"I'll leave you alone for a few moments," Aster said. "But we need to leave soon."

"Thank you, Delia said. "I won't be long."

Aster nodded and ascended the steps toward the entrance to the gardens.

Delia sighed. She pulled down a peach and bit into it. It was lovely, not quite like the ones she knew from home; a little tarter.

She sat, savoring it, and when she was done, she gazed up at the strange sky.

"Are you here, Kostye? Are you really here?"

There was no answer. She hadn't expected one. But then a motion caught her attention. A bird in flight, out over the forest. She thought it was an owl.

Okay, Delia, she thought. *Don't read into everything. There are always birds.*

But in a place that was the stuff fairy tales were built from, you could never know.

TWO

THE ITCH

V eronica Hale had been alive, once, until she was murdered
by a man she trusted. She had been dead for decades, a
nov who enticed evil-hearted men to their deaths in the forest
pool she inhabited. In that state, she had not remembered her
life or any of the emotions that went with living. But then a
sorceress named Aster Kostyena and a boy in a wooden body
named Errol Greyson restored her memory and eventually a
semblance of life. By day she breathed and ate food, and at night
her heart ceased to beat, and her blood ran cold.

She had fallen in love with the boy.

But that was not, of course, the end of the story. She had
travelled and fought through the distorted fairy tale lands of
the Kingdoms, and along the way she had become something
else yet again. She had no word for what she was. But she was
powerful, and growing more so each day, and whether she was
mostly alive or mostly dead no longer seemed like an important question. She was, and that was enough. But traveling that
path, she had also incurred a debt, a big one. In order to save
the boy's life she made a promise to a woman named Yurena, to
serve her for a year and a day. Yurena kept her end of the deal,

and Veronica saved the boy. They fought together once again on the Island of the Othersun and saved Aster's life.

Then Veronica left Errol and his friends on the island.

When she left, she still had time; her service to Yurena would not begin for days yet. She had chosen to give Dusk her life, knowing what the result would be. Dusk would replace her in Errol's affections. Given the terms of her deal, she could not tell Errol why she had to leave. If she could, he might promise to wait for her, but he probably wouldn't. And she could no longer be content with holding herself back just to be someone's girlfriend, which was exactly what she had been doing for Errol. So it was just as well he find someone else to press his affections on. But it wasn't as easy as all that. Her heart was mixed. She remembered being the girl who had lain under the stars with him one night and shared their first kiss. It had been her first real kiss, and even if his lips were made of wood at the time, it had been almost unimaginably sweet. Errol had helped her move forward before he began holding her back, and her love for him remained. It would have been hard to spend even a few more days with him, watching him dither between loyalty to her and the hard-candy sweets he had for Dusk.

So she went, to use her last few days of freedom for herself.

There were people beneath the sea, lots of them. Seal people, dolphin people, people with fish tails and human bodies, people who looked just like those above the waves, people who looked like the creature from the black lagoon. It made sense. The Kingdoms were the real stuff from which fairy tales were made, and there were plenty of wonder stories about mermaids and such. Heck, she had been one of those things, and she had lived in thrall of an even more malignant watery creature, a Vadras. But it has just been the two of them, in an old muddy creek. Here, in these seas of the Kingdoms she found splendid cities. She came upon one, bright and full of color, with towers and domes of living coral and inhabitants so beautiful it almost hurt to look at them. Deeper she found a kingdom of people with eyes like lamps who used giant squids for mounts, and they, too, were beautiful in her sight.

There were other wonders, too. For a time she trailed a Leviathan at least a mile long. It had palm trees on its back, and a small tribe of people that lived mostly by fishing. She encountered shoals of fish that glowed like an underwater rainbow. She swam to the edge of a whirlpool with no bottom and wove her way through reefs of living crystal.

A time came when she began to feel a certain path before her, a direction she was supposed to go. She didn't think much about it but followed her instincts. She soon found herself descending deeper than she had ever gone, into depths where no light penetrated, and water was heavier than lead.

When she realized what was happening, she tried to stop, but it wasn't possible. She realized her service to Yurena had begun.

And as she slipped into those darkest reaches, she began to feel something terrible, wonderful, and above all, familiar. The Itch.

When she was very young, before she was murdered, Veronica had been taught that the body was temporary, but that the soul was immortal. Her mother had said so, and her Sunday school teacher, and the preacher.

She now knew that was exactly backwards.

Veronica knew well the Itch before murder, the life that needed scratching until it went away. The killing brought an immediate satisfaction of creature desire, but her favorite part had not been the killing, but rather the corpses the slaughter left behind. They were like inside-out reefs, sponges and worms and jellyfish floating in a tiny sea enclosed by a flimsy nest of bone and paper-fragile skin. It was the undoing of them she had loved most, the process of decay, the smooth bones freed of the rough meat that concealed their beauty. In those days she had thought of deliquescence as an obliteration, the erasure of an existence, but now she understood that life was never unraveled by death. The sequestered waters of the body were opened back to the greater currents of the world, and the dead became gardens bursting with new life and growth. Everything a person had ever been was retrieved and put to use by some swelling, squirming thing, and something new created from it. Every atom of the corpse became a part of the living world.

Except for the shining inside, the thing that left behind those bones and guts and convolutions of brain. The soul, they called it where she had grown up. That could be repurposed, too. But it could also be destroyed without leaving a trace.

She felt that death-itch now, that yearning to put an end to something, but it wasn't inside of her. It was not her own desire, although it reminded her of those lustful thoughts. It was a cold current in the water, welling up from somewhere far beneath—as if reaching for her. Hunting her. Itching for *her*.

She transformed, became a swarm of sightless krill, her thoughts spreading out in the water like a cloud. Still she descended. The cold brushed by her and was swallowed by the lightless depths, like someone stepping over her grave. For a moment, she thought of ending her journey, of trying again to return to the wan sunlight of the surface. There were a hundred other things she would rather be doing, but in the core of her, she knew she couldn't. She had made a promise. And as it turned out, a promise was a big deal.

Her mother and the preacher had told her that, too, but she had never believed it. People broke promises all the time accidentally, purposefully, by omission. Her father once promised to bring her a donut when he came home from work, and he didn't. Her mother once promised to spank her but forgot. Her Uncle Charlie and Aunt Emeline had promised to stay married, but they got divorced. She had promised not to eat a cookie before dinner, but did it anyway, and nothing at all happened.

But that was there, in the Reign of the Departed, the lusterless world where she had been born. Here, in the High and Faraway, when you made a promise of a certain kind, it was a very big deal. And she had made a big one, to that strange and ancient queen, and although in the back of her mind she had always meant to betray that promise, it simply wasn't possible. The magic bands wrought by her words were pulling her here, to this deep, this hole in the bottom of the world. And there was nothing she could do about it.

This was not the place where she had met Yurena before, or if it was, it had become somehow deeper. That was hardly surprising; the High and Faraway was a changeable place, now more so than ever. It felt to her as if the whole universe was pulling apart, and maybe it was. Maybe, like mortal bodies, worlds could also lose the light inside of them, decay, become the food of future worlds. Maybe that wouldn't be so bad.

Except that she had friends in this world, and she hadn't had friends in a long time. As imperfect as they were, she wasn't ready to let them go completely.

But for now, she had made a promise.

The pull stopped. She felt something stir. She felt a question.

I've come back, Yurena, she said. *To serve you for a year and a day. Like I said I would.*

For a moment there was no reply, but then she thought the darkness became more grey than black. She swam forward, straining to see. She became herself again, or at least something like her human form, albeit one that could survive in these crushing depths.

Shapes appeared in the grey, and then a bit of color. And someone.

Yurena — the monster, or goddess — the snake/fish woman — wasn't there. But the face was familiar. And the place. Veronica was in a small, warm room, near a little table with a crystal dish of hard candy that looked like rubies, emeralds, and sapphires. Behind that was a window with white curtains, and a glimpse of a green garden beyond. To her right was an old black-and-white TV, with rabbit ears modified with tinfoil, and a rocking chair with a woman in it. Her face was framed in long grey hair worked up in a bun and her skin was like wrinkled paper. She peered at Veronica with piercing blue eyes.

"Grandma?" she whispered.

The old woman shook her head no.

"I am the one you made your promise to," she said. "Or part of what once was her."

"Yurena?"

The woman shrugged. "Many names. Many faces. Although I am forgetting all of them."

"Why do you look like my grandmother? Why does this look like her parlor?"

"I didn't choose this appearance," the woman said. "You did. Maybe it was easiest. I don't know. I'm growing thinner and thinner, child."

"Well," Veronica said. "I'm here to do my time. What am I to do?"

The woman grimaced. "I had plans for you," she said. "Schemes, some would say. I thought I would be stronger now, rather than weaker. But our gamble did not pay off."

Veronica narrowed her eyes. She remembered the Island of the Othersun, Dusk's mother, the Queen, the forms she had taken before the end.

"You're not just Yurena, are you?" she said. "You're the queen, too, right? Dusk's mother. You planned to kill Aster and end the curse. But we stopped you."

"That one," the one woman said. "Yes, she was one of us. My daughter, my cousin, my granddaughter, myself. Images in mirrors, through a crystal, all just bits and pieces. We could not end the curse. We never could have. It began too high, and too far away."

"Aster's dad made the curse, I thought."

The woman shook her head. "No. The curse made him. Higher, further away, nearer the beginning. It happened there, and we are drawn into imitation of it. We dance on the stage, that is all. We tell the story again and again with the motions of our lives. Until the stage itself breaks."

"This is getting awfully philosophical," Veronica said. "I'm supposed to do something for you. Just tell me what it is so I can get on with it or let me go." She reached over and took one of the candies, a bright red one, and popped it into her mouth. It tasted exactly like nothing.

The old woman's eyes fixed on her.

"I will tell you a story," she said.

"Great," Veronica said. "More stories. Is this one true?"

"All stories hold some truth, or they wouldn't be told," the old woman said.

"Uh-huh," Veronica said. "Like the time I broke Grandma's window and I told everyone Cousin Gary did it?"

"The truth was that the window was broken," the old woman said. "The more important truth to you at the time was that you didn't want to be punished."

"The truth was I did it and Gary didn't. So I get the sense of what you're saying. I expect you are about to tell me some kind of nonsense."

"My power is diminished," the old woman snapped, her blue eyes darkening to almost black. "It isn't gone. You will listen."

She sounded just like Grandma, and Veronica immediately felt her salt settle a little.

"Yes, ma'am," she said.

The woman reached over and turned on the television. The screen lit up with electronic snow, but after a moment an image began to form. It looked familiar.

The single channel their television picked up showed horror and monster movies late at night. She wasn't supposed to watch them, but one night, after everyone was asleep, she'd gone back to the living room, turned on the TV, and put the sound almost all the way down. This was the movie that had been playing that night. It had given her nightmares, but the very next time she saw a chance to watch the Midnight Feature, she had taken it.

It was about a giant monster. It stood on two legs like a man, but it was also scaly like a lizard, and had big horns like a bull. It was stomping on buildings and smashing army tanks. It looked really fake, obviously a guy in a suit running around in a toy-sized city. But she hadn't seen it that way when she was little. She'd been scared of the monster, which she now remembered had something to do with the giants mentioned in the Bible.

"There was a person," the woman said. "Neither male nor female, neither human nor beast. Some say they had the form of a giant, or a bull, or a serpent. But whatever form they took, they were the foundation, the stuff of the world. Everything."

The channel on the TV started changed. Now the monster was a dragon, breathing fire, and then it looked like a man, then a giant spider. Some were from movies she had seen; others weren't.

It went back to the first one, the giant horned monster. A bomb exploded on it, and when the dust cleared it had fallen over. The TV switched again, to a giant white baboon falling off of a tall building and splattering on the ground. In the next scene it was the reptilian giant again, surrounded by army men and workers, using chainsaws and cranes to cut the monster into pieces. That part, she did not remember from the movie; it had ended when the monster died.

The old woman kept narrating.

"But then that person died, or was murdered, or was sacrificed, and they were slaughtered out into parts. And from those pieces, the world was made. From their blood, the seas and lakes, from their veins streams and rivers, from their bones the spines of mountains, from their skull the sky, from their eyes the sun and moon and stars and from their mind — from their mind, the spirits of us all. The elumiris that inhabits matter and makes it alive."

Veronica stared at the woman, then back at the television. It didn't show the monster anymore. In fact, she didn't know what she was seeing. Like the earlier images, it was in black and white, but it was all shaky, hard to focus on. Like the camera was mounted on something moving extremely fast. There were swirls and blobs of white and grey and she thought that they might be clouds. But then a shape appeared, a curve against darkness, and now she understood she was looking down through clouds, with glimpses of continents and seas. Since it was all black and white it was hard to sort out, but more details emerged from chaos, and she understood she was seeing the Earth from space. Then the camera started to turn, toward something brighter and brighter. For an instant she saw the globe of the world, with the sun rising at its edge, and then everything was blindingly white.

The TV blinked off. The old woman didn't say anything.

"That's weird," Veronica said, after a while. "About the monster being cut up. I saw that movie, and that isn't what happened at the end. But on the way down here I was just thinking. How everything that dies becomes something else, how when a body rots it gives food and life to all of these other things. . . ."

"I know what you were thinking," the old woman said. "That is why I told you this story."

"Huh," she said. "I guess I don't get it. Who killed the giant? Who cut him up? God?"

"There are different stories about that. Some say it was suicide — they did it to themselves. Others say that one sibling killed another, or that its children or a hunter did the deed. That is all beside the point. The point is that this person was unmade to build the world we know. The High and Faraway, the Reign of the Departed, all of it. Now that ancient creature wishes to be made again."

"Oh," Veronica said. "It wants its parts back. Its skull, its eyes, its bones, its mind. Its soul. So, everything. And all of us."

"Yes," the old woman said. "They have wanted that for an exceedingly long time. From the beginning, in fact. But they were never able to act. Now they can."

"So to put themselves back together," Veronica said, "they have to tear all of this apart. All of *us* apart."

"Yes."

"That's a crazy story," she said. "Is it true?"

"As I said — "

"No," Veronica said. "No nonsense. Did it happen? Is it happening?"

"The truth is, the world is coming apart," the old woman said. "You have seen the signs of it yourself. The other truth is someone wants it to happen. Someone is helping it along. As for the details . . ." she frowned. "I forget."

"So this . . . person," Veronica said. "I'm supposed to fight him now, or what?"

"It has me in its hand," the woman whispered. "And soon it will close its fist. And it wants you. It needs you." Her eyes widened. Her mouth worked and her chest heaved as if she was having trouble breathing.

"What's wrong?" Veronica said.

"It's a trap," she said. "They used me to lure you here. You must flee. They must not have you."

"But what . . ."

Images began flickering on the TV again, these much clearer, less fuzzy than the last. A giant monster, tearing up a city, a strange jungle, a city of stone, another giant, this one cut in half and hanging in a cave, still alive, mountains, deserts . . . a young man's face, still in death.

She knew the face.

"Wait," she said. "Go back. That's Errol."

But the picture kept changing.

"Is he dead?" she demanded. "Tell me! Is Errol dead?"

"Not yet," the old woman said. "But he dies."

"You mean he might die," she said. "Like last time. But I can save him."

"No," she said, as the images moved so quickly, they became a blur. "He dies."

"Liar!" Veronica screamed.

Then something swallowed the old woman, the TV, everything. There was no mouth or teeth, nothing like that; more like the wall behind them became a hole and they fell into it.

And then Veronica felt it pulling her.

No! She screamed into the now lightless depths.

And she swam, as the whole dark of the universe came after her. The *Itch*.

But she was swift, and in time she outdistanced her enemy. She reviewed and ordered the images in her head, the things she had seen on the woman's television. They didn't tell her everything; but she knew for certain that she wasn't done with Errol and the others yet.

So she visited a friend, and she asked a favor. Then she went in search of the enemy.

THREE

HOMECOMING

To Delia Fincher, the real world didn't feel real anymore.

It all seemed normal enough; the sun was its usual size, not a fading mote in an ever-darker heaven. The sky was blue; perfectly reasonable white clouds drifted lazily across it. Whatever end-of-the-world weirdness was happening in the High and Faraway, the so-called "Reign of the Departed" seemed untouched by it.

Yet the colors seemed a little off, the sounds muffled. The breeze stank of papermill and diesel. The pines were green as always, but hardwoods clawed at the sky with leafless limbs. The atmosphere was chilly and damp. December, maybe, or February. The shoulder of winter. She had been gone a long time. But it was all as she remembered it. It just didn't seem *real*. It was like staring at the department-store knock-off version of the *Mona Lisa* after just having seen the real thing.

"I don't like this place," Billy said.

"Maybe you should go back," Aster said. "It may not be a good place for you."

Billy was a giant; Delia had seen him grow to hundreds of feet tall, but now he was of human height. His normally dark skin was paler than usual. People like Billy didn't exist here; what if Billy couldn't either?

"No," he said. "I'll stay with you. I'll be okay."

It had been a long trip home from Kostye's castle. How far, Delia could not say for certain. The shrinking sun did not move to mark the days. The seasons differed from place to place but did not change in cycles. Aster had built a large hourglass and calibrated it with her heartbeat, and that gave them a rough count of time. According to that, the trip had lasted no more than a week, give or take a day, and she trusted Aster's competence in these things. But it felt to her more like months or even a year they had sailed on the silver boat through all sorts of seas, until at last they reached the place Aster called the Pale, and from there they went on foot through forest and marsh, until the trees and plants resembled those she had grown up with, until pristine woodland gave way to beaten-up forest littered with rusting cans, barbed wire fence and pasture, and finally paved roads. High-flying jets left contrails across the sky.

The "real" world.

They emerged from a pine plantation onto an old, cracked, two-lane highway. She knew where they were — less than half a mile from little house she had once shared with her ex-husband. Home. She quickened her pace.

"Hang on," Errol said, putting his hand on her shoulder, pulling her back into the edge of the woods. "Car."

She heard it now, and for a moment was puzzled by Errol's reaction. Then she got it.

"Oh," she said. "Right." She looked at the others.

Dusk and Errol had left their armor and swords on the ship, but even so, they were all dressed as if they had just come from a renaissance fair. Here in rural Okatibee County they would certainly be noticed, and at least three of them were wanted by the police.

They withdrew into the woods and watched the car go by. The driver was a man with grey hair, another sign they were back in the realm of the normal. In the Kingdoms all of the adults were missing; transformed into beasts or stone or simply vanished. Some of the children left behind were now young adults, but none were old enough to have grey hair.

When the vehicle had passed, they resumed walking. The road wasn't a busy one; they only had to hide once more before reaching her house.

The key was still where she had left it, in a little box in the rose bed. She stopped at the front door to read the notice there that the bank was repossessing the house in a matter of days. She hadn't been able to make the payments from The Kingdoms.

She opened the door and ushered the others in. There was no electricity—that bill was also unpaid—but it was still light outside, and the little house had plenty of windows. Once she pulled back the shades things were bright enough.

To her relief, her car was still in the carport.

She made them a meal of canned ham and beans, with saltine crackers for bread. The water was still on, so they had that to drink.

Dusk looked dubiously at the food but began eating anyway.

"Thank you for the meal," she said. "It is good."

"It's not," Delia said. "But it's the best I can do out of the pantry. I'm not a great cook, but I can do better than this."

"It's great," Errol said. "I practically grew up on stuff like this. Mom didn't cook that much to begin with, and after dad died, I mostly had to fend for myself. I remember this one Thanksgiving . . ."

Delia studied Errol as he held forth. As his school counselor, she had tried to talk to him after his father died, but he'd been completely closed, unable to speak about his father at all. That was hardly a surprise; Southern boys weren't taught to share their feelings; they were taught to suck it up and soldier on. Errol had soldiered on for about two years and then attempted suicide. Looking at him now, her old instincts were kicking in; she found herself trying to gauge the young man's expression. But as he told the story of his lonely Thanksgiving meal of tinned corned beef and potato chips, he didn't seem sad, or angry. He was just talking to his friends. He seemed . . . okay.

"I like it," Billy said, when Errol finished.

"You like everything," Aster said.

"Giants don't eat," Billy explained. "At least, not like this. It's why we become little, sometimes. Every century or so. So we can taste food, feel heat and cold, and —uh, touch. Laugh." He glanced at Aster, who blushed a little.

"I once ate a half-rotten rat," Dusk said.

"That's disgusting," Errol said.

She shrugged. "I was able to cook it. It had a quality like certain cheeses."

"This story is not getting better," Errol said. "So when we've eaten what is thankfully not rotten rat cheese, what do we do next?"

"We go to my house," Aster said. "We get the astrarium, and from there — we figure it out."

"Your house is seven or eight miles from here," Delia said. "We'll need to take my car."

"I can drive," Aster said. "If you don't want to go."

"Thank you," Delia said. "I think I will take you up on that. I have some thinking to do."

"Are you going to stay?" Errol asked. "After, I mean?"

She shrugged. "I don't know. That's part of what I have to think about. The police will have a lot of questions for me. I've been a missing person for some time now, and Kostye and David are still missing. And Aster, and even you for that matter, even though that happened after I was gone. There will be suspicions. But there's no proof I did anything wrong, because I didn't. I probably won't get my job back, but I still have some savings." She tried to smile. The fact was, she didn't have the slightest inkling what she wanted to do now. Except be alone, in her little house, with her things. As soon as possible.

She looked them over. They were still dressed like the cast of a Robin Hood film.

"You'll need to change," she said. "Dusk, Aster, I think you can wear some of my old clothes." She looked at the boys. "You two . . ." she trailed off, then went to her closet. She found a denim dress for Aster and jeans and blouse that ought to fit Dusk. Then she reached up high and brought down a cardboard box.

Scott had left a few things. She'd put them away, imagining she would take them to Goodwill, but had never gotten around to it. She selected a pair of overalls she'd bought him for the garden, but which he'd never worn, a pair of khakis, a couple of t-shirts, and a plaid, long-sleeved shirt. The khakis fit Billy pretty well. The overalls were a little big on Errol, but they would do.

The stars on Aster's and Dusk's foreheads presented a bit of a problem. She remembered she had an old baseball cap someplace but wasn't able to find it.

But when she returned to the living room, everyone was changed, and neither girl had a visible birthmark.

"How did you do that?" she asked, pointing at Aster's forehead.

"I can work really little glamours here," Aster said. "It's a weaker version of the spell my dad used to keep my star hidden all of those years." She smiled thinly. "So I guess we're ready. I'm sorry I got you dragged into all of this, Ms. Fincher."

She shrugged. It was hard to sort out her feelings on that. In fact, she was aware she had been avoiding doing so. She'd made a home visit to Aster's house, because she suspected the girl's father was either unwell or absent entirely. David Watkins, a teacher at the school, had come with her. When they arrived, they found Aster's father, Kostye, raving drunk. Aster had magically conscripted Delia to look after him while she and her friends went off in search of an elixir to heal Kostye's memory. But before they returned, Dusk had shown up and forced her to conspire in the pretense that *she* was Aster in order to get Kostye to return to the Kingdoms.

Aster was to blame for everything that had happened since. But she had been working inside of a context that Delia mostly now understood.

"You should have asked for my help instead of forcing it," Delia said.

"I know," Aster admitted. But you wouldn't have."

"We'll never know, will we?" Delia said. "But it hardly matters now what decisions you made then. That's all done and can't be taken back. But you can make better decisions in the future."

"I can try," Aster said. She glanced around at the others. "I owe Errol an apology as well."

"I wouldn't be alive if you hadn't sucked me into all of this," Errol said. "So I think I'm good."

"Anyway," Delia said. "Be careful. Errol and Dusk are probably wanted for assault, given how you left here the last time."

"Yeah," Errol said. "Probably."

"Wait," Aster said. "I hate to ask for anything else. But do you have a clock, or a watch? A mechanical one, the kind you wind up? So when we go back to the Kingdoms, we'll have a better way of keeping time."

"Yes," Delia said. "There's one in the sunroom. I never bother to wind it, because I got a digital clock a while back."

"May I have it?"

Delia nodded. She went into the little room with its southern exposure. All of the potted plants were dead, which was a bit depressing. But the clock was there, a little alarm clock she'd gotten for Christmas when she was ten. She had asked for it specifically, picking it out of a Wishbook. It was gold, with a black face and hands and numbers coated in radium, so it glowed in the dark. She'd slept with it next to her pillow; the ticking lulled her to sleep.

As she picked it up, she had second thoughts. As a girl she had loved this thing. Sure, she didn't use it anymore. Maybe she had another timepiece, an old watch or something that would do.

She sighed and decided it didn't matter. It was just a thing. If it could be of some help to Aster and the others, why should she hold on to it?

Aster brightened when she saw it.

"This is perfect," she said. "You don't mind?"

"No," Delia said. "But take care of it. It keeps good time. Do you know how to wind a clock like that?"

"Yes," Aster said. "I do."

They stood there for a moment, and then hugged awkwardly. Their relationship had been strange enough when it had been that of school counselor and student, more so when it became that of captive and captor. Now she was—well, sort of Aster's stepmother. She and Kostye had never married, but whatever their relationship had been, it was in that ballpark.

And whatever it was, it was now over. Or would be soon.

"Listen," she said. "If for some reason you can't bring the car back, don't worry about it. This isn't that big a community. Wherever you leave it, it'll get back to me."

"We'll bring it back," Aster said, as she stepped back. "Who knows? You might decide to go back with us."

"I might," Delia agreed.

Aster nodded. "Okay," she said to the others.

They filed out the side door in the kitchen, and few moments later, she heard the car start up and roll down the driveway.

She did the dishes in cold water, wondering if she should call someone. Jenny or Abby or John. She should let them know she was alright. But then they would come over, and the word would get around. Her mother and father would be all over her. The police would come and ask questions. She had last been seen leaving the school where she worked with David Watkins. They would want to know where he was, where *she* had been for months or years or however long it had been. The principal and school secretary had known they were going to Aster's house. They would want to know about Aster—who had broken out of jail, and her father, and Errol, and the strange young woman who had assaulted and battered her way out of Laurel Grove.

Delia didn't have answers to any of those questions that the police would find acceptable. That was her problem, and she didn't want to spread it around. Better to wait until Aster, Errol, and the others were gone again, returned to the Kingdoms, and beyond the reach of Sowashee law.

She opened the back door, pushed open the screen, and walked down the red brick steps. Her garden was unkempt, but in better shape than she had feared. She found the hose and watered as the sun went down. Then she sat in the old metal sliding chair she'd picked up at a yard sale. Its familiar grating as she pushed the ground with her feet comforted her a little. Everything else seemed out of place.

I should be happy to be home, she thought. But she wasn't. She felt as she had left things unfinished; that Kostye would have wanted her to stay with Aster, help her end the curse. But what help could she be? She wasn't a warrior or a witch. She was just plain, mundane Delia. She had nothing to contribute. She was a burden to the others, not a help.

Over the metallic squeak of the sliding chair, she noticed a faint clicking whir, a little like a cicada, but deeper. She glanced around, wondering what it could be, but her yard was now crowded with shadows. Maybe the sound was coming from the Severs' house, but that was a few hundred yards down the road. This sounded close.

She got up to go into the house. A shadow stepped from beneath the pear tree.

She ran. It felt involuntary, as if she wasn't really in control of her body. She yanked the screen open, darted over the open threshold, then slammed the wooden door shut and locked it. She ran to the kitchen and pulled a knife from the block on the counter and backed up against the fridge.

What had she seen? A man? Some kind of animal? She'd only had a glimpse of something dark and moving. Or maybe it was just an illusion, a trick of the fading light.

She heard the screen door creak open. Then the doorknob on the back door tried to turn. She heard the chittering sound, muffled through the wood. Then nothing.

Until something slammed into the door and wood splintered. She ran for the front door, still gripping the knife, as something hit the back door a second time and it flew open.

A moment later she was sprinting down her driveway. She made it to the highway, but it was dark, with no cars in sight. No help to flag down.

She turned back and saw it coming.

Or him. It was a man with narrow shoulders and a receding hairline. Garret Wilcox, from down the road.

"Garret," she said. "What are you doing?"

Garret slowed but didn't stop.

"Delia?" He said. "Is that you? I thought someone broke into your place."

"It's just me," she said. "I'm back."

"Okay," he said. But he kept coming.

"What were you doing around here anyway?" She asked.

"Just checking in on the place," he said. "I've had to run some vagabonds off. Where have you been?"

"Could you stay there?" Delia said. "Don't come any closer."

"Why?" he said. "I don't mean you any harm."

"Stop!" She yelled, holding the knife out.

"Okay!" he said. He was only a few yards away. "Just calm down. I'm sorry about the door."

Her breathing slowed a little.

Headlights suddenly shown from behind her as a car came around the curve; it lit Garret fully. She saw his eyes, and knew it was not really Garrett.

He lunged forward and she scrambled back, waving the knife, but he didn't seem to notice.

"Hey!" Someone yelled behind her.

It was Errol.

The thing that looked like Garret stopped. Then he spun around and ran.

She turned and saw Errol running toward her. Dusk and Billy only a few feet behind.

"Ms. Fincher," Errol said. "Are you okay? Who was that?"

"Should we pursue him?" Dusk asked.

"No," she said. "No, I don't think so. He—did you see him?"

"Didn't get a good look," Errol said.

"He was in my garden," she said. "He kicked in my back door. I . . . I don't think he was human."

"No," Billy said. "He wasn't."

She looked back at the house. All doubts were gone. This was not her house now. This was no place for her.

"Can we go somewhere else?" she asked.

"Sure," Errol said. "I don't know where, but okay."

"Did you get what you came for?" She asked him.

"No," Aster answered. "My house has been sold. Everything in it is gone."

FOUR
ANOTHER'S TREASURE

ow that she knew it, Veronica felt the Itch everywhere. She saw it, too sometimes, like colorless seams running through the earth, the sky, the waters. She changed shape and nature, exploring the contours of it, until she saw that the stuff wasn't so much threads or seam or lines, but more like roots; they spread everywhere, they cracked the world the way sidewalks buckled up near oak trees. Or were they veins or sinews, the parts of the dead giant trying to grow again, to take hold inside of its own corpse?

Whatever they were, she suspected they had a common source. So she set out to find that.

She came to another undersea kingdom, but here the roots had taken hold, and she found it hollowed-out, bereft of life. She happened upon whale graveyards and schools of what appeared to be fish, but which no longer were.

Still further, and she became uncertain she was in water any longer; the transition happened slowly, but eventually she was walking instead of swimming. Here the roots became fewer but thicker, as if she was approaching the tree from which they sprang; except that the tendrils reached out in all directions.

Eventually she could go no farther without entering the Itch itself, so she stopped. She waited.

And eventually something came. A sort of impression of a man, or something that was trying to remember what a man looked like and not doing such a respectable job of it.

"I thought we'd lost you," It said. "But you've come to me. So you must sense it."

"I'm only trying to figure out what you are," Veronica said. "And how best to kill you."

"I'm already dead," the thing said. "Like you."

"I'm not dead anymore," Veronica said.

"You'd like to think so," the man said. "And yes, you have more of a seeming of life about you. But you are what you are."

"I am not a *nov*."

"No," It said. "No, you are so much more than that. Deeper, stronger than any such creature. But you are still a part of us. Of me. You must know this. And you must know that in time, you will come to me."

Veronica caught on then. She wagged her index finger at his face.

"I know you," she said. "You're the Raggedy Man. The bad, bad man that murdered me."

"He is here," the Raggedy Man said. "He is part of me. A piece come home. I am much more than I was, but there are still parts missing. And you are one of them."

"Did you enjoy being eaten by a shark?" she asked. "I sure enjoyed watching it."

"And yet here he is," he replied. "Here *we* are. We can be broken into fragments. We can be hidden away from each other. But we can't be destroyed."

"Uh-huh," Veronica said. "So you're just collecting the pieces to work your little jigsaw puzzle?"

"What?"

"My mom did jigsaw puzzles," Veronica said. "Sometimes I helped her. One time we did a big one of all these ships in a harbor. And we couldn't find the last piece. It drove my mom crazy, that one hole in that beautiful picture. She looked everywhere for that piece. But she never found it. And you know what? She had to get over it. And so do you, you piece of trash, because I am never going to come in there with you."

"Not even to save Errol?"

The image of Errol, dead, flashed again through her mind. It figured they would try to use him to get to her. She had to put that notion to rest. She couldn't let the Raggedy Man think had had an edge over her.

"I've done my part for him," she said. "He's on his own now."

"You belong here."

Thing was, he was right about that. She felt it in her bones. This was the place that had called ever since Aster and Errol had stolen her away from the Creek Man. This was where she could be what she really was, what she was meant to be. Every longing, every hunger she had ever felt came back, and if she went another step or two, she could indulge them all.

He can't make me, she thought, *or he already would have.*

But he didn't have to. She was already here, and she was only a single motion from finishing her journey. Trembling, she took a step forward.

No.

It was like ripping off a band-aid, or maybe more like a wolf chewing off its paw to escape a trap, but then she was rushing away, a stream of water, a school of fish, a dolphin, breaking the surface and feeling the air on her skin. The Itch grew weaker, but it did not fade entirely. It stayed there, at the top of her spine.

I can't do this alone, she knew. *Next time I will fail.*

So she searched the currents, she found a trail, and she began to follow it.

***

M s. Fincher, Errol had learned, was good at shaking things off. She was probably the most practical person he had ever met. For her, freaking out was a waste of time; she usually put her mind straight to finding a solution. He admired that about her.

So he wasn't surprised that she immediately moved from the shock of the attack to figuring out what was going on. She reversed her decision on leaving her house right away. She said they all needed sleep and a place to start from in the morning. They set a watch, just as if they were still in the Kingdoms.

His watch came right after Dusk's, and she did not leave right away. Instead, she paced to the window, looking like a caged tiger.

"Something the matter?" he asked.

"I don't know what I'm doing, Errol," she said.

"I don't know what you mean."

"For as long as I can remember, I always knew my purpose," she said. "I set the point of my arrow toward a target, and I followed it. I was always quite certain of my actions."

"Sure," Errol said, thinking that was an understatement.

Maybe she sensed something in his tone.

"I have apologized for all that," she said.

"I know," he said. "I didn't mean to imply anything."

She shrugged.

"Look," Errol said. "Before, you were trying to end the curse, right? I mean you were also trying to win a civil war against your siblings and all that, but we're still trying to, you know, fix the world. So your purpose hasn't changed."

She frowned and looked out the window.

"Oh, wait," he said. "It's because you aren't in charge."

She sighed. "You could put it that way," she said. "Aster undoubtedly knows more of this than I do. Our chances are best following her instincts. But I am unused to this. And thus far our meandering feels . . . aimless. There are other things I could be doing."

"Such as?"

"Hunting down my brothers and sisters and making them pay for their perfidy. Force them to tell me what they know."

"Oh," he said. "That is a plan. And I can't say that some of them don't deserve it. But if you feel that way why not ... why not do it?"

"I might yet," she said, not looking at him. Then she went to the couch and lay down.

***

The next morning, as promised, Ms. Fincher got busy on the phone. Hers was cut off, of course, so they drove to a convenience store in the next county, where hopefully no one would recognize her, and used the payphone there.

Aster's house and been repossessed by the bank only a week before; everything in it had been auctioned. Ms. Fincher discovered that most of the stuff had been purchased by a single buyer—Grandma's Chest, a junk and antique store in the Old Mall.

When Errol was younger, The Old Mall was the place to be. Everything about it was shiny, the stores were colorful and clean. He'd spent entire days there hanging out with his friends. They would watch a movie at the theater, play video games in the arcade, laugh at stuff in the novelty store, eat tacos or fried chicken sandwiches and drink orange-flavored milkshakes.

That was before the New Mall was built.

The faded, neglected façade of the Old Mall was depressing, but inside was much worse. They entered what had once been the department store where he'd picked out birthday presents for his friends, where before each school year his mom dragged him to get new clothes and tennis shoes. Where his dad bought him his first real suit.

Now it was a dingy bargain store with bins of plastic crap and cheap, "slightly" defective clothing in bins marked with prices mostly in the single digits. Only half of the fluorescent tubes that lit the place were still working, and of those that were, several flickered fitfully.

The long central hall of the shopping center was now lit only by skylights; wild plants pushed up from what had once been a fountain, straining toward the sky. Old people walked back and forth the length of the place in their sneakers, getting their daily exercise. The walls had been painted with festive scenes in places, in an attempt to rebrand the mall as a "community square." For a year or so there had been free concerts and dances and an indoor carnival. But now those murals were grimy and faded and the contrived parties existed — like so much else in Sowashee — only in memory.

Most of the stores were shuttered and dark. But where the record store had once been, the lights were on. A sign hand-painted with folksy letters identified it as Grandma's Chest. Below the letters was a painting of a busty older lady.

The greying, sallow-faced woman at the counter glanced up at them as they entered. She wore a salmon velour shirt with two puppies on it and pants to match. She had dark eyes, so dark he could hardly see her pupils. Her gaze picked across Billy before lingering on Errol. He knew the look. Like she was expecting one or both of them to pocket something. What, he could not imagine. Most everything was too big to steal — furniture, mostly, some antique but most just old. Maybe she worried he was interested in shoplifting porcelain figurines of men with ponytails in blue housecoats or monkeys made from coconut husks.

"Looking for anything in particular?" the lady asked.

"Just browsing," Ms. Fincher said.

"Well if you have any questions, let me know," she said.

Ms. Fincher nodded, and they all moved deeper into the store. Errol was a little surprised by how many people were already in the junk shop. All were older than Ms. Fincher, and some were really old. It was weird to see, after so much time in the Kingdoms, where anyone over sixteen or so had been disappeared in one way or another. It made him think again about what he had learned about the world of his birth—that it was the last stop in a long slide toward oblivion. Maybe that was why it hadn't been affected the way the Kingdoms had; everyone here was already a few wrong breaths from being permanently dead.

Beside him, Dusk touched a stack of old LP records, making a puzzled face at the art on the cover of the top one. She picked it up.

"That ax is absurdly large," she said. "It would never serve as a proper weapon, no matter how muscular the wielder."

"It's not supposed to be realistic," Errol said. "It's just an album cover."

"What is an album?" Dusk asked. "Some sort of farce, or comedy?"

"Music," he replied.

She frowned at the picture, shrugged, and put the album back. "What sort of place is this?" she asked.

"They sell old stuff," Errol said. "Things no one wants anymore."

"Why should anyone buy something another person discarded?" she asked.

"Well, they say one man's junk is another man's treasure," he said.

"Treasure is always treasure," she said. "Even if someone is foolish enough to discard it. And junk—"

"Yeah," he said.

"I know treasure when I see it," Dusk said. "I understand its value."

Oh, he thought. She wasn't talking about the stuff in Grandma's Chest, was she? Or was she? Crap, he hated it when he had to figure out what someone meant. But Dusk —she didn't usually beat around the bush. It wasn't her style.

Then she took his hand. It made him jump a little, but then he curled his fingers into hers, feeling the hard callouses on her palm. Warmth spread up his arm.

"Are you still thinking of her?" Dusk asked.

He didn't have to ask who she meant. Veronica.

"Umm," he said. "I wasn't."

"I meant in general," she said. "Is your heart still given?"

And that was the problem. He didn't know the answer to that. But it was clear she wanted one. At this point she probably deserved one. Veronica had been gone for a while now, with no explanation. From what he could tell that whole thing was over.

Dusk was—amazing. At one point he'd thought she was everything he desired. Now he sort of had her, if he wanted. But he felt guilty about his feelings, even now, with Veronica gone. But there was more to it than that. If you were in love with someone, and they were in love with you—well, it usually *went* somewhere. You either broke up or you moved on.

Dusk was a warrior and a princess of an ancient kingdom. She was not someone to be trifled with, and he knew that first-hand. Moving on with someone like Dusk—he wasn't certain about everything that entailed. But he was pretty sure there wasn't a big space between necking a little bit and marriage. Not for her, anyway. So if he actually did what he wanted, pulled her out of sight and started kissing her—he felt like they would be on that path. And with the universe and everything ending, getting married and all of that seemed really—complicated, and maybe pointless. So the risk was that they would get all hot and heavy and then break up. After Lisa and then Veronica, he really, really wasn't ready to do that again.

But he couldn't say all of that. At the same time, he didn't want to lie to her.

"No," he said. "My heart isn't . . . given. It's beaten up. It needs a rest."

She looked slightly vexed. "You don't trust me," she said. "With your heart. I understand. I did betray you once."

"It's not that," he said, remembering what she meant, the time she had cut his leg off. And Veronica's head. "Okay, maybe it's a little that."

"And this is why you haven't kissed me again?"

"No," he said, all the logical stuff he'd been thinking dissolving like a sandcastle before an incoming tide. "That's just because I'm stupid."

"I may not be very good at it," she said. "I haven't had much practice."

They weren't walking anymore. Somehow, they were facing each other, both hands clasped.

"No, you're—"

He knew she was going to do it. He could have tried to stop her, but of course he didn't really want to.

"Errol!" Someone shouted. Aster, in some other part of the store.

His lips parted from Dusk's, but their gazes stayed connected.

"Errol," she said, softly. "Last night you asked why I don't strike out on my own to search from my siblings. Do I really have to say?"

It was too much. He didn't have anything to say back to her.

"Aster's found something," he said. "I think we'd better go."

***

"Oh, crap," Errol said.

The back corner of the store was crammed with a bunch of stuff he recognized from Aster's house. A lot of it was furniture. But that wasn't what had stopped him in his tracks.

"It looks like you, Errol," Dusk said. "When we first met. Not exactly . . . "

"Yeah," he said. His mouth felt dry.

They were staring at rough model of a man, built of wood, wire and various scraps of metal. It was articulated like a human-sized puppet, but there were no strings.

"Oh, that," Aster said, from nearby. "Yeah, that was an earlier model. Errol got the improved version."

The main difference was the face. The automaton Aster had summoned his soul to animate had been carved to look something like him. This thing's face was as blank as that of a crash-test dummy.

"Anyway," Aster said. "That's not what we're here for. This is."

His gaze shifted over.

"I remember that," he said. He had only seen it once, in Aster's workshop. It resembled a picture frame, but it was several inches deep, a shallow box. It was hanging on the shop wall, just as it had been on the wall back in Aster's house.

Behind the glass was something like a clock, with lots of gears. In Aster's house, it had been running, so the golden sun, the silver moon, and one little shining star had moved in an elaborate dance. Now the two disks and the jagged representation of a star were still.

"The Sun, the Moon, the Morning Star," Dusk murmured.

"This is it," Delia confirmed. "I . . . don't know how I know."

"Twenty dollars," Aster said, reading the little white tag on the thing. She sounded cross.

"Is that too much?" Billy asked.

"My father built this," Aster said. "It's worth far more."

"I'm sure it is," Delia said. "But do you have twenty dollars? I don't. They don't take credit cards here, if mine are even still good, which I doubt."

Aster shrugged. "I think I can work something out. If one of you guys can carry it."

Billy lifted the thing off the wall. Errol wondered how heavy it was; Billy seemed to be straining, which was unusual. He wasn't a giant right now, but he was strong guy, even like this.

They made their way back to the front of the store, where the lady was still watching them suspiciously. He noticed the other people in the shop were also looking at them, apparently curious why so many young people were in here. It was morning, and probably a school day, but Errol figured all of them could pass as old enough to be out of high school.

Maybe it was their purchase that was drawing so much attention. It was fairly weird.

As they reached the counter, Aster reached into a pocket of the denim dress Ms. Fincher had given her. She muttered under her breath and pulled out something green.

She placed it on the counter. It looked like money.

"Twenty?" Aster said.

The woman looked at the paper, but she didn't pick it up.

"You're sure that's what you want?" she asked.

"I'm sure," Aster said.

The woman nodded. She stood up.

"It's not for sale," she said.

"Yes, it is," Aster said. "It's got a tag on it."

The woman shrugged. "I changed my mind. I don't want to sell it."

Aster frowned.

"Billy," she said. "Hang on to that."

"*Esenteyese!*" she shouted.

The fluorescent lights flickered.

The old lady at the adding machine was no longer an old lady. She was a young woman with jet black hair, eyes that were so pale as to be almost white, and a five-pointed silver star on her forehead. Her clothes hadn't changed — she was still in the puppy-shirt which was maybe weirder than the fact that she had been magically disguised in the first place.

"Nocturn!" Dusk snapped.

The curious strangers in the shop had also changed. Nocturn was one of Dusk's sisters. They were now surrounded by her other three siblings. There was Hawk, with his coal-dark skin and golden hair under a trucker's hat, dressed in walking shorts, polo shirt, and sneakers.

Dawn, about thirteen, red-headed and freckled, was clothed in blue scrubs, like a nurse. Long-armed, rangy Gloam, with his dark eyes and fine brown hair, had on a tan polyester leisure suit with coat sleeves and pants far too short for him.

As it turned out, Dusk didn't have to go looking for her brothers and sisters. They had found *her*.

"Wow," Errol said. "You people have really terrible fashion sense."

Hawk lifted his hand, and Errol saw he had a sword in it, and not one he'd picked up around here.

"Still very quick of tongue, I see," Hawk said. "Perhaps if I cut it off, it will run off on its own. Join a footrace, or something."

"Your jokes kind of suck, too," Errol said. But he didn't feel quite as brave as he was trying to sound. Hawk had more-or-less killed him once, as casually as one might crush an ant. And he wasn't the only one armed. All of Dusk's siblings had swords.

"Do not," Dusk warned them. "They are under my protection."

"But you are under no one's protection, sister," Nocturn said. "And you have run up quite a debt with this family. Not the least of which is forcing us to come here, to this dingy, awful place."

"If you've come for Aster, you're wasting your time," Errol said. "Killing her won't fix things. Your mom's plan was bonkers."

Nocturn shrugged. "Her plan had merit, based on what we knew then," she said. "How well it would have worked, we do not know. At the very least it would have given us more time to find a real cure to the world's ills. But that is all past. The blood of Kostye's daughter is worth nothing to us now." She nodded at the shadow-box Billy was holding. "That, however, will be of value to us."

"You didn't even know what it was," Aster said. "You've been sitting here with it, waiting for us."

"That much is true," Gloam said. "We don't need your blood, but the things rattling around in your head — those we need."

"I won't be coerced," Aster said.

"We're on the same side in this," Hawk said. "We want the same thing."

"Yeah, you said that last time," Errol pointed out. "Then you tried to cut her head off and murder the rest of us."

"That's unreasonable," Gloam said. "We would never have hurt any one of you if you had but let us have her head."

Billy settled the shadowbox on the ground. He was frowning, which was rare for him.

"Billy —" Errol cautioned.

Billy took a step toward Hawk, who lifted his sword to point at him.

"You would be advised against taking another step," Hawk said.

By now, Errol thought he knew Billy pretty well. He was normally one of the calmest people Errol had ever known. He was not given to anger.

Now he was trembling with barely contained rage. Someone who didn't know him as well as Errol did probably wouldn't see it at all. But to him, Billy was a volcano a few seconds from erupting.

"Hey," Errol said. "Let's everyone just calm down a bit, okay?"

Behind Nocturn, Errol noticed someone else had just walked in. A young man with his long dark hair worn in a ponytail.

Nocturn noticed it to. She turned to see who it was.

"We're closed," she said.

"Apologies," the fellow said, and ducked away.

Errol thought he looked familiar. Someone he'd gone to school with, maybe? He thought about yelling for help. Did the mall still have any guards?

Probably not. But it gave him an idea.

"What's your plan?" Errol asked Nocturn. "The way he ran off, that guy probably saw you with those swords. You might not know it, but that's not normal around here. It's not even legal. Ask Dusk. When she came here after me the police caught her and threw her in the pokey."

"That's true," Dusk said. "The authorities here are not tolerant of such things."

"In that case," Hawk said, "our time might be short. By the time the authorities arrive—if they arrive at all—four of you will be dead, and we will once more be disguised in illusion. Unless Aster agrees to go with us."

"No chance," Errol said. Nocturn was nearest. All he had to do was get past the sword. Knowing these guys, there wasn't much chance of that, but it was better than just letting them take Aster away. And it wasn't like Aster was helpless. Any minute now she would do some sort of spell. . . .

Nocturn fixed her gaze on him.

"Aster, *Keidi!*" Dawn suddenly shouted. Aster hissed and grabbed at her throat.

"Hey—" Errol began.

"*Steledi!*" Nocturn said. Errol felt his limbs tighten, as if his tendons had suddenly been turned into wire.

Billy jumped Hawk, knocking his sword aside with his arm, but Hawk backpedaled and clocked Billy in the jaw with a left; and an instant later Gloam clobbered him on the head with the pommel of his sword. Billy dropped, moaning. Dusk was just behind Billy; she slammed Gloam with an elbow and followed through with a punch that caught Hawk in his armpit. Both men dropped. She kicked Hawk in the head and leapt toward Nocturn.

She never got there. Nocturn hit her with the same hex she had him, and she landed on the floor with a solid thud, her arms and legs frozen in the act of jumping.

Dawn immobilized the mute Aster and Delia as Hawk and Gloam slowly recovered from Dusk's attack.

Hawk looked them over, panting.

"What now?" Gloam asked.

"Kill them," Hawk said.

"Our sister, too?" Gloam said.

Hawk shook his head. "No," he said. "But I will hamstring her. We cannot have her following."

Errol fought to move, but he couldn't even crook a finger to make the gesture he wanted. He watched helplessly as Hawk approached Dusk.

"I think you had best not do that," a voice said, from the door to the shop. At his angle, Errol didn't have to turn; he saw it was the boy from before. He noticed more details now; he was dressed in a vest, a long-sleeved white shirt with lots of buttons, and black pants stuffed into boots.

He held a revolver in one hand and a curved sword in the other.

Errol thought he recognized him now—one of the gypsies from the camp where he and Veronica had spent the night.

Hawk straightened and regarded the gypsy. Nocturn turned toward him, too.

"*Steledi!*" Nocturn shouted, gesturing toward the guy.

But the fellow just grinned a little. "It's not wise to repeat yourself," he said. Then he raised his gun and fired.

The bullet hit Nocturn in the shoulder and turned her half around. She screamed and clutched at the wound.

Hawk started forward, blade ready, but the gypsy drew a bead on him.

"This goes in your head," he said. "As easily as that one might have hers. I've no wish to send anyone across the flood today, so all of you had best keep your peace."

"You stink of the Pale," Hawk sneered. "March-dweller. Half-thing."

"I'll not dispute my nature," the young man said. "I am Shandor King Minko, a Prince Regent in my own country, which is maybe not so High and Far Away, but far nearer here than your rightful place. And as such, I put all of these here under my hand."

Shandor. Errol knew that name. This was the guy who had been sweet on Veronica. The one who had tried to take her away from him. What the hell was he up to?

"If you do that," Hawk said, "You'll make enemies you don't want."

"I'm right good at deciding what I want," Shandor said. "And right good at defending what I have."

"You shot my sister," Hawk said. "I will not forgive that."

"What? You mealy-tongued worm. You were just about to cripple another sister of yours. Your outrage is a cracked bell, so far as I'm concerned. Anyway, you're as welcome to try and kill me as the last many that failed. Sister, would you?"

The girl next to him stepped quietly into the room. Errol was nearest, and she touched him first. The magical paralysis instantly vanished. Aster was next, then Dusk, Billy, and Delia. Hawk and the others watched in obvious frustration. Nocturn took a seat. Blood was seeping through her fingers, but she looked more furious than pained.

Dusk didn't waste any time. Ignoring his sword, she took two steps and slapped the hell out of Hawk.

"That's for you, brother," she said. "Hamstring me, would you? Try it now."

Hawk glowered at her, but he didn't attempt to raise his weapon.

"You betrayed us," he said, softly.

"And you, me, and mother all of us," she snapped back. "When was ever one of us born without a dagger in hand for the back of another. I'm done with all of you."

"The world is dying," Nocturn said. "You must think larger than that."

"You should have considered that yourself," Dusk replied.

Shandor kept his weapon trained on Hawk as Billy picked the astrarium back up. Then they all left the store.

"This way," Shandor said. "Go down to the theater. I will make certain they do not follow us."

"You're aren't going to kill them?" Errol said.

"If I meant to do that, I would have done it already," Shandor said. "I'll be right along."

The theater was at the far end of the mall, looking some-how more abandoned and forlorn than the rest of the place. He remembered when it had been new and smelled of popcorn. He had watched a lot of matinees here with his friends. Some of his favorite movies, and more he couldn't even name now.

True to his word, Shandor arrived a few minutes later.

"We should hurry," he said. "They have others with them, waiting just beyond the Pale. They will be after us soon."

"Hang on," Aster said. "I know who you are. Veronica's friend. Did she send you? Have you seen her?"

"She came to my camp some days ago, yes. She said I should come and help you from your troubles. She had, as she put it, other matters to attend to elsewhere."

"How did she know we would have troubles?" Aster asked.

"I did not question her about that. She is a person of consid-erable power, as you ought to know."

"How did you know we were here?" Errol asked. "We've been back in Sowashee less than a day."

"My kingdom is in the Marches of this place. You came through it on your way here. You left your ship docked there. You were not hard to track."

"Yeah," Errol said. "Well, anyway, thanks."

"You are very welcome."

He touched the locked door of the theater and then pushed it open.

"We'll go now," he said.

"This isn't how we came in," Aster said.

"Nor I," Shandor replied. "But your siblings have their gang waiting on that path. We must take another."

"There is a way here," Billy said. "I can smell it."

"Aster?" Errol said.

She nodded. "We got what we came for," she said. "It's time to go back."

Errol nodded. Then he saw Ms. Fincher, standing a few feet away.

"Wait," he said. "What about her? Will she be safe if we leave her here?"

"I cannot account for what my brothers and sisters might do," Dusk said. "But if you hide, Delia, I'm sure they will think you went with us. They will not return here once they have gone."

"Right," Errol said. "You could hide in a closet or a storeroom or the manager's office or something."

"I think I'm going with you," Ms. Fincher said. "That man — or — whatever it was. At my house. Dusk, do you think your siblings sent that?"

Dusk shook her head. "No," she said. "That was something else."

"From very far away," Billy added.

"Something that came just for me," Ms. Fincher said. "Why?"

"I don't know," Aster replied. "You were my father's lover. He had many enemies. It could be any one of them."

"So I'm not safe here. Or possibly anywhere. I'm better off with all of you — if you'll have me."

"Of course," Errol said.

"If this is all settled now . . ." Shandor said.

"All of us then," Aster said.

FIVE

THROUGH THE KUDZU

S handor led them into one of the theaters. It was dark inside, but the handrail was still there, leading them down toward the screen and the emergency exit. Shandor pushed it open. Outside, the parking lot stretched out, cracked and broken, grass pushing up through the seams, and kudzu had crept from the nearby fields to cover not only much of the parking lot, but the back part of the mall, as well. It made him a little dizzy. How long had it been like this? Not the last time he was here. But he wasn't sure how long ago that had been.

And the parking lot seemed much bigger than it had. He couldn't see the interstate, or any buildings south or east, because the Kudzu had engulfed all of the pines around the perimeter.

When they finally reached the edge of the lot, Shandor used his sabre to cut a hole in the kudzu, and they went in. They sloshed across the shin-deep Sowashee Creek that gave the town its name, and then into more kudzu.

Fifteen minutes later, they were still in the vines, although they should have hit the frontage road about fourteen minutes earlier, followed quickly by the interstate. Instead, they were in a forest of dead and dying trees, under a green, crawling canopy of kudzu.

"Oh," he said.

"Yeah," Aster said, understanding him. "Me too. We're back in the in-between."

Errol wondered what it said that parts of his hometown were so run down that he couldn't clearly tell where urban decay ended and wilderness began. The High and Faraway was falling apart because of a curse. It seemed like his world wasn't affected by that, but maybe it was. Maybe it always had been falling apart. The Kingdoms were on the verge of death, but his world had been dying for years.

"Is it just me, or is it getting easier to pass through?" Errol said. "I mean the first time you had to build me that body, and then we had to find Veronica — "

"Veronica was a creature of the Pale," Aster said. "The in-between. So is Shandor. It's the same."

"I don't know," Dusk said. "Before I met you, I searched endlessly for your world. The Pale is vast and mazy. Finding the way through is no simple matter. This feels easier to me. As if the two are drawing closer. The Kingdoms are pulling apart, but they and the Reign of the Departed appear to be nearer. It seems a contradiction."

"I don't know," Errol said. You said the Reign — my world — is like the bottom, as low as you can go. Maybe the Kingdoms aren't just falling apart — maybe they're also sinking."

"Like a broken ship," Dusk murmured. "And everything will pass into oblivion. An awful thought."

"Except we're going to stop it, right?" Errol said. "Break the curse."

"My father's curse isn't the cause of this," Aster said.

"Wait, what?" Errol said. "I thought everyone pretty much agreed on that."

She shook her head. "My father was a powerful sorcerer, and he did make a curse. But as powerful as he was, he couldn't cause all of this. No, it's something deeper. His curse is a symptom of something else, a shadow of something much higher and farther."

"What do you mean by that?" Errol said.

"Look," Aster said. "You were just talking about your world being the "bottom." So think of it that way, for a moment. Think of one of those wedding cakes, the ones that are stacked up, each cake a little smaller than the last. The higher up you go, the more elumiris is present. The more magic. Where I'm from—where Dusk is from—that's maybe the second or third layer of the cake. On this cake, that's only about halfway up, maybe not that. There are layers way above that. Each world is sort of a shadow of the one above it."

"What's at the top?"

"The real thing. Pure magic. I don't know exactly. But the point is my father's curse—my father himself—is a shadow of something even higher up. We can't fix things by taking on his curse—we have to find whatever the real problem is. We have to go farther up. And that can be harder than moving from your world to the Marches."

"So how do we do it?"

"That," she said, pointing to the thing Billy was carrying. "I hope."

"How?"

"I've no idea."

He digested that for a few moments.

"So my world, the Reign—it's the bottom layer of the cake?"

She shook her head. "When you get that far down, there is no cake. It's the table, or the ground, or—well, it's just an analogy."

"But not cake," he said

"Right."

"Great."

***

The Kudzu eventually played out, and so did the forest, replaced by fields that stretched off as far as the eye could see, unbroken except by a few trees that probably marked the course of streams. Whatever had been farmed here was long dead, taken over by thistle and broomsedge, but the remains of furrows left little doubt that this had been fields and not pasture. Their passage through the weeds flushed bobwhites now and then, sending them into quick, low, reluctant flight before they dove back into the vegetation for cover. Errol noticed a few deer in the distance. Shandor eventually brought them to muddy road that sucked at their shoes but was easier going than the grass and brambles.

The sky was dark blue, with inky banks of clouds on the horizon. They were sluggish and slow to change, as if there wasn't much wind up where they were. The sun, when it was visible, was about half the size it ought to be, and stuck just above the clouds, halfway to noon or so.

A road turned off to their right, and in the distance, Errol saw a few big oaks and a house. It was a big house, with Greek columns and three or four stories.

Shandor didn't take them that way, though. They stopped to rest when they came to a sizable creek, lying under a willow.

Billy heard it first. He was lying with Aster's head on his arm, when he gently disengaged and sat up.

"What is it?" Aster asked

"Something coming," Billy said.

Shandor stood up, alert, gazing off into the distance.

"He's right," the Gypsy said. "I don't know what. Those from back in the shop, probably. We should go."

The fields continued, seemingly without end, a sea of weeds stretching to every horizon. They saw a few more houses, large and small, but Shandor avoided all of them.

They reached the clouds, or the clouds reached them, Errol couldn't tell which. But it began to rain. By that time, Errol was tired. He and Billy had been taking turns carrying the astrarium, and the damn thing had gotten *heavy*. But Ms. Fincher looked like she couldn't go any further.

"We've got to rest," he told Shandor.

"It's not much farther now."

"It's here," Billy said, pointing back the way they'd come.

Errol looked back through the rain. The road stretched like a line to the horizon, but since the land gently undulated, parts of it were hidden from sight. Billy was pointing at someone running toward them, just at the edge of their vision.

Running fast, crazy fast. He vanished behind a dip of in the landscape and then reappeared, way sooner than he should have.

Shandor turned, too.

"Go on," he said. "All of you. This road runs to a river. Your ship is there. I'll stand here and settle this."

"Not alone," Dusk said.

"No," Errol said. "Dusk, you go with them."

"Errol, I'm the better warrior."

"I know you are," he snapped. "But you don't have your armor, or your sword. They're on the ship. You get those, and you can deal with anything that comes at you. If whatever-this-is is something easy, Shandor and I can stop it. If it's something nasty — really nasty — you would be wasted here, just like I would be back at the boat."

"We'll all stay," Aster said.

Errol eyes the thing again, a bad feeling growing in his belly.

"We came all of this way to get that astrarium thing and save the world," Errol said. "What if it gets busted in the fight? Get to the boat and get it safe. Then worry about us if you want to."

"He's right," Shandor said. "Leave this to us. We will rejoin you. There isn't time for disputation."

Dusk's knitted brows showed her displeasure, but she sighed and stepped up to him.

"Stay alive," she said. "I will return for you."

"I'm counting on it," Errol said.

She kissed him, then nodded to the others.

"Errol's right," she said. "Let's hurry."

Errol watched them jog off through the rain, then turned to face whatever-it-was coming their way.

"You're a brave fellow," Shandor said, after a moment.

"Hey," Errol said. "One of him, two of us."

Shandor smiled grimly. "I suspect it will not be that easy," he said. "But we shall see."

"Okay."

"I must confess something to you," Shandor said.

"What's that?"

"Veronica. I asked her to be my queen. She refused, but I will persist. You should know this, if you still have designs on her."

Errol didn't answer right away.

"That's all up to her," he told Shandor. "I had my chance. I blew it."

"Dusk seems an admirable woman."

"Yeah. She is," Errol said. "Maybe we can talk about this later."

"I thought you should know," Shandor said. "In case one or both of us should not survive this."

Shandor pulled his pistol from his belt. "You know how to use this?" he asked.

"Yes," Errol replied. It was a heavy gun, a six-shooter. Most of his experience was with hunting rifles. He had only fired a pistol once, shooting at cans. But he knew how it worked.

"Take it, then." Shandor said, drawing his sabre.

The rain slackened slightly.

Then the runner came over the last hill. Errol suppressed the urge to fire immediately. He knew he would miss, and he wasn't that happy about the prospect of shooting someone, anyway.

Then he saw what it was and opened up. His first shot hit the road; his second was dead center; the runner staggered and lost a little momentum, so it was almost still for a second. Errol shot it again, still not quite believing what he was seeing.

It was Aster's automaton, the one from the shop in the mall. It was working. But that meant someone — or something — was in it.

It zigged to the left when he fired again, and he wasn't sure if he hit it or not. Then it was on them.

Shandor was fast, too; his sabre flicked out, cutting at the thing's throat. The only problem was, there were no blood vessels there, only wire. The automaton swiped at Shandor, but he danced back, slicing like mad. Little bits off wood flew off the thing, but none of the "wounds" looked critical.

"Cut its legs off!" Errol yelped.

Dusk's sword had gone through his wooden leg like butter; Shandor's wasn't as sharp, or magical, or whatever.

Errol stepped back, trying to aim at its head, without putting Shandor in the line of fire.

When the moment came, he missed. His next and final shot dug into the barrel of its torso, which didn't do much. Just after that, the automaton got a punch through Shandor's guard, sending him reeling.

Errol dropped the gun and jumped the thing, tackling it below the waist and hurling it to the ground. He managed to change his hold, grappling it from behind, pinning its arms to its sides.

That wouldn't last long, he could tell. It was hideously strong, squirming and slamming him against the ground. It was hollering, too, not in English and not in any of the languages Aster's spells had taught him to understand.

Shandor didn't mess around. He got an opening and used his sword like an ax, chopping at the thing's ankle joint. Two quick blows had it off, and he started on the other. Errol didn't get to see if he was successful there, because the automaton managed to heave off the ground and slam him down hard enough that he lost his grip. He rolled away, lungs burning, scrambling up for a re-match.

The thing was back on its feet too — or rather, foot. Shandor cut at it again as it started forward, and the leg with a foot still on it came off at the knee.

That didn't stop it, though. It skittered toward them, looking like some kind of insect. Shandor shouted, a drawn-out battle cry, cutting at its neck again, but it bowled him over. Errol jumped on its back and put it in a sleeper hold. It didn't breathe, so . . .

But the head popped off. The body dropped flat. The head was screaming, so Errol tossed it aside.

He stood, panting, as it rolled to a stop, its empty eyes staring at him.

"Holy crap," he muttered.

The head quivered, then began rolling toward the body. Shandor yelped and kicked it away. It went about thirty feet, and then started back.

"Its foot," Errol said.

The severed foot was reattached.

Errol ran over and grabbed the head. It kept pulling toward the body, like a magnet toward iron. The body shifted, too, until Shandor threw himself on it to prevent it from moving. He was only partly successful; it dragged him slowly cross the wet clay.

Errol dug his heels in. The pull was almost too strong for him to step back, but he managed it, and there the tug felt slightly less. Finally, after he'd gotten about twenty feet away, he could just hold the head without it threatening to overbalance him.

But it wasn't over. The severed leg re-attached, and the headless body stood back up.

"Get farther away," Shandor said. "Get to the river and throw it in. I will stay here and keep the body from following."

"Okay," Errol said. He was aching from the fight, but it was a good ache. He'd spent months in a coma, and it had taken a long time for his muscles to come back. But now they were better than ever.

Maybe because of that, opening up to a full-on run felt great. He remembered when he was little, how he'd loved to run across a field just to do it, to jump and feel like he was flying, if only for an instant. Or that he was a deer or a lion or superhero. When he'd been trapped in his own automaton, he'd been stronger and faster than in his human body, but he hadn't really *felt* it. Now, the rain didn't bother him, or the clay sucking at his shoes, or anything else, past or present. He was in his body, healthy, whole—and despite everything, *happy*.

The fields finally ended as the road dropped into forested lowland. He sailed over puddles like an Olympic jumper, and the bigger ones he just splatted through, each footfall hurling mud and rainwater into the air. He smelled bruised hickory and sassafras leaves, and thunder rumbled in the distance. The rain was growing colder.

And now things looked familiar as he ran through forests of cane as thick as his thigh alternating with blackwater swamps of cypress, black gum, and bay. This was where they had come into the Pale two days earlier.

He found the ship without much trouble. Dusk was there, fully armored but still adjusting her straps. Billy had a long rifle trained on him as he emerged from the woods, but quickly let the barrel drop away when he recognized him. Aster was on deck, too, but Ms. Fincher wasn't in sight.

"Where is Shandor?" Dusk shouted, over the din of the rain.

"Coming," Errol shouted. He held up the wood-and-metal head. "This is what was chasing us. Part of it, anyway."

Aster came down off the ship. She took it from his hands and muttered a few words. The head pulsed a faint purple color.

"*Zhedye*," she swore.

"What is it?" he asked.

"Remember when I first woke you up, how I was worried something other than you had gotten into the automaton?"

"Yes," he said. He wasn't likely to forget the fact that Aster had been able to turn him on and off like throwing a light switch.

"They've summoned some sort of *dves* to inhabit it," she said. "Something really — awful and strong."

"The body and head were trying to get back together," Errol said. "Shandor thought I should throw it in the river."

"It'll just keep following us," Aster said. "This close to the Pale, I can't do anything about it. But deeper in, I can probably break the enchantment, send whatever-this-is back to the hell it came from."

"Your call," Errol said.

Aster nodded, took the head on board, and vanished below decks.

"Are we waiting on him?" Dusk asked.

"Shandor?" Errol said. "Yes. He saved our butts."

"I did the same, when we first met," Dusk replied. "You trusted me because of that. You were wrong to do so."

"Well, it's hard to argue with that," Errol said. "But it did work out eventually, right?"

"That time," she said. "What do we know of this man?"

"He's sweet on Veronica," he replied.

"That does not recommend him to me," Dusk said.

"Yeah. But Veronica saved your life, too."

"And yet, where is she?" Dusk said. "Why did she abandon us?"

Errol shrugged. He wasn't sure of that himself. Veronica hadn't told him. She'd just *left*.

"Anyway," Errol said, pointing at Shandor, emerging from the trees. "There he is."

"Indeed," Dusk said.

By that time Aster was back on deck. Seconds after Shandor set foot on the boat, she spoke the magic words, and they were underway, moving out into the deepest part of the channel. Tired, Errol slept, and when he awoke, they were at sea, and the sun shrunken to about twice the size of Venus, in the middle of an indigo sky, and the Reign of the Departed was once again far behind them.

SIX:
PICNIC

V eronica had wondered if she could swim in the Hollow
Sea, whose vast depths contained only the memory of
water. She had first crossed it with the others in the silver ship
and had been bemused to see water form in front of them and
vanish behind, so that the ship could sail. She remembered dol-
phins leaping from the water and turning into skeletons as they
crossed the boundary of the ship's magic.

She was not the silver ship; the sea did not spring into existence around her as she swam. Instead, she became like it—a
ghost, with less substance than a breath of air. But in that state,
the sea was more wonderous to her than ever. It was overflowing
with colors her human eyes could never have seen, and which
no words she had in her could describe. The sea had a strong,
deep memory of itself, of when it had been filled with water
and life, colorful creatures like mimosa blossoms, drifting in the
recollection of currents, schools of things with corkscrew shells
and tentacles like squids, gigantic sea serpents that shimmered
with internal light. This place was like her, caught between
being and not being. She wanted to explore its depths, learn all
of its secrets. She could spend years here, if not centuries.

But when the Raggedy Man pulled the world apart, the Hollow Sea would be just as gone as everything else. So she kept her focus and found her destination.

As she emerged, she saw a colorful figure descending from the sky, twirling a little, like a falling leaf, so his felted and embroidered robe spread out around him. His red hair was longer than she had seen it last, and it too fanned out in the turning breeze he himself was creating.

Haydevil, one of the Children of the Winds.

"Well, look who it is," Haydevil said, settling down on boots that curled up at the toes. "I rather hoped we'd seen the last of you."

Veronica felt heavy again, as her substance returned. It hurt, but she tried to stay bright.

"Oh, Haydevil," she said, "You know that's not true. Everything is always so interesting when I show up."

"To say the least," Devil replied. "I can only imagine what kind of trouble you're bringing me this time."

"Well, I've come to ask a favor," she said.

"Let me check in my pocket," Haydevil said. He stuck his hand into the red, gold, and black robe. "Nay, no favors there. I'm fresh shed of them."

Veronica glanced up at the young woman floating down toward them. Her gown was brown and copper, like leaves in late autumn, and her black hair was put up in complicated braids.

"Hello, Mistral," Veronica said.

"What sort of favor?" Mistral asked as she too came to ground.

"Well, I'm in a bit of a pickle. I'm afraid I've misplaced Errol and Aster again."

"We haven't seen them since they brought us here and made off with our ship," Haydevil said. "And after all we've done for them."

"I gave them leave to take the ship," Mistral said.

"You what?"

"What need have we of it?" his sister said. "We can fly, can we not?"

"Well—but it's the principal at stake," Haydevil said.

"It's the flying thing I came to talk to you about," Veronica cut in. "I have become quite good about getting around in the water, but I need to go back to the Watchtower, and that's rather high above sea level."

"Can't you swim up from beneath?" Haydevil said. "You said the pool goes down quite deep."

"Not anymore, it doesn't. It's all changed now. Maybe the whole thing has—I've got to try."

"Oh, spare me your lovelorn devotion," Haydevil said.

"This isn't about that," Veronica said. "This is about getting the sun moving again. About keeping the world from tearing itself apart."

"Do you know something about that?" Mistral said. "Because if you do, you'd best tell us."

"I feel like maybe we can trade," Veronica said. "And Brume, you'd best not even consider freezing me. I know you're there."

"Why ever would I freeze my best friend in the whole wide world?" the Brume said, stepping around from behind her. She was the youngest of the siblings, looking to be only about ten years old, and her dark, tangled hair had a greenish tinge. She was dressed in what appeared to be the remains of a ball gown made for a taller person; the hem had been ripped in a ragged fashion. "I think we ought to have a tea party, and you can tell us your story. And if these two don't take you where you need to go, I'll do it myself. How's that for a deal?"

"I like that deal, best friend," Veronica said.

There was an argument about where to have the tea party; the Brume wanted it down in her dank caverns, but Mistral and Haydevil argued against that. In the end, it took place in the apple orchard where Veronica, Errol, Dusk, and Billy had confronted a giant and learned that Billy was also one.

"I like it here," the Brume decided, after a little pouting. "With the sun all shrunken, it's almost as dark as my caves. And I feel like I can hear Mum's voice in the leaves."

"Well, this *is* what she went into,' Haydevil said. "I reckon there's something left of her yet."

"None of them are really dead," Veronica said. "Your parents, all of the elders in the kingdoms who were changed by the curse."

"You know this for certain?"

Veronica thought about it for a second. "Yes, I do," she said. "Don't ask me how. But I'm as certain of that as I'm sitting here."

"Go on then," Haydevil said. "What you were going to tell us."

So she told them, between sips of the tea she was nearly certain had been brewed from dirt and dead leaves and cakes that were almost too hard to eat. When she was done, no one said anything at first.

Finally, Mistral spoke.

"I don't think you need to go the Watchtower at all," she said.

"What do you mean?" Veronica said. "Have you seen them? Do you know where they are?"

"No. We've been busy here, putting things back in order after Nocturn and her goblins messed the place up. But listen; you said you sent your friend Shandor to protect your friends in the Reign of the Departed. But what makes you think that they're there? Last we saw of them they were hunting for someplace Aster's father used to live."

"I don't know about that either," Veronica replied. "That's just where I thought they would be."

"Did you go check?" Mistral asked.

"No," Veronica replied. "Because they aren't there anymore."

"And how do you know that?" the Wind persisted. "If they were there for Shandor to find, why wouldn't they still be there?"

"Well, I . . . I see where you're going with this," Veronica said, starting to feel stupid.

"When you went into the pool, on the Watchtower," Mistral said. "What happened? We never heard."

"I met this woman," Veronica said. "Yurena. She told me she would help me find Errol if I would promise to serve her for a year and a day."

"And how did this Yurena find Errol? Did she tell you where he was?"

"No, she didn't tell me anything," Veronica said. "I just knew. Where he was going to be."

Oh, she thought. *How stupid. How could I not have seen this for myself?*

"The spell stuck on you," The Brume said. "Maybe it got weaker, but it's still there."

Veronica thought about it for a moment, trying picture where Errol was. That didn't work, and for a moment she thought Mistral's logic was all wrong. But then she saw her mistake.

"I see," she said. "I don't know where he *is*. But I know where he's *going* to be. All I have to do is go there and wait for him."

"That's perfect," Haydevil said. "We don't have to do anything at all, then."

"I guess not," Veronica replied. "I've just wasted everyone's time, including my own."

"Nonsense," Mistral said. "Sometimes it just takes a wind from a different direction to fill your sails and send you on your way. It's easy to get bound up by the things you think you know."

"My sister the poet," Haydevil said. He stood up. "Well, this has been grand. The most charming part of my day."

"Always a gentleman," Veronica said.

"I'm sorry we can't do more," Mistral said.

"I understand," Veronica said. "Thanks for your help."

"I'll go with you anyway," The Brume said. "It's been awfully dull hereabouts."

"I think you had better not," Veronica said. "You need to help your brother and sister."

"Help them with what?" The Brume said.

"Fight the enemy," she replied. "What I call the Itch. The Raggedy Man. It's coming behind me. It will offer you things. It will make promises. But you must not listen. You have to fight it."

"You led it here?" Haydevil snapped.

"I'm sorry," Veronica said. "It would have come regardless. It will come sooner, that's all. Chasing me."

"We can flee," Haydevil said. "Return to our refuge in north. We can stay ahead of it."

"No," Mistral said. "We were driven from here once. Never again. We will hold it on that side of the sea. For a time. We will keep it from tracking you through here. And you, Veronica, your payment to us will be to see this thing done. Bring back the sun. Give us seasons again."

"I will," Veronica promised. "Brume?"

"I sort of like it with the sun like it is now," The Brume said. "But fine. I'll do as you say, Veronica."

"Thanks, best friend."

***

"Are we sure we got the right thing?" Errol asked.

Aster sat cross-legged on the floor, fiddling with the clockwork in the astrarium.

"Yeah," she said. "Or as sure as I can be, anyway—which I guess isn't very."

"But you found something," Errol said. "In the castle. Your dad's old place."

She kept her eyes studiously on the machinery.

"Not exactly," she said.

Errol stared down at her. "What does that mean?" he said. "We fought our way clear across the Kingdoms, nearly got offed by your cousins and one of your old Pinocchio-men, and you aren't sure about any of this?"

"The world is ending, Errol," she said. "I couldn't just wait around forever, going through my father's library."

"So you just took a guess."

She sighed. "It was more than a guess. But if I had tried to explain it then, you would have thought I was crazy."

"What then?"

"My father told me to come get it," she said.

"Your father," Errol said. "You mean before he died?"

"No. After."

"So—like a ghost, then?"

"More like that," she said. "Delia—Ms. Fincher. She told me. But the way she talked—and . . . other things. It was Dad. It had to be."

"Why would that sound crazy?" Errol asked. "Your dead father possessed our old high school guidance counselor and gave you some hint vague enough that even now you aren't sure it was right?"

"They were lovers, Errol," Aster said. "They had a connection. He spent his last hours with her. It might not have been a ghost, but some sort of spell to make her tell me something at the right time. But ghosts are real, here. You understand that by now, yes? You *were* one. More or less."

"Yeah," he said. "I just—I thought we were on firmer footing here, is all. So what is this thing?"

"I always thought it was a toy. I used to watch it when I was little. All the time. Dad never said where he got it."

"I've seen it work," he said. "It's like a sun, and a moon, and a star."

"It tells a story," she said. "Dad told it to me once. Just once. But I remember it."

"How does it go?"

"It's like a fairy tale," she said. "About how the Moon was a handsome prince and the Sun a beautiful princess. He sought after her, overcoming many obstacles, and succeeded where many failed. He found her, and they were married, but then she was taken away by a terrible demon. The Moon went after her again, fought his way across the kingdoms, and finally won her back. They became King and Queen. And that's where the happily-ever-after would come in, right? Except in this story, the Queen had a servant, the Morning Star, and her husband the Moon began to fall in love with her. When the Sun heard about their affair, she hid herself, and the world became an eternal realm of night and winter. But then the Sun's brother learned what had happened. He was pissed off; he found the Moon and hit him in the face with his sword, cut him down until he was nothing. But the Moon was a powerful sorcerer; he put himself back together, a bit at a time. It's supposed to explain why the Moon goes through phases; during the New Moon, he's completely cut to pieces. But he couldn't totally heal—so even when he's full, his face is covered in scars. He's no longer handsome."

Errol frowned. "That reminds me of a story Billy told me," he said.

"Really?"

"The details weren't the same," he said. "But it was about the Sun and the Moon, and how the Moon got those splotchy marks on his face."

"Tell me."

"Billy tells it better," he said. "What I remember is that the Moon and Sun were brother and sister. Some guy kept coming to the Sun at night to . . . you know. But it was dark, so she couldn't see who it was. So one night she put her fingers in some ashes and touched his face. The next day she saw the Moon had ash all over his face."

"Huh," Aster said. "And she knew she'd been having sex with her brother. That's sort of disgusting. But I see your point. In both cases the Moon was fooling around with someone he wasn't supposed to and ended up getting his face marked for it."

"Yeah," Errol said. "Anyway, what does any of this have to do with the curse and all of that?"

"I'm not sure," she said. She patted the astrarium. "But the story in this is sort of like my dad's story, at least what I've learned of it the last time we were here. Think about it. He was married to Dusk's mother, the Queen. But then he met my mother and fell in love with her and they had me. The Queen had my father attacked and my mother murdered. They meant to kill me, and that's when Dad made the curse."

"I guess there are some things in common," Errol said. "You were talking earlier about how your father's curse was the shadow of some other thing that happened, higher and further away. You think he's a shadow of this Moon guy? That your dad's life was a version of that story?"

"Or the story about the Moon and my father's life are both echoes of something deeper in and higher up. Closer to the source of everything."

He gestured at the clockwork. "So then, maybe this thing is supposed to lead us to wherever that is. The real thing, I mean — where the curse was really made."

"That's what I believe,' she said. "I just don't know *how*."

"I guess that is the tricky part," Errol said. "Have you tried asking Ms. Fincher? I mean, if you think your dad somehow spoke to you through her before, I think that's where I would start."

"I had the same thought," she said. "But . . ." she trailed off.

"What?"

"I'm afraid," she said.

***

Delia watched as Aster set the clockwork in motion. At first, she thought it was charming, the golden disk of the sun dancing with the silver disk of the moon. But then the star danced with the moon, and a feeling of dread snuck up on her and began to grow. Like she knew something terrible was going to happen but was helpless to stop it.

As the moon moved to dance with star, the sun turned her bright face away, and the feeling of dread multiplied. By the time the moon flipped about to reveal his dark, scarred face, Delia was sweating, although it was not hot in the slightest. Her stomach was uncomfortable, like rats were gnawing at it, and her breath tasted sour in her mouth.

"Ms. Fincher?" Errol asked. "Are you okay?"

She shook her head. She wasn't okay. She had been trying not to think about it, to deny what was happening, but she knew now. And she realized something else. It just appeared in her head and settled there as if she had always known it. She understood what this box was, and what to do with it.

"Take it to the ship's bridge," she said. "Put it on the shelf below the wheel. Tell it to steer."

"It's a guide?" Aster said.

"I believe so," Delia said. She felt dizzy again and put her hand against the bulkhead to steady herself.

"Are you okay?" Errol asked. "You're really pale."

"I just need to be alone," she told him. "I'll be fine."

When they were gone, Delia sat on her bunk, trying to fight the sick feeling, but it was no use. She went up onto the deck, around the back of the castle. There she leaned over the rail and vomited into the grey-green sea. She did that for a while, until she had the dry heaves. The motion of the ship didn't help, the high swells, the flying fish skipping from wave to wave, all in the strange twilight that had befallen this world. When she could finally lift her head, she traced her gaze off to the horizon. The sails snapped and swung around as the ship changed course. Aster had done as she'd been told, and now they were on their way. What that meant eluded her; something she did somehow know but hadn't remembered yet.

She realized she was weeping, and she didn't care. After Kostye's death, after the strange battle on the Island of the Othersun, she had felt at first incredibly open to the world, but as the darkness crept into the sky, she had felt herself increasingly closed. Distant from everything. She'd thought going home would free her, but she'd been wrong about that. Now, more than ever, she knew she belonged here. It was all back— hope, terror, desire, disgust. She had always assumed she would have a child one day, but as that day moved further and further down the road, she had told herself she didn't have to. Not everyone did. And that had been a relief. She had seen the friends of her youth marked and changed by motherhood in ways that, frankly, repelled her. After a while, she had stopped thinking about motherhood entirely.

Until now, when she knew a child was growing in her. His child. Kostye's child. The child of the man who had cursed an entire universe and made it stick.

THE PALACE ON THE EDGE OF THE WORLD

The astrarium took control of the ship, as Delia said it would.

"She was right," Aster murmured.

"You really think it's your dad?" Errol said.

"It has to be. He built the astrarium, early on, before his mind started to go. He must have made it to do this. But that doesn't make sense."

"Why?" Errol asked.

"Because he always told me we would never come back," Aster said. "That the Reign of the Departed was the only place we would be safe."

"That *you* would be safe," Errol said. "He probably never meant for you to go back. Just him. He must have figured out what the curse was doing. Remember how he freaked out when he first saw me? He knew what you were up to. He knew you needed me and Veronica to return to the Kingdoms. How would he know that if he hadn't had it all worked out?"

She shrugged. "You didn't know Dad very well. His strength wasn't his intellect. I mean, he was smart, but that isn't where his power came from. He was driven by passion and intuition. I figured when he saw you he just . . . put it together, just like that. It's how he operated." She glanced back at the astrarium. "Clearly I was wrong. The thing is—I don't think he would have gone back to try and fix things unless he believed . . ." she trailed off.

"Unless he thought you really weren't safe," Errol said. "That the curse would affect my world, too."

She nodded. "Yes. And he was right. The curse caught up with him and made a wreck of his memory. And when he did come back here, it killed him."

Her voice cracked a little on the last two words, so Errol let it sit there for a moment, looking away as Aster struggled to master her grief.

"So where is this thing taking us?" he asked, after a few moments.

Aster swallowed and then let out a long breath. Her face cleared. "I don't know," she said. "I doubt Dad did either. He just built what the elumiris in him wanted him to."

"Well," Errol said, "I guess we'll find out soon enough."

***

I t wasn't soon, though. The ship conducted them across a seemingly endless sea. Now and then, the coasts of islands and continents appeared in the distance, but the silver vessel ignored all of these. There was no pressing need to make landfall on some strange and probably dangerous coast, since each day the table in the ship's mess produced food and drink.

But at times Aster was tempted anyway, to wrest control from her father's dead hand, land on some island, just so she could be *alone*. It had been so long since she'd had that luxury. The ship was small, and they had been on it for a long time. Everyone could use a bath; washing from basins was fine, but it didn't really do the job long term. But more than that, she needed a break from the expectation of conversation, from the constant surveillance by other people, from the voices incessantly intruding on her own. She loved Billy, she truly did, but it would be good to be out of even his sight for a while.

But it would also be good to be alone with him, too, which had never happened for more than a few moments at a time. His love was undemanding, as love went, but true intimacy was something they could never have unless everyone else was out of the picture. She wasn't even sure how intimate she wanted to be, but she wished she could work that out on her terms and his, without the constant presence of observers.

It was frustrating to have so much free time, and so little she could actually *do* with it. She kept thinking when it was all over, there would be plenty of space to live her life. But would anything ever truly be over? Was the curse something that could really be ended, or was its end a mirage she would chase for her entire life? When would she be free from the sins of her father?

***

The sky changed as they traveled, but not with regularity. They would pass through a heavy mist, or several hours of utter darkness, and when they emerged, it was just different; a watercolor haze of a sunset, a cerulean dome with a half-sized sun stuck at noon, a copper sky and golden clouds but no sun at all, a night with stars bright enough to read by.

But Delia's clock worked just fine, just so long as Aster remembered to wind it. So she knew they had been on the sea for two weeks, moving fast. Since the astrarium had taken control, the wind was always in their sails, and at its fastest the silver ship was extremely fast, cutting though the water almost as if it wasn't there. The swells hardly affected her, except in the worst of storms.

It had been eight days since they had last seen land of any sort.

On the fifteenth day, they saw the storm ahead. It blotted out half of everything, the mile-high thunderheads flaring fitfully from the lightning within. The ship, rather than slowing or turning to avoid the storm, instead hastened toward it with increasing speed.

The rain came, and then hail that grew worse until it was the size of apples. They huddled below decks as the silver ship rang like a bell without letup for three days. They ate, they played games, they slept. They pretended not to be going mad.

And on the fourth day, the pounding stopped. They went above to find it freezing, and the ship climbing what at first seemed to be a huge swell. But after several hours, it seemed there was no end to the wave. Aster wondered if it was some sort of illusion, but if so, it was good one. Every sense told her the deck was tilted from prow to stern. Billy placed a pistol shot on the deck and it rolled toward the back of the boat.

The sun was a tiny yellow spark in the mist. No other lights could be seen in the sky. The sea grew darker as they traveled, and sightings of land more common, and in all directions, suggesting that they were now in a large inland sea or lake. Whatever the case, the ship continued to see the coasts only as obstacles to be avoided, until it last it sailed into a bay, and then the mouth of a river. Marshland stretched out in all directions, a paradise for the waterfowl which they saw in vast numbers. It reminded her of the dream of birds she'd had when she was the captive of Vilken, the vision that had given her the hope she needed to live through that dark time.

Billy pointed out that they weren't sailing against the river's current, but with it; it wasn't flowing into the sea, but out from it.

As they moved downriver and the banks grew higher, the marshland gave way to short grass prairie with tiny yellow flowers riffled by occasional breeze. Herds of shaggy horses for-aged near the riverbanks, along with cattle and deer. Mountains lay on the horizon, white-capped but otherwise blue-grey with distance. Eventually they saw small villages—collections of domed tents and houses of earth, stone, and wood. Once, they saw some children fishing and playing on the banks, but as the ship approached, they quickly vanished into the scrubby growth along the river. A few times they saw riders on horse-back, always at a distance. Once they passed what could only be described as a wagon train—seven or eight colorful covered carts pulled by oxen, accompanied by many riders and a herd of horses.

The land grew rougher, more mountainous, and the river dug deeper into the earth and stone, until they were in a steep-sided canyon, where small spidery trees clung to the stone. The tiny sun, always in the middle of the sky, began to move again; with each mile it grew lower, until they could no longer see it at all. A sickle moon rose over the canyon walls, huge but dim, dark blotches covering most of its light.

The flow of the river quickened, then became a rush. When they heard the hushed roar of a waterfall ahead, Aster com-manded the silver ship to stop.

Obedient to her authority, it went still in the water, unaf-fected by the powerful current. Ahead, they could see the flat line where the river ended, and mist kicked up by its plunge into whatever deep lay beyond.

"What now?" Aster wondered.

"We could climb up," Billy said, nodding his head toward the chasm wall. The scale had been so great she hadn't notice it right away, but Billy had a keener eye for that sort of thing. His gaze indicated a stone landing and stairs ascending the side of the cliff.

When they pulled their ship up to the mooring, she saw the scale was still fooling her. Everything was big: the quay, the stone pillar for tying up the ship, the stairs carved into the canyon wall. All had been made for beings of more-than-human size.

"Did Giants build this?" Dusk asked Billy.

"Not my kind of giants," he said. "We don't build things. Besides, these people weren't so big. Hardly bigger than you."

He was right, Aster reflected. The stairs would be tiny for Billy at his full size. Each was about three feet above the one below.

"This is going to be fun," Errol said.

Aster closed her eyes. She could feel the elumiris humming and rattling the air, like a symphony only she could hear. It was extraordinarily strong.

"I think I can make it *actually* fun," she said.

They all turned to look at her.

"Just give me a few minutes," she said. She kept her eyes closed, ordered her thoughts. Then she opened them again.

"All of you look me in the eye," Aster said.

She waited until they had all done that and then she composed her Whimsy.

"*Lenghyemas!*"

The syllables weren't even fully off of her tongue before she felt light, as if she'd been pumped full of helium.

"Oh," Errol said. He flexed his knees and jumped, not too hard, but it carried him nearly a foot from the ground.

"I can think of some other times this would have come in handy," he said.

"We've never been this far in," Aster said. "I can only do what the elumiris allows me to do in any given place."

"Maybe you should put us back the way we were before until we get our stuff packed up," Errol suggested. "Otherwise, we might just float out into the river."

She nodded and returned their full weight to them.

The boat would be okay on its own; it could guard itself. When she'd found it, her father had left it with the command to kill anyone who tried to board without the proper password. She wasn't comfortable with that, so she simply told it to make anyone who messed with it unable able to see or remember it. She didn't fancy cleaning up dead bodies on their return.

***

Aster was right; her spell was not only useful, it was fun. Jumping up the giant steps was like being in a dream, even with his armor and backpack on. Errol always wondered how the guys who walked on the Moon felt; now he thought he was getting at least a taste of that.

The spell didn't do anything to quell his vertigo, however, and even before they were halfway up the cliff, his gut and monkey-brain told him he was unacceptably far from the bottom. He wondered just exactly how deep the canyon was. As deep as the Grand Canyon?

He kept his eyes forward and tried not to look down. His upward leaps became far less experimental, and he settled on mostly pulling himself from step-to-step. Dusk, of course, had no such qualms, and by the time she reached the top, he was more than ten steps behind her. When she got there, she stopped, waiting on them.

"Anything?" he called up.

"You'll see," she said.

A few moments later he stood beside her.

The moonlight plain had been hidden from them, but it was still there, silvery grass rolling off to a horizon of snow-capped mountains that must reach most of the way to the heavens. To his left, the vast dark depths of the canyon wound off across the land. Just at its lip, a few steps from where they stood, apple trees grew, some gnarled and ancient, others just saplings. They weren't spaced regularly, as one might expect in an orchard, but neither did they crowd one another. Many were laden with fruit of many colors — ruby red, yellow-gold, green and some that were as black as obsidian. From the top of the stairs and off through the trees a road ran, a big one. And the road followed along to the edge of the same cliff the river tumbled over. Beyond that, a castle floated in space.

It was golden, but not made of gold. Errol thought it might be amber, because it had a translucent quality, and light seemed to shine from inside of it. And on second look it wasn't a castle, at least not the kind with lots of towers and pennants and crenelated walls. *Palace* or *fortress* might be a better word. Cyclopean gates opened from a circular outer wall. Within that, there rose a second, higher wall. It was big, really huge, but it was not all that tall relative to its width; he wasn't even sure if the structure in the middle qualified as a tower.

But whatever you called the structure, it was massive, wider than several football fields.

And sitting on a freaking floating island. Or at least that's how it looked. Maybe it was really on spur of rock, and the cliff in front of him just obscured that fact.

But when they got closer, he could see underneath it, and there was nothing there.

A *lot* of nothing. Standing on the edge of the precipice, he could see the river pouring over off to his right. He could watch the stream of water, which he knew to be at least two or three hundred feet in width — dwindle down to the size of a pencil, a lollipop stick, a sewing thread — nothing. It was as if they were standing on the edge of the world. But he had been someplace like this before.

"Is this the Hollow Sea?" He asked Aster, as she arrived.

"Maybe," she said. "But it doesn't feel like that. I think this is something else. Or maybe the place the Hollow Sea is a shadow of."

The island was connected to the mainland by a bridge that looked as if had been spun from spider silk; it appeared far too delicate to be practical.

Everyone was up now. Aster murmured something and their weight returned to normal.

"Are you sure that's a good idea?" Errol asked. "We're about to walk out on a floating island."

"If the island holds that up," Aster said, pointing at the huge building, "I don't think it will notice us."

"It seems sturdy," Billy said.

Errol still hesitated at the edge of the bridge. What if the island was holding *exactly* as much weight as it was meant to? If he had learned anything about magic, it was it that it was not fair and certainly wasn't always designed to be helpful. After all, the silver ship had killed a fair number of people who did nothing more sinister than try to board it. It was hard to believe a palace like this would be left unguarded.

The bridge didn't collapse, nor did the island when they set foot on it. But when they approached the doorless gates, fire suddenly flickered in its threshold, quickly rising until it filled the entire opening with white-hot flame.

"There's the catch," Errol muttered.

But Aster didn't hesitate. She spoke a sentence he didn't understand, and the flames immediately dropped down. The air was still roasting hot when they stepped into the palace, but as they moved a little further in, it quickly cooled down.

"You think this place was built by the same people as the castle where we found the water of health?" Errol asked. That place too had been built for something larger than human. It had been made of golden metal.

"Not the same," Billy said. "But—not so different."

"Were you here before, too?" Aster asked.

"This place?" Billy said. "Maybe. I can't say for sure."

"I think I know where we are," Dusk said. She sounded subdued, as if afraid to speak too loudly. "*Ghartas Sauvens.*"

"And where is that?" Aster asked.

"They say my great-great-grandmother ruled here," Dusk replied. "My ancestors fled this place long ago."

"Fled?" Errol said. "As in 'ran away'?"

"Yes," Dusk said.

"Why?"

"To avoid being eaten," she replied.

"That's a good reason," Errol said.

"This is where Dad's astrarium brought us," Aster said. "This is where we're supposed to be. I'm sure of it."

"What now, then?" Shandor asked. "Shall we explore this place?"

Aster nodded. "But we stay together. Don't anyone go off on your own."

"Don't worry," Errol said. "I won't."

EIGHT

ANOTHER QUEEN

The palace was a fortress within a fortress. Once through the first gate and its fiery defenses, there was another, with a ramp leading up to the central part of the building. Or they could go left or right and wander around the lower level, which they elected to do first.

Between the outer and inner fortress ran a broad curving corridor, open to the sky. The Moon and stars provided a little light, but the amber glow of the walls allowed them to make their way. Numerous rooms and compartments opened from the passage, many of which were empty. Those with contents were disturbing. The first of these, Errol recognized almost instantly, was a huge stable, with stalls, feeding troughs, and so forth, all oversized. There were no living horses, but there were plenty of bones, mostly of very large horses, all laid out in piles as if the animals had collapsed and rotted in place without being disturbed by scavengers. Leather bridles hung on pegs, along with ornate felt blankets and what he guessed were saddles, although they definitely weren't the western-style saddles he'd grown up with. For one thing, they didn't have stirrups.

The horse bones predominated, but there were human-looking ones, as well. If a human stood nine feet tall.

They found more oversized bones in some of the other rooms. One held something what appeared to be a stove or a furnace. The swords, knives, and spears hanging up an on the tables suggested it was a foundry. Another space was full of half-built, two-wheeled wagons. Others held looms or tools for working wood. Some were obviously apartments, with bedrooms, courtyards, kitchens, and stairways that led up to the flat roof. Like the horses, the people in those rooms seemed to have died in the middle of their daily tasks.

"It's a good thing this isn't creepy," Errol said. "Or else I might be creeped out. I mean, at least in the other Kingdoms, the adults had changed into things. Monsters, statues, birds. This is a little too . . . real."

Aster shot him a funny look but didn't say anything.

Crap, he thought. Aster's father had turned into stone and been swallowed by the earth — while she was holding his hand. That was pretty real.

They didn't explore the entire outer part of the citadel — it was the size of a town and seemed to be more of the same. When they saw another ramp moving up to the second tier, they ascended, through a corridor carved in panoramas of chariots and wagons, some carrying spheres with rays shooting from them, others depicting warrior men and women. In what seemed to be the dead center of the palace was another open square, maybe a hundred yards across. It was paved in white stone, but the core must have been filled with earth, because a magnificent tree grew in the center of it. Its massive, gnarled trunk twisted up, tapering sharply as it went; its limbs sprawled everywhere. Some of the thicker, lower ones had come back to earth and taken root, where smaller trees had sprouted. On its limbs hung round, coppery fruit.

The inner palace had four entrances from the courtyard.

The rooms in the upper palace were bigger. One full quarter of it was a single huge throne room. The ceiling vaulted high above, and in the domed center of it was a huge sun made of what appeared to be gold. The sphere sent out waving rays of metal, veined into the amber, radiating across the arched ceiling and down the walls, which were themselves carved and painted with cranes, hawks, geese, swans, deer, bulls, lizards, snakes, bees, butterflies, dragonflies, flowering trees, bushes, and vines, each stylized blossom resembling smaller versions of the sun. The floor was inlaid with images of hundreds of fish and sea creatures carved from many sorts of stone.

The throne was also of gold, and by contrast with the rest of the room, rather plain.

A giant woman sat the throne. Her robe was white, hemmed in flowing gold patterns. She wore no crown, but the shimmering yellow of her hair cascaded in ringlets. She wasn't a skeleton, like the others they had seen, but her skin was almost as white as bone. Her eyes were closed, and her head tilted down to rest on her chest. Despite the colors and her fair skin, after he had been looking at her for a few seconds, Errol felt his sight dim, as if darkness were emanating from her somehow; not shadow exactly, but the opposite of light.

"Is she alive?" Errol murmured.

"There is something there," Shandor whispered. He seemed in awe, which was out of character for him. "Something more like death than life."

Aster spoke a few words and took a step forward, but the darkness suddenly intensified; Aster gasped and stumbled. Billy caught her before she could actually fall.

"Out," Aster said. "Everyone."

"What happened?" Errol asked, once they were out of the room.

"I'm not sure," Aster said. "I felt something watching us. And then it reached for me, touched me. Something terrible." She shook her head as if to clear it. "I don't know what we're supposed to find here. But I hope it isn't her."

"Let's look around some more," Errol said.

The rest of the upper story was filled with lavish banquet halls, vast bedrooms, and baths. A staircase led to the roof, which — aside from the dome above the throne room — was flat. There they discovered fountains and gardens full of withered flowers and trees, along with a very large, four-wheeled wagon made to be drawn by draft animals of some sort — horses or oxen, maybe. But they would have to be the size of elephants.

In all of this, they found no sign of anything actually living. Not a bird, lizard, or bug.

"Where are the children?" Delia asked. "I understand the lack of adults, but everywhere I've been, the curse spared the children."

"Yes," Dusk replied. "Usually, anyway."

"The city of pyramids," Errol said. "We didn't see anyone at all there, not in the city itself."

"They were there at first," Dusk said. "My brother Hawk conscripted them all, either keeping them in his entourage or sending them elsewhere to fight his wars."

"Maybe the ones here left, too," Aster said. "Maybe they didn't want to stay here, with the skeletons of their parents."

"Yeah," Errol said. "I can understand that. On the other hand, we haven't searched the whole place yet. Have you figured out why we're here?"

"Not yet," Aster said. "But I'm sure this is where my father wanted me to go.."

"It could be her," Dusk said. "The woman. She's the only one who isn't a skeleton. And if this is some higher and farther away version of the lands I know, then this place — my mother's palace might be a shadow of it. And my mother a shadow of . . . *her*. And a descendant, if this place is what I think it is. "

"You called it *Ghartas Sauvens*," Aster said. "The Demesne of the Sun Queen."

"Yes."

"So, hang on," Errol said. "Dusk's Kingdoms—to me, they seem like fairy tales. Snow White. Jack and the Beanstalk. There's magic and such, but the people are basically people. But these guys—"

"Would be more like what we think of as gods," Aster finished. "Like those of the Greeks or Norse. The amount of elumiris here is incredible. We are fortunate they're all dead, or—whatever state *she's* in. If any of them were around, I think we wouldn't last ten seconds if they wanted to kill us, or enslave us, or turn us into pigeons."

"So this is it?" Errol said. "The top? The highest and farthest away? Where we're trying to get to? Could the woman on the throne actually be the Sun, like in the story? Hidden away in her castle?"

Aster shook her head. "I don't think so. A sun queen, yes. The actual personification of the sun—I don't think so. Not yet. I think we have further to go. Dad's ship got us this far. From here, I think we're on our own."

"Maybe the wagon," Dusk suggested. "Perhaps it can take us further."

"Maybe," Aster conceded. "Let's take a break, eat something, and have another look."

They rested on the roof; it was chilly, but they were loath to break up anything there to make a fire. Aster was able to conjure one that burned right on the stone, without need for fuel. They ate cheese and dried meat they had packed up with them and sat talking for a little while, but after a bit, Aster and Billy wandered off, and Ms. Fincher said she was going to sleep. A little after that, Dusk tugged at his hand.

"Let us keep watch," she said.

Errol glanced over at Shandor, the only one remaining at the fire.

The Gypsy nodded. "I will rest," he said, "and relieve you in a bit."

"Okay," Errol said.

***

Aster remembered the first time she had kissed Billy. It had been — important. It wasn't the first time she had kissed someone, but it was the first time she had liked it. And she had really liked it. This thing people had talked about, love, had for most of her life been beyond her. She had loved her father, of course, but that was sort of the point. For her, love was all tied up with pain and loss, and was never an entirely good thing. Good things didn't last. Billy hadn't lasted; she had just decided she loved him when he vanished from her life.

Now he had returned to her, against all odds. And now, when they were alone — at her father's ancient tower, and now here — his kisses felt . . . hungrier. His hands moved on her body more freely each time. Sometimes it felt good, sometimes his choices were . . . puzzling. She wanted more and less at the same time. She knew where this was going, in one sense. Billy was restrained and respectful, but whatever he had been born, he currently owned the body and yearnings of a young human man. And that body wanted hers, there could be no doubt of that. But like love, her feelings about sex were — fraught. All twisted up with violence and control. She was both curious and repelled by the very idea of it, of letting someone not just close, but *inside* of her. The one time it had nearly happened, there had been a knife at her throat.

And if they had sex, and it was okay, and she didn't hate it—what then? Where did they go from that? Nothing good lasted, right? Everything had to end. Zhedye, what if she got pregnant? Were there spells to stop that happening?

Their lips parted, and she had no doubt what she saw in his eyes. But as much as she wanted to embrace it, to just let it be, it wasn't in her nature.

"Why did you come back to me?" she asked softly.

"Because I love you," he said. It came out immediately, which was weird. Billy almost never answered a question without thinking about it for a *long* time. It was both one of his most endearing and most annoying characteristics.

"I know," she said. "but—you said giants don't feel love—not like this. Not for something or someone—so small."

This time he did take a while to answer.

"You're right," he said. "I wandered distant places, waded in the sea whose far shore is the stars, where everything is very big, and very slow."

"Yes," Aster said. "You've told me this. That sometimes giants become curious about the little things, and become small, so they can experience what... *we* experience. But then you become big again and forget the little things. But you didn't forget me."

"Because I learned that love is not a little thing," he said.

"Yes, you said that, too. But I don't understand it," Aster said. "It's wonderful, but I don't know what it means. Has this happened to other giants?"

"I don't know," Billy said.

"How can you not know that?"

"I have seen other giants," he said. "We know when another is around. But we don't—talk, or touch, or . . . kiss. We don't go looking for company. We don't like or love—or hate."

"Really? Then how do — umm — how are more giants made?"

"We just — *are,*" he said. "We always have been. There are no giant children."

"It sounds lonely," she said.

"It's not, when you're a giant," he replied.

"And yet you chose to be like this? Small?"

"I didn't choose it," Billy said, touching her cheek with the palm of his hand. "It chose me. You chose me."

"What do you mean?" she asked. "You think I cast a spell on you, or something?"

"No," he said. "It's more — basic — than that. I can't explain it. I can only feel it."

"So you're saying this isn't so much something you want as something the universe is forcing you to do?"

"I . . . you're confusing me," Billy said. "I love you."

"Yes," she said. "I hear that. I just — that's a word, Billy. Everyone means something different by it."

"You say it," he said. "What do you mean?"

"You know what?" she said. "I don't know."

She disentangled from him. He tried to pull her back, but she wouldn't let him; he didn't force it; he let her go. But what if he didn't? Even as a human, he was stronger than she. Of course, she had her magic. . . .

She needed to be alone. Now.

"What's wrong?" he asked.

"Nothing," she said. "I just remembered, there's something I need to do."

NINE

THE CHILDREN OF GODS

T he silver ship was where Aster had left it. She murmured the password and boarded, went down to her quarters, and opened the box she'd put the automaton's head in. She had tried several times on the voyage to destroy it or dismiss the spirit that inhabited it but had been unable to do either; any physical damage to it repaired itself in relatively short order. And the spirit in it was *strong*.

The body was probably following. It might be a year behind them or a few days. But either way, keeping the head around seemed dangerous. It was time to deal with it.

She took it from the box, then wafted her way back up the stairs and walked to the edge of the cliff with no bottom. She stood there for a moment, ready to pitch it in. But she paused. She lifted it in front of her so the eyes she had carved were looking at her.

She had made it for Errol but hadn't been satisfied with it. She'd thought she could do better, and she had. The model Errol had worn not only looked more like him, but had several improvements, including a little homunculus of bone that contained his soul, in case he had to leave the bigger body. But obviously, she had built this one well enough to carry a passenger of spirit.

She wondered which of Dusk's siblings had summoned this thing. Nocturn seemed the likeliest bet, and yet—how had she managed it? It was difficult working magic in a world that held so little of it. Aster had spent years learning to do it, but she had had one of the greatest sorcerers ever known to help her along. How had Nocturn—or any of her cousins—been able to turn such a trick?

"*Speledi*," she murmured, commanding it to speak. She had tried before, without result. She didn't expect it to work this time, either.

The eyes remained vacant. She sighed, and drew back her arm to throw it into the gulf, even as all of the hairs on it pricked up.

"What shall I say?" the head asked.

The lips did not move, the eyes did not light. But she heard the words as clearly as when Errol had spoken, housed in his automaton.

"Tell me who you are," she said.

"I am not worthy of a name," the head said. "I have never been given one."

"What are you, then?"

"I am sent to fetch," it said. "To fetch what my master desires."

"Who is your master?"

"Why would that person tell me their name? It would only loosen their power over me. I know their command and their desire but cannot tell you who they are."

"Then what did they send you for?"

"Why should I tell you that?" the head said. "You made me speak, but I already have a master."

"Tell me or I will cast this head into the abyss," she said.

"You can do that," the head said. "It is in your power."

She didn't like the sound of that. It reminded her of a story about a rabbit, a fox, and a thicket of briars she had once heard.

She still wasn't strong enough to destroy it. Until she was, it was best she keep it under her control.

She put it back into the box, latched in, and then put the strongest Utterance of Sealing she could muster.

As she prepared to return to the others, she became certain of one thing. The automaton that had followed them from the mall had not been animated by Nocturn, or Hawk, or any of her cousins.

Something else was after them.

***

Veronica was dozing in the cave when she felt someone arrive.

Someone had come to see the Severed Giant.

That's what Veronica called him, anyway.

She had been in this place for a while, long enough to become bored of waiting for Errol to arrive. She had even begun to worry that Mistral might have been mistaken about her ability to find where Errol was headed. Or maybe he *had been* coming here but hadn't made it. She had sneaked past some things at the boundary of this Kingdom, wild, insane things that might have been people once, if people had lightning or molten metal or ice for blood and spent their time in constant rage, shifting forms from more-or-less human to titanic wolves, bears, and storm clouds. They hadn't noticed her slip in, but they were always looking, like dogs sure there was a scrap of meat on the floor someplace. They were infected by the enemy, and so was the silent queen on her golden throne. The castle wasn't safe. But down here, in the Severed Giant's cave, near the water, she felt hidden. And she was starting to understand what the giant wanted.

But now someone else had arrived. Delia Fincher.

She hadn't seen Veronica yet; in fact, her eyes were strangely vacant as she began walking on the huge chains that held the cavern's occupant.

The Severed Giant was at least a hundred feet long, maybe more. His skin was grey and withered and clung tightly to his bones, his long, lank hair was the color of dishwater. He was suspended by an arm and a leg, on huge metal chains, so he hung like a hammock, just a few yards above the water basin in the middle of the cave.

An eye was turned in Delia's direction as she approached, huge, white, and opaque, like that of a long-dead fish. He did not have another eye; in fact, half of his head was missing, and half of his body, as if he had been sliced in two by an unimaginably large knife or saw and the right side discarded. He was twisted and his back bent the wrong way into an arc; she could see his severed insides, still red with blood.

But he was not dead. His veins were pulsating; blood still flowing in them. She watched his single lung sluggishly inflate, pushing out of the open chest cavity, then diminish back into the riven cage of his ribs.

Delia completed her trip across the chain, made her way up to the creature's head, and then closed her eyes and snuggled up against him.

Even given everything Veronica had seen, been through, and done, that seemed a little weird. But it confirmed the notion that had been growing in her gut.

But that would wait. If Delia was here, Errol must also be.

***

Errol and Dusk sat on the edge of the palace roof, right at one of the corners. It gave them an excellent view of the plains and mountains, as well as part of the depths that surrounded the place. In the High and Faraway, you never knew what direction trouble might come from. It could as easily arrive by dragon or flying ship as by land, so a good watchman tried to cover all of his bases.

He was a decent watchman. Dusk was excellent.

Together, they left something to be desired.

Despite his misgivings, they were kissing again. It was weird, at first. Dusk had plenty of enthusiasm, but not a lot of practice. It felt like she was trying to prove a point or win a contest, at times. But eventually—after a minute or so—he warmed up to it. His mind stopped trying to talk him out of it, and the back part of his brain that was concerned mostly about things below the waist kicked in. He began moving his lips across her cheek, to her ear, down to her neck. . . .

She knocked him back so hard his head went light.

"What the . . ." he gasped. She was staring at him, wide-eyed, touching her neck, panting. "What's wrong?"

"You were . . . my neck. What were you doing?"

"Kissing you," he said.

"Surely not!" Dusk said. "Kissing is for the lips."

"Okay, well, maybe technically it's called necking," Errol said. "But it's a thing we do where I come from. If you don't like it—"

"Like it?" she said. "I feared you were going to bite me."

"What, like a vampire?"

"I don't know what that is," she said. "I meant like a wolf, or a lion. The neck is . . . vulnerable. A single well-placed bite, and I would be dead in a matter of heartbeats."

"But why would I do that?" Errol asked.

"You wouldn't, of course," Dusk said. "I know that. But . . ."

"It's meant to feel good," Errol said. "You didn't like it at all?"

"It felt dangerous."

He shrugged. "Maybe that's why people like it," he said. "I never thought about it like this, but maybe it shows trust. You know, that you trust the person you're kissing."

She looked dubious. "So you would let me do that to you?"

"Ah — well, yeah. If I have to. You know, to prove I trust you."

"Very well," she said. "Bare your neck."

"So," he said, "you probably don't want to start that way," he said. "You do what I did, just sort of move down there — "

"You mean sneak, like a thief?"

"You've stolen things," he pointed out.

"No," she said. "I've *taken* things. That's different. Bare your neck."

"Fine," he said. He leaned his head back and a little over to the side. She started kissing him.

"Like that?" she said.

"Ah — maybe slower. Gentle. Like you're looking for something with your lips."

She frowned, but then bent back to him.

"Oh!" he said.

"That's right?" she said.

"Umm. Yeah," he said. "That's — good."

He reached up and stroked her long, auburn hair as her lips moved up his neck. He felt like he was melting. He tried to keep quiet, but he couldn't help a gasp now and then. His skin had always been sensitive, and it had been a long time . . .

She came back up and faced him, smiling.

"Well?"

"That's fun, Errol," she whispered. "You're so helpless. Like I could do anything to you, and you couldn't stop me."

"Right," he said, trying to calm his breathing. "Like that."

"I could bite off your ear or slit your throat. Anything."

He blinked. "We need to work on your pillow talk," he said.

"My what?"

"Never mind," she said. "You want to switch, let me try now?"

"You want me to be helpless, Errol?" she asked, lowering her lips toward his.

"Well, not *helpless* . . ." he said.

She kissed him, and it went on for a while. She was catching on.

They parted and looked into each other's eyes for what seemed a hundred years.

"I'm not helpless, Errol," she said. "I cannot be."

"Okay," he said. "But can you trust me?"

"I'm trying to do that," she said. "That also does not come easily to me."

At first, he thought the noise he heard was some sort of sound effect in his head, to go along with the pounding of his pulse. But then he realized it was something else, something familiar.

Dusk heard it too. "It sounds like horns," she said.

It did, a little. And there were lots of them. Some were almost below the range of hearing, and others sounded something like the distant screech of jet engines. They rose and faded and rose again, dissonant and unsettling.

The horizon lit with lightning, and again, as if a storm were coming over the mountains. There was another jagged line of light, and another, then tens and hundreds of them.

"If it is a storm," she said. "I think it an uncanny one."

"What?"

"I think someone knows we're here, and they don't think we ought to be."

"Someone? Who?"

"We were wondering what happened to the children," she said. "That might be them."

The children of gods, Errol thought. He remembered reading some Greek and Norse mythology. He remembered thinking that most of those characters weren't the sort you wanted to meet or even see from a distance. He looked back. The flashes seemed to be getting closer, albeit slowly. And the horns were getting louder, wilder.

"This is interesting," Shandor said, coming up behind them. Errol wondered how much he had seen and heard, and again felt a brief twinge of guilt. Shandor made no bones about his feelings for Veronica. He would certainly mention all of this to her.

But that didn't matter, did it? Veronica was gone. Let Shandor pine after her.

The storm — if that's what it was — drew nearer.

"We'd best put our armor back on," Dusk said.

"Probably a good idea."

***

Dusk's armor was just beside them, and she was still wearing the padded cloth gambeson that went under it. Errol, on the other hand, had to strip down to skin to get his armor on, since it magically melded to his flesh. He went around behind the wagon to change, then went to alert the others. He almost bumped into Aster as he came around the wagon.

Had anyone actually gone to sleep? Across the roof, he saw Billy coming their way. That left Ms. Fincher, who was probably best left out of whatever-this-was anyway.

The flickering grew brighter and brighter, and in its light he now saw shadows, and as they drew even nearer, huge shapes in the sky.

Then the entire plain lit up with a terrific flash of lightning, and as the light faded, he made out four people on horseback, galloping toward the fortress, the hooves of their steeds striking sparks on the ground. They road across the bridge and in through the gate. After that, he was unable to see them.

"Dusk," he said. "If you're right, and these are the . . . kids . . . what do we do?"

"I see no point in hiding," Dusk said. "They must be coming up the way we did. They obviously know we're here."

"Aster can cast her floaty spell on us and we can jump off the wall and beat it back to the silver ship," he pointed out. "By the time they figure out we're not up here anymore, we would be most of the way there."

"We haven't got what we came for," Aster said. "We don't know that they mean to attack us. Maybe they can help. And if things do go badly, at least we're all here."

"I agree," Dusk said. "We have no where else to go. We should stand our ground."

"Fine," Errol said. But look—we aren't all here. Where's Ms. Fincher?"

"I don't know," Aster said. "But it's probably better she's not involved."

"Yeah, but where is she? I don't think she would just wander off in a strange place."

"She's a grown woman," Shandor said. "She can do as she thinks best. And this is not the time to worry about that. The strangers have arrived."

Errol followed Shandor's gaze and saw them coming up the ramp.

It was immediately clear which of the four was the leader, not only because she rode a little ahead of the other three, but by her bearing. She looked to be around his age—you never saw anyone much older in the High and Faraway—but she was considerably taller, probably about nine feet in height. Her hair was black, shot through with white here and there. Her eyes, even in the dim light, were steel blue. She wore a long, sleeveless shirt of what looked like wool, leather leggings and boots, and a cloak pinned at one shoulder. She held a spear in one hand and had a round shield slung on one flank of her horse. A leather cord with a bit of gold dangled at her neck. Her bare arms were covered in tattoos of stylized wolves, horses, and snakes.

Her companions were all female, dressed in roughly the same way, but although they were all as tall or taller than him, they looked younger — nine or ten.

All of their horses were gigantic, of course. The saddles were ornate affairs of wood, leather, and brightly patterned felt, like those he had seen in the stables. Like those in the fortress, they did not have stirrups.

The woman did not dismount; she stared down at them like they were rats or maybe cockroaches that she had discovered in her house.

"*Kwes yus heste?*" she demanded.

Errol understood the tone, but not the words.

"*Viemes,*" Aster said.

The woman frowned at Aster. "Are you trying to talk?" she asked.

"Now we can understand one another," Aster replied.

That didn't seem to give the woman any pleasure.

"Name yourselves," she demanded. "You who have invaded this sacred place."

"My name is Aster. We have not come to trouble anyone. Who do I have the honor of addressing?

"I am Daughter of the Thundering Sky and the Grain That Ripens in The Field," she declared. "I am The Oak on The Height, She Who Strikes from Heaven. You must be from far away not to know this."

"Very far away," Aster said. "Can you tell us what happened here?"

If possible, the woman looked more annoyed than ever. She dismounted and signed for the others to do so was well. Standing, she was even more intimidating.

"Who sent you?" she demanded. "One of my wayward cousins? The Covered One? Who?"

"I don't know what you're talking about," Aster said. "I came here seeking something. I have no quarrel with anyone here."

Dusk's sword whisked from its sheath. "But if you bring a quarrel," she said, "we will answer it."

"No, Dusk," Aster said. "We're not here to fight her."

The tall woman actually cracked a smile.

"A brave one," she said. "That is not in itself a terrible thing. But do not confuse bravery with insolence, for then we will have to come to terms."

"If you take on her, you take me on, too," Errol said.

"I have never been more frightened," the woman said. "I wonder if I should offer you my surrender?"

"Now you show *your* lack of manners," Shandor said. "We have done nothing to earn such contempt, no matter who you are or what your station."

The tall woman's face softened a little, and her voice dropped down.

"It is not contempt, you know," she said. "It is affection. I have always been fond of you Smallings. I have many in my service and treat them all well. It is my duty as your superior to do so."

"Are you sure you know what contempt means?" Aster said.

The tall woman stared at her then barked out a short laugh.

"Let's get back to the matter at hand," the woman said. "Can it be you are ignorant of what you have done? That you have broken the truce?"

"We don't know anything about any truce," Aster said.

"Ah," the woman said. "Yet you came through the fire that guards the gates. You should have taken that as a sign that you were not wanted here." She tilted her head. "And yet you did pass, didn't you?"

"That wasn't too hard," Aster said. "Just a little spell."

"And blood," the woman said. "There is blood somehow. We are kin, though distant, as the regal swan and the lowly grouse are of the same clan. But I believe you. It is not malice that brought you here, but ignorance and ill-luck. Nevertheless, you have brought on the season of slaughter. There is no halting that now. So we had best prepare. You are armed, at least, although in a most peculiar manner." She bent over and tapped on Dusk's armor. "Like a little turtle, aren't you?"

"Aster," Errol said, "what the hell is she talking about?"

"We may have just started a war," Aster said.

"Well, it's not our war, is it?" Errol said. "I mean, does this have anything to do with — you-know-what?"

"I don't know," Aster.

"I stand before you," the woman said. "Do not speak in riddles to one another. Here is the plain truth; you *have* brought war upon this place. That is not to be despised. War tests what is best in us. You will fight with my koreos, my war-band. At my side, when the time comes."

"And if we don't?" Errol said.

"Do you know who I am?"

"Well, you said a lot of names," Errol replied. "All of them pretty long."

"You may call me Tempest," she said. "And you are not my equal. I am your battle-lord. You will fight for me, and I will guide you to glory."

Errol wanted to tell her she was full of it, that there was zero chance he was going to do anything just because she said so, much less fight in a war he didn't understand in the slightest.

He opened his mouth to say so.

"Yes, Lady," was what he said.

That was bad enough, but he heard Dusk say it, too, and Aster, and even Shandor. Billy didn't say anything at all.

Tempest nodded, and then she turned to her attendants. "Ready yourselves," she said. "Call the charioteers and other Smallings and prepare to receive my kindred." Then she turned back to them.

"Gird yourselves," she said. She pointed at Errol. "You ride with me in my chariot," she said. "The rest of you will be assigned. I shall go to find the lay of our enemies."

She mounted back up, and in moments, all four of them were out of sight.

TEN
IMMORTAL FAME

"What the hell just happened?" Errol said.

"An Obligation," Aster said. "More powerful than any I ever imagined."

"But you can break it, right?" Errol said.

"Well," Aster said. "I don't think so. The Obligation itself prevents me from trying."

***

The next day, Tempest returned with reinforcements. A lot of them seemed human—or at least they were no taller than he was. But she also brought more of her larger-than life clan. They gathered on the ground in front of the fortress, setting up round tents and building bonfires. By the end of the day, he figured there was maybe a thousand of them down there. At that point he could see they broke out into individual camps; Tempest and her warrior-women were at the center of one, surrounded by maybe forty or fifty people-sized types. The latter arrived in wagons, like those he had seen when they were still on the river.

After a while, a man in a felt shirt and pants came up onto the roof and told them all Tempest wanted to see them.

"You can tell her to screw off," Errol said.

"Follow me please," the man said.

"Right," Errol said. But even as the words left his mouth he stood up and started walking. So did Dusk, and the others.

"Shit," he said. "Aster, is there really nothing you can do about this?"

"We've already been through, this Errol," Aster said.

"Right," he said. "Sorry. It's just hard to deal with my mouth saying one thing and my body doing the other."

"She's going to regret this," Dusk said. "I am not to be treated in this fashion. When the times comes, she will learn that."

Errol remembered a time not so long ago when Dusk had compelled him to follow her; he had been just as helpless to say no as he was now. That had been before he and Dusk got . . . friendly. But part of him was amused that she was getting a taste of her own medicine.

"So who are you?" Errol asked their guide.

"I am called Handler of Horses," he said.

"And you work for Tempest?"

"I am the Lady's charioteer," he said. "It's a great honor."

"So you've fought in one of these things before?" Errol asked.

"No," Handler said. "I was too young last time there was a war. My father was her father's driver then."

"How did that go?"

"He died stained in glory," Handler said.

"That doesn't make you think twice about this whole business?" Errol asked.

Handler seemed surprised at the question. "What better fate than to fight and die with the gods themselves?" he asked.

"I don't know," Errol said. "I can think of a few."

Handler ushered them into the biggest tent Errol had ever seen. Tempest was there, seated on a gigantic stool, drinking something from a huge bull horn. Her warrior woman and a number of smaller people sat around her, attentive.

"Ah," she said. "Our newcomers. You have questions, I'm certain. I will answer them, if they are not impertinent."

"A plea first, Lady," Aster said. "Before we met you, we were on a quest. Our intent is to restore the days and the seasons, to end the curse that has come upon the world."

Tempest took another swig of her drink.

"I see," she said. "You would restore our mothers and fathers to their thrones? Recall them from the dead?"

"Not specifically," Aster said. "The world is falling apart. The Sun is fading. Soon everything and everyone will die. We hope to prevent that."

"You tiny creatures aspire to accomplish what the mightiest gods could not?" Tempest asked. "Do you think we made no effort toward those ends?"

"No," Aster said. "I'm sure you did. But I am asking—begging— your leave to try."

"I see," the woman said. "You have finished speaking?"

"That's all I have to say for now," Aster replied.

"Good. Then now hear my words. Behind us is the castle of Sahual, the great Lady of the Sun. Once this was a place of glory, the gateway of the Sun itself, favored palace of the Daughter of the Sky. But then the Weird came upon us, and all of the first and second generations of gods died, leaving only us, their children—and Sahual. But as you have seen, while she did not die, she is not . . . well. After the elder gods perished, there was much fighting among us, their children, each lord and lady, eager to claim their glory and the fortresses of our fathers and mothers. Eventually the quarrel became so great we met here, and we all swore an Oath Unbreakable, that this place should be sacrosanct, that none of us should take it for our own. For this palace is our only hope. Sahual yet lives, as does her handmaid, Hausas. One day they will wake, and the heavens will again become ordered. Until that time, this place was to be left alone. But then you came here."

"Knowing none of this," Dusk interrupted.

"Granted," Tempest said. "But it matters not. I thought someone had broken the truce; in coming to see who it was, I broke it myself."

"I'm sure you could explain to the others," Aster said. "We can help you."

"Yes," Tempest said. "We might explain, if our enemies could speak. But they cannot, I fear. Monsters lurk outside the boundaries of our gardens. Some of my cousins have pledged faith with them, broken bread, lain amongst them. In so doing they have become monsters themselves and lost the gifts of speech and reason. The only thing that has kept them from this place, from destroying our last hope, is the power of the Oath, made before they fell to their low alliances. Now that is broken, and they will not care what pretty words I put in their ears. So I have gathered my brothers, sisters, and cousins who remain faithful to our old ways. We have called to us those who invoke us and give us gifts, and who we in turn protect. And we will hold this place against the army of Night that advances upon us. And because you have a part in this, you will stand with us."

"But what if I can figure it out?" Aster said. "How to bring Sahual back?"

"That's easy," Tempest said. "We all know how to do that. To bring her back we need her Handmaiden. But Hausas is nowhere to be found, though we have searched ceaselessly for her."

"Maybe—"Aster began.

Tempest waved her off. "No more talk of this. If we triumph in the coming battle, we will discuss it again."

She looked them over. "Four of you are armed. You will fight in my cohort." She nodded her head toward Aster. "You, without a weapon. I sense you have some sorcery. Is it of war-like nature?"

"I have used it to fight," Aster said.

"Then perhaps an apt place for you is behind the walls, were you can do your work without worry about defending your body." She nodded at Dusk. "You will fight with my vanguard."

"Very well," Dusk said.

Then she pointed at Errol. "You shall ride with me in my chariot."

"I don't know anything about fighting in chariots," Errol said.

"You needn't worry about that. I shall do the fighting, and my charioteer will drive. In that kit you're wearing, you're a walking shield. You need only defend my back."

"Whatever," Errol said. "But maybe I should have a look at one of these chariots first, so I don't go in completely cold."

"An excellent idea," she said. "Handler will show you."

***

It seemed to Errol that *chariot* was a fancy word for what looked more like a two-wheeled box on wheels. In fact, it wasn't even a box—it was open in the back. A long wooden shaft protruded from the front, with two yolks fastened to either side of it at the end. Handler explained those would go on the two horses that would pull it.

"So I'll be up front here, handling the horses," he said. "Our Lady will stand in the car and fling javelins. When she is out of those she'll go to sword. Now, usually there's no room for a third in the car, but since we're both little, she can take an extra. While's she's hurling javelins, you'll cut down those coming behind or from the side."

"That sounds great," Errol said.

***

T hat night he, Dusk, and Shandor camped with Tempest's *Koreos*. The wagons they had arrived in were drawn up in a semicircle with the open side to the fortress, guarding the entrance to the bridge. They reminded Errol of the wagons in old westerns, with big spoked wheels, but they were more colorful; the wood was painted with stylized animals, sun symbols, eyes, and dragons. The felt awnings were similarly dyed. After setting up Tempest's tents, they put up more of their own, some of which were big enough to hold twenty people and more. These too were beautifully decorated. Beyond these things, their weapons, and a few tools, these people didn't seem to carry a lot of permanent objects. It made sense they would make the most of the ones they had. In fact, he had seen something like this before.

"This reminds me of your people," Errol told Shandor.

"Similar," Shandor said. "We also are a people always on the move. Tents, horses, wagons—it is how such people live. It is the only way to live, in my opinion."

"Don't take this the wrong way," Errol said. "But haven't you been camped in the Pale outside of Sowashee for a long time?"

Shandor smiled. "Because you encountered me there?"

"Well, it just that local legends—"

"Yes, my father and mother are buried in your town, on your side of the Pale," Shandor said. "And so I return there to pay tribute to them. We make camp, and I cross into the Reign, and honor them. But then, me and mine, we move on. Even in the Pale, there are many and varied countries, things to see, bargains to be made, adventures to be had. And at the end of the year we come back to that spot near your town."

"Do you miss your people?" Dusk asked.

"Very much," Shandor said.

"And yet you are here, all for the love of a girl."

"Veronica?" Shandor said. "She is magnificent and would be a fitting bride for me. Together we could make the many tribes one and rule an empire as grand as any. An empire of caravans and wagons such has never been known. But I know I have little hope of winning her, and that is not why I am here. I am here because she believes you will end this curse. And if she believes it, I know it to be true. So I am here, with my sword, for you and not for her."

"If she thinks we're going to end the curse, why isn't she here? Why isn't she helping us, too?"

"I suspect she is, in her own way," Shandor said. "After all, she sent me to your aid."

"Sure," Errol said. "But why not come herself?"

Shandor hesitated. "I'm not certain of this," he said. "I may be speaking more than I know."

"So we'll take it with a grain of salt," Errol said.

Shandor nodded. "There is, in the heart of this universe, a sickness. We call it *Mamioro*. My grandfather's people, they called it *Na Lusa Chito*. And this thing, if it touches you in a certain way, you become a part of it. Sometimes you don't even know it's happened; you just start doing evil and don't know why. Now, knowing that, you must consider what a prize Veronica would be to *Mamioro*. And there is in her heart a yearning to be a part of it. I believe that yearning is offset mostly by her love for you, her friends. But she fights that battle — against her own will — far from you, so that if she yields . . ."

"She doesn't kill us all," Dusk finished. "Yes, I can easily see that. So in your mind, if she approaches us, it might not be with good intentions? It could mean she has become the instrument of the ill?"

"Or, perhaps not," Shandor said. "It is just as possible that she fears my good looks and abundant wit will finally seduce her to my side."

Errol smiled, but Dusk was not ready to let the subject go. "Either way, it is a matter of discipline," she said. "Of self-control. Which, sad to say, Veronica does not have in abundance."

"She has more than you think," Errol said. "I've seen her tempted. I've seen her right on the edge. And she always came back."

"I grant you that," Dusk said. "But then she always had something — no, someone — to come back *for*. What if she no longer believes that to be the case?"

"She saved your life," Errol said, feeling a little heated. "After you tried to take hers. And that was after she knew that you and I had . . ." He stopped. This was a dangerous topic, and it was a personal one, and although he liked Shandor fine, he didn't want to get into his love life in front of him.

"Anyway," he said. "Let's hope she stays on our side."

Across the tent, a musical note sounded, and then another. Errol looked up and saw Handler had a crowd of mostly younger — and mostly female — admirers gathered before him. He held a stringed instrument made of a turtle shell and two antlers with a wooden crosspiece. From where he sat, Errol thought it had seven, maybe eight strings.

Handler struck a chord, and then he began to sing.

I sing of those
Of Ancient Fame,
Of the fame of gods and heroes
Swift horses and Man-killers
Who flew to battle unafraid
In chariots with wheels like the Sun
And in their deaths found Immortal Fame
In the tales of their deeds,
In the songs we sing of them.

Errol sighed.

"What's the matter?" Dusk asked.

"We're screwed," Errol replied.

***

A ster saw the enemy arrive from the rooftops; they came without lightning or the fanfare of trumpets of Tempest and her kin, but they brought a fog with them, and pale green lights burned in the mists. A stench drifted on the wind, but it was nothing she recognized; not the stink of putrefaction, or the throat-itch of smoke, but more like sickly sweet flowers or honey somehow gone bad. Tempest and her brothers, sisters, and cousins had their chariots in a line, facing the enemy, with their foot soldiers in roughly square formations behind them.

The enemy had chariots too, big ones, and they were not drawn by horses, but by much stranger things; lions with beaks like eagles, monstrous leopard-spotted bulls, snake-headed dogs the size of elk. Those that rode in the chariots, from what she could see through the mists, were also an odd mix. Most were even bigger than Tempest, and some were truly beautiful, their wild features framed by tumbling locks of dark hair, eyes a little too large, even given their proportions, and features that wouldn't have looked out of place on Greek statues. Others appeared a little off, as if the bodies beneath their cloaks weren't exactly human shaped. Some were a mixture of human and wolf or bear or both.

Alongside the chariots were what she at first took to be centaurs, and she supposed they were, sort of; their lower bodies were those of very large goats, with a human torso attached, finished off with goat heads. They carried spears with shafts as big around as fenceposts and at least a dozen feet in length.

Behind the charioteers and goat centaurs was what could only be accurately described as hordes. They were on foot, and they outnumbered Tempest's infantry by thousands. Some were hulked up larger than elephants and carried uprooted trees for weapons.

The enemy army stopped a couple of hundred yards from Tempest's line, and for a moment there was a long, terrifying silence.

It was time to do something. Aster felt the elumiris flash through her, and almost with thinking she shouted an Utterance and threw out her hands. In the midst of the enemy army, the ground split open and fire spewed out; the crack quickly grew larger, cutting off the massive back end of the army from the front. It wasn't something she planned; she just did what she felt, and the results left her gaping.

This is what it must have felt like to be my father, she thought.

On both sides, the chariots started forward, quickening at an alarming rate.

A dark form rose out of the army, flapping black wings, aimed at her.

I am Aster Kostyena, she thought. *Come and get me.*

***

Errol's teeth rattled together so hard he thought they would break; whoever built the chariots had never heard of shocks, or springs, or any other device to dampen the jolting of the wheels against the uneven earth. It reminded him of rolling down the steep levee of the Reservoir in his little red wagon when he was six. That hadn't ended well. He didn't imagine this would, either.

He gripped his sword one-handed as the air filled with javelins.

Tempest had maybe fifteen of the throwing spears, carried in a leather sheath inside the chariot. She let them fly, shrieking at the top of her lungs, and the enemy returned in kind. He twisted from the path of one, but a second struck his armor. The bronze-tipped weapon glanced off, but it left him seeing spots and fighting for breath. And the other line was still a hundred yards away.

He saw one of Tempest's javelins break the spine of a goat-centaur as she batted away another incoming with the shaft of her next weapon. Beside them, one of the horses drawing another chariot was hit in the head, which essentially exploded as if it had been hit by a bazooka round in a war movie. Still they crashed on, the ground between them closing with dizzying speed. The infantry on both sides were advancing at a trot but were now far behind them.

What's the strategy here? Errol wondered. Surely they weren't just going to slam into the enemy line.

But that's exactly what they did. He had a nightmare vision of Tempest hitting an enemy charioteer in the eye with one of her javelins thrown from nearly point-blank range. Handler wasn't in the wagon at all; he was balanced on the pole that the horses were yoked to. He snapped the reigns and the horses crashed directly into a pair of beaked lions, which tried to dodge aside at the last moment. They scrapped along the left flank of one, and suddenly the beak snapped down at him. He yelped as his sword swung itself, decapitating the beast, and nearly gagged at the smell; then the sides of the two chariots slapped together, and he was off his feet flying through the air—until Tempest hand fastened onto his arm and yanked him back down. The chariot tipped up on one wheel, but Handler got it under control as they turned through the churn of the lines. Tempest tossed another javelin at a warrior in an enemy chariot; then she drew her bronze sword and leapt from the car, landing on the yoke of an approaching vehicle drawn by draft-horse-sized wolves. She struck the charioteer at the junction of his neck and shoulder, cutting down through this sternum. Then she yanked out the blade and split the beautiful head of the warrior beyond nearly in half. As the now unpiloted chariot struck another and caromed away, she leapt back into her own car.

The enemy infantry, perhaps fifty yards away now, broke into a run.

Handler got the chariot into motion, and they ran hard toward them, turning at the last moment so they paralleled the advancing line allowing Tempest to savage them broadside.

It wasn't really fighting; the footmen were armed with spears, club, knives, and short swords, but Errol's reach was longer, and while he didn't know a lot about sword-fighting, the sword knew quite a lot, and it left a trail of severed limbs and slashed torsos behind them as the chariot turned again. As Tempest murdered another dozen of them, he slaughtered those coming from behind them.

They turned and made another pass; Tempest had switched her sword out for a long-handled ax and was wielding it to awful, bloody effect.

It was like being on a rollercoaster going through a hall of horrors, and he hated it. Fighting was okay, but he hated killing. If he could have stopped, he would have. But the ride wouldn't let him off.

About this time, their own foot soldiers were showing up. He had a glimpse of Dusk, auburn hair flowing from beneath her helm, cutting the legs out from under a monster bull pulling a really monstrous chariot, then dancing aside as the contraption crashed to a stop. A giant with almost comically huge eyes roared and leapt from the broken car, cutting at her with a spear that had a blade the size of Errol's sword. Then he lost sight of Dusk in the sweep of battle.

An instant later, the bulls pulling an enemy chariot hit them from the side, and the impact tossed Errol from the car. He fought to his feet and saw Tempest a few yards away, enemies swarming toward her from all sides. He leapt forward and cut down a footman coming at her back.

"I'm here!" he shouted.

"Well you should be," she said. "Keep there."

The next minute or so was the hardest fighting he'd ever been in, and every second of it he thought he was about to die. If it weren't for his armor, he would have. The miracle streak ended when he slipped and fell sideways, looking up in time to see a twelve-foot tall, ape-like fellow raising a tree-trunk to make an end of him.

Then Dusk was there. She danced inside of the monster's guard and butchered him.

***

The black-feathered wings, Aster realized, belonged to the steeds, horses with dragon's heads and scales instead of hair. The two of them pulled a chariot of unusual size even for this battle. The werewolf charioteer was balanced on a web of ropes fixed to the yokes and harness of the "horses."

The warrior in the car was a woman, bare from the waist up. Her skin was either blue or dyed that color. Her eyes were white, with black pupils. Her obsidian hair crawled around in the air as if each strand were the tentacle of a sea anemone.

The chariot rushed toward Aster, wheels spinning like mad, as if somehow finding traction on the air.

The woman flung a javelin. Aster summoned the wind, blowing it aside so that it hit the fortress wall. The amber shattered under the force of the blow; Aster felt bits of it sting her left arm and cheek. She felt a jag of anger, and the elumiris surged, turning white hot inside her mind. A nimbus of red-gold light sprang up around her.

The warrior in the chariot hurled another spear; Aster spat out a Dictate of Immolation. The javelin burst into flame, and a bow-shock of heat and light blasted into the chariot, knocking it back so that it first stalled and then started to fall, as the winged steeds fought for equilibrium.

The ashes that the spear had become hit Aster in the chest; there wasn't enough of it left to penetrate, but the *force* was still there, enough to knock her down.

By the time she stood back up, she saw the chariot was back under control and on its way back to her.

"*Eza azmi areles mezhes,*" she shouted.

Time seemed to slow as she exploded, expanded into a sphere a thousand yards wide, and then slammed back together into a new form. She snapped her wings down and leapt into the air, surprised at what she could see of herself. Her wings were blood red, which wasn't what she had intended. Her target form had been eagle.

But she was huge, and that was intentional.

Another javelin cracked against the stone where she had just been, striking sparks, and an instant later the chariot itself hurled past. The charioteer leaned into his pull on the reins, and the chariot struck one wheel on the roof of the fortress and started back up, turning as it came, the horse dragons furiously beating their wings. Aster fought for more altitude, finding that changing direction wasn't much easier for her than it seemed to be for the chariot. Last time she'd been a bird, she's been a raven of regular size. Now she was larger than a small plane.

She climbed, barely dodging another javelin; then she turned down and closed her wings.

The chariot was still in a turn; Aster saw the woman draw back for another throw and knew the spear would hit her before she could reach her enemy. She opened her wings again, for just an instant, catching the air and causing her to jump up and stall; the spear hissed by just below her.

Then she dropped again, claws out, stooping on the chariot as if it were a field mouse.

Of course, it wasn't a field mouse, and when she hit it, it nearly knocked the breath out of her. Her target was the charioteer, or rather the shaft and ropes that connected the chariot to the horse that was his seat. He leapt back, but not quite far enough; one of her taloned feet struck him; she felt bones snap. The shaft cracked, too, and the car was suddenly connected to the hellish steeds merely by the rope webbing, so it began to buck up and down wildly. She saw the woman in the chariot draw a sword that shone with a dark, bronze light. As she swung, Aster hopped forward, over the blade and caught the warrior in her claws. She yanked her from the tumbling car. Screaming, the woman twisted in her grip, reaching high enough to stab upward with her blade. The pain was almost unbelievable as the sharp point slid in. Aster dropped the woman and careened through the air, trying to regain control. She saw the fortress and started toward that, but then she realized the ground had found her; she felt the impact, and then everything faded away.

ELEVEN

ELEVEN
THE SEVERED GIANT

T empest and her troop pushed forward, and standing side-by-side with Dusk, Errol felt as if they could beat any odds. The enemy was in disarray, not so much retreating as simply running. It felt as if they had already won.

But that was a trick of the mist, which continued to roll forward. And with that mist came the second wave, twelve-foot-tall titans swinging tree trunks like the one Dusk had slain earlier, but dozens of them. He watched one of Tempest's sisters go down beneath two of them; Tempest buried her ax in the skull of one of the monsters, and it stuck there. The second hit Tempest with its huge club, sending her staggering back; but then she drew her short sword and buried it in one of its eyes.

Beyond these guys Errol could see even more monster infantry rushing toward them, having finally circled around the volcano or whatever Aster had conjured up.

Time to retreat, Errol thought.

"For immortal fame!" Tempest shouted, charging.

***

A ster's own breath woke her, rasping in and out of her chest. Where was she?

Then she remembered and looked wildly around. She saw the chariot, and the broken beasts who had pulled it. One was still struggling, weakly, to rise. By the way it moved, she thought it might have a broken back. The charioteer was sprawled in a pool of blood not far away. But where was the woman?

Her neck tingled as something moved in her peripheral vision.

She was only two yards away, dragging herself forward with a spear for a walking stick; one of her legs looked was bent the wrong way — twice — and her leggings were dark with blood. As Dusk scrambled to her feet, the warrior pulled strength from some unknown depths and somehow sprang forward, following her spear toward Aster.

This time she didn't have to say the Dictate of Immolation; it just happened. White hot wind struck the woman and knocked her back, stripping her skin and flesh. Incredibly, as the blast subsided, the warrior — still burning — took a step toward Aster, and then another. Then she collapsed into a pile of blackened bones.

***

Tempest's foot soldiers formed a line with shields overlapping and pressed forward, Tempest using her reach to cut over the shield-wall at the enemy. Dusk, Errol, Billy, and Shandor fought on Tempest's left flank, where the line was weakest. They didn't have shields or training in how to us them, so they stood near each other. Shandor used his sabre like a surgeon, finding the weak spots of things that did not look like they had any. Dusk, rather than tiring, seemed to be gaining strength, and at times he was certain he saw her eyes flash, as if she was taking pictures with them. Billy had a pair of bronze hatchets which he wielded methodically and without passion.

Incredibly, they inched forward, taking ground. The enemy foot wasn't organized; they didn't have shields. Tempest didn't have much of a strategy, but these monsters had none at all. This could still work.

But whatever the gods were made of, Tempest's infantry were just men and women. They grew tired, and the enemy numbers seemed greater than ever, and the shield line started to thin. And ahead, in yet a third wave Errol made out several massive shapes that looked like rhinoceroses roughly the size of elephants. No, bigger than that.

The first to reach them crashed through the shield wall like it was a bunch of playing cards held up by toy army men, flinging broken warriors in every direction with a wicked, curved horn longer than Errol was tall.

Errol was taking a step back, strongly considering a strategic retreat, when Dusk careered past him, straight at the beast.

"Dusk—" he shouted. But there was no point. She was fully aware of what she was doing. Of course she was.

He had two choices, he figured.

Except he didn't. Not really.

There was nothing between him and the rhino but Dusk and a scattering of corpses. Cursing under his breath, terrified half out of his mind, he charged after his friend.

The thing was, he liked rhinos. The idea that he could kill this one was laughable, but even if could, he didn't want to. But then he saw its eyes, and understood that whatever this looked like, it was not a rhinoceros. What he saw in that gaze was a window straight into the rotten heart of the world Shandor had been talking about. This thing didn't feel, or think, or remember. Not anymore. Something or someone had taken all of that away from it. Made it *this*.

The behemoth lowered its head as Dusk raced up. It jabbed its horn at her, lurching forward. Anticipating that, Dusk suddenly jerked backward so the horn missed, then sprang up onto the lowered head. Just behind her, Errol didn't have to do any fancy footwork; he just followed her, hoping for the best. He landed just above the horn, and, gripping the coarse hair of its coat, hung on like the ground was lava.

Dusk, impossibly, had landed in her feet, right on top of the rhino's head. Scrambling to retain her footing, she thrust her sword in one of the rhino's eyes. Errol stabbed the other eye, just as it let forth an unholy bellow, tossed its head, and sent Dusk and him flying.

Errol smacked down on its back, grasping wildly, his hand finding renewed purchase in its hair. The monstrosity was too big to buck like a horse or a bull, so once he had a grip—and was off its head—it wasn't that hard to stay on. He chopped at its spine; the sword cut into the hide, but not deeply enough to do any real damage.

But it was clear the rhino was blind. It had veered from its forward charge and now seemed to be stomping about randomly.

Errol saw Dusk appear ahead; she must have clung to its flank and then climbed back up; now she made her way back towards its head. Why? It was already blind. Did she think she was going to decapitate it?

But when she got there, she slapped the hairy beast with the flat of her weapon, just below its ear.

Bellowing again, the rhino suddenly turned that way seeking the source of its pain. Dusk slapped it again. She was making it turn—into the enemy ranks. In moments she had it charging straight back the way it had come from. Furious, shrieking, its head swinging this way and that, the titan butted and trampled a swath through the enemy. Errol doubled his hold on the rough coat and made his way toward Dusk.

She grinned at him when he got near.

"I've got to hand it to you," he told her. "I never saw this coming."

"Thank you," she said. "I aim to entertain."

"The question is, where do we get off?"

He nodded at the sea of monsters around them. The good news was that the mega-rhino was leaving a trail of crushed foes. The bad news was they were now far behind enemy lines. In the mist, he could no longer make out where Tempest and everyone else was. He couldn't even see the fortress.

"Take heart," she said. "We will know the opportunity when we see it." She leaned down and decapitated some sort of human-lizard hybrid. The enemy was finally catching on to what was happening, and they were trying to grapple the rhino and pull it down by sheer force of numbers. So far it was not working. But in the near distance, something bulked in the mist.

Another rhino. And it clearly had its course set on them. If nothing changed, it was going to gore their mount in the ribs.

"You keep to this beast," Dusk said. "I'll try and duplicate our feat on that one."

"You're nuts," he said.

She leaned over and kissed him. "So I've been told." She straightened up to her full height and then ran along the ridge of the behemoth's back, shouting.

Even though blind, the rhino they were riding sensed something; maybe it smelled the other animal, or maybe the earth-shaking thud of its hooves gave it away, but it suddenly turned, trying to meet the newcomer nose-to-nose. Errol had a view of a horn three feet around at the base and longer than him growing bigger with every heartbeat. He hunkered down, trying to hide behind the hump of muscle on his mount's shoulders.

Dusk, correcting her earlier trajectory, leapt past him, flying through the air as the behemoths collided. The impact was so shockingly powerful that Errol's grip failed instantly, and he was flung into the air, this time away from the creature. He landed hard on one shoulder and rolled, biting back a scream; it felt like he'd broken his collar bone.

The two mountainous brutes had locked horns and began grinding against each other, shivering the earth with each stamp of their hooves. Smaller abominations scrambled away from the combatants for fear of being crushed underfoot. Errol didn't see Dusk. She didn't seem to have made it to the back of the new rhino, but that was the last direction he's seen her going, so he ran that way. A nearly naked warrior covered in black tattoos leapt at him, stabbing at him with a bronze-tipped spear. His sword beat it aside, and he grabbed the shaft with his left hand as his weapon continued to do its thing, burying itself below the fellow's sternum.

He had once sworn off killing. Now it seemed like it was all he did. It was easier when the enemy didn't look human, but this guy could have been his first cousin, except with weirder tattoos. Of course, he was trying to kill Errol, but . . .

The battling giants had cleared the area, but now the dozens of nearby warriors were aware of Errol, and soon he would be surrounded. He did the only thing he could do; he retreated underneath the nearest monster.

"Like minds," someone said.

"Dusk!"

She was crouching a few feet away, grinning.

"I misjudged my jump," she said.

"Well, no one is perfect," he said. "Although you come pretty close. That was a wild ride."

A spear glanced off his armor. The crowd was creeping closer.

"Any ideas?" he said.

"The fortress is in that direction," Dusk said, pointing with a nod. "Beyond these here, this army is moving that way. We can punch through them, and then we'll be at their backs."

"I count about a two dozen," Errol said. "You think we can take them, huh?"

"Side-by-side," she said.

She was serious. On the other hand, if they stayed where they were, the crowd was only going to get bigger. They would eventually either be speared or stepped on.

"Okay," he said. "Ready when you are."

Their sudden charge surprised the nearest warriors; Dusk was like a dervish, her sword whipping in impossible arcs. Errol went with her, guarding her left. He got hit—a lot—but he and Dusk were warded head to foot in plate armor, which easily deflected the wooden and bronze weapons. Their opponents, on the other hand, were wearing mostly skin. It was a huge advantage. But although the blows didn't breach his armor, they hurt; the shock of the hit still traveled. And he was bone-weary. A woman with snakes tattooed on her arms managed to get past his sword and try to wrestle him down, but Dusk sent her reeling away.

And then they drove forward, taking down the last of their immediate attackers. Once through, Dusk's prediction proved correct; coming from behind, the enemy did not see them as opponents, at least not most of them. They didn't draw further attention by attacking anyone, but instead wove between the disorganized brutes, as if they were in a hurry to reach the front line. A couple of the bad guys caught on and took a swing at them, but for the most part it looked like they were in the clear. The fog was thinning, and he could see heavy fighting ahead.

And that's where things turned on them. When they reached the front, they couldn't simply dodge around their opponents anymore; they were all piled up against shield walls. They chose a weak spot to hack through, but unsurprisingly, these guys didn't like being stabbed in the back, and they began turning to face them. At the same time, the enemy kept arriving behind them, and soon he and Dusk were back to back, trying to keep the foe at bay.

"We've been here before," Dusk said.

"Seems familiar," he agreed.

"There's none I would rather stand with, Errol."

"Same here."

The enemy surged around them. Errol stabbed one, and then had to kick whatever-it-was off his blade. While he was doing that, a wolf-faced woman leapt in deep and tackled him at the waist. He slammed her in the head with the pommel of his sword, but she held on, and then someone else came at his legs, toppling him off-balance. A dagger hit his armor inches from his gorge, trying to work through to his throat, and he knew it wouldn't be long before one of them found a way into his flesh. He wished he could see Dusk.

Two of them started trying to tear his helmet off. He was almost completely immobilized under a pile of bodies.

But then his antagonists fell away, or rather, were thrown away. He heard war cries and a fresh clash of arms. Chest heaving, he pushed himself up, sword still gripped in his hand, ready to fight.

Then he saw what had happened. Tempest and what was left of her war band had swept past him, slaughtering his attackers and pushing the front line another fifty feet. He saw Dusk, also rising.

"Are you okay?" he asked.

She nodded, wearily. "We should—"

"Yeah," he said. "Just catching my breath."

They were alive, and that was great, but they were also about to be overwhelmed again, Tempest or no Tempest. There seemed to be no end to the enemy; Tempest's line, such as it was, was now far too short, and the bad guys were working around it. In moments they would all be just as surrounded as he and Dusk had just been.

Tempest saw it too.

"Give ground," she yelled. "But do not turn your backs. We'll fight our way back the fortress."

They drew their ranks tight and did that, though it was slow going. They backed through the camp where they'd spent the night and then began filing onto the bridge. The tents and wagons were empty now, but it was still a terrible thing to see them go up in flames. Finally, they reached the gates, entered the fortress, and closed the massive portals behind them.

Surprisingly, the enemy didn't follow them across the bridge. Instead, they backed off, formed a perimeter around the fortress, and camped.

Inside, Tempest gathered what was left of her war band. Errol guessed that was less than a fourth of what they had started the day with.

"Well done," Tempest told them. "My instincts about you were right. The poets will sing of you, in the ages to come, my brave, death-taunting band. Refresh yourselves. Rest. Tomorrow we return to the field."

"Why not just stay in here?" Errol asked.

"Two reasons," she told him sternly. "The first is that it is not our way. We fight on the field, not hiding behind walls."

"Then what are the walls for?" he asked.

"To keep out the wind," Tempest replied. "Besides, unless you have some way to fill the empty larders of this place, we will begin starving tomorrow, and each day be weaker for the final accounting. I have no intention of dying like that. I would take as many of these with me as I can."

"So you don't think we can win?"

"No," she said. "But we can die like gods, and you like heroes. It will be magnificent."

***

All of the army camped inside the walls that night, most on the roof. Exhausted and sore to the bone, Errol sought out Aster, hoping she had survived, and was relieved to find that she had.

"We need to talk," Errol said. He found Dusk and Shandor, and together the four of them went down into the castle, found a room where they could have some privacy. Aster started a fire; they ate some of their dwindling rations.

"Has anyone seen or heard from Ms. Fincher?" Errol asked.

"Hopefully she's hiding someplace," Aster said. "She wasn't there when Tempest obliged us, so she's free to go. Right now, I don't think there's much we can do for her. If we bring her to Tempest's attention, she could end up as trapped as we are."

"This is true," Shandor said. "She is better off without us right now."

"Okay," Errol said. "Moving on. Tomorrow we're all gonna die. Tempest and her bunch have no interest in saving the world. They just want to go down fighting. They're going to get their wish, and we'll be right there with them. Is there *any* way we can get out of this deal?"

"The ship," Shandor said. "We could return to it, set sail . . ." then he gasped and set his hands to his head. "No," he gasped. "I see. Even trying to make plans . . ."

"If I had time, maybe," Aster said. "But between now and tomorrow—"

"What if we solve the problem between now and tomorrow?" Errol asked. "You know, figure out what your dad's machine brought us here for in the first place."

"We could try and wake the Queen," I suppose," Aster said. "Although from what I felt earlier, that seems . . . wrong, and incredibly dangerous."

"Tempest said we need her Handmaiden," Dusk said. "Perhaps we could trick her somehow? One of us could impersonate the Handmaiden?"

"How would we even know where to start on that?" Errol asked.

"In our stories," Dusk said. "The Sun had a handmaiden — the Morning Star. Or Dawn. Sometimes they are the same person. Aster and I are both of her bloodline. If Aster could somehow . . ." she trailed off. "I'm not sure. It's all I can think of."

"Y'all sound like you could use a little help," a voice said, softly.

It was a familiar voice; one Errol wasn't sure he would ever here again.

"Veronica!" Shandor said, as Errol turned and saw her. She looked small in the cavernous room, but her hair almost seemed to glow in the dim light.

"Where did you come from?" Aster said.

"That's not really the most important thing now, is it?" Veronica said. "What's important is that y'all have gotten yourselves, once again, in a big ol' mess. What's important now is that you follow me."

"Wait," Dusk said. "How did you come to be here? What do you know of this place?"

"We can catch up later," Veronica said. "Right now, it's best your new best friends don't notice us."

"Veronica," Aster said. "We are compelled to help them. Magically."

"I'm not asking you not to help them," Veronica said. "Surely you should help them with their own little version of Armageddon. I wouldn't expect any less of you. I just want to show you something, okay?"

"Veronica," Errol said. "Do you know where Ms. Fincher is?"

"What a good question," Veronica said. "And I know the answer. Come along."

***

E rrol dithered, of course, before giving her a perfunctory hug. Shandor did not. He took Veronica's hand and kissed it.

"I am glad you are well," he said. "And I'm glad you found us."

She started walking; Shandor kept up, staying at her side. The others straggled, but then they followed.

"Good job fetching them," she told him. "I didn't really expect for you to tag along."

"Didn't you?" Shandor said. "You should have. I've made my interests quite clear."

"Yes, you have," she said, lowering her voice so the others couldn't hear. "And it's very sweet. So I'll be plain with you. I'm not interested in romance just now. With anyone. It's a waste of time we don't have. And if we don't figure all of this out, and quick, no one is going to be necking behind the shed. Or proposing marriage, or anything else. So if you like me like you say, let up on all of this. Be my friend. Let's help each other. Or go away. But let's not go steady, sugar. I'm not up for it."

He sighed and nodded. "I will respect your wishes," he said. "But I will not leave your side."

"That's great," she said. "Because I think we'll need all the help we can get. And still fail, probably."

When they entered the cave, Veronica allowed herself to enjoy the collective jaw-dropping.

"Holy crap," Errol said.

"Wait," Aster said. "Is that . . . is that Delia?"

PART TWO

THE BLOOD OF DAWN

ONE
BIRDS OF A FEATHER

Aster stared in horror at the cloven body, at Ms. Fincher tucked against the creature's ear, apparently asleep. When they came into the cave, the monster had been still, but now he began to squirm, yanking at his chains, and letting loose weird, airy moans from his half-formed lips.

"Jesus," Errol said. "What the hell is that? Veronica, how did you know about this. Or us. Or where we were?"

"A girl needs some secrets, Errol. I know things. Mostly dreadful things, but now and then they come in handy. I got here a few days before y'all."

"Why?"

"Well, Errol, that would take a lot of explaining. I'm trying to fix this mess, just like the rest of you."

"And this . . . this . . . is going to help us?"

"Listen," Aster said. "Hush. I think . . . I think it's *saying* something."

Everyone fell silent, and she listening to the wheezing from the giant's single lung.

Hhhhheeeeehhhguuuuee . . . he moaned. His single arm reached toward the water below.

"That doesn't sound like anything," Errol said.

"No," Aster whispered, the hairs on her neck pricking up. "I know this language. He's asking for a drink. For water."

Dhhmteeyy Hhhheeeghhueee! The half-thing boomed, louder. Pleading.

"Okay," Veronica said. "Let's give him a drink."

"Wait," Dusk said. "That is not wise."

Veronica didn't gesture or even move, but her eyes were suddenly holes into the ocean, and her blond hair lifted up as if she was under water, drifting about her head.

Below the giant, the water in the pool heaved, lifted, and exploded, dousing the huge body head to foot.

And the giant changed. His withered flesh began to fill out; his dull eye shone with an awful light. A stench of death rose, so strong Errol almost vomited.

The water rose twice more, splashing the monster, and each time he looked bigger. With a metallic snap so loud it hurt his ears, the chains holding the creature parted, and he plunged into the water, vanishing beneath the surface, with Ms. Fincher still on his shoulder.

"Veronica," Aster said. "What have you done?"

"What I do," Veronica said. "I couldn't let the unfortunate thing go thirsty, could I?"

"It might have been best," Dusk said, grimly. She had drawn her sword and had it held ready.

"Ms. Fincher," Errol said. "She'll drown." He started toward the water's edge.

Before he went three steps the surface of the pool erupted, inundating them, knocking Aster off of her feet. Before she could clear her mouth, something gripped her, yanked her up. Everything whirled about as the half-monster vaulted up, taking her along with him. And not just her; everyone else as well.

The wall of the cave shattered and broke away and they were over the gulf, then rising above it with terrible speed. She had a glimpse of the palace below dwindling to almost nothing before they were into the clouds, and then all she saw was white, then grey, then a starless black. The giant hadn't gripped her with his hand; it was the air itself, and it kept her fast, as if frozen. She could not form a spell, even if she knew what spell to say, although she felt the power inside her well almost beyond comprehension. She had never imagined a place could be so rich in elumiris.

This could not be, she thought. They could not go. They had to help Tempest. Her head pounded with awful pain, and writhed in the insubstantial grip, try to go back, do the thing she had to do. Her breath came quick; she felt like she was suffocating, like she had ants all over her body.

And then, it became less horrible. She began to think she might live after all. Finally, she felt no urge whatsoever to do Tempest's bidding.

The Obligation was of a place and time, and they were no longer there, nor were they in some lower place where it would trickle down. They were going higher and further away, and here Tempest's spell had never been and never would be. They were free.

Just as Veronica had known they would be. But she couldn't have told them, could she? Because if they knew the Obligation would be derailed, they couldn't have gone with Veronica to see . . . this thing.

Of course, there was no reason to expect the situation they were headed for would be any better. From the spit to the fire, as her father said. Used to say.

Light began seeping into the darkness, and then it began coming in bands; she saw flashes of distant landscape, very green, with dark winding rivers and broad lakes or seas. None of the light was daylight, but in places it was nearly as bright as the sun.

And then, in a moment, the ground came up to them, quickly. She couldn't help but close her eyes and wonder if she would even feel the impact.

But then it was over. They lay on bare stone, all of them, the mutilated giant, too. As she watched, he pushed himself up with his single arm and leg, groaning in agony. He wasn't looking at them, but toward the edge of the stony hill.

Before she could wonder why, something came over it.

***

Errol lay with his cheek pressed into the stone for a moment, trying not to retch. The surface was cool, and a little damp, and it smelled like earth. Best of all, it was not moving through the air at a trillion miles per hour.

He didn't want to look up. He just wanted to lay there, feel his breath go in and out, maybe take a nap. Was that too much to ask?

Apparently. With a sigh he rolled over.

Venom green eyes peered from behind the curve of the hill, perfectly round and without pupils. The mouth below them yawned so wide, he thought the whole head would split open. It was mottled black and green, , and reminded him of a frog he's seen once in the herptile house at the zoo in Leflore.

Of course, this thing was more the size of the house than the frog…

As he watched, he realized it was bigger than that, because there was more to it than its head, which was now rising on a neck that kept coming and coming. So no, not a frog, but some kind of worm or eel or legless salamander.

Or, given where they were, the god of those things.

And it wasn't just curiously observing them. It was coming for them. Quickly, too quickly to run from.

He yanked out his sword, knowing it wouldn't feel like more than a fleabite to this thing.

Something moved in his peripheral vision.

The giant. Crawling along the hilltop. Putting his mutilated body between them and the worm. The giant reached up, took Ms. Fincher from his shoulder, and placed her on the ground, an oddly gentle movement. Then he stumbled forward and threw himself on the monster. His single arm was long enough to wrap around its body just below the head, and he threw his leg around it further down. It was without doubt the weirdest wrestling match Errol had ever seen.

Bhhheegtehhh! the giant croaked.

"Does that mean . . .?" Errol began.

"Yes," Aster said. "Run!"

The worm's body bunched and coiled and still more of it came over the ridge.

"Yeah," Errol said. He darted forward, intent on gathering up Ms. Fincher, but she was already standing.

"What?" she said. "What is all this?"

"No time," Errol said. "Let's go."

She glanced back, saw the monsters grappling, and did as he said. He went right after her.

He hadn't had time to take in much of their surroundings. It was night, although the sky blazed with unnaturally bright stars. The moon was huge, taking up a good chunk of the sky, and even though it was a thin crescent, the light it gave off was far more than any full moon he had ever seen. In its light, he saw that the stone sloped away from them in every direction and vanished into what looked like a sea of clouds. Aster had already begun running, directly away from the worm and the giant, and everyone else was quickly following her. In moments they had plunged into the mist, though, and that slowed them considerably. They were hindered even more when the slope steepened to the point that they couldn't run anymore but had to pick their way carefully down broken shelves of stone. The stone shuddered from the force of the fight above them, but there was little sound; the worm made none, and the giant seemed to have used up all of his breath on his warning to them.

He and Billy were the most practiced at moving in this kind of terrain, and so they ended up ahead of the rest, yelling back when they came to a descent too steep and searching for a better path. The mist thinned, and finally they passed out of it entirely.

The view was incredible. And very bad news.

They were near the top of a mountain that must have been miles high. Below in the moonlight, he could make out a dark, verdant land, the pearly glow of a moonlit river.

The cliff below them was sheer for at least a thousand feet, and after that the slope still looked appallingly steep.

"Aster!" he said.

"I'm not sure," she said. "The elumiris here; it's so strong. I can try something, but I can't be sure what will happen."

"Perhaps we should go back and fight," Dusk said.

"You saw that thing, right?" Errol said. "What about you, Veronica? You got us into this mess, can you get us out?"

"Mountains aren't really my forte, Errol." She brightened. "*Forte.* I had forgotten that word. Mom used to use it a lot."

Shandor drew his sword. "Perhaps I can slow it down."

"You can't," Veronica said. "It's part of the enemy. We have to keep ahead of it."

"Just make us light, like when we were going up the steps," Errol told Aster. "Then we can just jump and sort of float down."

"I can try," Aster said. "Or . . ." she closed her eyes.

"*Mes petyendar,*" she said.

Errol's head spun, and to his horror he realized that he was falling. He yelped, but it sounded weird, not like his voice at all. He flailed about helplessly, knowing there was nothing he could do.

Then the air pushed up beneath his arms, and he felt himself lift.

No. Not his arms. His wings. He looked around wildly and saw he wasn't alone; there was a whole flock of birds with him. Crows . . . no, they were too big for that. Ravens. Aster had turned them all into ravens.

Then it really sank in; he was flying. And it felt great.

He didn't know if a raven could smile, but if it could, he would be grinning ear-to-ear.

His elation didn't last long, though. One of the other ravens croaked out a few sounds.

Behind us.

Not only did he understand her, he knew it was Aster. She looked different from the others; the shape of her beak, the way her feathers ruffed at her neck. In fact he could tell all of them apart.

He wheeled about to see what was behind them.

The worm. It was pouring over the side of the cliff like a dark waterfall; it seemed to go on forever. For a moment he was relieved, figuring the beast had doomed itself and was going to wind up as a pile of meat at the bottom of the cliff. But then its head turned up, and its body followed and then it just . . . broke apart into thousands of pieces.

And then the parts began flapping wings and came after them.

"That sucks," Errol said. "What the hell is that thing?"

"That's the enemy," raven Veronica said. "Or part of it."

"Fly!" raven Aster croaked.

"Where?" Errol demanded.

"Follow me."

Raven Ast—Aster? In his mind, her name was getting shorter, like he couldn't hold on to the whole two syllables. Raven Ast dropped into a steep dive. Whether or not she knew where she was going, he couldn't say, but he knew he didn't have any idea what to do, so he followed.

The things behind them were *fast,* and as they drew nearer, he saw they were also big. And they weren't birds; their wings were more like those of bats.

The enemy. Ver had said that on the mountain, too. They had plenty of antagonists, but no one had ever said anything about *the* enemy. And he might be reading too much into those few words. But if it was true, it would be a relief, for him at least. Up until now most everyone they had runs-ins with had some sort of agenda, but none of them had been trying to end the entire world. Each, in their own way, had been trying to *stop* the curse, reverse its affects, or take advantage of them. The possible exception was whatever the thing that had once been Mr. Watkins was. He hadn't shown much concern about the curse one way or another; he was just some kind of pedophile-rapist monster who only seemed interested in his own twisted needs.

But if there was something he could confront, fight, beat— that would be great. Even if it was a four hundred-foot-long worm that could turn into bats. Even if it was the Devil himself. Because it gave him something to focus on. A goal. He'd spent too much of his time not knowing what the hell was really going on or who he should take a swing at. It would be nice if things were . . . simple.

Like right now, for instance. It was all really simple. They just had to get away from these things chasing them and they could . . .

Could what? What had they been doing before? They had been in one place, and there had been a half-of-a-giant that brought them here, and . . . but that all seemed vague now. Things he didn't need to know. What he needed to know was how to elude these bat-things.

They were nearly to the treetops of a vast forest when the quickest of their pursuers caught up. Errol saw the motion out of the corner of his eye as it came down on one of his companions. He screeched and turned his wings against the fall, cutting back around toward the thing.

It was like a bat, but furless, or nearly so; it had a collar of coarse hair on its neck. The head was more human than bat, with horrible, beady eyes. When its mouth swung open, it looked less human; the mouth was too big, and the teeth as sharp as needles. It was four times his size. It reminded him of a gargoyle.

He flew full in its face, pecking at its eye. It screeched and snapped at him, but although it was fast, it was less maneuverable than he was. It turned, coming after him—

—and crashed into the top of a tree as Errol ducked and wove through the branches, down into the shadow of the forest, where only the faintest moonlight penetrated.

As it turned out, ravens couldn't see all that well in the dark. But he could still make out Raven A ahead.

The gargoyles were beating down through the trees, now, everywhere. He and the others broke back for the canopy, striving toward the moonlight. He understood the plan now; it was harder for the gargoyles to reverse direction. While they were trying to fly back up out of the forest, the ravens could build a lead.

But when they burst back into the open sky, his heart sank. There were still plenty up here, and now they were spotted, and hundreds of pairs of wings turning their way.

He kept following Raven A, hoping she had another plan, but he was starting to wonder why he was sticking with these other birds. Why were they staying together? They would each probably have a better chance of escaping on their own.

Or maybe not. He now saw some of the nightmares had gotten in front of them.

So it would be a fight no matter what. Not a fight they could win, obviously. . . .

Raven A dove again, and he followed, this time toward a clearing on the ground. They reached it just ahead of the closest gargoyles.

He hit the earth much harder than he expected, and his wings were suddenly not lifting at all. In fact, they weren't wings, they were arms again. His head seemed to explode and then come back together, and realization returned.

Aster was Aster again, too, and she shouted something that set the sky on fire. The gargoyles screamed as they combusted, hurtling into the ground like flaming fighter planes. He reached for his sword and found it wasn't there. Nor for that matter, was his sheath. Or his armor, or any single stitch of clothing.

A quick glance showed him that everyone else was in the same condition, even though the only one he could see very well was Aster; the flame was coming from her, rising up in a column that surrounded her and then mushroomed up into the sky.

He had witnessed her do some stuff before, but this—this seemed like *more*. Way more. Hell, they might even have a chance. Could she burn up all of the gargoyles?

For a moment he continued to think it was possible. Then the flame around Aster flickered as increasing numbers of the monsters came through. As they burned, they melted, like tar, and then became black smoke, and the smoke was everywhere now; it seemed to be smothering Aster's fire.

And there were still hundreds if not thousands of gargoyles.

But then came a rush of air, and the smoke spun into a tornado lying in its side, and he was off his feet once more, tearing through the air, trying not to puke.

TWO

THE ALABASTER PALACE

A ster came around between walls and beneath a ceiling of ivory-colored stone that seemed to glow slightly; there were no shadows anywhere. She was lying on a bed, covered in sheets so light they might have been woven from damselfly wings. She stayed there, continuing to examine her surroundings, and letting her memories rush back into the dark hollows left by sleep. She had been overwhelmed, her power failing, when something again swept her away, just as the half-giant had done below the fortress. In the fury and darkness she had not been able to make him out, but she was certain it was the same strange being. He must have survived the fight with the worm and come back for them. But where was she now?

She was still naked from her transformation to bird and back to human again, but clothes of some sort lay across the end of the bed. On closer examination, there were two garments; a calf-length skirt and a sleeved robe that wrapped and was held closed by a sash, sort of like a bathrobe. Like the sheets, they were made of a silky fabric, a light red orange, bordered in black. They were so light, it almost felt like she wasn't wearing anything, but the fabric was completely opaque so that although she felt naked, she didn't look it.

Once she was dressed, she turned her attention back to the room. It was not terribly large. Two arched doorways opened opposite one another, one leading into a long hall with similar doorways, the other to a balcony nearly as large as the room itself. The balcony overlooked a fantastic forest. The tallest trees rose on improbably thin stalks and spread feathery tops that reminded her both of ferns and of mushroom caps. Most where white, some tending toward yellow. The understory was just as weird; giant mosses and scaly plants that had purple spheres instead of leaves, flowers that looked and wriggled like sea anemones. Some were blue and yellow or red, some opalescent and changeable, others as white as the trees. But in the whole of the forest, she saw no shade of green.

It was curious, but she didn't linger. She had to find the others. Had the giant brought them, too? Or just her?

Her fears eased a bit when she found Errol in the next room. He was breathing, but she could not wake him; her fingers tingled when she touched him; the enchantment was so powerful. She thought about trying to wake him magically, but so far, her powers here were unpredictable. Or rather, she got results far more robust than what she was shooting for. What had been meant as a mere Whimsy of Flight had transformed her and her friends into ravens, perhaps because she had once made a similar transformation. Her Dictate of Immolation had set the sky on fire. No, if she tried to countermand some other powerful magic, there was no telling what the results would be. Best to leave that as a last result.

Dusk, Billy, Veronica, and Shandor were in the same deep sleep.

But Delia was missing. Aster found an empty room with rumpled covers. She must have awakened first. But how long ago? Hours? Days? Longer?

She stood in the hall for a moment, eyes closed, trying to sense where she ought to go. After a few breaths, she thought she felt a slight warmth on the left side of her face. When she turned that direction, the feeling moved to front. When she opened her eyes, she was facing down the corridor, which she now realized was not straight, but curved ever so slightly. She shrugged and began walking.

The place, she discovered, was enormous, far larger even than the fortress of the Sun Queen. The corridor continued to curve, and after a time, its walls and ceiling dropped away, and it became a bridge over an indoor lake that reached so far into the distance she could not see the end of it. Other bridges crossed it, all held aloft by tall, delicate-looking arches. Here and there, light glowed beneath the water, but she couldn't tell from what source.

The bridge—and many of the other bridges—converged on an island, where the high roof opened to the stars above. She stopped when she reached the edge of it.

Carved of the same translucent stone as the rest of the place, the island was perfectly round. Artificial trees of smokey crystal were placed around the perimeter, spreading branches that divided into smaller ones, and those into even smaller, and so on, eventually becoming as fine as human hair. Just past the trees, a stone bench described the island's circumference, open in the places where the bridges arrived.

In the center was a large stone divan figured on the sides with moonflowers, lilies, and jasmine. A man lay on it. Delia lay next to him, apparently asleep, just as she had been with the half giant.

When Aster stepped into the courtyard, the man's eyes opened, and he pushed himself up.

He was dressed much as she was, but his robes were all black. But what drew the eye was his face. At one moment it was that of a handsome young man, but in the next, most of his features were missing, replaced instead by utter darkness. And between that, she saw yet another face, this one hideously scarred, with one eye socket empty, a wound in the skull, skin wrinkled and papery, hair all grey.

He nodded at her.

"There you are," he said. "I've been waiting."

"What are you doing with Delia?"

He looked over at the sleeping woman and lay his hand on her shoulder.

"She is in no danger, and I mean her no harm of any kind. She keeps me here," he whispered. "Her presence . . . it makes me better. Able to converse with you. And I *must* speak with you."

"Are you the one that brought us here? The giant we found cut in half in that cave?"

"I am who you see," he murmured. He rubbed his head as it changed. His tone had altered as if he was uncertain. "I am wounded yes, cut deeply, yes. That is the trouble. With me like this, the others . . . there can be no reconciliation. And it is my fault, yes. And the remorse, it eats me alive at times. At others I do not care. My nature is not fixed, ever, but . . ." he trailed off. "What are you asking?"

"Who are you," Aster said. "What's your name?"

"I am not a name," he said, as his face became a cracked skull. "I am . . ." he sighed, as if in surrender. "Call me Tuulgun, if you must. It will do, if you need that." He drew himself up, and his voice strengthened again. He wagged a finger at her.

"We know each other," he said. "Can't you feel it? We are kin, of a sort. It is how you found me."

"My father led me to you," she whispered.

"Yes," he said. "Your father. I see him. Yet he is not there."

"He died."

"Nothing dies," Tuulgun said. "Not yet, anyway. But soon, everything . . ." He turned away and staggered, almost falling. Then he slouched back onto his couch and turned back to her.

"You're looking for the sacrifice," he said. "To put it all back together."

"You mean end the curse."

"I mean set things right," he said. "Start it over. You must find the sacrifice and take it to the place where it all happened. You must heal the rifts that pull apart the world and remake it. Where the world became the world."

"I don't understand," Aster said. "What sacrifice? Sacrifice to what? What place are you talking about?"

Tuulgun shuddered and lay back.

"In time," he said.

"Why me?" Aster asked. "Why must it be me? I'm not a goddess."

"There were others," he said. "Many others. Shadows, like you. Images of the original. But only you remain. And you have the companions."

A chill crept across her scalp, as she imagined dozens, hundreds, maybe thousands of versions of herself, all striving, all failing. For a moment she could see them passing before her — some male, some female, some both. Faces in every human color; faces that were not human at all. Each one of them became vapor and drifted away.

When it was over, she felt tears on her face.

"And if I fail?" she whispered.

"It pulls apart," Tuulgun said. "Life and light fail."

"Then tell me how not to fail."

"I can't," he said, his voice barely more than a whisper. "Find your companions. You must do as I say, or all is lost. Do as I say, Streya."

The nickname struck deep.

"Father?" she said. She thought of the half-thing in the cave, and stared at his mutilated changeable face, searching for her father's features. At Ms. Fincher, her father's lover, lying next to him. "Are you my father? Kostye Dveses?"

"You name a shadow," the man said. His eyes closed. "I too am a shadow. But not exactly the same, you see. Go."

***

E rrol woke in a forest of tall, slender trees. He woke already standing.

He knew he had been here before, or someplace like it. And when he saw the woman in the distance, he recognized her, too. He had seen her when he had been in a coma, and again just before he came out of it. He did not know her name, but he knew who she was. Or what she was.

Death. Or at least somebody that worked pretty closely with death. He had never seen her face, and he didn't see it now, but he knew all the way to bottom of him that when he did, that would be it. One day it would happen of course, and he had sort of come to accept that. But he wasn't exactly eager.

"You don't scare me, anymore," he said. He knew that was a lie the moment he said it. Of course he was scared. But he wanted her to know he at least had a handle on his fear.

She turned toward him; he lifted his chin in defiance, but refused to look away, because he knew that wouldn't help. The least he could do was put on a brave face, even if it was partly an act.

She turned enough that he saw she was smiling, just a little, but her long hair still hid her eyes. Then she turned her back to him and slowly walked away.

And now he was in strange bed, naked, covered only by a sheet thinner than tissue. And there was still a woman with blond hair there, with her back to him, standing out on a balcony. But she wasn't dressed in white: she wore a dark green robe. And he was fairly sure he recognized her.

"Veronica?" he said.

She nodded. "It's me," she said. "You can get dressed. I'll keep my back turned."

He blinked and realized there were clothes of some sort at the end of the bed.

"What kind of trouble are we in this time?" he asked.

"The worst kind, of course," she said.

"So we're right on track."

"That is true, Errol."

He held up a piece of the clothing.

"This is a skirt," he said.

"Yes, it is," she said. "But unless you want to walk around without bottoms on . . ."

"Yeah," he said, pulling it on, then spent a bit of time figuring out the ties and sash on the top. "So is everyone else here?"

"I imagine so," she said. She still hadn't turned around.

"Okay," Errol said. "I'm decent."

"Well, let's not exaggerate," Veronica said, glancing at him over her shoulder.

"Veronica—"

"Aren't you glad to see me?" she asked. "I don't get a welcome back kiss?"

He felt as if his legs had turned to wood and his feet to stone. He *was* glad to see her. That was the thing. He just didn't know how to handle that right now.

"Where did you go?" he said. "Why? You didn't explain. You just *went*."

"So no kiss?" she said.

He couldn't tell if she was serious or not. What if she was?

Then she laughed. "It's okay, Errol. I knew when I left what would happen. You and Dusk. And I didn't come back for a kiss."

"Okay," he said. But that didn't help. He was still unsure how he felt. But she had shut that discussion down, hadn't she? And it was probably not the most important thing to be talking about anyway.

"So about that, then," he said. "You coming back. You nearly got us all killed. What the hell was that all about? And where are we now?"

She sighed and took a few steps forward. "We're where we have to be," she said. "You guys might have made it here on your own. Eventually. But we *are* in a bit of a hurry, you know. No time to waste. So I could have shown up and spent a lot of time answering questions about where I have been and what I've been doing. Then I could explain about the Severed Giant, and how we had to break him out of there so he could carry us here. And then y'all would have spent a day or two trying to decide if you could trust me, and it would have all been so *tiresome*. Not to mention the spell what's-her-name put on you would have kept you fighting Armageddon until you were all dead. This way it got done quick and tidy. We're here. And no one got killed."

He didn't bother to tell her they might have been. She knew that. She'd been there.

"Okay," he said. "So we're here, wherever here is. Are you going to tell me what comes next, or are you going to surprise us again?"

"I don't know what to do next," she said. "It's out of my hands. At least for right now."

"So you're leaving again?"

"I'd like to tag along," she said. "If it's okay. I'm quite sure I can be useful."

He didn't doubt that. He had never known Veronica when she was . . . human. When he'd met her she'd been a *nov*, a kind of siren that lured men to watery graves. She wasn't that anymore, but whatever she was, she was much more powerful, especially if she was anywhere near water.

He nodded. "That would be great," he said. "I have a feeling we're in way over our heads. I know I am. At least before I had my sword and my armor. Now I've got nothing."

"That's silly," Veronica said. "You've got that nice skirt."

"Uh, yeah," he said.

"And you've got friends," she said. She stepped closer. "I am still your friend, aren't I, Errol?"

"Yes," he said. "Of course. And uh, speaking of which . . . do you know where everybody else is?"

"Aster and Delia aren't here," Veronica said. "Everyone else is sleeping in the other rooms down this hall."

"I wonder why they haven't woken up yet?" He said.

"Because I didn't want them to," Veronica said. "I wanted a little alone time with you."

"What?"

She stepped closer, and he remembered kissing her through the bars of his bedroom window at Laurel Grove Sanitarium.

"I know things have changed," she said. "I'm sorry I couldn't tell you why I had to leave. And I'm not interested in starting things up again, not like they were. But you are always going to be special to me, Errol. I want you to understand that."

Now she leaned up, and his heart quickened. He still felt frozen in place.

The kiss landed on his cheek. It was warm, and stuck there like honey.

"Let's go wake up everybody else," she said. "Maybe your girlfriend won't try and cut my head off again."

"Well, she doesn't have a sword anymore, either." Errol pointed out. "And you did save her life, so I don't think she's so keen to do that anymore."

Veronica arched one eyebrow and sighed.

"Errol," she said, "I'm sure you are perfectly infatuated with her, and I think she likes you an awful lot. But I don't believe you *understand* her at all."

"Yeah," he conceded. "You're probably right about that."

She smiled and started toward the door.

"Speaking of infatuated," he said. "Shandor seems a decent sort."

"He is quite a decent sort," Veronica said. "Maybe you should date him, too."

"Veronica," someone said. Aster, coming down the hall.

"Hey there," Veronica said.

"What do you know about all of this?" Aster snapped. "You knew he would bring us here. How? What are you up to?"

Veronica's brow creased. "Is positively no one happy to see me?"

Aster closed her eyes and took a deep breath.

"I am delighted to see you, Veronica. Now please tell me what the hell is going on."

Veronica smiled. "Let's wake up the others, shall we. It's story time."

THREE

STORY TIME

They all gathered in Errol's room. Veronica stood near the balcony, facing them.

"I was trying to find Errol," Veronica said. "You remember, Aster, after you abandoned him?"

"I was trying to find my father first," Aster said. "I would have gone after Errol."

"Of course," Veronica said. "Eventually. But I was trying to find Errol, and I met a queen, deep beneath the water. And she told me she could help me find him, but that he would be dead before I got there. Unless I made a promise." She looked around at them all.

"Well, isn't anyone going to ask what I promised?" Errol was too busy processing what she was saying. He *had* been on the verge of drowning when she showed up out of nowhere.

"To serve her?" Shandor ventured.

Veronica touched her nose. "Yes. Five points to the man from the Pale. Yes, I had to promise to serve her for a year and a day."

"Doing what?" Errol said.

"Well, she had big plans for me, I think. But she was expecting the curse to end when I made that promise, and it didn't. Thing's haven't gone so well for her since."

"It was my mother you promised, then?" Dusk said.

"Well, you know your mother was kind of bound up with a lot of other queens," Veronica said. "You know how when light goes through one of those triangular glass things and makes a rainbow — "

"A prism," Aster said.

"Five points," Veronica said. "But minus two for interrupting. Yes, a prism. So the queen I met was like one of those colors. She got broken up, you see, by the curse. But the white light coming into the prism, that was Dusk's mother."

"I met one of the other 'colors'," Errol said, remembering an encounter with a woman in a tomb in the Kingdom of Pyramids.

"Well, now she's all broken up again," Veronica said. "And she's in even worse shape this time. She's fighting for her existence, and she's really too scatter-brained to give me orders. I don't think she would even know what orders to give me. But you know how magic is, I still have to serve her. So I'm doing what I think she wants, which is to end the curse and save her life."

"And you know how to do that?" Aster said.

"No. But I think I can help you figure it out. "

"How?"

"I promised you a story," she said. "So here it goes." Her voice dropped into a mock singsong. "Long ago and far away, there was a giant, or a bull, or a dragon — or something. Something big. And someone killed it, cut it up into bloody pieces and made the world. The sky from his skull, the stars from his eyes, the oceans from his blood — you get the picture. And now the dead monster wants all of his parts back. That's it. Not a very long story."

"That's nuts," Errol said.

But Veronica was looking at Aster, whose eyes had widened just a bit.

"Is it, Aster?"

Aster frowned, but she didn't answer.

"Okay," Errol said. "Let's pretend that story makes a lick of sense. If this guy could put himself back together, why didn't he do it a long time ago. Why now?"

"Because now he can," Billy said.

Everyone turned toward Billy, surprised. He didn't speak that often, but when he did, it was usually worth listening to.

"What do you mean?" Aster asked.

"We giants know this story," Billy said. "To us he is the Elder, and we too were made from fragments of him. He was a willing sacrifice; he gave his body and soul so the world could be made. His severed parts were bound together by the cycles of the sun, moon, and stars. By the invention of time. Now something has gone wrong with that. The cycle of days and nights is broken. The seasons do not change. The bonds are weak, and the will of the enemy is great."

"But if he gave his life willingly," Aster said, "why is he doing this?"

"The best part of him became elumiris, the soul of the universe," Billy said. "But no being, not even the Elder, has only best parts. Every person has a dark soul as well as a bright one. The Elder's dark spirit was also broken into shards and hidden throughout creation. But now, maybe, those shards are coming back together. And they believe that they are *him*."

"And Billy wins the grand prize," Veronica said. "The dark soul—I call it the Itch—has been pulling in all of its parts for a while now. We even know one of those parts."

"Mr. Watkins," Aster said. "Vilken."

"Everyone is a winner," Veronica said.

Aster turned to Billy. "Why didn't you ever say anything about this before?" she demanded.

Billy shrugged. "This story never came up, and I had forgotten. Those thoughts are from my life as a giant. They do not come easily to me unless I am reminded."

"And so that thing," Errol said. "That thing that was a worm, and then a bunch of gargoyles? That was all the dark stuff?"

"Yep," Veronica said. "Well, some of it. There's a lot more where that came from, but it still can't go wherever it wants."

"The army; the one Tempest led us against," Dusk said. "Also a part of the Itch?"

"Another splendid example," Veronica said.

"No," Errol said. "I don't believe any of that. Even for here, that's ridiculous. The universe isn't made of a chopped-up corpse. Water isn't really blood. Stone isn't bone."

"You don't have to take it that literally," Aster said. "You don't have to believe the Elder was literally flesh and blood, like you and me."

"What was he then? The Big Bang?"

She tilted her head, thinking, then nodded. "If you wish. I had not thought about it. If you're trying to reconcile this place with the science of the Reign of the Departed, I guess you could go that way. Before the big bang there was no spacetime, at least as we know it. Or elements. Or forces like gravity and magnetism. After the big bang there was all of that. A primordial state that diversified into everything. And those forces—time, gravity, and so on—hold it together, just like Billy said."

"Or maybe all of this is just fairy tale," Errol said.

"Myth, not fairy tale," Aster said. "There is a difference."

"And the enemy is no fairy tale either," Veronica said. "This isn't my first run-in with it. I've seen it up close, where it lives. It's getting into everything, like a cancer, or a virus. It has infected Dusk's brothers and sisters. Their mother too, by now. And the queen back in the fortress. It's starting to really mess with everything."

"If you serve my mother," Dusk said, "or some version of my mother, and she has now become a part of the Itch, how can we trust you?"

"I think she spent the last of her free will to send me to you," Veronica said. "But the promise I made to her is still there. So the truth is, you can't trust me. *I* can't trust me. The Itch might reel me in. But right now I'm the best chance you've got. You just have to keep an eye on me, is all."

"How could we know?" Dusk said. "You're asking a lot."

Veronica smiled. "Errol will know," she said. "Won't you, Errol?"

Dusk turned to look at him, and he knew he was blushing. She frowned but seemed to accept Veronica's assertion.

"This is too much philosophizing," Dusk said. "We must discover where we are. We must have a plan of action."

"I know what we're supposed to do," Aster said. "I was confused before, but I think I see it now. Or the shape of it."

Aster kept going, telling them about the man in the courtyard, about what he'd told her.

"He said we have to make the sacrifice," she said.

"You mean find another monster and kill it?"

"Something like that. To reinforce the order of things. To start everything moving again."

"Okay," Errol said. "I'm with Dusk. This is all making my head hurt, too. Just tell us what to do. Where do we find this sacrifice?"

"That, I don't know," Aster said.

***

Delia woke weeping from a dream she could not remember, in a place she did not know, lying next to a man she did not recognize, dressed in clothes she had never seen before. She sat up, slowly, trying not to disturb whoever it was. Trying to remember what had happened to her, how she got here — where everyone else was. The last thing she could remember was the fortress at the edge of the world. Aster and the others had been trying to figure out why Kostye's ship had brought them there. She'd been tired and had lain down to sleep.

And that was it. When she woke, she was here.

She couldn't see the man's face, so she carefully stepped down from the stone divan and padded around to peer out him, hoping it would jog her memory; but she did not know his face. He was nice-looking, beautiful really. But a stranger.

Her eyes blinked, and his face was different, mutilated. She stifled a shriek and stepped back as the man's eyes flew open. One of them was missing. Then his face changed, and again. She felt bile rise in her throat and all of her blood seemed to rush to her head at once. She backed up two more steps, then turned and ran.

No, a voice said. *Remain.*

The words did not come from the man on the bed. They did not come into her by her ears at all. In fact, she realized, they weren't even really words. They were more basic than words, but her mind was assigning them meaning, the way you tried to impose sense upon a dream after waking from it.

"Oh," she said. She stopped, closing her eyes, trying to understand what was going on. But the voice was calm, and somehow familiar, although she could not place it.

She turned slowly around.

The man sat there, watching her. Their gazes locked, and in a few breaths the horrible changes in his face slowed, and finally stopped on the features she had seen when he was sleeping.

She realized she had placed one hand on her belly.

Stay with him, the voice said. *He will not harm you.*

"I . . . are you speaking to me?" she asked the man. "In my head?" He shook his head. "I speak to you like this," he said.

His lips moved. Words came out. They weren't English or any other language she'd ever heard, but she understood it.

"Why was I lying with you?"

"You help me," he said. "Without you, my mind wanders. I cannot focus, and there is no hope. With you here, my mind works. I can think, and plan. It's been a long time since I could do that."

"I don't understand," she said. "How can just my presence be of help to you?"

"I am wounded," he said. "Badly so. Part of me is missing. What you carry in you . . . it is like a piece of me. It doesn't make me whole, but it helps. And it will help me get you and your friends to the next place. And perhaps if the one there is healed and forgiven, so too can I be."

"What happened to you?" she asked.

"There was a woman," he said. "I sought her, I found her in her vast dwelling. We were married and were happy for a time. For a long time. But then I fell in love with another, a servant of hers. She was . . . splendid. When it became known, my wife was humiliated. She went into the inner chambers of her castle and she stayed there, alone. Brooding. Her humiliation became anger, and her anger became a poison inside of her. She had a brother who dwelt far away, but when she sent for him, he came. He struck me down and left me for dead, but I did not die. My lover nursed what life I had in me until I was somewhat restored. And for this, my wife slew her."

"I've heard this story before," Delia said.

"I know you have," the man said. "It is an old story. It gets around. But it isn't finished. It needs finishing."

"How am I to do that? By staying with you?"

"No," he said. "You must go with Aster and the others. Once I have sent you on your way, I will have done all I can do."

"But if what you say is true, if me being here helps you . . . "

He shrugged. "I once thought only of myself and my wants. See where that got me, got all of us. It is good to have this time, to feel like myself again. But if I were to keep you here, I foresee no good end for this. If I let you go, there is a chance. Perhaps not a great one. But a chance. I must make what amends I can. I must send you soon. But until then, please—would you lie beside me?"

"You frighten me," she said.

But it wasn't actually true. She knew she should be terrified, that there was nothing normal about this. And yet she trusted him, somehow.

But that wasn't her, was it? It was the child growing in her. Kostye's child. And the child was somehow connected with . . . this person.

He was sad and broken and somehow determined. If she was really the only thing that made him whole, how could she believe he would really let her go? If she went back to him, she might not be able to leave again.

But the voice inside of her would not be silenced; weeping, she returned to lie next to the stranger on the couch. And after a time, she fell asleep.

When she woke again, he was asleep. He did not stir as she rose and left him, although she felt a tremor of anguish. She wondered if she was just dreaming that she was awake, that she knew what she was supposed to do. Because she *did* know. Just as she had known that they needed the astrarium.

She found the others easily; they were all asleep, in one room, most of them on the floor. When she entered the room, they stirred awake.

Aster rose first.

"Mrs. Fincher?"

"Come with me," she said.

She was becoming increasingly convinced she was dreaming. All of them rose and followed her; they asked no questions. They didn't bicker among themselves, or theorize, or make nervous jokes. They just followed her to the edge, where the palace suddenly ended, as if cut in half by a sword the size of a planet. Beyond the broken hallway lay a night sky and stars.

Until they stood on the precipice. Then she could see the honeycomb of rooms, all ended halfway, all missing a wall on this side. But the cut did not stop with the building; the forest below ended as abruptly, and the stone below that. And beyond that, there was mostly shadow — but in the distance, some light. Distant shrouds of blue and green.

And still she had no fear of what she was supposed to do. She lifted her arms out and stepped onto nothing.

And she fell. Not with a terrible rush of air or the feeling of weightlessness, but with a wonderful lightness, and the faintest of pulls, as if something were just tugging at her toes. She turned, quite slowly. She felt like the feathery seed of a dandelion, caught in a breeze, destined to reach the ground but in no hurry at all about it.

She looked up to see the others, outlined in the silvery light of the palace, drifting as easily as she. Convinced now that she was dreaming, she settled into the long, slow fall. Below her, a landscape gradually took form. It was dark, but her eyes were adjusting, so the faint light from above was more than enough to make out mountains and valleys, and in the distance, a coast. When she looked back up, she didn't see a palace anymore, but instead an enormous crescent moon.

The landscape gathered detail; grasslands, hills, and forest. Herds of animals still too distant to make out, and as they got lower, birds of prey and carrion gliding in their own unhurried

patrols. They descended further, to the side of a broken plateau sloping down into a river valley where the wind rippled
through tall grass and a group of antelope or deer bolted at
their approach. She heard the long, low call of a nightbird, and
the distant howls of what might be dogs or wolves, the croaking and chittering of frogs and insects. Finally, when her feet
touched the earth, she found herself wondering if, like a dandelion seed, she was going to take root now. The thought didn't
frighten her at all, and in fact she felt disappointment as the full
weight of her body returned.

FOUR
THE TWINS

Errol had assumed their long, slow fall from the palace had been a dream, but now that they were on the ground, it was gradually becoming less dreamlike. The air was heavy and wet, and sweat began to bead on his forehead. A mosquito or gnat bit his bare arm, and then another.

"Well, that was interesting," he heard Veronica say. "Nice work, Delia."

Everyone turned to stare at Ms. Fincher.

"How did you do that?" Aster demanded.

"Is this not a dream?" Delia said. "It felt like a dream."

"Yeah," Errol said. "It did. But it doesn't anymore. Where are we?"

"Higher," Aster whispered. "And much further away."

Errol heard something weird in Aster's voice. Then he saw it wasn't just her voice that had gone strange. Aster was starting to glow. Her eyes gleamed a bright coral color; her hair was yellow shot through with streaks of rose, and even her skin looked like amber, with lights shifting inside of it.

"What's happening?" Errol said.

"No," Aster whispered. She took a step forward, mumbling under her breath, but then she screamed, flaring briefly so bright it left spots in Errol's eyes. Then she went dark and crumpled into the tall grass.

Billy was at her side before she even hit the ground, and Errol an instant behind. Frantically he put his finger to her neck, and to his relief felt the artery pulsing.

"She's alive," he said.

"Wake her up or pick her up," Veronica said. "She might as well have sent up a flare. The Itch knows, now. It's coming. We need to get out of here. Delia, are you still in charge of this?"

Delia looked confused, but after a breath or two she nodded. "That way," she said, pointing down along the valley. "That's where we have to go."

Billy started to lift Aster up, but she gasped and opened her eyes.

"Billy?" she said.

"You're okay," he breathed.

"I think I am," Aster replied. "There's no need to carry me. I can walk."

"I think running, not walking," Veronica said.

***

Run they did, through the grass, beneath the bright crescent moon, occasionally splashing through streams and over low hummocks. Off to their right, the land first sloped up and then became cliffs. To their left, Errol caught glimpses of what was either a river or a lake, mostly hidden by a screen of trees and bushes.

Behind them he heard nothing, but he didn't doubt Veronica in the slightest. He felt a sort of tingle at his back, the breath of a wolf he could not see or hear.

They had to slow to a walk sooner than Errol would have liked. Ms. Fincher, in particular was having difficulty keeping the pace, and Aster—despite her protestations—was pretty shaky as well.

"I don't like this," Errol said. "Veronica, can you tell? Can we outrun it?"

"No," Veronica said. "He's getting pretty close."

"Can you —there's a river or something over there. Can you—you know—do your thing?"

"I could," she said. "But I might get . . . lost."

"What do you mean?" Errol asked.

"You saw what happened to Aster," Veronica said. "She almost—went. Became something else. The magic stuff is so strong here, and it is calling out to us to change. Haven't you noticed Billy is taller?"

He hadn't, but he did now. Billy was at least a head taller. And Aster's eyes kept flashing. And Dusk, too, seemed to have a faint umbra.

"I can change, like I've done before," Veronica went on. "Or stretch my power out to the river and call something. But I don't know if I can control it. I might become worse than what is coming after us. I might become *part* of what's coming after us."

"She's right," Dusk said. "I feel it too."

Shandor nodded. "It's not so strong for me, but there is also something trying to bend me," he said.

"But I don't feel anything," Errol said.

They all looked at him.

"Oh," he said. He got it. Nobody had to explain to him. They were all connected to the Kingdoms, the High and Faraway. They all had real souls that could live on after their bodies died. They were magical.

He was just a lump of clay from the Reign of the Departed. There was nothing in him ready to become something else, no caterpillar waiting to be a butterfly.

Maybe that made things easier.

"Maybe I can lead them off," he said. "Slow them down."

"I will stand with you again," Shandor said.

"And me," Dusk said.

"No." Aster snapped. "No. We're not going to be separated again. We are staying together. Nobody is going off anywhere. Besides, what are you planning on fighting *with*? You don't have any weapons or armor — and you don't even know what's coming, exactly."

"It can be anything," Veronica said. "It's got no real form. You saw — it was a giant worm, and then it was those flying things. It can get into animals, people — and it's getting faster, stronger. More awake."

"And it has found you," a voice said, from behind them.

Errol turned to face the voice.

It was the automaton; the prototype of the wood-and-metal body Aster had made to contain his soul. But it had changed a little. Weirds symbols flowed up along its limbs and digits; maybe writing of some sort, maybe just patterns. But he did not like the look of them. And it seemed to have aged, the wood weathered to a grey, the steel spotted with rust.

"Don't come closer," Aster said.

There was something else behind him. Several somethings, four-legged things, hump shouldered, pacing back and forth. Wolves? Jackals? Sabre-toothed tigers? Hell, they could be anything. And they were big.

"I'm just here to talk, Aster," the creature said. He sounded eerily familiar. And he was speaking English. But for Errol the strangest thing was that when it spoke, its lips moved. When he'd been in a similar constructed body, he'd been able to talk, but the sound just came out of his head.

"Mr. Watkins?" Aster said.

"He's here," the thing said. "And what you called the Sheriff or Vilken. And many more of us. Broken apart so long ago, scattered, hidden in places we were never supposed to escape. But now the gods have broken the heavens, and we are finding each other again. It is really quite wonderful. Veronica, Errol, Delia, Dusk. Even you, Shandor. It's good to see you again."

"What is it you want?" Errol said.

"What do I want? Well, let me see. I want to stop you from whatever you think you're doing. From, you know, 'fixing' things. You, Errol, were you happy with the way things were? You were just thinking about it, weren't you, how you will become dust, like your father, while your friends all find shiny new homes? Is that fair?"

"I'll take that over whatever you have to offer," Errol said.

"That's because you've no idea what I have to offer," the automaton said.

"This is deception," Dusk said. "He's only talking to us to keep us quiet while his beasts surround us."

Errol had noticed that, too. But what could he do? Aster was right. He didn't have a gun, or a sword. Or even a stick. He could punch him in his stupid wooden face, but he didn't think he was going to get very far in that fight. But he might distract him for a second, give Aster a chance to blast him with some sort of spell. In a moment, it might be too late for even that.

Off to his left there was a sudden howl. The automaton snarled and looked that way.

Errol jumped.

It was like hitting an ice sculpture, except the ice ran up his arm and into his chest. He tried to scream but his lungs closed up. He wobbled back, a little surprised his legs were still holding him erect.

The automaton's wooden lips parted in a smile and kept parting until his toothy grin went all the way back to his ears. Then he leapt toward Errol.

But he didn't reach him. He fell back; Errol saw something sticking out from him, a long, slender pole. The automaton landed on all fours and then straightened back up. He reached up and pulled the pole from his chest, and Errol realized it was a spear with a stone point.

"I think you're going now," someone behind him said. "This is where *we* live, and you're not welcome."

It wasn't English. It wasn't any language Errol had ever heard before, full of weird clicks and pops and whistles. But he understood it. He looked to his right and saw a boy standing there. He might have been eleven or twelve years old. He was intensely brown, his skin as close to truly black as Errol had ever seen. His ebony hair fell in rings to his shoulders. He wore a loincloth supported by what was more of a thick string than a belt, leather shoes that looked something like moccasins, and nothing else.

"You can't stop me," the automaton said. "You might send me back now, but soon—"

"Soon is not now," the boy said, and hurled a second spear. The monster tried to dodge, but the point hit him in the eye. The automaton's head bent to the side, then began to slide off, and his whole body followed, collapsing into a pile of mud. In the distance the dark, wolf-like forms receded quickly and vanished.

The boy looked around at them. "That's a bad fellow," he said. "You ought not to be messing with him."

"Yeah," Errol said, as everything started to white out. The last thing he saw was another boy approaching, one who could be a double for the first one.

***

E rrol never fully lost consciousness, but for a while he wished he could. The cold festering in his arm and chest now felt alive, like maggots, squirming toward his head, trying to get into his skull. He knew he was vomiting. He tried to concentrate on what everyone around him was saying, but he kept hearing the automaton, talking about how he would be dust.

Whether they succeed at this moment or not, there is no future for you. It is only my victory that holds any hope for you. You can be nothing or you can be everything . . .

The maggots seemed to quiet down, then, he saw something, a face, dim, insubstantial.

You can have everything.

It was his father, he realized, as he had seen him, just before he came out of his coma. If death was forever, what had he seen? What was he seeing now, if his father had no soul?

You people in the Reign die so those in the High and Faraway can have eternal life, always reborn, always renewed. At your expense. But it doesn't have to be like that. If you come with me . . .

Then suddenly the voice cut off, and he was aware of heat, and hands on him, and someone singing.

He coughed. One of the boys was just in front of him. He handed Errol a bowl.

"Drink it," he said.

It was just water, but it was good, like water straight from a spring. He remembered ages ago, his father scooping sand back from a rivulet bubbling out of the side of a hill, waiting for the water to go clear as crystal, how it was more delicious than iced tea or a Coke.

"Thanks," he said.

Everyone else was there, too, and the other boy. They were all ranged around a small fire in a circle of stones, under the eaves of a rock shelter.

"Who are you?" he asked.

"Well, we're the Twins," the boy said. "Children of the Sky, The Antelope-Boys, Brothers of the Dawn. You can call me First and my brother there Second. If you don't like that, we have other names. Sweet Water and Hunter, for instance, Dog and Lion, Shelter and Open Sky."

"And where are we?"

"Why, this place," First said. "We camp here sometimes, in winter. It isn't winter now but it's dark, so we came here. And now here you come along."

"They're going to help us," Aster said.

"Help us what?" Errol asked.

"Help start up the sky again," Second said. "Get mom out of her hole."

"Mom?"

"The Sun," First said. "Our Mom is the Sun."

Errol closed his eyes, but that just made him dizzier. "Right," he said. "Of course. So what's the plan?"

"Well, when you're up to it," First said, "we'll do a bit of walking."

***

Errol stayed awake for only a few hours before he fell back into a fitful sleep. One of the boys went to front of the cave and set watch, while the other one lay down. Aster decided to stay up. She kept feeling like she was going to explode, and she feared if she went to sleep, she might. Besides, there was too much to think about. And questions to answer.

The moon was almost gone; it had widened from the thin sliver when they arrived to a fuller crescent, but now it was a sliver again, and still shrinking.

She saw Delia sitting beyond the edge of the firelight and, after a moment, went over to join her.

"I think we need to talk," she said.

Delia nodded. "That's probably true."

"Do you remember any of it?" Aster asked. "Lying with the giant in the cave, and then with Tuulgun in the palace?"

"I don't remember a giant in a cave," she said. "And I don't know that name. But I remember the man on the couch."

"Did you know him?"

"No," Delia said. "But he was . . . there was something familiar about him."

"Familiar like my father?" Aster said.

"Something like that," Delia replied.

"And the way you know things," Aster said. "Like where to find the astrarium or how to get us down to this place. You called me Streya, once. Only my father ever called me that, but first you and then Tuulgun — the man you were lying with — he called me that too. I think he is connected with my father somehow. Remember when Veronica was talking about a prism?"

"Yes, "Delia said. "You believe your father was a . . . version of him."

"Yes," Aster said. "But what I don't understand is Tuulgun's connection with *you*. Do you remember if he did any sort of ritual, cast any sort of spell, had you repeat any words he spoke?"

"No," Delia said.

"Did he ever write on you? Or — "

"Aster," Delia said, "I'm pregnant."

Aster just stared at her, wondering if she'd heard right, and at the same time wondering why Delia was changing the subject.

But then she understood.

"Oh, zhedye," she said. "Pregnant by . . . "

"Kostye," she said. "There was no one else." She smiled thinly. "Anyway," she said. "There's your connection."

Aster started to reply, but realized she had nothing to say. Emotion welled up in her so quickly, she didn't know what it was until the tears started in her eyes.

"I'm sorry," Ms. Fincher said. "I should have told you sooner. I only found out when we were on the ship. I'm just starting to really show, and in these clothes, and with so much happening, I'm not surprised none of you noticed." She paused. "But *he* knew. The man up there."

"He said you made him better," Aster said. "Closer to whole. Because—because he is connected to my father. And you are carrying something of my father inside of you. Is that how you know things? How you know what we should do?"

Ms. Fincher nodded. "She's started speaking to me," she said. "Or . . . maybe it's more like something is speaking through her, like a telephone . . ." she shrugged. "Or I'm crazy."

"She?" Aster said.

"I think so," Delia said. "It feels that way."

"You're not crazy," Aster said. "You've been right each time. Things like this happen here. And this might mean, in some way, part of my father remains alive, able to guide us."

"Aster . . . "

"Yes?"

"What if she's a monster?"

Aster thought about that for minute. "You're asking because my father was a monster? No, don't deny it. Sometimes he was. There are entire epics about the terrible things he did."

"He did monstrous things," Delia agreed. "But from what I understand, after you were born, he changed."

"He made the curse after I was born," Aster said.

"To save you," Delia pointed out.

"Then why do you think your child might be a monster?" Aster asked. "She's going to be a person, like you, like my father. Like me. She may have abilities others do not. But what she does with those, what sort of person she becomes—that's probably the same as anyone. I've done some awful things for what I thought were the right reasons. You know that. But I like to think I'm not a monster. I'm my father's daughter. And so will she be. She'll be my sister."

Aster noticed Errol had come up behind them and was waiting out of earshot for them to finish.

"What is it, Errol?" she asked.

"The Twins say we need to move out," he said. "We've got someplace to be."

"Okay," she said. "We'll be right there."

Above, what was left of the moon vanished entirely, leaving only the stars to light the world.

FIVE
MOON

T hey came down from the rock shelter and walked under moonlight through the river valley. The ground was hard on Errol's bare feet; it had been a long time since he had gone without shoes. When he was a boy, he'd seldom worn them, and as a result his feet had become as tough as leather. He wished they were that way now. But at least there didn't seem to be any thorns or stickers on their path.

The moon had come back and broadened back to a crescent; it seemed there was a day and night here of sorts. Right now the moon was as orange as a pumpkin, painting the landscape in dull sunset colors. That might be nice if it had been proceeded by a blue sky and a yellow sun. He'd almost forgotten what real daylight looked like.

Antelopes sprang ahead of them. Herds of wild cattle moved along the river, and Errol saw what he thought were ele- phants in the distance. It made him nervous; from experience he knew that big predators tended to shadow herds like that, and if they saw easier prey—say, a human with no weapons or armor—they might choose that over a ton or three of muscle with horns or tusks. The Twins seemed wary, too, but they also seemed confident. If anything was stalking them, it never made itself known.

Later that day, they ran across more elephants, although they were a little weird looking—bigger than Errol remembered elephants being, with longer legs, and their tusks were straighter, only curving up a little. His first thought was that they were woolly mammoths, but they weren't furry at all, and he remembered mammoths had *very* curvy tusks. They also saw giraffes and zebras that looked pretty much exactly like they were supposed to.

Aster and Billy were walking a little to his left. Dusk was to his right, and Veronica was lagging back talking to Shandor.

"So, look," he said to Aster. "I know this is no place on Earth. But . . . being in the Kingdoms—I know it wasn't like our past exactly, but it was like versions of our past. The Middle Ages, ancient Egypt—you know what I mean."

"I do," Aster said.

"And here—this place—this all seems like the stone age."

"Closer to the beginning," Aster said. "Closer to the top, I should say."

"Then why are we seeing giraffes and zebras? Where are the saber-toothed tigers and woolly mammoths?"

"Well, it's not cold here," Aster said. "The stone age was everywhere, not just in Europe. Wherever we are, we're the in tropics, so no mammoths. And I think saber-toothed tigers were only in the Americas, and this is maybe more like Africa or India. Or maybe we just haven't seen one, who knows? You know how geography is in the High and Faraway. It doesn't follow the same rules."

"It's odd," Dusk said. "Sometimes I don't understand the two of you when you speak of the Reign of the Departed. Having been there, I think I now understand more. But you have seen animals like these?"

"Well, in zoos," Errol said. "And in books and on television."

"That's marvelous," she said. "I've seen elephants of course, but those long-necked things . . ."

"Giraffes," Aster said.

"Very strange. Yet compelling. I'm glad to know there is some beauty in your world."

"There's plenty of beauty there," Errol said. "Of course, we tend to wreck it. A lot of these animals are nearly extinct."

"It's hardly surprising," Dusk said. "Your home is so close to the end of things. It is a world made for death."

"Let's not get too high and mighty," Veronica said. She and Shandor had caught up. "Death is coming here, too. Real, permanent death. The kind you never get better from."

"I know that," Dusk said. "I can see it. Perhaps not so clearly as you, who have been dead yourself. Some part of you must be torn. I should think it would be in your nature to cooperate with the enemy rather than fight it."

"You don't know anything about my nature," Veronica said. But to Errol, she didn't sound as certain as she usually did. As if Dusk's words actually bothered her.

"I've certainly been wrong about you in the past," Dusk said. "I will try not to misjudge you again."

Errol felt his face flush a little; that had *not* been an apology; it had been a promise. This was exactly what they didn't need now; the old feud between Veronica and Dusk to heat up.

"I know that," Veronica said. Then she smiled and pointed. "Is that a zebra?"

It was, and to his relief, that was also the end of that conversation.

***

They made camp by the dark of the moon, and the Twins built a small fire. Aster watched as the little tongues of flame spread from the kindling to the twigs and larger branches. Along with the pops and crackles of the burning wood, she also heard a voice, singing.

I am the little fire god. I live, I die, I am reborn. We are kin, you and me.

"Do any of you hear that?" she asked.

"Hear what?" Errol asked.

"She mean's the fire," Second said. "Yes, they can be right garrulous, especially when they're young."

Everything is alive here, Aster realized. *Everything has consciousness. The rocks, the trees. All of it.*

"I don't hear anything," Dusk said.

"Give it time," Second said. "But listen, it's time we have a talk."

"Okay," Aster said.

"This is what we're after, to be plain," First said. "The reason it's all broken—the reason there's no daylight, no seasons, or anything like that is because our Mom is hiding in her hole and our sister is dead."

Aster nodded. "Your mother is the Sun, you said."

"And our sister is the Dawn," Second said. "It started way back. There was nothing, much. Something like Earth and something like Sky, but not really. They were stuck together. But after a while, jammed together like that, they had kids. And the kids pushed them apart. And then those kids had kids. But still, not a lot going on. No water, no trees, no grass, no animals. There were plenty of first people, but they didn't have form, no bodies. So then our sister did it. She went to our three uncles and told them she was going to make a whole world, but she needed their help. She needed a sacrifice. Our uncles were First Man, Twin, and Thunder. Thunder offered himself, but Sister feared the world would be too turbulent, and that he would be needed later. First Man and Twin were twins, like us. Our mother was their sister. Twin stepped up and said he would be the sacrifice. So she killed him, and the true nature of the world was revealed. It just rolled out as he fell, as he went into it. Everything became real. Everyone became real. They became what they were already, inside. Our sister, she became the Dawn, and when she rose up from the sacrifice, she began traveling across the new world. And our mother, she woke up too, knowing she was the Sun, and she came right after our sister. And as they traveled, other things came to be. Trees. Grass. Our Uncle Thunder became *the* Thunder, and he released the waters beneath the world to make streams, rivers, oceans. He released the animals, too. Had to fight a big snake to do it, strike it dead with lightning. And all the while the world kept stretching out, getting bigger."

"Now our sister is dead," Second said. "And everything she and Twin created is coming apart. Evil entered the heart of our Uncle Twin, and without Dawn he can't be consoled. Without Dawn, our mother won't leave her hole."

Second looked Aster directly in the eye.

"What we need is a new Dawn," he said. "And a new sacrifice to clean up this whole thing. I'm the second twin, so we reckon I'll do as the sacrifice. But we need a Dawn. And you're it. You're the only one can do it now. So we're going to where our sister is, and we'll get her things. Then we'll go to the hole where our mother is, and you'll do the sacrifice. And when it's done, she'll come out of her hole and light up the world again. She'll forgive the Moon and he'll heal up. Everything will start up again. And that will be that."

Aster had been listening with growing horror. She didn't question that any of this was real; she could feel it happening already; there was a vacancy in the universe, and it was trying to make her fill it. But the idea of becoming a goddess was terrifying; it meant losing herself and everything she was. And it meant something worse than that.

"I have to kill you?" she asked Second.

"It won't be hard, since I'm willing."

"No, I don't mean that," she said. "I mean, I don't want to kill anyone."

"You've killed before," First pointed out.

"Only to protect myself and my friends," she said.

"You'll be protecting the whole entire creation," First sputtered.

Aster stared at him for a moment before conceding that with a nod. Of course she could do it. In the end, she would do whatever she had to do, wouldn't she? She had to see this through. She didn't have a choice.

***

E ventually they came to a village. It was situated on a high bank of the river in front of a line of wooded hills and was comprised of a bunch of small cone-shaped huts. Errol counted twelve with walls and roofs of thatched grass, but there were several open-air arbors as well. The people curiously watching them arrive looked a lot like the twins. As in the Kingdoms, they were all of ages between about eight and early twenties. The men wore loincloths. The women wore kilt-like affairs made of animal skins decorated with painted images of animals. They didn't wear tops, although the older ones had patterns painted on their upper bodies in red, black, yellow, and ivory. Both men and women wore jewelry of shell and carved bone. Some of the younger kids ran out and stopped when they got close, then reached tentatively to touch the silken clothing he and the others still wore.

"Like spiderweb," one of them said.

"Well rest here a bit," First said. "Get you some proper clothes and some other things you'll need for the trip."

"We need weapons," Dusk said. "I feel uneasy with no sword to fill my hand."

"Don't know what a sword is," First said. "But I can get you a spear and a throwing stick. You know how to fight with a spear?"

"Yeah," Errol said. "We had that in fourth grade gym class."

"This is a yes, or a no?" First said.

"It's a no," Errol replied.

"Throwing stick? Bow and arrow?"

"I actually did take archery in P.E.," Errol said. "I don't know what a throwing stick is."

"Bow and arrow is okay," First said. "But if we have to fight something big, you'll need a spear. We'll work on that, then. And the rest of you?"

"I have been instructed in most weapons," Dusk said. "Including spear. But the spears I have used are not like yours. I am interested in learning more about them."

"Same for me," Billy said.

"So it's the whole bunch of you," Second said. "Okay. Get rested and fed. First and I are going for a hunt."

***

The food consisted of figs and several other kinds of fruit Errol didn't recognize, but they were good. Best of all, they villagers had collected dozens and dozens of decent-sized freshwater clams from the river, which they placed on flattish rocks right as the edge of the fire until they popped open. They pulled out the juicy insides with their fingers.

Until then, Errol had not realized how hungry he was. They hadn't eaten since leaving the fortress. But how long ago had that been?

"Where did the Twins find you?" Pearl asked. She was one of the older ones, maybe twenty, maybe a little older. Her brown eyes were flecked with gold, and she had a big smile when she chose to show it. She seemed to be the closest thing the little band had to a leader. "Or where did you find them?"

"Out in the valley," Aster said.

"But you're not from there," Pearl said. "You must be from very far away."

"We are," Aster agreed.

"We came from up there," Veronica said, pointing at the moon. Errol saw Aster shoot Veronica a nasty look.

"From the house of the Moon Man," Pearl said. "Truly?"

"Yes," Veronica said.

"So no wonder," Pearl said. "The Twins are his sons."

"And the Sun is their mother," Skink, a boy of about eight put in. "But Moon goes with lots of other women, you know."

"Do tell," Veronica said. "How many?"

Pearl blinked. "Well . . . all of us girls," she said. "When we reach a certain age, he comes to us in the night. And that's when we start our bleeding. After that, every month, he comes back."

"Wait," Errol said. "Literally? He actually comes down here in person and rapes every one of you?"

"He doesn't ask, if that's what you mean," Pearl asked. "I've never seen him—I'm always asleep. But I've heard tell of some who woke up and caught him at it."

"But he couldn't really . . . it's some sort of metaphor, right?"

But even as he said the word, he heard it as garbled nonsense, and Pearl and the others looked puzzled. They didn't have any word in their language that meant "metaphor."

"Never mind," he said. He was tired of trying to sort all of this out. He was looking forward to getting a spear in his hands.

But Veronica wasn't done with the subject.

"I want to hear a little more about this," she said. "So, what does the Moon's wife, the Sun think about this gadding about?"

"Well, actually, he doesn't anymore," Pearl said. "He just stays up there, these days. So none of us bleed anymore. But as for the Sun, she's not properly his wife. She's his sister. He tricked her one night and got her with child. That was the Dawn. It happened again, and the Twins were born. After that, Sun said she didn't want to see Moon anymore, told him to stay on his side of the sky. And he pretended to, and they had a truce. But then he went too far."

"If getting his sister pregnant and jumping on every one of you is okay, I'd love to hear what *too* far is," Veronica said.

"Well, it's not okay what he does to us," Pearl said. "It's how we teach boys *not* to act, to not follow his bad example. He's a bad man, the Moon. He can't control himself. He doesn't follow the rules. But what he did that no one could bear, was he came to Dawn, one night. His own daughter. His sister's daughter. That's too far."

"Are you kidding me?" Errol said.

"Oh," Aster said. "It wasn't just an affair."

"It was incest," Dusk said.

"Double incest," Veronica put in.

"That's a new twist on the story, for sure," Errol said.

"That can't be right," Ms. Fincher said. She looked troubled.

"So then what happened to Dawn?" Veronica asked. "How did she die?"

"The Sun got really mad," Pearl said. "She was shining too bright, burning everything up. Nobody could calm her down. So the Moon sent a snake to bite her. The snake sat outside her cave and waited for her, but it was Dawn who came out first, so the snake bit her, and she died. The Sun lost her anger, but she crawled into her cave and hasn't come out."

"That's when the sky stopped," Pearl said. "And our elders all walked away and never came back. We tracked them for days, but they weren't there."

"But that's not the worst of it," Skink said. "That was okay for a while. But then the Under woke up. And some normal animals started going nasty. And some nasty animals got worse. And it's been hard. The Twins protect us, but without them, we'd all be gone by now."

"You didn't come to take the Twins from us, did you?" One little girl asked. "'Cause then we would just be dead."

"They are going to take us somewhere," Veronica said, "but I'm sure they'll be back. Meantime, what if I tell a story?"

"Yes, please," the boy said.

"It's about a boy all made out of wood," she began, darting a sly glance at Errol.

SIX

A LITTLE ELECTRICITY

After the moon went dark, the villagers excused themselves to their huts. Pearl offered Aster a spot in hers, and she and Billy joined the four other people crowded into it. It was uncomfortable and smelly, and her mind was awhirl, wondering what it all meant. Delia's revelation felt like it changed everything, but maybe it really changed nothing. She just didn't know.

The story about the Moon nagged at her, too. It sounded crazy, but one thing about it, at least, rang true; her periods had stopped, too. And then there was incest. If her father was an aspect of the Moon they were talking about—the way he told the story, her mother had been a servant of the Queen, not their daughter. Had he lied about that? Was she also the product of incest?

She couldn't tell if she didn't believe it or didn't want to.

She didn't expect to sleep, but she woke realizing she had. And not only that, but that she was the only one left in the hut.

Once outside, she saw the Twins were back, and had brought a dead antelope with them. Everyone in the village was at a task; butchering the animal, scraping the skin, cooking, twining cordage, making stone tools. The Twins were some distance off with Billy, Errol, Shandor, and Dusk, practicing with spears. She noticed with some amusement that they had traded out their silky clothes for garments more in keeping with the locals. The boys were in breechclouts, while Dusk sported one of the kilt-like garments the young women of the village wore, although hers was longer, coming just to her knees rather than mid-thigh. Also unlike the women in the village, she also wore a band of her former garment tied around her chest.

"We've clothes for you, too," Pearl said.

The hide skirt, as it turned out, had a loincloth under it. In addition to that, she was given a cloak — just a big rectangle, but it could be tied at one shoulder, and it reached nearly to her ankles. It was some sort of animal skin, worn with the hair-side in. On the skin side, white feathers had been sewn so that when worn it looked almost like wings.

"The Twins said for you take this one," they said.

She considered asking them to make her a top, too, but with the cloak on, if she tied it right, her breasts didn't show. When she saw Veronica, she saw she had adopted the same philosophy.

"I spent decades naked anyway," she said. "I kind of want to laugh at the boys, though. It looks like they're running around in their underwear."

"When in Rome," Aster said.

"Honey, we're a long way from Rome," Veronica said.

"So what now?" Aster asked.

"I think the boys play with their spears for a while, and then we go."

"Should we help these people out with something?" Aster asked.

"I already did my part," Veronica said. She pointed to where a couple of the younger villagers were cleaning two dozen or so fish. "I wouldn't worry too much about it. It would be more trouble to teach you how to do any of this stuff than for them to just do it themselves."

"Probably," Aster agreed. Still, she didn't like doing nothing while everyone else was doing something. It was not in her nature to be still for long.

She went into the empty hut and sat down cross-legged, trying to think, to put everything that was happening into some sort of sense.

Then it happened again.

It was like a wave of heat that started in her toes and quickly swept through her entire body, but it wasn't exactly heat. Light flashed; the interior of the hut lit up with a coral glow, and she realized that the light was coming from beneath her skin. She could see the veins and bones, not as shadows, like when you held a flashlight behind your hand, but as white light.

All of the thoughts trying to form in her head blew away, and for a moment, she felt peaceful — almost blissful.

But then the noise began, like the clicking of insect mandibles, like voices made of circular saws cutting tin, like whales speaking the language of devils, and the light in her suddenly went out, leaving her gasping and breathless, the horrible din fading in her ears.

What's happening?

It hadn't been as bad the first time. Just a flash, here and gone. This time it had felt like an eternity.

The tent flap lifted, and Billy came in.

"Your fire is burning hotter," he said.

"I know," she said. "But what does it mean?"

"I feel it in me, too," he said. "I'm trying to become a giant again. I have to fight it."

"You're a foot taller than you were."

He nodded. "It's difficult. But I know both ends; I know what is happening. But you've never been what you're becoming."

The Twins had said she had to become the Dawn. Was that what this was? But if that was the case, why did they have to go find the grave of the old one? Because if they didn't, she would become something worse? Something bad?

"I don't want to become anything," she told Billy. "I want to be me."

"Whatever you're trying to become, it *is* you," Billy said.

"Not the me I want to be," she said. "Like you don't want to be a giant."

"I *do* want to be giant," he said. "I just want this more."

She closed her eyes and touched her head to his. It wasn't that Billy always knew the right things to say. He just said the right things because they were true.

She had never considered that Billy was giving up anything that mattered to him to be with her. She had always thought of his being a giant as more of a *condition* like dementia or something, a thing to be cured. But now, when she thought back to the few times he talked about his life as a giant, it all turned around in her mind. Being a giant was pure existence, living the majesty and beauty of the universe as no human being ever could. He talked about becoming "small" to experience "little" sensations, like touch and taste, but what senses had he given up? With what sort of gaze did he engage the world when he was truly what he was meant to be? What was it like to hear the very earth and sea breathe? Billy was hundreds, maybe thousands of years old, but he came to things with a kind of innocence, boundless acceptance — and wonder. A human who lived that long would probably be jaded beyond all measure.

She realized then that she should let him go. But she also knew that she couldn't. She needed him now, more than ever.

She needed his calm and his strength and his unwavering love for her to get through this.

"I love you, Billy," she whispered.

"And I you," he said.

"I'm scared."

"So am I."

***

Delia thrust her spear at the target, a patch of rawhide wrapped around a tree; the resulting jar of impact sent her stumbling back.

"Your feet," Second told her. "You have to set them. Look at me."

She glanced over. His knees were bent, his feet spaced at about the breadth of his shoulders.

"Your strength comes from the Earth," he said. "You must plant yourself on it. And when you move, you have to keep the connection. If your legs are straight and your feet too close together, you can't put the shock back into the ground, where it belongs."

"Okay," she said. She bent her knees, spread her feet out a little, and tried again.

Part of her found this all hard to take seriously. She had done what she could to satisfy her modesty, but she felt awkward, exposed, and ridiculous in the garments they had given her. And she felt embarrassed every time she saw one of the boys. She'd thought about trying to get some kind of sewing kit together and make something a little less Paleolithic but had decided her time might be better spent trying to learn at least the basics of how to use the spear. Not that she thought she would ever be good at it or stand a chance against anything that might attack them, but she was needed to carry one as backup for those that *could* make themselves useful in a fight. And if she was going to carry one, she ought to be at least reasonably conversant with it.

By the end of the "day" she was tired and sore from head to foot, but pleasantly surprised at her progress. She had even sparred a little with Second. The practice was with spears that had not been tipped with stone blades; they were too fragile, she was told, and too hard to make to use in practice. It seemed secondary that one also risked a significant injury bouting with sharp weapons. Still, a wooden pole could hurt, too. But Second was so skilled that when he "hit" her she hardly felt it.

There were basically three ways to fight with the spear. When fighting another person with a spear, the Twins usually did so holding the weapon with one hand, down around the waist, with an underhand grip. They would dance in, out, and around their opponent, looking for a chance to come into thrusting range while ducking or turning their bodies to avoid their opponent's thrust. There were three main thrusts—an underhanded stab that came up, an overhand that came down, and a backhand stab that started from the other side of your body—she was right-handed, so that meant holding the spear near her left shoulder and then thrusting toward the right. They used their other hands to try and catch or bat away the wooden shaft of their opponent's weapon—sometimes they used another spear to block instead, but that required more coordination than she thought she had. A two-handed grip was favored for hunting big animals, and sometimes for fighting, in which case there were a few parries, with the pole part of the weapon blocking a thrust and then following up with a return jab. The Twins cautioned against this except in extreme cases; the spears weren't all that long—about five or six feet—and it would be easy to get knuckles rapped or slashed.

Finally, they could be thrown, always from short range. The two opponents stood several yards apart, the spear held overhand, near the shoulder. They would skitter toward each other, feinting throws, until they caught their opponents over-balanced or dodging the wrong way, and then hurl the weapon. The problem with this was that you could really only carry a couple of spears, and if you missed you were in deep trouble.

After her bout with Second, she watched the others training. Unsurprisingly, Dusk was doing the best; by the time they stopped she was moving almost as well at the Twins. Shandor, Billy, and Errol were doing okay, but none of them looked as comfortable with their weapons as the warrior-woman.

Veronica and Aster didn't practice with the spears at all. But they didn't really need to, did they?

***

Two days later, they set out. Errol felt a little better equipped than before, although he still felt pretty vulnerable. He was getting used to the loincloth and mantle, but they were no replacement for his armor. It felt good to have the spear in his hand, although he wasn't that great at fighting with it. He was okay at throwing it, but most of the training the Twins had given them was on how to use it as a hand-weapon. He had a flint knife hafted onto a piece of antler, as well, and a throwing stick. A throwing stick, as it turned out, was a boomerang, a curved piece of wood carved so it was something like an airplane wing. These didn't come back, the way the plastic boomerang he had back at home did, but if you threw it right, it would glide a lot farther than you could throw a normal stick. And it was heavy, heavy enough to use as a club.

The village had only four bows among them. He'd tried one out and saw what the Twins meant about their effectiveness. The staves were only about a yard long, and the pull probably wasn't much more than thirty pounds. The arrows were sharpened river canes. That would be okay for taking down something small to medium game but would probably just annoy something bigger.

Shandor, Billy, and Dusk were similarly equipped, although Dusk had managed to make herself impressive. Lacking armor, she had fashioned a round shield of saplings and rawhide, and she had cobbled together leggings that were suspended from the belt under her skirt. They offered her some protection, but he was pretty sure it was mostly to cut down on the amount of skin she was showing. She carried two spears in one hand and a boomerang in the other.

They camped a few hours before "night" came. There wasn't much camp to set up; First started a fire. Errol and Billy went out to scavenge a little firewood.

They hadn't gone far before the came over a hill and were looking down a little stream valley at a small herd of pig-like creatures. They were maybe sixty feet away, snuffling around on the bank.

Errol carefully placed the firewood he had gathered on the ground and pulled out his boomerang. Billy glanced at him and nodded, taking his out, too.

Let's see if I can do this, he thought.

The pigs hadn't noticed them yet. He cocked to throw it as he had been shown.

"You want to try first?" Billy whispered.

"Best we try at the same time," Errol said. "The first throw is likely to spook them, right?"

"Yes," Billy said.

"Okay," Errol said, setting his stance. "On three. One, two . . ."

He whipped the stick toward the pigs and watched it hopefully. He'd tried a few throws back at the village and knew that it wouldn't fly in a straight line; it spun like a returning boomerang, and its course bent first right and then left. He missed the animal he'd been aiming at by two yards. Billy came closer, but also failed to hit anything. As predicted, the pigs scattered.

Errol shrugged. "Oh, well. I got closer than I thought I would." He picked up his spear and went to recover the weapon.

They reached the general area, and Errol began hunting in the bushes along the stream, while Billy stood by. He was wondering why Billy wasn't looking for his own throwing stick when he spotted a blur from the corner of his eye.

"Hey!" Billy shouted.

Errol swung around, pulling the spear in front of him, but he wasn't fast enough. The blur slammed into him, and jaws closed on the arm he threw up in defense. The weight of whatever it was knocked him off of his feat. The animal thrashed, worrying his arm, and Errol had only fragmentary images of fur and fangs, and one glimpse of eyes that seemed horribly human. It felt hot, and it stank. Claws raked across his body, splitting skin.

Then his attacker screeched, horribly, and leapt off of him, skittering back.

"What the . . ." he sputtered. Billy was next to him, pointing his spear at it as it circled them.

He'd thought it was a lion or something, but now he saw it was some kind of monkey. In fact, it looked like a baboon. But it was *huge*. Standing on all fours, it was nearly as tall as he was. He saw it was bleeding from its flank. Billy must have stabbed it.

Its gaze flicked back and forth between him and Billy. It looked insane. In fact, it reminded him of the rhino, back in the other place. Like it wasn't really a baboon anymore.

"Brother, leave us in peace," Billy said. "We've no wish to harm you further."

Speak for yourself, Errol thought. His arm was bleeding freely, and he felt scratch marks over most of his torso.

It didn't matter anyway. The Baboon screeched again and launched itself at him.

This time he got his spear up, and as it leapt, he hit it in the throat. The stone blade went through it like butter. The weight of the beast yanked the weapon out of his hands. He stumbled back as it kept coming for him, but Billy hit it again. It sputtered and fell over, huffing quick, shallow breaths.

It turned its eyes back to him. It smiled. Then it died.

The spear had gone out the back of its neck, so he had to push and pull it on through to get it out. It couldn't have been smiling, he thought. That was just my imagination. But he'd felt a connection, as it died. It had felt like . . . contempt.

He looked down at the corpse. "Should we field dress it?" he asked Billy. "Take it back to camp?"

"I don't think it would be a very good idea to eat that," Billy said.

"Probably not," he said.

Billy found the boomerangs while he tried to staunch the bleeding from his arm, most of which came from two holes made by the beast's huge canines. Then they went back to camp.

***

"Those don't do that," Second said, as he rubbed some kind of smelly paste into his wounds and then wrapped it up with a strip of soft hide. "Mostly eat fruit and bugs, a few small animals. They don't go after big things."

"The Under had a grip on it, I think," Second said. "That's the likely explanation. Unless it had the Fear-of-Water sickness."

"Rabies?" Errol said. He hadn't thought of that. He was so used to fighting dragons and whatnot it hadn't occurred to him that what would kill him would be a disease they had back home. He'd been vaccinated, right? Did they vaccinate humans for rabies? He didn't know for sure. Whenever the doctors had given him shots, he had always been more interested in getting through it than wondering what they were for.

Veronica squatted down next to him. She touched him lightly on his wounded arm.

"I don't know about rabies," she said. "But that was definitely something the Raggedy Man sent your way."

"The villagers said some animals had been made bad by the Under," Aster said.

"Yeah," First said. "More all the time. Me and my brother, we can smell it. We can tell. Best not go off to hunt without one of us, right? Otherwise next time you might run into something really dangerous."

Errol looked at the boy, thinking the giant baboon probably outweighed First by twenty pounds. But of course, though they looked no older the twelve, they were twelve-year-old gods. So when they said something "really dangerous," what did they mean? He shuddered to imagine what else was out there. Lions and tigers, surely. And maybe things that were worse, that were extinct in his world. But this wasn't his world; if the Kingdoms could have dragons, there was no guessing what might live here.

They ate jerky and figs the Twins had collected. Errol stared at the fire for a while, mesmerized by the brightening and darkening of the coals. But he was tired and shaken, and soon took his rest.

He had wondered why they had been given cloaks. Pearl and most of the others hadn't worn them, and in the tropical weather they didn't seem necessary. But now he realized they were ready-made bedrolls. He stretched out on his, trying to ignore the ache in his wounded arm, the sting of sweat in the lesser scratches on his chest, and the mosquitos and biting flies that were not entirely deterred by the smoke from the small fire. He watched the blaze of stars for a while, then closed his eyes. When Dusk put her cloak next to his and lay down, he pretended to be asleep, and soon he actually was.

He woke to being kissed. It was startling, but pleasant enough, and certainly unexpected.

"Hey," he said. Dusk was lying next to him.

She smiled. "Do you mind?"

"Let me think about that," he said, and kissed her back. She shifted so she was half on top of him, and he winced; the cuts on his torso might be shallow, but they stung.

"Oh," she said.

"No, it's okay."

She kissed him again, then suddenly bounced to her feet. She held out her hand.

"Come on," she said. "Bring your cloak."

He did, his pulse pounding. She led him out of sight of the fire, so there was only starlight.

They laid their cloaks down and started again. She was warm, then hot, and he felt like their skin was melting together.

Then he realized why. She'd taken her top off.

"Dusk," he said. "I'm not sure . . ."

"Hush," she said. "I've waited long enough. Who do I have to answer to? My mother? My siblings? My kingdom and its people? That's all gone. I can make my own rules now."

He felt like he should say something else. At least one more thing. Because he had a feeling that as much as he wanted this, in the end it was not a good idea.

"You might—uh, what if you get pregnant?"

"Like the girls back in the village, my menses stopped months ago," she said. "I do not think it is possible for anyone to become pregnant now."

That sounded reasonable, but how could they be sure? But he was all out of willpower, and she kept kissing him. Not like she had before, but really fiercely. She was starting to get rough, too, and she was *strong*. He realized he was actually a little scared of her. But then she softened, as if realizing that. She giggled a little.

"What?" he asked.

"How do we do this?" she said.

"I, uh . . ." he sighed. "I'll show you."

He started to roll her over, but she shook her head. "I told you," she said. "I cannot be helpless."

"Okay," he said. "Then I think . . ."

***

E rrol looked up at the stars, trying to clear his head. Dusk lay against him.

"Are you okay?" she asked.

He wasn't sure. There had been a flash, and then it felt like he had touched an electric fence, but with his whole body.

"Is that not what is supposed to happen?" she asked.

"Maybe with electric eels," he said. "Not with people. There's no lightning involved, usually. Not literal lightning, anyway."

"I'm sorry," she said. "It must be this thing happening to me. Like it is to Aster and Billy. But what we just did . . . is new to me. All of the feelings were . . . good, but unfamiliar. I've never felt any of that before. Next time I will be more careful."

Next time? He thought. He'd barely survived this time. Still . . .

"Okay," he said.

She propped herself on an elbow.

"You've done this before, then?"

"Once," he said.

"With Veronica?"

"No," he said. "Another girl. Back home. A long time ago."

"But you are no longer with her?"

"No," he said. "She dumped me."

"That can't mean what it sounds like," Dusk said.

He chuckled at that.

"No," he said. "I mean she didn't want to continue the relationship. But it feels like being dumped off of a cliff or something."

"I see," she said. "Perhaps when this is all over, I will seek her out and punish her for hurting you."

"No," he said. "There's no need for that. I'm over it."

Out in the darkness, something howled. It didn't sound very close, but Dusk grabbed her clothes and started getting dressed.

"What?" he said.

"This was foolish," she said. "We are easy prey out here. This isn't like me. I wasn't thinking."

"My fault," he said. "I didn't have to come."

"No, it's not that. It's that my passions are so *strong*. My lust, my anger, my . . ." she trailed off. He wished he could see her face better.

"I lost control," she said. "I fear I will do it again. Do you understand?"

"I do," he said. He started dressing, too.

"But Errol?"

"Yeah?"

"I'm not at all sorry about what we just did."

"I'm glad," he said, hoping she was telling the truth. Hoping it stayed that way.

SEVEN

ON THE COAST

When the moon shone again, they moved on. Errol found himself glancing often at Dusk, searching her face for signs she was having second thoughts, but whenever she noticed she just smiled a little, and once she shook her head. Mostly she seemed focused on the terrain, and on trying to get what information about the dangers they might face from the Twins.

Soon they were in hills, winding through a broad valley, and the air took on a little chill, making their cloaks useful for more than sleeping bags. The grass gave way to trees. Errol couldn't identify any of them; they looked more like they belonged in a jungle than the forests he's grown up with, although it wasn't all that hot. Maybe it would be warmer if the sun came out.

Which brought up an interesting question.

"Aster."

"Yes," she said.

"Why aren't all of these trees dead? If there isn't any sun, how can they keep on . . . you know, photosynthesizing and all of that?"

"I don't know," she said. "You keep trying to make sense of this place in terms of what you know. You'd be better off trying to understand the way things actually are, here."

She sounded irritated. But she also sounded uncertain. As if she could almost be talking to herself.

"Are you okay?" he asked.

"No," she said. "Something's happening to me."

"Like when you lit up like a road flare?"

"Yes," she said.

"What's going on, there?"

"It's like . . . like I'm this tiny light bulb, the kind you put in a flashlight. And someone is trying to plug me into a wall socket."

"Like you're going to explode?" Errol said.

"Sort of," she said.

"Light bulb? I thought we weren't supposed to refer to science or whatever to—"

"Oh, shut up," Aster snapped. "I'm just trying to use an analogy that would make sense to you."

Aster had a habit of talking down to people. In their time together, it had not become more endearing.

"Whatever is happening to you, it's because you have a real soul," he snapped. "Not this second rate thing I have."

"You have a soul, Errol," she shot back. "It's what I animated the automaton with."

"You know what I mean. You're giving off light. Billy's getting taller. Dusk is—she's stronger. And she shocked me last night."

"I don't want to hear about whatever kinky stuff you guys are into."

"No," he said. "A literal shock. Electricity."

"Oh," Aster said. "Don't make out with her, then."

"Like you can talk about *that*. "

She shrugged and looked down. It wasn't a big gesture, but he realized then just how worried she was.

"So are you turning into a god or something?" he said, more softly. "Into the Dawn goddess, like the Twins said. That might not be so bad."

"It might be *really* bad," Aster said. "How much reading have you done about gods?"

"A little."

"Some of them are really nasty. Didn't you listen to Pearl's story? And where we are . . . things are much more *basic* here. Much more elemental. Further away from anything human and much closer to the stuff the universe is made of. Imagine me, with unthinkable power, but no empathy or kindness, feeling not much more for you than I would for a pet at best or a tick at worst."

"That's sort of how I think of you already," he said.

She stopped and stared at him for a moment. Then a tear suddenly ran down her cheek.

"Hey," he said. "I'm just kidding."

"No you're not," she said. "Not really. And you're right."

"No, I'm not right," he said. "Listen—"

"No, you listen. If it happens—if something happens—run, Errol. Get away from me. Please." She paused. "And keep your eye on Dusk and Veronica. Especially Veronica."

***

I n the next few moon days they made their way from hills down to a rocky seashore, a long flat of tide pools with surf rolling in the distance. The moon was as close to full as it ever got, painting the puddles in sunset hues; beyond the irregular white line of waves, the ocean faded into the sky. The breeze smelled of iodine and seaweed. Delia loved it. She had always adored going to the seashore, but the only one she'd ever been to was on the Gulf Coast. When she was a girl, her parents had rented little beach cottages down there, and she'd spent hours beachcombing and swimming. Her favorite time to go had been at night, when the winds were cool, and the sun wouldn't burn her skin. Those beaches had smelled of sewage and algae bloom and papermills, and were all of sand, mostly dredged up artificially.

This beach was not like that. She had seen pictures of places like this, wild coasts in exotic places, and always hoped to visit one. And now here she was.

And the birds! Gulls she recognized, and terns, gathering in argumentative flocks; sandpipers or something similar, darting between the shallower pools. Cormorants perched on rocks and dead trees, long necks preening. Huge, heron-like birds stalked the deeper pools. Pelicans skimmed over the distant waves. When the rocky coast gave way to mudflats, they came upon enormous flocks of flamingos. Once, in a surprise that made her laugh aloud, they saw penguins lining the strand.

Although the moon did not move, tides still came and went, forcing them toward the hills when they rolled in. They ate well: oysters and crab, fish speared in tide pools, huge sea snails, nuts and fruit when they moved nearer the hills.

They were having such a meal one night when Errol asked how far they had left to go, and Delia realized she didn't want to hear that answer. It was so peaceful here, so calming. At times it felt like they were going nowhere, caught in an eternal present, which was fine by her. When they got where they were going, she knew there would be mayhem, fighting and killing and other terrible things. She was in no hurry to reach the end of this journey.

The child in her was becoming heavy, too, and although it was at times uncomfortable, it somehow fit with the contemplative nature of their trek by the sea. What better place for a child to be born than amidst all of this beauty?

That the universe was ending, that they could somehow stop it, seemed ludicrous to her. This seemed real.

But Errol asked the question, and First gave something like an answer.

"So, our sister Dawn is right near the Under," he said. "Not in it, or at least not deep in. But it's going to be trouble when we get there. So we're going to get our other sister to help us. She lives right on the border, you know, and she's strong there. She can get us there safely."

"Your other sister," Aster said. "You haven't mentioned her."

"Our other sister is Night," they said. "The Evening Star, the Shadow."

"She tends to keep to herself," Second said. "But she's a good sort. And her country is called the same: Night."

"But Night isn't part of the Under?" Aster asked.

"Nah, but's on the border. Maybe they were once the same, I don't remember. But the Under is where the Bad Soul lives, where the dead go. Night is . . . well, night. A normal kind of thing."

"But everything is night right now, isn't it?" Aster asked.

"Sort of," Second said. "But that's what's wrong. Nothing is properly divided anymore. It's all running together."

Like a sidewalk chalk drawing in the rain, Delia thought, gazing out toward the ocean.

"So how long until we get to your sister's place, then?"

"Depends," First said.

"On what?" Errol asked.

"On how far away it is now," Second replied.

***

D elia got up in the dark and went a few steps from camp so relieve herself. The stars were beautiful, bright, and unfamiliar. She knew most of the major constellations and didn't see any of them in this strange sky. She wondered briefly if they were in the Southern Hemisphere, but quickly dismissed that as a pointless question. There was obviously some relationship between this place and the world where she had been born and raised, but there was no one-to-one relationship in anything. Anyway, her lack of knowledge about this sky freed her up to name her own constellations. She wasn't particularly sleepy, so she lay down on the water-smoothed stone and started doing so. She named one the Hedgehog, and another the Model T. She had just worked out that one celestial grouping looked like a stinkbug when she heard a slight sound. She sat up, looking out into the darkness. In the starlight she saw something moving; at first, she thought it was some sort of animal, but then she realized it was two people, clasped together.

Errol and Dusk.

Embarrassed, she lay back down and hoped they hadn't noticed her. Given what they seemed to be doing, she doubted that they had.

In a group this small, together for this long, it was impossible to hide everything. She had known for some time that Errol and Dusk were together, and Billy and Aster. Shandor wanted something to happen with Veronica, but she wasn't interested. She'd also gathered that Errol and Veronica had once been together. But how adult these relationships were, she didn't really know. But she should have guessed. All of them had faced death dozens of times, and world itself was apparently ending. She remembered with some amusement a boy who had tried to talk her into sex when she was sixteen by pointing out a nuclear war could start any day, and did she really want to die a virgin? For these kids—no, strike that, they were all adults at this point—that was literally the truth. Who could blame them for wanting to feel everything they could feel? The problem was, sex almost always complicated things. It magnified jealousy, possessiveness, and pretty much every other emotion, which in people their age really didn't *need* any magnification.

She smiled slightly, thinking about how many times she had made a speech to that effect back when she had been a guidance counselor. And about the more substantial worries of unwanted pregnancy and STDs.

But that wasn't her place anymore, or her role with these people. Anyway, who was she to talk, a woman well on her way to being an unwed mother?

Still, she thought, maybe she should find some way to broach the subject to either Dusk or Errol. It seemed very unlikely that they had any form of contraception available to them. Of course, if Pearl and her kin were no longer menstruating, it was probable that Dusk wasn't either, which meant pregnancy wasn't an issue.

She eased back up, ready to move back to camp. The two were still there, no longer moving, hopefully asleep. But as she began to stand, she saw a faint green phosphorescence. For a moment she thought it was some sort of sea creature in one of the pools, but then she realized it was Veronica, submerged in a tide pool except for her head. She was looking at Errol and Dusk, but then her eyes turned slowly to settle on Delia.

Delia walked quickly back to the camp, lay on her cloak, and tried to go to sleep.

***

The next day, after about an hour of walking, Veronica came up beside her. They tended to string out as they walked, and Delia's place was usually near the back, with someone tasked to keep an eye on her. Today it seemed to be Veronica. One the Twins was about ten yards behind them, while ahead the nearest was Billy, about the same distance.

"How are you feeling?" Veronica asked.

"Tired," she said. "I didn't sleep that well last night."

"Yeah," Veronica said.

"And this baby is really starting to get heavy."

"Sure," Veronica said.

They went on a few steps in silence.

"We can talk about it," Veronica said. "About what you saw."

"Look," Delia said. "It's none of my business. I wasn't trying to spy on anyone."

"I was," Veronica said.

"Ah . . . okay," Delia replied. "Are . . . I mean, are you okay?"

"You mean because my ex-boyfriend is playing doctor with a girl who tried to murder me?"

"Yes."

"I don't know," Veronica said. "I guess I don't know how I feel, exactly. How I feel keeps changing. It's one reason I wanted to see it for myself. So I would know."

"Are you still in love with him?" Delia said.

"I love him," Veronica said. "I don't know that I'm in love with him. Even if I was, I'm not . . . "

She hesitated, but Delia didn't push, figuring if Veronica wanted to finish the thought, she would.

"I don't know that I would ever want to do *that*," she finally said. "With anyone. I know people are supposed to like it, but just thinking about it—all I can see is the blood on my shoes. And later, when I was a *nov*, all those men that came to me, and the things in their minds, the revolting things they were planning to do to me. And what I did to them, for that matter. And the one time Errol and I ever came close to doing . . . that . . . it felt like I was about to be raped. Even though he would never have, even though I could have easily stopped him if he *had* tried to—that's how it felt."

Delia absorbed all of that for a moment.

"Here's the thing you need to know," she finally said. "You're not alone, and you're not abnormal. Not wanting to have sex is as normal as wanting to. You have to trust your own feelings on this. And you should absolutely never do anything with your body that you don't one hundred percent want to do."

"That's nice of you to say," Veronica said. "I appreciate it. And agree. Except for one thing. I *am* abnormal. I've been alive, dead, and everything in between. I look like a person right now, but I could be a dragon or a school of fish or a current in the water if I wanted. I am in no way normal. I don't even know what I am."

"Right," Delia said. "I hear what you're saying. But that's just it—whatever it is you are now—maybe you're perfectly normal for whatever that is. Comparing yourself to Dusk, or Errol—or me—what's the point in that? From what I've seen of you, you're strong, powerful, mostly comfortable with who you are, and you defend your friends fiercely. I can't imagine any version of you that might be better."

Veronica smiled, reached over, and took her hand. "Maybe that's because you don't know what's going on in my head sometimes."

"I have enough trouble knowing what's going on in my head without worrying about what's going on in yours," Delia said. She squeezed Veronica's hand, as they skirted a tide pool, where a bright blue eel sought cover from their shadows.

"This was actually good," Veronica said, after a moment. "I mostly meant to ask you not to tell them I was watching. I know that's not okay."

"It's probably not healthy, either," Delia said.

"No, it probably isn't," she said. "But what I'm trying to say is—I couldn't have talked to anyone else here about this. I didn't want to talk to you about it, but I sort of had to. What I didn't expect was that I would feel better after we talked."

Delia turned to face her fully.

"Thank you," she said. "You can't imagine what that means to me."

***

Another few lunar days passed; the coast grew narrower, the hills taller. The streams rushing down from higher ground grew more numerous, deeper, and wider, until they finally reached one they couldn't cross by wading or swimming.

"We're going to need a boat," Second said. "There were some reeds back there we could use to build one."

"How long will that take?" Errol asked.

"A couple of days," Second said.

"Hang on," Veronica said. "I think I've found us some boats."

Delia saw them then, approaching with just their eyes above the water.

"Those are crocodiles," she said.

"They're my little sweethearts, that's what they are," Veronica said. "Aren't you, my little snookums?"

One the huge reptiles raised its head from the water, and Veronica scratched the pale scales under its neck.

A total of four crocodiles came up to the banks of the river. They were all big, but the one Veronica had called snookums was huge, more than twenty feet long, maybe closer to thirty.

"Come on," Veronica said, taking Delia's hand. "You ride with me. Shandor, you too. The rest of you, take your pick."

"Well, those are nice boats," First said, hopping onto one of the beasts without the slightest hesitation. His brother joined him an instant later. Errol, looking much more hesitant, followed Dusk onto their mount, while Billy and Aster rode the last.

"How do we steer these?" Errol asked.

"I'll do all of that," Veronica said. "Y'all just enjoy the ride."

It was like sitting on one huge muscle, Delia mused, gripping the beast with her legs and she might a horse as it carried them out into the river by broad sweeps of its tail. Her legs were mostly under water, which felt cooler than she had thought it would.

The crocodiles did not take them straight across the river, and as they drew near the middle of the stream, Delia saw why; there was no bank on the other side to speak of, but instead a marsh that seemed to go on for some distance. Instead their mounts took them downstream, toward the mouth of the river, where mudflats fanned out on either side. Once past the mouth, the sea was still calm, as the ocean swells were absorbed by a chain of barrier islands on the horizon, leaving a tranquil waterway paralleling the marshy coast.

"We could get off and walk now," Errol observed.

"Sure," Veronica said. "But I'm a little tired of walking, aren't you? And that mud won't be any fun. First, are we going in the right direction?"

"Yes," First replied. "Just keep along the coast."

***

They camped that night on a barrier island; the crocodiles swam off to hunt, but Veronica assured them they would be back in the morning. On the sea side of the island they found the first sandy beach they had seen, and while the strangeness of the early strands had taken Delia in, nostalgia now brought her to the water's edge and then into it, playing in the surf like a girl, riding the waves up to their tops by kicking, occasionally having one break over her and fill her nostrils with brine. The Twins built a big fire with driftwood, and Veronica brought them a haul of some sort of big fish. Nobody knew what they were called, but roasted over the fire they were wonderful, with dense white flesh that reminded Delia of grouper or even chicken. They washed the fish down with the sweet liquid from some green coconuts the Twins had turned up.

"We're close," Second said, tossing another stick in the fire. "There's a bend in the coast up ahead, and the mouth of another river. Once we cross that, we're in her territory."

Delia fell asleep as cool breezes stroked the palms. She dreamed of her father, whom she hadn't dreamt of in years. He was young, like she usually remembered him, but his face was vague, blurred like an old polaroid. He was trying to tell her something, but she couldn't understand him. Finally, he put one hand on her shoulder and pointed up to the sky, at the full moon.

But there was something weird about it: the moon was all there, but an orange-looking shadow covered part of it, and as she watched, the shadow engulfed more and more of the slivery sphere.

Lunar eclipse, she thought. *I remember this.*

And even though the sky was clear, she felt a drop of rain hit her shoulder, and then another. One struck her hand, and she saw that it wasn't rain at all.

It was blood.

She woke, gasping. It was cold, and the weird, sickly light that passed for morning was filtering down. Everyone else was up, breaking camp.

"Are you all right?" Errol asked her. "We thought we would let you sleep a little longer."

"I'm okay,' she said. "I'll be fine."

She walked down the seaside for one last look at the surf. Veronica and Shandor came along behind her a few moments later.

"Is it time to go?" she asked.

"Our rides are on the way back," Veronica said. She seemed a little distracted.

"There's something out there," Shandor said.

"I know," Veronica said. "It's been coming for a while."

"It's one of yours?" Shandor asked.

"No," she said. "It's coming over water, but it's not *of* the water."

"Is it the enemy?" Delia asked.

"I don't know."

Delia thought she saw it now, something extremely far out to sea; not on the water, but above it, a spot darker than the rest of the sky.

"What's that?" First asked, coming up behind them. "Something coming?"

"Yes," Veronica said. "Something strong. You know what it is?"

"Oh, let it not be," First said.

"We have some suspicions," Second admitted. "This should be a good time to make our way back to the mainland."

"Okay," Veronica said. "Our boats are ready."

EIGHT

FIRE THIEF

D elia couldn't help looking behind her as whatever-it-was drew nearer. Its appearance kept changing. At one glance, she saw a flock of crows, at another a raft with a triangular sail navigated by a long human figure. Then a tall, spindly giant wading through the deeps. It seemed in no hurry; less like it was chasing them and more like they happened to be going in the direction it was already traveling.

When they reached the coast, the apparition was still some distance behind them.

"It's on foot from here," First said. "See how the coast bends, to the south? Go there and cross the river. That one is slow and shallow, and you can swim it, no trouble. There are some cliffs with caves in them. There are some Before People living there, but they won't bother you if you don't bother them. After that, there's a land out on the water. At low tide you can walk to it. Go there and wait for us. It's our sister's country."

"Wait," Errol said. "Where are you two going?"

"We got to go back and deal with this one," Second said. "We set the winds against him, slowed him down, but they're getting weak. He'll get through and then he'll move as fast as a bee. Brother and I will send him packing, then we'll be back with you for the rest of this. You'll be fine. Just stay on your toes."

"Who is it?" Aster said. "Who is coming."

"We thought he was dead, or turned to stone or something," First said. "But it looks like he's just been away. Like us, he's got lots of names. Some just call him Fire Thief. The thing is, he went mad even before the curse. He might do good, he might do bad, you never know. But in his case, I might think bad. He was always a little cozy with the Under. I wouldn't make a bet on his good nature. So get going."

Then the two boys sprinted off toward the water—and when they reached it, across it.

"Let's go," Errol said.

"Shouldn't we stay and help them fight?" Dusk asked.

"I can't walk on water," Errol said. "Can you? I'll bet they can handle it. And if they can't, I kind of doubt we can."

"You doubt?" Dusk said. "The rider of the great Unicorn?"

"Unicorn?" Errol said.

"The one-horned beast?"

"Oh," Errol said. "I get it. We have a different name for . . . anyway, I think we should go."

"I second that," Aster said. "We need to do what we travelled all this way for. The Twins know that."

Dusk nodded, and without any more debate they moved out.

The hills were now mountains, the beach was dark, fine sand, littered with seashells and wave-polished bone. The birds seemed fewer, and in the distance they often saw what appeared to be packs of wild dogs. They soon turned the bend the twins had spoken of, and not long after that reached the river mouth.

Or mouths, rather; there was no obvious central channel, but instead a series of braided streams. The Twins were right, in that none of them were very deep or very wide, but it was still a hard, muddy slog though often dense stands of reeds and seemingly solid ground that swallowed their legs to mid-calf. It seemed to take forever, and when "night" came, they didn't try to camp, but kept going, until they finally reached higher, drier ground. There they took a break of just a few hours, sleeping in turns, before setting out again.

Toward the end of the next day, they reached the cliffs the Twins had spoken off, but they didn't see any people. That evening, Errol and Billy scouted out a rock shelter, and when they found it uninhabited, led everyone up to it. There Aster started a fire while Dusk, Shandor, and Billy went hunting. Errol stood restless guard at the cave mouth; Veronica just settled into a corner. Outside, the moon's light faded. Delia found a rock to sit on and leaned back against the cave wall.

"They ought to be back by now," Errol said, after a while.

"They ought to be," Veronica replied. "Errol, I think you'd better—"

She didn't get to finish. Everything just—stopped. Veronica's mouth was frozen open. The fire looked like a sculpture carved of yellow and red crystal. Errol was as still as a statue.

But Delia could move. She stood up.

"What's happening?" she asked.

"Hey," someone said. "Look at you. Not expecting that."

The voice came from the cave mouth.

He looked like a teenager, maybe seventeen or eighteen, and he resembled the Twins, except that he was an albino. And very tall. He carried a long pole over his shoulders, so he looked almost like he was bearing a cross; on each end of the pole, bound hands-to-feet, the Twins were suspended.

"Are they alive?" she asked. "Did you kill them?"

"No," he said. "Why would I kill my younger cousins? What a shame that would be."

"Are you the Fire Thief?" Delia asked.

"I am that," he said. "And much more. But what are you, going so quick, like me?" He squinted at her. "Ah," he said, after a bit. "It's her inside you. Now I see. Look, I'm going to have to ask you to sit still for a moment."

He lifted the pole from his shoulders and wedged it between two shelves of rock, so the Twins remained suspended above the ground. Then he went over and tied up Errol, Veronica, and Aster with more of the cordage that, like a magician, he seemed to produce from nowhere. She tried to move to at least try and stop him but found she couldn't.

When he was done securing them, he left the cave and returned with Shandor, Billy, and Dusk, one at a time, and tied them up as well.

"Now there," he said, returning his attention to Delia. "Let's think about you."

"Why are you doing this?" Delia asked.

"They're off to see their Sister Night," he said, nodding at the Twins. "Can't have that. Can't have any of you going there, for that matter. It's a bad business."

"Why?"

"Why?" the Fire Thief said. He cocked his head. Then he laughed. "You said one of my names. But who am I? Can you tell by looking at me?"

"I don't understand what you mean," Delia said.

His form broke like a reflection on suddenly disturbed water. Then it was one of the Twins standing there. Then Aster. Then he returned to the way she had first seen him.

"So who am I?" he asked.

"I don't know," she said. "But whoever you are, please let us go. We're doing something important."

"Oh, yes," he said. "I see that. You should have asked me about that." He nodded at the Twins. "*They* should have asked me about that. So. Right now I'm going to check on something, and I'll be back. Don't untie them or let them get eaten by wild dogs. And don't leave the cave."

Then he distorted again, and was a large, black raven. He flew out of the cave and was quickly out of sight.

The flames began flickering again. The sounds of insects and frogs and nightbirds returned. And almost immediately, the Twins began to struggle with their bonds.

"Cut us free!" First said.

Delia reached for her little stone knife, but then stopped.

"I can't," she said.

"Of course she can't," Second said.

"Can't you break free?" Delia said.

"Not from these bands," Second replied. "Fire Thief is an elder. The only elder besides Moon that's still walking, I guess. We thought he wasn't. We can't undo what he's done, at least not easily."

"I see what you mean," Veronica said. "I can't change," she said. "Aster, can you do anything?"

"No," Aster said. "It's like I'm cut off from elumiris. I can sense it out there, but I can't touch it. Why did he do this?"

"Who knows?" First said. "He's crazy. He's always been crazy, but now it's worse. He's hard to talk to."

"I noticed that," Delia said.

"You talk to him?" First said. He seemed surprised.

"Yes. He . . . froze time or something. But it didn't affect me. He said he had to go check on something, and that he would be back."

"I don't doubt that," Second said. "We need to be loose by then. If we get to our sister's place, he won't be able to follow us."

Then it seemed like everyone was talking at once. Delia moved toward the cave mouth until Fire Thief's compunction forced her to stop, seeking quiet.

Sing, the voice inside of her said.

She looked behind her, but no one was paying attention. She didn't need to ask what she should sing; she heard it in her head. She started, softly at first. There wasn't much of a tune — three notes rising, four falling, five rising, four falling, three rising, and so on. And the cadence was strange; it sounded off to her ear. But she kept going anyway, getting louder, and she did so, the song began to make a strange sort of sense. Gradually behind her, the quarreling broke off.

"Ms. Fincher, what are you doing?" Errol asked.

Unwilling to break off the song now, she ignored him. It was if the melody had taken on a life of its own, as if her throat was just a conduit bringing the music from somewhere long ago and faraway.

And now, in the distant hollows of the night, she heard an answer; a sort of sliding whistle that reminded her of a whippoorwill's voice singing a different song, matching what she was singing at times, striking dissonance at others. After a moment, another voice joined in — and odd, chittering bark, quickly joined by a deep, growling that formed the baseline of their quartet. That omnipresent buzz of insects and cheeping of frogs shifted subtly, so that they, too were humming along.

The song grew louder, cacophonous but weirdly beautiful.

Then she stopped singing, and so did everything else.

Eyes appeared in the darkness, and then three creatures came into the cave. One was a puffy grey and brown bird with huge black eyes. Another was a foxlike creature with long ears. Finally, and most worrying, was a tiger.

"Welcome, Before People," First said.

There were no longer three animals standing there, but three people. Of a sort. From the neck down they looked perfectly human, made more than obvious by the fact that they were naked. Two were women and one was a man. They had wide mouths, receding chins, heavy brow ridges, and not much in the way of foreheads. If Delia had to guess, based on what little she remembered from her anthropology class in college, they were some sort of early human—*Homo erectus*, maybe. Of course, they had been animals a moment ago, so it wasn't likely that they were actually anything that had ever existed in her world.

The three gazed around at them for a few moments. Then they went over to the twins and began touching the cords that bound them. They unraveled instantly. The Before People made their way around the cave until everyone was free.

Then one of the women came over and took Delia's hand. She felt the Fire Thief's prohibitions drop away.

"Thank you," she said.

The woman gazed into her eyes, then used the middle knuckle of her index finger to point at the moon, which was just starting to show again.

"Yes," Delia said. "We mean to fix that."

The woman nodded, and then she was the nightbird, again, on the wing. The other two Before People were already gone.

"We've got to get going," First said. "Now. Before Fire Thief returns."

***

They alternated running and walking, following the shore until they saw another landmass, out across the water, connected to the mainland by a small strip of land.

"We get across that, we're fine," First said.

"Run hard," Second said. "Because Fire Thief is coming up behind."

So they ran. Despite the child in her, Delia felt her footsteps fall lightly, and she realized someone—probably Aster—was doing something to make the going easier.

She heard something behind them that at first sounded like the angry croaking of a raven; but as it drew nearer and louder, she realized it was Fire Thief, ranting into the night.

No, no, you can't! It's not supposed to be like this! I know the way. The broken road, the crossroad, the place where the dead whisper . . .

"Don't listen to him," First said. "That's not the way. If we go that way, the Under will snatch us up in an instant."

Delia looked back and saw a cloud of black birds, descending toward them. She ran faster, but the island still seemed impossibly far away.

Then Fire Thief was suddenly standing in front of them. Almost instantly, the others began to slow down, like before. But then she saw a glow surround Aster, rose-colored rays— and then the wind came rushing from behind them. It lifted Fire Thief into the air and blew him away. Delia watched him grow smaller and smaller until he was just a speck, then gone. And with him went the slowing of time.

The hurricane wind diminished, dropped to a breeze, and then they all stood in eerie silence.

"Wow," Errol said.

"I almost didn't make it," Aster said. "Another second, and he would have had us."

"Close," Second agreed. "But well done. Still, he will return."

They resumed their run, and did not see Fire Thief again before they crossed into the Land of Night.

NINE
∩IGHT

The Land of Night didn't look any different to Errol, at least not at first. The trail took them through tropical forest, open, tall-grass meadows, and fields of ferns. The sky was still the same, with its stationary stars and weird moon. But then he began to notice the shadows fluttering against that sky and realized that they were not birds. Many of them were moths, some glowing with a faint phosphorescence, while others described the frantic, jittery motions of bats. The midnight chorus was the strangest he had ever heard: peeps, clicks, and high trilling songs that might have been birds or frogs or neither. One rasping call sounded like someone talking on a scratchy old phonograph record, too low to make out the words. Another reminded him of the lowing of cattle, and one awful call was almost—but not quite—like the scream of a child.

They gained altitude as they went along, and the ocean was soon far from sight. They followed a trail upward to a highland valley. The air was cool and clear, and he was glad he had his mantle. Aster's feather-covered cloak glowed in the starlight. Dusk's eyes flickered now and then, as if she had lightning in her head.

"Can you feel that?" he asked her, tapping his head.

"The lightning?" Dusk said. "Yes. But not as you do. It's more like an emotion."

"What sort of emotion?" Errol asked.

She smiled. "It's different depending on what else is going on. When you and I are . . . together . . . it feels like passion. Like love. But at other times it's closer to rage."

"What does it feel like now?" he asked.

"Something in between," she said. "It's hard to explain. But whatever is happening to me is happening . . . more."

"Do you think you can control it?" he asked.

"I haven't shocked you again, have I?"

"No," he said. "And thank you, by the way."

She took his hand. "I can control it," she said.

***

Eventually they came to a village, if four buildings could be called that. They were more substantial than the simple shelters in Pearl's village. Wooden posts lifted the houses about ten feet off the ground, supporting bamboo floors and pitched roofs of thatched grass, but no walls. They were much longer than they were wide. Three of the buildings he guessed to be about twenty feet long. The fourth was much larger, maybe twice that, and stood higher than the others. In the square between them, a pool of clear water bubbled out of the ground, spilling out to create a stream that ran off downhill.

He wasn't sure what he was expecting, but the people didn't have bat wings or owl eyes, or anything like that. They just looked like people, and they wore loincloths and cloaks a lot like the ones he had on.

As they arrived, a young woman appeared at the edge of the largest longhouse, watching them. She took a step into the air, and her cloak billowed up as she dropped slowly to the ground and then came toward them. Her face was round, her eyes dark and wide, her smile like the crescent moon. Her hair was piled up in complicated braids.

"Brothers," she said. "So good to see you." Then she turned her gaze to the rest of them. "I am Night," she said. "Welcome to my home."

"I am delighted to see you, Sister," Second said. "Your lands are as inviting as ever."

"And you are as welcome as ever," she replied. "As are these cousins you bring with you."

"You know why we're here," First said.

"Of course," Night replied. "You seek our other sister, in her grave at the border with the Under."

"Exactly," Second said. "And I hate to say so, but we are in something of a hurry."

She clucked with her tongue. "Always in a hurry, you two. No time for manners. You know I will not have you just passing through, without offering you hospitality. It's not my way."

"Well," First said.

"And you must tell me your stories of your travels here," she added.

"Fire Thief is still alive," Second said. "He nearly kept us from getting here."

"Yes, he has been troubling me lately as well, or trying to. I banned him from this place long ago, and he has done nothing to change my inclination. Come. Let us eat together."

***

The cooking pits were dug into the ground underneath the longhouse, so the smoke filtered up through the bamboo floor, making the inside of the building fairly smoky. It was unpleasant to breathe, but it seemed to discourage the mosquitos and biting flies Aster had been slapping at for so long she had almost forgotten they existed. They sat on mats woven from some sort of grass with banana leaves spread out for plates. Younger kids brought the food up in baskets, climbing the rickety ladders that led up from the ground.

First course was hot tea of some sort served in a coconut half, accompanied by shriveled, sour smelling leaves. Aster muttered a small Telling under her breath, to make certain the food didn't contain anything toxic. She knew it was paranoid, but despite the Twin's vocal certainty about their sister, something seemed off to her.

Thus reassured, she tasted the tea. It was bitter, but not excessively so. The leaves tasted weird, sweet and sour with an aftertaste like wet leather smelled.

First and Second talked about their travels, with Night occasionally asking someone else a question. It was light conversation until they reached the part about Fire Thief and the Before People, which coincided with the second course, several huge crawfish cooked in their shells.

"Brothers," Night said, "It must be asked. Has Fire Thief become one with the Under? He has always been attracted to it."

"As a source of amusement," First said. "To taunt the masters of that place. To trick and steal from them."

"Perhaps he went too far," Night said. "Perhaps the trickster tricked himself."

"It's possible," First replied. "And yet he existed before the Under — or any of us, for that matter. He is nothing if not a survivor."

"Perhaps he has made alliance with enemy precisely *so* he can survive," she replied.

"Perhaps," First said.

"Wait," Aster said. "I don't understand. Fire Thief existed before the Under? Before the giant was slain and the world made as it is?"

"Yes," Second said. "He was once one of the Before People, like those who freed us from the caves. But when we came along, he became obsessed with us, and with our human family. As the other Before People withdrew from the world, Fire Thief became more and more of it. He was here before any of my kin."

"But if there wasn't a world . . ." Errol began, obviously as puzzled as she was.

"Well, there was always *something*," Second said. "Or the image of something. The Dream of it."

"But doesn't that mean if the Itch gets its way, there will still be *something*, too?" Veronica put in.

"Sure," First said. "But you won't be in it. Or me, or any of us."

"But what about Fire Thief, and the Before People. They survived one new world. Will they survive another?"

Second mused that over. "They might," he said. "They might at that."

"So maybe Fire Thief *is* in league with the enemy," Dusk said.

"Could be," First reluctantly agreed.

A boy of about five or six placed something on her leaf. Honeycomb, dripping with honey. Again she whispered the Telling, then took a bite. It was the best thing she had eaten in a while, and like no honey she'd ever had before. It tasted like vanilla and honeysuckle, lemon, lime, and orange.

"Sister," First said, licking honey from his fingers. "What became of Racer, your dog?"

"Indeed," Second said. "You once had many dogs, but now I seen not one."

"They died," Night said. "Protecting us from the Under."

"Has the Under penetrated your territory so deeply?" First asked.

"No," Night began, but Shandor interrupted her.

"Veronica!" he said, sharply. "Do not eat that."

Veronica blinked and held up her honeycomb. She frowned, and then Aster saw she was holding a chunk of meat wriggling with black maggots. And from it stretched a dark line, worming its way across the room to Night.

"Sister!" First shouted. Shandor leapt to his feet, drawing his knife, but suddenly a spear appeared in his back, and then another, one thrown by the boy who had brought the honeycomb and the other by a young man who had just come up the ladder.

"Shandor!" Veronica yelled.

But Aster was watching Night. Still sitting cross-legged on the floor, her eyes went white and the top of her head began to wriggle. Then the skin covering her skull split down the center, and another head pushed out of it, followed by a torso and arms, pushing Night's skin down as if shucking off a dress. A puff of air escaped from her skin, and with it, two words.

Flee, brothers . . .

It seemed to go slowly but it only took seconds. Veronica had just started to move toward the wounded Shandor when the woman inside of Night's skin stepped out of it.

"Nocturn!" Dusk shouted.

"Dear Sister," Nocturn said.

Now besides Nocturn she saw Hawk and Gloam, both armed with spears. The boy who had brought her the honeycomb had changed, too; he had sunken, glassy eyes, and flies buzzed around fatal wounds in his belly and throat. And the black tendrils were in him, too, wriggling toward her. In fact, now that she looked, they were everywhere, coming from the roof, the floor, the walls, all reaching for Veronica.

"Veronica!" she shouted.

Veronica was kneeling over Shandor, but now she straightened.

"No!" she said.

Aster had no doubt of what was happening. All the real villagers were dead. Nocturn and the others were part of the enemy now, and they wanted Veronica with them, too.

Dusk leapt at Nocturn like a panther and sank her spear into her sister's chest. Apparently unconcerned, Nocturn batted Dusk aside with the back of her hand. She reached out for Errol with blinding speed and caught him by the throat as he, too, rushed at her. Aster stumbled forward, dodging around them, as the dark tendrils touched Veronica.

Aster grabbed Veronica by the arm and let the light inside of her do what it was trying to do. In an instant it ran into Veronica's bones and burst from her eyes, her mouth, the pores of her skin. The black tendrils shrank back, curling away.

"Damn you!" Veronica screamed at Nocturn. "Damn you!

Nocturn flinched back, but she was still sitting, and Veronica was fast. She plunged her fingers into Nocturn's chest, and Aster's light suddenly flashed inside of her too, a sickly glow, but growing. Nocturn screamed, a hideous unearthly sound. The roof of the building burst into flame.

From the corner of her eyes Aster saw Hawk rush at her with his spear and knew she would never be able to stop him in time.

But she didn't have to, because of course Errol was there.

***

As was often the case, Errol had only the vaguest idea what was going on. Nocturn had been in the process of crushing his larynx when Aster and Veronica went all glowy. Nocturn turned him loose, but he still had spots in his eyes when he saw Hawk was about to stab Aster.

"Screw that," he said. Four quick steps, building speed, then Errol ducked under the spear, hit Hawk just above the knees, heaved him up, and then rammed him straight over the side of the longhouse. He wasn't sure where his own spear had gotten off to, but his boomerang was still in his belt, and without much thought he jumped right after Hawk, landing on him before he could recover from the fall. He rolled to spend momentum and then bounced up.

He'd fought Hawk before and lost, badly. He knew he couldn't give him time to recover. If anything, Hawk was faster than before. He had almost gotten back to his feet when Errol came at him, bludgeoning him on the side of the head with the boomerang. Hawk's head snapped back, and Errol hit him again. The heavy weapon should have split his skull like a cantaloupe, but it didn't, which was not a good sign.

Hawk dodged the third blow and hit Errol with his fist, right in the ribs, so hard that everything went white. He remembered the last time—Hawk's smug satisfaction, his certainty that Errol was no match for him, and infuriating reality that he was right.

Not this time, Errol thought. *Not even if it kills me.*

As Errol staggered back and his vision cleared, Hawk came on, grinning. He threw another punch.

Errol dodged to the side and clocked him at the base of his skull with the boomerang, putting his whole body into it. He heard the gasp of surprise and followed up with a blow to the ribs. Hawk hit the ground, heavily. Errol kicked him in the side, and again. Hawk struggled to get back to his feet, but Errol had no intention of letting that happen. He was vaguely aware that everything was on fire, but he was going to finish it this time.

Someone grabbed his arm, and he spun around, cranking the club back before seeing it was Billy.

"We've got to go," Billy said. "Now."

"But . . ." Hawk was climbing to his feet.

"We don't have time for you to kill him."

"I wasn't . . ." he started. Panting, Hawk started to step toward him. Then he turned and ran.

Errol cocked his arm to hurl the boomerang at the fleeing man, realizing that he really did want to kill him.

The fight was over. He'd won. He let his arm relax at his side as Hawk vanished into the woods.

"Okay," he said to Billy. "Where to?"

"Back the way we came," Billy said. "And quick. They will all be back. I don't think we can kill them."

***

"How did Nocturn do that?" Errol asked later. They were back on the mainland, where the Twins said they ought to be safe. They had started a fire, and were tending to Shandor, who was in bad shape. Even Veronica, who had once healed Dusk of mortal wounds, couldn't seem to do much for him.

"He was wounded by a ghost," First said. "It is difficult to return from that."

"So Nocturn is a ghost? Those guys are all dead?"

"The one in our sister's skin?" Second said. "She must have *become*. As Aster is becoming. In Aster's case, she is trying to replace Dawn, who is dead. Nocturn *became*, I think, inside of our sister Night, as she was still alive. She is also a thing of the Under now, but not a ghost. Her brothers and sisters, however, are ghosts. And it was one of them that wounded Shandor."

"My brothers and sisters, too," Dusk said. Errol put his hand in his shoulder, but she didn't react. She just kept staring into the fire. "I had a younger sister, also named Dawn. She wasn't with them. I think they may have murdered her."

"Maybe because she might have served in Aster's place," Second said.

"Yes," Dusk said. "That's my reasoning."

That killed the conversation for a minute or so.

"Hawk was pretty solid for a ghost," Errol finally said, rubbing ribs that he was reasonably certain were cracked.

"Ghosts are often solid," Second said.

Not where I'm from, Errol thought. Even ghosts were less in his world. It made sense, he guessed.

"I did try to stop you," a familiar voice said.

Errol sprang to his feet before the sentence was complete, heart hammering in his chest. Fire Thief was just suddenly *there,* leaning against a tree.

"You!" he snapped.

"Calm yourself," Fire Thief said. "If I had come to do more than talk, you would already know it."

"What is it you are saying, Uncle?" Second asked.

"I told you not to go there, to your sister's place," he said.

"No," Errol said. "No, that's not what happened. You didn't *tell* us anything. You put us under some sort of spell and then tied us up."

"I think my message was more than clear," Fire Thief said.

"Uncle, it would have been much clearer if you had simply spoken of the danger," First said.

"And maybe I would have done just that, small Nephew, if certain children I know of hadn't set the winds against me and then assaulted me with their little spears."

"Looking back on it, perhaps we made a mistake," Second admitted.

"You were disrespectful," Fire Thief said. "You needed to be taught a lesson. And you should not have gone to see your sister, as you now know. Look at your friend."

"Can you do anything for him?" Veronica asked.

Fire Thief squatted down on his haunches and sniffed the air around Shandor.

"Something, maybe," he said. "But first, we should discuss what to do now."

"Hang on," Errol said. "Why did the Before People help us escape you? I thought you were one of them."

"I was one of them, long ago. But no more. That was my mistake, you know? I no longer think like them, so I didn't understand. I thought they would respect me in this matter. But here is how it is: they wanted you to go there, to fail and die. They have never been fond of the world we made. They would be happy to see it gone. I didn't anticipate that. My mind slips a lot, these days. I'm not quite the same since the Dawn died."

"None of us is, Uncle," First said. "So what do we do now?"

Fire Thief pointed off into the darkness with his lips. "We go my way, on the ghost trail."

"We might not survive that," Second said.

"Well, you can't go through your sister's place, can you? And I've been on the ghost trail. I've been there and back."

"They say you used to harass the dead for the fun of it," Second said.

"At one time or another I've harassed everyone for the fun of it," Fire Thief replied. He squatted down by the fire and warmed his hands. "Go my way or fail."

"We'll go your way, Uncle," First said.

"And Shandor?" Veronica said.

Fire Thief bent and touched Shandor. After a moment, the Gypsy's eyes flickered open.

"You are ghost wounded," Fire Thief told him. "Do you know what that means?"

Shandor nodded.

"This is what I can do for you. I can give you the strength to walk, and fight, and all of that. For a few days. Then you will die. Or I can let you die here. If you die here, we can get your soul safely to where it's going. If you die near the Under, there is no telling. Probably you will be devoured and entirely cease to be. Do you understand?"

"Give me the strength to continue," Shandor said.

"Shandor," Veronica said. She knelt by him.

Shandor smiled, faintly. "My sister told me," he said. "She is rarely wrong."

"Told you what?"

"That if I found you, it would mean my doom."

"Then why?" Veronica asked.

"You know," he sighed.

"Oh, Shandor," she said. "I'm sorry."

"You have no reason for sorrow," he said. "Let Fire Thief give me a few more days. It will be enough for me."

"The cost," she said.

"I don't care."

She cupped his face in her hand. "Thank you, Shandor Mingo King Michaels," she said. "Thank you for everything."

Then she kissed him. When they parted, Shandor's head lolled to the side, his eyes now sightless.

Tears trickled down Veronica's face.

"You . . . you killed him," Errol said.

"I saved him," Veronica said. "Or what I could of him."

"It's not what he wanted," Dusk said.

"No," Veronica replied. "But it is what was best."

Then she turned and walked away from the fire.

TEN

THE GHOST TRAIL

Now following Fire Thief, they continued along the coast for a while and then struck off into the interior, quickly gaining altitude before eventually reaching a river valley carved into a rocky plateau. They entered a forest of towering tree ferns, stands of pale bamboo, meadows of moss and lichen, strange, thorny plants with large, beautiful flowers, ferns like lace. Veronica wondered if there was anywhere in the Reign of the Departed so strange and beautiful.

No one had spoken to her in days. She didn't really blame them, and she didn't really want to talk to anyone, anyway.

That evening, after camp was made, she retreated to a stream she sensed nearby. She took off her clothes and bathed in a shallow pool she found there, feeling the small lives of fish and crawfish, snails and frogs. She closed her eyes and tried to find a moment of peace.

She knew Dusk was there before she said anything. She was surprised; she had thought Errol would be the first one to approach her.

"Hello," Veronica said. "Join me for a soak?"

"No," Dusk said. "I came to talk."

"I don't suppose I can stop you," Veronica said.

"You can ask me to leave," Dusk replied.

"No, that's okay," Veronica said. "Talk away."

Dusk sat down cross-legged on the mossy bank. "I wanted to you to know I understand why you did that for him," she said. "For Shandor."

"Do you?" Veronica said. "You objected at the time."

"I didn't say I approve," Dusk replied. "Only that I understand."

"That's okay," Veronica said. "I didn't ask for anyone's approval."

Dusk nodded. "Good for you," She said. She stayed seated.

"Is there something else?" Veronica asked.

"I'm becoming something," Dusk replied. "Just as Aster is. I'm not sure what. But it isn't like I feel something being *forced* on me. It is rather like something already inside of me is becoming *more*. Is that how you feel?"

"Yes," Veronica said. "I've been feeling that way for a long time."

"But what is it, do you think, that is becoming *more* in you?"

"It sounds like you want to tell me," Veronica said.

"You can take life," Dusk said. "You can snuff it out with a kiss."

"You've taken plenty of lives, my dear Dusk."

"Yet you can also *give* life," Dusk continued, ignoring her. "You gave it to me."

"If you're suggesting I could have kept Shandor alive, you're wrong. Fire Thief was right. Your soul hadn't strayed all that far from your body. It wasn't that hard to keep it there. Shandor's was all but adrift. If his soul left him in the Under, he would have been destroyed completely. No rebirth for him. Just food for the Itch."

"That's not what I'm suggesting," Dusk said. "I believe you have a choice, Veronica, in what you are becoming. You will either be a creature of life or one of death. And I believe that choice will be before you soon. I hope you make the right one — for all our sakes."

"Very well, Dusk," Veronica said. "I'll take that under consideration. And I promise, you will be the very first to know what I decide. Now, if you don't have anything else to tell me about myself, I would like a little quiet time."

"That was all," Dusk said. "Enjoy your bath." She stood and walked back toward camp.

Veronica did not enjoy her bath. Dusk had just said what she herself had been thinking for some time. But what Dusk didn't understand was what that choice would hinge on. Or rather, who.

Errol.

***

A few more days passed, and Errol began speaking to Veronica again, and once he did, so did the others. No one mentioned Shandor. It was not like it had been before, and was never going to be, but she was no longer isolated.

The forest began to feel different to her; she could not decide just when it had begun, but after half a day she was sure something was wrong. It didn't look different; the trees, bushes, and ferns were the same. A photograph taken here and one from a day behind them in their travels would be nearly indistinguishable from one another.

It was more like the material the pictures were printed in were different. And then she began to understand.

"We're on the ghost road," she said.

"We are," Second said. "You feel it?'

"Very dangerous here for the living," First added. "I still worry about this."

"I've done this dozens of times," Fire Thief said.

"I recall you got caught at least once," First said. "Isn't that right? You were imprisoned, or something."

"Well, sure," Fire Thief said. "For a little while. A century or two."

"I don't think we can afford a century or two," Errol said.

"Well," Fire Thief said. "We'll just have to be careful. And quiet."

"Look there," Dusk said.

Veronica looked, and saw a tiny light rising in the forest. And there was another, flickering, reminding her of something, something she had loved when she was little.

"Lightning bugs," she said.

"No," Fire Thief said. "That isn't what they are at all."

"Those are a very bad sign," First said.

"What do they do?" Errol asked.

"They bring the Walkalongs."

"That doesn't sound all that threatening," Errol said.

The "eyes" drifted along, pacing them. They still looked and acted like lightning bugs, but she was starting to feel something else, a greater presence, as if the little lights were holes in a wall that something much larger was peeking through.

It began raining; a few fat drops at first, bursting like frog eggs on the forest floor, but quickly escalating to a steady downpour. Normally Veronica would have been glad of that; she was more powerful when she was in water, or near it. But this was a cold, sterile rain, with no life in it, and instead of strengthening her it numbed her senses.

Eventually, the movement of the lights became less random, and soon it became clear that they were traveling in pairs, just a few inches apart. Shadowy faces began to appear around them, and then ephemeral bodies. With each step the phantoms gained color, depth, substance. She was reminded of a self-developing camera her grandfather had, the way the image gradually became real.

For the most part, they looked like people, but as they grew sharper and more visible, she realized that none of them was entirely human. One had the head of an owl, another a dog's head. A normal human head and body but a snakelike tail, a woman covered in feathers and a beak instead of a nose . . . they were everywhere now, dozens of them, their eyes still shining and flickering like the fireflies she'd first believed them to be. They came closer, darting forward and reaching out as if to touch them, but then retreating back from range. Errol took a swipe at one of them with his spear — a monkey-headed woman — and she bounced from range, venting an odd little *hoot*.

"What's going on?" Errol demanded.

"Don't stop," Fire Thief said. "And don't talk to them. Don't answer them."

"Talk to them?" Errol said. "They aren't saying anything."

But that wasn't true, Veronica realized. The ones nearest her were whispering. She couldn't understand them at first, but the syllables became clearer as they continued.

You will have to choose, they were saying. *Very soon, you will have to choose. We can tell you what to do, if you will only ask.*

Yeah, right, Veronica thought. But it was weird; she sensed the danger, but what she did not feel was any connection to the Itch or the Raggedy Man. This seemed older to her, maybe — like Fire Thief — relics of a more ancient order.

"Jesus," Errol said. "I hear them now."

"Me too," Dusk said. "It's maddening."

"Can't we do something about them?" Errol asked. "Aster, can't you blast them or something?"

"Do nothing," Fire Thief said. "We are on their ground, in their territory. We dare not attack them here. We will pass through this place soon enough. Be resolute."

"Not as easy as it sounds," Errol said.

His death is coming, the creatures told Veronica. *Coming soon, unless you choose. Ask us how to stop it, how to save his life, and we will tell you."*

Veronica pressed her lips tightly together, but the voices only became louder and more insistent.

Errol, the voices said. *Errol will die unless you act.*

So they were telling her the same thing Yurena had.

She wondered what the others were hearing. Was Errol being warned of his own death or of hers? Dusk's? Or something else entirely?

What made it all the more horrible was that she knew what the voices were saying was true. Her mind couldn't help responding, telling them to shut up, or asking them for help, admitting that she knew they were right. And she knew that eventually, those thoughts would slip into words, maybe without her even knowing.

And if she didn't, one of the others would break.

She had to do something. It was like when her mother made her play the quiet game. It never worked for long.

But there was another game, one they had played during long car rides.

She took a deep breath.

And she sang.

"Ninety-nine bottles of beer on the wall, ninety-nine bottles of beer . . ."

Everyone looked at her like she had lost her mind. But then Errol's mouth formed an "O," and he smiled and joined in. "Take one down, pass it around, ninety-eight bottles of beer on the wall!"

Then Delia joined in. The others continued looking puzzled, but neither the words nor the tune was difficult. Fire Thief started bellowing his own version of the song, which sounded more like "blobbles of deer," but he had the idea. By ninety-six bottles of beer the Twins were singing, grinning ear-to-ear, and Dusk had joined by ninety. Even the normally taciturn Billy eventually took up the song.

They pulled down all ninety-nine bottles of beer and started over, and each time they sang it, it became easier to ignore their spectral antagonists, until eventually the cajoling voices receded into whimpers, and the Walkalongs themselves gradually faded, becoming once more like lightning bugs bobbing in the trees, and then vanished from sight. When she was quite sure they were safe, Veronica stopped singing, and all of the others trailed off, too, except Fire Thief, who kept going for several minutes. When he finally stopped, they all took a moment to enjoy the relative silence, the return of birdsong, the murmuring of wind through the branches.

"That was smart," First said, after a time. "Second and I would have been okay, but other kinds of people have difficulty."

"Thanks," Veronica.

"But it raises a serious question," First said. "One that needs answering before we go on."

"What's that?"

"What is beer?"

"Yes," Second said. "And what is a bottle?"

***

T he forest grew deeper and the fronds of the tree ferns overhead knitted together, and they soon found themselves no longer in a shallow valley but enveloped by a deep, steep-sided ravine. Moss, lichens, and ferns covered the rocky ground and clung to the sheer cliffs. Things the size of large dogs skittered away at their approach; now and then they would climb the walls, and Veronica could see that they had more than four limbs, sometimes many more.

They camped twice more, and the next day reached the opening to a cave, plugged by a huge boulder. The Twins and Fire Thief set to pushing it aside, which seemed ludicrous, but when everyone joined in helping them it rolled away, leaving the way into the cliff open.

"This is as far as I can go," Fire Thief said. "But I can scout ahead to the Hole of the Sun and make certain nothing awaits you there. Keep to the trails you know. Don't be led off."

With that he became a raven and soared away.

"Thanks, Uncle," First called after him. Then he turned his gaze back to the cave.

"So she's in there," Aster said.

"She's in there," First confirmed. "We also can accompany you no further. This place is taboo for us. But we'll wait for you here."

ELEVEN

THE TOMB

O nly a few steps into the cave took them beyond what little illumination the moonlight provided, so Aster worked
a Whimsy of Heatless Flame, but as with everything here, the
results were outsized and strange. It should have made her
hand glow like a lantern, but instead, wherever she placed her
feet, the stone flashed white, and illumination spread out from
her in a ring, fading quickly toward the red end of the spectrum;
she figured they could see about sixty feet before the light vanishing into wavelengths too long for the human eye to perceive.

The passage descended at a relatively constant angle, and
the black stone it burrowed through was almost featureless; no
stalactites hanging from the ceiling, no stalagmites jutting from
the floor, no columns or curtains or mineral formations of any
kind. They walked on, speaking seldom.

Eventually the tunnel opened into a much larger space. The
radiance from her Whimsy showed no ceiling, but before them it
revealed the flat black mirror of an underwater lake. The light from
her feet traveled further on the waters than on stone, so she could
see a dark silhouette of an island rising up above the surface.

"Why do I have the feeling that what we're looking for is on the island?" Errol asked.

"It is," Aster said. She felt it, an almost magnetic tug.

"Where are we?" Errol said. "The Twins keep talking about the Under. I've been figuring that was a stone age version of Hell, or Hades or whatever. An underworld. And what I remember about all of that was that there was water you had to cross, right? Like the River Styx?"

"In Greek mythology there were several rivers," Aster said.

"Right," Errol said. "But they did stuff to you, right? Like took away your memories and such?"

"I have heard of such waters," Dusk said.

"I'll take your word for it," Veronica said. "I never learned all of that. And I don't remember our preacher ever saying anything about water in Hell. Sort of the opposite—lakes of fire and seas of lava is what I remember. But anyway, I've been to the Under. This isn't it. It's out there, all around us, but it can't get in here. Something is keeping it out."

Aster nodded. "I think she's right."

"So this water isn't going to suck out our souls or whatever when we try and cross it?"

"I don't think so," Aster said. "But crossing it might be a problem, anyway. It's still water, and that's a good distance."

"Not to worry," Veronica said. "There aren't any crocodiles here, but I think I can make do. Somebody take care of this stuff for me."

So saying, she began stripping off her clothes. Errol turned away, quickly, tossing a nervous glance at Dusk, who Aster noticed was watching Errol, not Veronica. Errol couldn't have Dusk getting jealous, could he? Dusk had betrayed them once, spectacularly, and Aster was sure that jealousy had been at least a minor part of her motivations. The incident had ended with Errol missing a leg and Veronica beheaded. And that was all before Dusk and Errol had become involved. Now that they were together, and Veronica was back, there was no telling what was going to happen if Dusk started feeling slighted.

Errol had always been an idiot when it came to females. It didn't look like he was getting any better.

When she was down to skin, Veronica waded into the lake, each step taking her deeper. After six steps her head vanished beneath the surface.

For a moment, nothing happened. Then something came up from beneath, something huge, and moving toward the shore. Eyes appeared, an inhuman face, and then a long sleek body emerged from the pool.

"It's . . . an otter," Errol said.

And so it was. The very largest otter Aster had ever seen. It crawled up out of the water and waited, watching them with intelligent brown eyes.

"We're supposed to get on your back, I take it?" Errol asked.

The otter nodded. Errol waved Aster forward.

"After you," he said.

Aster shrugged and climbed up just behind the otter's head. Otter-Veronica's fur felt slick and oily, and difficult to hold on to. She squeezed with her legs, as if riding a horse, hoping that would save her from a dunking.

Dusk climbed on next, with others just behind.

Veronica had her fun with them on the way, dipping below the surface of the lake now and then, drenching them completely. She circled, threatening to barrel roll, but eventually they made it the other shore intact.

The otter vanished, and a few moments later Veronica came out of the lake and put her clothes back on.

"Sorry about all that what-for," she said. "I thought being an otter would be fun. And it was—too much fun. Turns out they just can't help being playful."

"Can't they?" Errol said.

"We're here," Veronica said. "At least we had a little fun on the way."

"I wouldn't use the plural pronoun," Delia said. She looked a little unsteady.

Aster was only barely paying attention. The circle of illumination spreading from her feet was brighter now, causing the entire island to glow. The light was now strong enough to see the vaulting stone ceiling as well. And up ahead, toward the center of the island, the glow was even stronger. And in that center lay a corpse.

Aster was powerfully reminded of another island, the Island of the Othersun. There, in a castle of pink and white shell, the undecayed remains of her mother had lain in a crystal coffin. Here was another island, another body. Or at least the remnants of one.

Dawn lay on her side, knees tucked up to her neck, wrapped in a beautiful mantle of white feathers very much like the one Aster was wearing. Rings and necklaces of coral and amber adorned her fingers, and strings of glimmering yellow, red, orange, and white beads encircled her wrists, ankles, and throat. Her hair remained, a red-gold pile on her skull. Some sort of red powder had been sprinkled all over the body, which was reduced almost entirely to bones, with only a few bits of sinew and dried flesh visible.

"So this is their sister?" Errol said.

"Yes," Aster said. "The daughter of the Sun and of the Moon. Dawn." She reached up, unpinned the mantle the Twins had given her, and reached down for the one the dead girl wore.

It felt strange to the touch, thin, and she realized the feathers had not been sewn to it, but that it was in fact the preserved skin of a large bird.

"No!" Errol shouted. "Watch out!"

None of the others had noticed, so silently had it come from the water.

It was mostly snake, but plated like an alligator, and feathered around its neck and along the ridge of its back with oily black water-fowl feathers. It was reared up now, staring down at them.

"It's not the enemy," Veronica said. "It's something else. But . . ."

Errol whipped out his boomerang and hurled it. At this range, against a monster this big, there wasn't much chance of missing, and he didn't. The wooden weapon bounced off of the dragon's snout.

Quick as a cobra, it darted its head toward Errol, who yelped, leaping to the side, not quite fast enough. The jaws didn't catch him, but the head hit him in his already sore ribs, sending him flying.

A flash like lightning filled the cave, and Aster heard an unholy shriek of a war cry. "Dusk, no!" Veronica shouted.

But by that time the monstrous head was darting down. Aster saw that Dusk was glowing, crackling really, as if she had lightning inside of her. And she looked . . . bigger.

She jammed her shield in the monster's face and stabbed her spear into it, underhand. The cavern filled with an enormous shock of thunder. Billy ran up to help her.

"Aster," Veronica said. "Finish, fast. We have to get the hell out of here."

Aster finished taking off her cloak. She took the dead Dawn's mantle and placed it on her own shoulders, then covered Dawn's remains with the one she'd been wearing. She felt it settle into place, and at once the wildness surging inside of her subsided. She felt contained, in control, no longer at the mercy of the elumiris that filled her to bursting.

Visions began racing through her mind: a hundred dawns, crossing the sky in chariots pulled by red bulls, by horses, by swans, *as* swans and more colorful birds, as a herd of buffalo. She watched bare earth beneath her spring to life, trees, bushes, grass growing at the touch of her light. She felt beautiful, delirious, playful, filled with lust for sex and food and drink, and the reach of her arms was the universe.

***

E rrol climbed shakily to his feet, getting his breath back, watching his girlfriend, now apparently some sort of thunder-god, whale at a monster a hundred times her size. And she was winning. Her hair was like flame, and her eyes dripped white fire. She had buried her spear in the monster on her third thrust and was now beating at it using the boomerang as a club. She was shouting, ranting in a language he didn't know. She seemed completely berserk. He honestly did not know which he was most frightened of; the dragon-thing or Dusk.

But he had to do something. He ran up and jabbed his spear into the scutts of the reptilian belly, but the stone point didn't penetrate. He tried again, aiming for the seam between two scales; this time he managed to lodge the spear in long enough for the writhing of the beast to yank the weapon from his hands.

Billy, now almost seven feet tall, was doing a little better, at least until one of Dusk's wind-ups accidentally caught him in the side of the head and sent him sprawling.

Errol was stumbled back, fumbling the boomerang from his belt—recalling belatedly he'd already thrown it—when there was a terrific flash of light; as his vision cleared, he saw Dusk had split the snake's head open. It was stretched out on the rock, still twitching.

Dusk hit it again, and again. The look on her face was terrifying.

"Here we go," Veronica said.

The cool air in the cavern suddenly dropped by several degrees, and an awful stench drifted on it, like rotten fish boiling in piss. Errol's ears popped.

For a moment, everything seemed still. Then Dusk leapt forward, flaring like a lightning bolt. In the snapshot of light, Errol saw them, oozing from the walls of the cavern, thousands of squirming creatures, things like spiders but with too many legs, hyaenas with eyes like saucers that stood as tall as horses.

And him, the guy in the wooden body. Dusk reached him and struck at him with her spear. It went through him, but he didn't seem to care. He smacked her in the forehead with his palm, and she flew backwards, landing on her back and skidding a few feet.

"Damn it," Veronica said. She flew past Errol toward the fallen Dusk.

Veronica stopped next to Dusk and drew herself up straight.

And the lake came out of its bed.

***

Veronica became part of the stream, stretching herself out, gathering Dusk and Errol and the rest within her waters. As long as they were in her care, they would not drown, but if something happened to her, they were now all doomed. A vast wave beat back the Raggedy Man and his creatures, but she knew better than to think he or any of his monsters would perish. The best she could do was get her friends out.

She rushed across the lake and into the flooding passage that had brought them here, picking up speed, until finally they blasted from the cave mouth in a jet of water. She released her companions and sent the water back down, dropping the entire lake back onto the Raggedy Man.

Veronica felt a moment's elation. She done it.

"Dusk!" she heard Errol shout. She glanced over and saw him kneeling next to the warrior-woman.

Slowly Veronica stood and went to Errol.

"Is she dead?" she asked.

"No," he said. "She's got a pulse."

"That's good," she said, and sat back down.

"What you just did," Errol said. "Getting us out of there like that. That was incredible."

Veronica shrugged, not sure what she felt. She wanted to rest. She wanted to sleep for a week. But she couldn't.

She took a few breaths, pushed her wet hair out of her face. Then she forced herself back to her feet.

"No rest for the wicked," she said.

"That's it," Second said pointing to the mantle Aster had on. "That's what we came for. Now we should be off to Mom's hole. I hear creepy things coming from the Under."

"Yep," Veronica said. She put her hand on Errol's shoulder and nodded toward Dusk.

"Watch her, when she wakes up," Veronica said. "I'm not sure what we have there."

"Yeah," he said. "That was crazy. Almost as crazy as pulling a lake up a tunnel."

"That's where we are," Veronica said. "Take care, Errol." She leaned down and kissed him on the lips, watched him as he slowly toppled over.

"What the hell?"

It was Delia, standing a few feet away, drenched. "Did you kill him too?"

"No," Veronica said. "Dear Errol is just taking a nap. You know him. It'll be easier this way. A lot easier."

She turned to the Twins. "You boys get them out of here. Now."

***

Aster watched as Veronica turned and started back toward the cave.

"What are you doing? She asked.

"Good luck with that goddess business," Veronica said. "Bring back the sun and all that if you can. But seriously, you guys need to get going, or you won't have a chance. Watch out for Errol, will you?"

"Veronica . . ."

Veronica stepped into the cave mouth.

"Bye," she said. Then she vanished into the cavern.

"Veronica!" Aster started running toward the cave.

Before she'd gone two steps, Second caught her arm.

"No," he said. He nodded up.

The cliffs above had splintered, and water was spraying out like forty firehoses.

"Let's run, as Veronica suggested," he said.

Billy lifted up Dusk in a fireman's carry, draping her over his shoulders, and Second took Errol up, which—despite Errol probably weighing twice as much as the boy—didn't seem to present a problem. As they ran back down the ravine, all three walls of the cul-de-sac collapsed, burying the cave entrance under tons of rock and mud.

"Veronica is giving us a chance," First said, running alongside Delia, glancing back at the rockslide. "We'd best take it. We get to Mom's hole before the Under catches up with us, this is all sorted, and the Under goes back to being a normal place, at least for what it is. If they catch us, though, that's the end of all this. So we won't let 'em catch us, right?"

"Right," Aster said.

"You feel it, our sister's mantle."

"I feel it," Aster said. "I understand now."

TWELVE
THE UNDER

W hen Errol came to his senses, the first thing he saw was the ground, a few feet below him; it took a few seconds for him to realize he was draped over the shoulder of one of the Twins.

"Hey!" he said.

"You can walk now?" The Twin asked.

"I think so," he said, struggling to remember what had happened. He remembered lips, a familiar kiss.

"Veronica," he said, as the boy set him on his feet.

"Yeah," the boy said. "She gave it a good try, but I reckon they're past her now."

"What are you talking about?" he demanded, looking around. He saw Billy carrying Dusk, and there was Ms. Fincher, and the other Twin, but Veronica was nowhere to be seen.

"She went back into the cave, Errol," Ms. Fincher said. "She collapsed the canyon on the opening to give us time to escape."

"Well, screw that," he said. "I'm going back for her."

"She's in the Under now," First said. "Alive or dead I don't know, but she's way past your reach. Or mine. Not to mention there's a whole gang of them on our heels as we speak."

"Let's get to our mom," First said. "Do the thing. If your friend is still alive, I'll help you fetch her. But until after Dawn, there's nothing to be done."

Errol's breath caught in his chest; he couldn't breathe. "No," he said. "There must be something we can do. We can't just leave her."

"She made a choice, to help us out," Second said. "I we fail, what do you think she'd feel about her choice?"

"Goddamn it!" Errol shouted. Rage mixed with grief swelled in him until his throat was raw and he thought his skin would split. But he nodded and put one foot in front of the other, and again, until they were all back in motion.

Not much later, Dusk came around, too, and they were able to pick up the pace, alternating jogging with walking.

***

O nce out of the ravine, they didn't go back the way they had come through the forest, but went parallel to the mountains, traveling across a vast plain. They passed a huge herd of wild cattle or buffalo; Errol didn't know which, and he didn't care. It was hard to focus on anything because his mind kept going in a tight circle. He remembered his first kiss with Veronica, underneath the stars, her visits to him at Laurel Grove, long moments of silence together. And then he would come around to the fact that she was dead, and the whole thing would start again.

He remembered he had felt this way after his father died. How he kept thinking he could just go into the next room and ask him something. How his dad had lingered in his dreams. His mind refused to accept he was gone. He still had those thoughts and those dreams from time to time.

And the thing was, Veronica might not be gone. She might be fighting still, or have found a way out, slipped away through some underground river. She might be hurt, or dying, waiting for him to come for her, like he had come for her after the Sheriff buried her head-down in a rocky shaft. Those images kept coming, too. What did Aster and the Twins need with him? He wasn't required for the horrible ritual they had planned. When he had been the automaton, and later in his magic armor with a sword that knew how to fight, he had been useful. But without them, he wasn't much of a threat to anything. He wasn't a god or a superhero or turning into one like everybody else. If they had more trouble, he would be exactly as useful as he had been back in the cave. Which was not at all.

But by the same measure, he wouldn't survive ten seconds against something that could take down Veronica. She didn't need him to rescue her.

But it still felt wrong, running away from where she was.

***

Veronica continued to fight, but she knew the end was near. The tendrils of the enemy were all around her, trying to force their way in. And the Raggedy Man would not let up.

"Let me show you again," he said.

She saw Aster, shining like the light before the rising sun. She saw Errol die, the life struck out of him, his eyes like pieces of glass.

"You can save him," the Raggedy Man said. "All you need to do is join me."

"And help you destroy the world," she said.

"Help us become what we were," he said.

Suddenly she saw two lightless eyes and a creature without a form; and stars, black stars, strung together in perfectly exquisite constellations. Only they were not stars; they were a collection, The Raggedy Man's collection. Like her collection of bones at the bottom of the creek. But these were not the bones, or the bodies — these were the parts that always got away. The parts that really made people what they were. Souls.

"They're not gone," the Raggedy Man said. "They have been here all along, trying to get out. Denied. Waiting for eternity to join back together, to become the thing they are all fragments of, to be whole. But they—we—need you. And you need us. You can't deny it any longer. You belong here."

She started to protest, as she had a hundred times already. But everything was so beautiful, the vision so perfect—it sent shivers through her as nothing had in an awfully long time. Not since she had last taken a life, passed its essence through her . . .

Yes, she remembered. Through her. The act of murder had nourished her, strengthened her, but she had not really eaten the souls of the dead. It was more like she had been a doorway, a hole in the ground that led . . . here. She was and always had been a part of the Itch. Everything else, everything she wanted to believe about herself, was just moonbeams.

The Raggedy Man was right. Everything that had happened to her, everything she had done had been meant to bring her here, to this place and this moment. It was time to stop pretending.

"Errol does not die," she said. "Not here. Not now, not at your hand or mine or any other creature of yours. It is my only condition. But it's an absolute one."

"I accept," The Raggedy Man said. "Errol lives. But Aster is about to become the Dawn. If she does, it is out of my hands."

"Don't worry," Veronica said. "She's not going to do that."

***

Errol was aware that Dusk had been avoiding him. He had tried to strike up a conversation several times when the group slowed to a walk, but she hadn't responded. So when they stopped at a spring to drink and eat what little rations they had left, he was relieved when she came over and sat next to him.

"We're close," First announced. "Take a little rest. From here on we have to run hard."

The water tasted better than anything he'd ever drunk, and the dried meat might as well have been filet mignon.

"I'm sorry," Dusk murmured, so low only he could hear it.

"For what?" he asked.

"My rage. If I had not slain the serpent, everything would not be in such jeopardy. And Veronica . . ." she sighed. "It was as if I was someone else. I saw the beast and could think of nothing but to slay it."

"I saw," Errol said. "It was pretty fantastic. I thought I'd seen you fight before, but that was a whole other thing."

"It's this place," she said. "The elumiris . . ."

"It's pushing you," First—who had apparently been eavesdropping—said, "You're a Thunder. You just didn't know it."

"I ruined all," Dusk said.

"Well, you've made it harder," First said. "But it's our fault. We should have known Moon would put something down there to guard her bones. We should have prepared you better. But it's all done, you see? You can walk backwards, but it won't get you back to your starting place, not really."

Dusk nodded. First walked off to talk to his brother.

"I know you still loved her," Dusk said.

"I guess," Errol said. "I mean, in a way."

"I should be glad she's gone," Dusk said. "I find that I'm not. It's not clear to me why."

"It doesn't change how I feel about you," Errol said, knowing he had screwed up the instant he said it.

"How *do* you feel about me, Errol?" Dusk asked, softly.

He was silent for a moment. "I think you're incredible," he said. "I've never known anyone like you. Sometimes I'm afraid of you."

"As you should be," she said.

"You're not making this easy."

She drew up straight and placed her hands in her lap.

"If you do not love me, Errol, it would wisest to say so now. I won't like it, but I will get over it. But if we continue as we . . . as we have recently, if you let my affections for you deepen based on a falsehood — that would be difficult to bear."

"Dusk, just because I'm afraid of you doesn't mean I don't love you."

She frowned. "Can you say that more plainly?"

"I love you," he said.

"And her too?"

He paused, then nodded. "Yes."

She smiled slightly. Then she leaned in and kissed him. Gently. No lightning this time.

"No time for that, you two," Second said. "We've got to go."

***

Aster could sense their destination now, the emptiness, the cold Sun in her hideaway of stone. The cloak of swan's feathers felt alive, as if it were growing from her skin, and memories that were not hers continued to pass through her mind. She saw the light of creation, caught in a nutshell, in the belly of a monster, in a cedar box, in the eye of an aurochs, in an amber palace below the sea. She felt light, and she felt beautiful. She felt like dancing, like drinking wine. She wanted to make love, to feel every pleasure her body could afford her. With each footstep they traveled, her inhibitions, so much a part of who she was, were shedding off like an old skin.

This isn't me, she thought. But she did not care. The quest to cure her father and end the curse laid on the world had consumed so much of her life, and she had rarely tried to look beyond it, because when she did she didn't see anything there. Nothing, perhaps, except the luxury to rest, to stop thinking, to do nothing for a time. But now she saw the future opening like a flower, like a field of flowers, a continent of them.

She felt a smile on her face, and knew it probably looked foolish. She didn't care about that either.

The grass gave way to lichen-covered stone, sloping up toward a rocky line of hills.

"It's just there," Second said.

He was in the rear, and Aster looked back at him. And saw it coming.

The stars in the sky behind them were going out—not one-by-one, but in a wave, as if a cloud were covering them. A darker shadow moved across the land, as well, and swiftly.

Errol saw it too. "What's that?" he asked.

First stared. Then he turned and looked ahead of them.

"Well, that's that," he said.

Aster turned and saw the shadow coming from there, too.

"The Under," Second said. "They didn't send out a hunting party. They're bringing the whole place to us."

"What can we do?" Aster said.

"Nothing," Veronica said. She was just *there*, all of a sudden.

"Veronica," Errol said.

The girl smiled thinly. Her eyes looked weird, like black fire. She reached out and touched Billy.

"Take them, Billy, Veronica said. "You know where."

"Veronica," Aster said. "what are you—"

But then Billy started growing. Fast. He reached out with his hand and gently scooped Aster and Errol up, and kept rising toward the sky.

"No!" Aster shrieked. "Billy, stop!" Everything she had been feeling was stripped away as Billy began walking. She felt the light and life leaking out of her, the potential of Dawn dwindling away.

"What the Hell?" Errol shouted. "Billy, what are you doing?"

Billy was now as tall as Aster had ever seen him, which was very. His features had simplified, bereft of expression, and his eyes looked only outward, toward his destination. He strode over the hills, through a gap in the approaching darkness, gaining speed as he went. Horrified, Aster pronounced a greater Utterance to recall him, but he didn't even glance down at her. Veronica had done something, laid a compunction on him, and he wouldn't stop until he had fulfilled it.

When had Veronica learned to do that?

She beat at his palm. "Billy, please stop."

He would forget her again. He would go away to those distant places he longed for. Maybe he would remember her eventually. But if he did it would probably not be for decades or centuries, and she would be long dead of old age.

But of course, she would not die of old age. The whole universe was about to come apart. So it didn't matter anyway.

"We have to do something," Errol said. "Turn us back into birds, or . . . get us to the place where the Sun is. We might still be able to pull this off."

"No," Aster said. "It's over, Errol. We lost. There's nothing more we can do."

***

It all happened so quickly, Delia wasn't able to sort sense into it until later. Billy, becoming a giant, whisking Errol and Aster off and leaving the rest of them behind. The arrival of the darkness, with all of its teeth and scales and claws. Veronica, grinning like a demon, more terrifying than any monster there. First whirling about with his spear and shouting at Second to take her. The younger Twin embracing Delia, pulling her close, wrapping her into his cloak.

The sky pulled them up. She watched First, surrounded, keeping the Under back, growing smaller and smaller until she couldn't see him anymore.

She knew their destination before she saw it; the slight thin sickle of the moon. At first it was just a sliver of light, but as they drew nearer, she made out his features. Part of an eye and a mouth, a spine. Most of him was missing, and what was left was only bone, twisted into a crescent.

Up close, she saw the vast sliver was hollowed out, like a canoe, and water stood inside, a long, narrow lake. Second settled her down near one pointed end, not far from the water. Her mind was hardly functioning. And as she touched the stone, she felt shocking pain, fathomless remorse, and beneath all of that, rage. It shook her to her bones, and she cried out.

Second sat cross-legged in front of her and sighed. He took her hand. The pain, the soundless scream began to fade. Behind him she saw Fire Thief carrying Dusk as Second had carried her. He also settled down next to them.

"Sorry," Fire Thief said. "I thought I could keep the Under from coming to the Sun. My powers are weakening."

"No shame to you, Uncle," Second said. "It was a hard thing. So much harder than we thought. Why is that?"

"Because she has joined them at last," Fire Thief said. "With her, the Under is unstoppable."

"Veronica?" Delia said.

"She had a choice," Dusk said. "To become a creature of life or one of death. I hoped she would choose life." She sighed. "I should have killed her when it was possible."

The great wave of pain had subsided, but Delia could still feel it, down in her marrow.

"I don't understand," she said, through her tears. "What are we doing now? Why are we here?"

"The Under can't come here yet," Fire Thief said. "Not until Moon is completely dead."

Delia gestured at the weird landscape.

"Is this alive?" she asked.

"Look," Fire Thief said.

At first she didn't know what he meant; then she saw a mist had begun to rise around them; and then water—apparently coming from beneath them, drawn up from the world below—began spilling over the rim of the Moon and into the long, narrow hollow. She slid back on the stone as the water rose, but even as she did, the stone shifted beneath her, and the moon—grew. A little. The pool of water was bigger, deeper, and wider.

"Before, he would fill all the way up," Fire Thief said. "The tides, you know. He would get round and fat and full. But now. . . ." He shrugged.

"You're helping Moon out," Second said. "He's still dying, but it will take longer now. Give us some more time."

"More time for what?" Dusk demanded, sparks flashing in her eyes. "To find Aster? To lure your mother from her cave?"

Second shook his head. "Mom's in the Under now. That plan is finished."

Dusk shook her head. More electricity danced in her eyes, and a few arcs jumped along the surface of her bare arms.

"Why did you bring me, then?" Dusk said. "I could have helped First. We might at least have killed Veronica. I could have died with honor."

"Wouldn't have mattered," Fire Thief said. "And you'll be needed here. The Under cannot come here yet. But they will try, and as his life fades it will become easier. They'll come for Delia. And we will fight them as long as we possibly can. Then you can have your honorable death."

Dusk stared at him silently, her face twisted in anguish. Then she nodded and began climbing the horn of the moon, perching about fifty feet above.

"So what is the plan?" Delia asked.

"Well," Second said. He nodded at the water. "There's fish in there. I'll catch us a couple. Anyone comes up here after us, we'll kill it. And we'll see what happens."

"That doesn't sound like much of a plan," Delia said.

Second shrugged. "It's what we've got for the moment. Plans are maybe overrated, as we just found out, I reckon. The simple ones are best."

With that, he took his spear and started walking along the water's edge. Fire Thief rose into the air and settled on the Moon's opposite point.

Delia closed her eyes, took a deep breath, and let it out. She felt a stirring inside her. Nothing big; maybe her baby's first kick.

Are you still there? she wondered.

She felt another little movement, and then, without words, she knew something. She knew that she was where she was supposed to be. That the stars were still there. And she was still alive, and well, and for the moment, in a place of peace.

She thought about what Pearl and the others had said about the Moon, all of the terrible things he had done. Rape. Incest. Murder. How could this—place—be a place of peace? But it was. All the anguish she had felt when they arrived was gone now.

She opened her eyes and saw the stars, like gems in the sky.

And Second, bringing a fish.

PART THREE

THE WOMAN
IN WHITE

ONE
DEFEATED

A ster was sleeping when Billy settled them on the ground, and he did so so gently she almost didn't wake. But she did, and she remembered, and she leapt up, trying to grab one of his fingers.

"Billy!" she shouted, as loudly as she could. "Please stay!"

He paused for an instant, staring down at her with his expressionless face. Then he looked off in the distance. He took a long step, and then another. She watched as he disappeared a little at a time, from the bottom up, like a ship sailing over the horizon.

"I'm sorry," Errol said.

She nodded. "So am I."

"Where are we?" Errol asked.

In answer, Aster pointed. The top of Billy's head was the only part of him that remained visible. The sky was now aglow with rosy light, and as he finally passed from sight a sliver of a rising sun appeared.

"Did they—did they somehow do it without you?" Errol asked. "Did we win after all?"

"No," she said. "Look behind you."

He turned to see what she meant. There was a road behind them, an asphalt road. Across it was barbed wire fence and pasture.

"We're back in Sowashee," she said.

***

After those first few words, Errol couldn't get much out of Aster, but she followed him when he started walking. His first thought was to go after Billy, figuring that the giant would lead them back into the Pale. He was able to for a while, moving from one huge footprint to the next. But then the ground got boggy, and then actually swampy. They pushed through that, but when they came out, they ran straight into another road. This one had a sign designating it as highway 393. He knew where that was. They weren't in the Pale; they were still squarely in the Reign of the Departed.

But pretty far north of Sowashee. Closer to where his grandmother had lived. He thought about that for a few minutes, looking down the north and south.

"Do you have any ideas about where we ought to go?" he asked Aster.

She just shook her head no.

So he started off north, away from Sowashee.

Just like the last time they'd been here, they were dressed to be noticed. But in what was probably more than an hour of walking, they didn't encounter anyone either on foot or in a car. Finally they did have to duck into the woods to avoid being seen by the driver of a car pulling out of a long, country driveway. He watched as a woman in jeans unhitched a cattle gate, drove her car through, got back out and closed the gate, then returned to her car and drove off.

The driveway wound up through a pasture to a little house on a hill. When they continued on, Errol noticed a clothesline just barely showing from behind the house, heavy with garments.

Dogs barked inside the house as they approached, but when Errol knocked on the door, he got no answer. When he was pretty certain no one was home, they went around back and took stock of the clothes hanging to dry. He found a pair of jeans and t-shirt that fit him. Nothing on the line was a great fit for Aster, but even pants way too big for her would draw less attention than the near-naked condition she was in.

They undressed and dressed behind the house, where no one would see them from the road. Errol took a sheet from the line and wrapped up their stone-age clothes. He carried it over his shoulder like a sack, and they hurried on, lest someone return before they were safely away.

Midday, they reached their destination—an old house built of weather-greyed planks and a streaked tin roof.

"Where is this?" Aster asked.

"My grandmother's house," he said.

"Is she still here?"

"No," he said. "She died a few years ago. Nobody else wanted to live here. It's barely got water and electricity. Anyway, all the neighbors moved into town years before she died. There's nobody around for miles. Sowashee is twenty-five miles away or more. We should be safe here."

"Safe?"

"From being recognized," he said. "From the police."

"Errol, we aren't safe," Aster said. "The world is about to end."

"Are you sure about that?" he said. "There's still a sun here, and it's still moving. Maybe *here* is so cut off from *there* that we'll never know it when the Kingdoms and all of that go kablooie."

"We'll know," she said. "And we'll die, too."

"Fine," Errol said. "Then we can't just wait for the end of the world. We've got to figure something out. Meantime, we need a place to stay that isn't jail. Okay?"

She nodded, but he thought it wasn't so much that she was in agreement with him as she wanted the conversation to be over.

The house didn't have any locks other than the inside latches of the screen doors, so getting in wasn't a problem. But as soon as they were inside, he wondered if he hadn't made a mistake.

He hadn't been here since Grandma died. He had never seen the place empty. The big feather bed was gone, the rocking chairs, the dining room table. Even the old stove had been taken out. The house had always seemed so warm, as if it itself was alive. But now . . . it made him feel sad, and empty.

But it was dry and safe. They still had a little food in their leather packs. The house got water from a deep well, and while the electrical pump that served the kitchen tap was probably turned off, he remembered that there was a little hand pump outside.

Days passed. He tried to draw Aster into conversation, but she wouldn't even look at him. He went on walks in the woods and pastures he had grown up with. He made a bamboo fishing pole, dug some worms, and caught a few sunfish in the pond, which was starting to turn into a marsh. He managed to talk Aster into starting a fire so he could cook them, but she still didn't say anything.

Finally, on the fourth day, as he was sitting on the porch watching the sunset, she came out and sat next to him.

"Sorry," she said.

"It's okay," he said. "I get it." He looked off across the yard. It was warmer than when they'd been here last time, and green buds were appearing on the apple trees by the fence, so he figured it must be spring. Things were coming back to life.

"They're dead, aren't they?" he said.

"Dusk and Ms. Fincher?" Aster said. "Probably. But the Twins were there. And Dusk has all of that thunder stuff. Maybe they got to someplace safe."

"Those things were coming from everywhere," he said.

"I'm sorry," Aster said. "I know you and Dusk were . . . close."

"Yeah," he said. "I guess I don't believe it. It's hard to imagine Dusk dying. I thought Veronica was dead, after the cave. She wasn't. Not only wasn't she but—why did Veronica do that? Make Billy bring us here? I don't understand what happened."

"She's with the enemy now," Aster said. "She went over. She was always on the razor's edge, right from the beginning, because of what she was."

"But every other time she chose not to go there, become that," he protested. "What was different this time? And if she is part of *that* now, why didn't she just kill us?"

"Maybe it was her last human act," Aster said. "To save our lives. She didn't have to kill us to stop us from waking up the Sun. She just had to put us so far away we would never make it back in time. She could have had Billy take everybody else with him, but she didn't. Just us."

"Because we're her friends," he said.

She nodded, and they sat there silently for a moment, listening to the familiar songs of the frogs and a not-too-distant whippoorwill.

"So," he finally said. "How do we get back?"

"We don't," Aster said. "Get it through your head, Errol. We failed. There isn't a do-over."

"This world is still here," he said. "You said it yourself, it shouldn't be. So it must not be over. There must still be a way. There has to be."

"I love your optimism," she said. Her tone said otherwise.

"So you're really giving up?"

"Exactly."

He wanted to be mad at her, but he had really never seen her like this. She had always been the one that drove them on, that always believed she could find a way, no matter what.

"You know I can't do that," he said. "Dusk and Mrs. Fincher might still be alive. If for no other reason than that, I have to get back. Or at least try. So help me out. Give me some ideas. One step at a time. How do I get back?"

She sat in silence, eyes focused on nothing. Finally she sighed.

"I don't know," she said. "As the High and Faraway is torn apart, the Pale will be affected. I'm not sure how. The ways in and out might get harder or easier to find. Eventually the destruction will reach here, but I'm not sure how that will play out. This place—this world—is deluded, Errol. It thinks it is the whole universe; it is in denial everything else exists. I suspect that when the Reign of the Departed ends, it will be very quickly, like a person having a stroke or a heart attack. Everything will seem fine until it isn't."

"So if I go back to Sowashee and try some of the places we went in before, maybe I'll be able to see a way through?"

"You're missing my larger point," she said.

"I'm not," he said. "I'm ignoring it."

"Then sure," she said. "You have crossed often enough. You might be able to see your way in."

"I'd have a better chance if you were with me," he said.

She shrugged.

"Do I have to go all the way back to Sowashee?" he asked. "Surely there's a way through to the Pale around here someplace."

"Of course. But you aren't familiar with any of them, and neither am I. I think you have to go to Sowashee."

"And what will you do, if I leave you here?" He asked.

"I don't know," she said. "Don't worry about me."

His empathy had been keeping his anger in check. No longer.

"Fine," he snapped. "I'm leaving in the morning."

He left her on the porch. It was dark inside the house, and he was tired, so he laid out the cloak the Pearl and her people had given him and tried to go to sleep, with no luck. All he could think about was Veronica and her strange eyes, Dusk facing a wall of monsters, and a thousand imagined versions of her death. Helplessness felt like fluid in his lungs.

After a while, he heard the screen door open and close, then the wooden door shut. He heard Aster take a few steps toward him. He lay on his side and pretended to be asleep.

She laid down next to him, and he realized she was crying.

"Aster . . ."

She reached around from behind him and pulled herself tight against his back. He was frozen at first, wondering what it meant, feeling the quake of her body against his as she continued crying.

"I've lost everyone, Errol," she finally gasped. "I don't want to lose you too."

His throat tightened.

"I know," he said. "I feel the same way. It's why I got mad." He was crying now, too. "Remember your first day at school?"

"Yes," she whispered. "You gave me an apple from your lunch."

"You didn't have anything to eat," he pointed out.

"My dad said I could eat the school lunch. The money he gave me was just some leaves with an enchantment on it. Once

I left the house, it turned back into leaves. Dad was still figuring this place out, and I guess he screwed up. But you gave me your lunch."

"I liked your accent," he said. "I liked that you were different." He chuckled. "You called the apple an 'ahabowl'."

"A'bol," she murmured. "I didn't know the English word yet. Anyway, they're almost the same in both languages." She paused. "I liked you, too," she said. "Everyone else just thought I was a weirdo, and they never changed their minds. They were used to everyone being the same."

"I thought you were a weirdo, too," Errol said. "But I like weird."

"Because you're a weirdo, too," she said.

"Yeah," he replied. "I guess I am."

"I'll go with you tomorrow," she said. "I still don't think there's anything we can do. But I will go with you."

"Thanks," he said.

They fell asleep like that, and for the first night since their return, Errol didn't have any nightmares.

TWO
DEBTS

T he next morning they packed everything up and walked up the long dirt road until they reached the highway. After about a mile they reached a convenience store. They were out of food and had nothing to drink. Errol reluctantly agreed to let Aster pay with enchanted leaves.

"I'm better at working here than dad was," she said. "It'll still look like money a few days from now."

He remembered the store. It had new gas pumps and bright new sign, but inside it retained some of the character of the country store it had been when he was little. Big jars of pickled pig's feet, sausages, and eggs sat on the polished wooden counter. On the wall behind it were shelves of cigarettes, rifle and shotgun ammunition, hair cream, and various cures for head and stomach aches. Half of the place was a hardware store, and there was a butcher counter in the back. Long open coolers full of soft drinks and ice cream treats invited him to stick his head down in them and have a breath of refrigerated air.

Errol grabbed some tins of sausage, chips, and drinks, trying not to draw attention.

"Is that the Greyson boy?"

It took a second to register. Errol hadn't heard his last name in so long it sounded almost alien. He looked over at the old man behind the counter.

"Mr. McKee," he said. "Yes, sir. Errol Greyson."

"I thought so," Mr. McKee said. "You're a foot taller, but I remember you. Used to come in here with your grandmother."

"Yes sir," he said. "I remember that."

Mr. McKee looked out the window, surveying the empty parking lot.

"How did you kids get here?" he asked. "Did you walk?"

"Yes sir," he said.

"Are you living out this way now?"

"No sir," Errol said. "Still in Sowashee. We're headed back there."

"That's a long walk, son," McKee said, scratching his chin.

"Yes sir," he agreed. He glanced at Aster who was now following the conversation. Looking like she might do something. He decided he had better head that off.

"Mr. McKee," he said, "Uh, the fact is, we're sort of in a bind. Some friends dropped us off up in Highlasha and left us there."

"Not very good friends," the old man observed.

"And I don't have any money on me," Errol went on. "I was wondering if I could do some chores or something to pay for this stuff."

"Well . . ." the old man said. "Hang on."

He pulled up a little metal box full of index cards and started digging through them. After a minute he pulled one out.

"Your mom still has a tab with us. She hasn't used it in a while, but I can put this stuff on that, if you want."

"Yes, sir," he said. "That would be great."

***

"It would have been fine," Aster said. "The fake money would have stayed fake long enough for him to put it in the bank."

"He's a nice old man," Errol said. "He always used to give me an extra piece of candy when I bought some there. Grandma liked him."

She shrugged. "Knowing your mom, she'll probably never pay it anyway. He's still out the money."

"Yeah," he said. "That's true."

A car blew by them, doing ninety miles an hour if it was doing ten. He took a sip of his Coke.

"How much further is it to town?" Aster asked.

"I don't know," he replied. "Twenty miles?"

"So we'll be there before sundown," she said.

"I think so," he said, kicking an empty bottle. "I've never walked it."

Another car was approaching, this one coming from town. But instead of passing them, it screeched to halt. Errol smelled burning rubber as the door flung open, and woman stepped out.

"You!" She said. "Get in this car. Now!"

Errol blinked. He had seen some unbelievable things in the past few years, but this *had* to be a hallucination,

"Mom?" he said.

"Oh, zhedye," Aster murmured.

***

"Are you going to tell me where you've been?" Errol's mother demanded, after he settled into the cracked upholstery of the front seat and Aster slid into the back.

It took him a few seconds to process the question, to fight through years of outrage and anger. He had imagined this confrontation many times, and as it played out in his head, he always had a biting, clever answer that left her devastated.

"What?" was what actually came out.

"This last year? No, more than a year. Since you broke out of Laurel Grove."

He was familiar with his mother's angry voice. He'd heard it plenty of times, over the years. This wasn't exactly it. She sounded less angry and closer to hysterical. He looked at her straight on, for the first time since she pulled up.

His mother had had him when she was young. She wasn't quite forty yet, but she looked older than that to him; thin and sort of dried out. Maybe it was because she didn't have a lot of makeup on; she usually had way too much.

He had been angry with her for a long time. For the way she acted when his father was sick, and after he died. Later, when he had been in a freaking *coma*, but by all reports, she almost never came to see him. And when he beat the odds and woke up, she immediately stuck him in Laurel Grove, for "rehabilitation."

So he didn't owe her anything, least of all an explanation.

"I've been away," he said.

"No shit," she snapped. "You're wanted by the police, you know. For what you did at Laurel Grove. And now you turn up out here. Mr. McKee called me, in case you haven't figured that out. He was worried about you. Said something didn't seem right. Have you been at Granny's house this whole time?"

"You know what, Mom?" he snapped. "What do you care? Where is this motherly concern coming from all of a sudden?"

It felt good. It wasn't as strong or damning as some of things he thought of over the years, but it would do. He was ready to do this, now. He knew there was nothing she could say in her defense, nothing he couldn't come back at twice as hard. He had been both dreading this moment and anticipating it, but now the dread was gone.

But she didn't come back at him. She didn't answer at all. Instead, a tear worked itself from the corner of her eye and started down her face.

"No," he said. "Don't. Don't even."

She nodded, but the tears kept coming.

"Are you guys hungry? she finally asked. "Mr. McKee said you got some snacks, but . . ."

"I'm hungry," Aster said.

**

They went through a drive-through on the outskirts of Sowashee and got some burgers. He had only taken a few bites when they pulled up in front of an unfamiliar house.

"Where is this?" Errol asked.

"It's where I live," she said.

"Oh," he said. "You and what's-his-name?"

"No," she said, killing the engine and pulling up the parking brake. "What's-his-name is no longer in the picture. It's just me. Come on inside. Finish your food."

"Are you going to call the police?" he asked.

"No, Errol," his mother said. "I'm not going to call the police."

He wasn't sure he could believe that. Anyway, he and Aster were in Sowashee now. They had things to do, things he didn't want to explain to his mom even if he thought she would believe him. Which she would not.

The house was small, just two bedrooms, a kitchen, a living room, and a bathroom with a cabinet shower. It was surprisingly neat, albeit lightly furnished.

She waved them to a small kitchen table—an old one, with a Formica top. They finished eating their burgers and fries in silence, and then Aster excused herself to the bathroom.

His mother sighed. "You're right," she said. "I had no business asking where you've been. I get that."

"Okay," he said.

She nodded and looked at the floor. "Will you stay here? At least for the night. There's a spare bed." She nodded toward the bathroom. "Are you and she . . .?"

"No," he said. "I can sleep on the couch."

He realized as he said it that he'd agreed to stay there.

Stupid, he thought. But he didn't have to make it stick. He did not owe her honesty, not at this point.

"It pulls out," she said. "It's Aster, isn't it? From your school."

"Yes."

"I saw her once, in the hospital. Visiting you."

He nodded.

"She's been missing too."

"Yes."

"And her father is missing, and two teachers—"

"You said I didn't have to talk about this," he said.

"Right," she replied. She patted the table with both hands. "Okay. I'm going to go lie down. Maybe you should get a shower and offer Aster one too. You both reek." She attempted a smile, and he realized she was trying to lighten the mood. It wasn't going to work.

"I'm sure we do," he said.

"I think I can find her some clothes that fit better. If you look in the chest-of-drawers in the other room, you'll find a few of your old things."

"Okay," he said.

She stood up and turned, but then looked back at him.

"Can we talk later though, Errol?"

It was afternoon already. "Later" usually meant wine and slurred words. He wasn't sure he was up for that. Maybe he and Aster could get a shower and a nap, then sneak off and do what they had come for.

"Sure," he lied.

***

Aster didn't remember when she'd last had a shower. The water pressure was weak, and the hot water not very hot, but it felt so good she didn't want to get out. She just wanted to stand in it, let the shower head massage her scalp and shoulders, until all of the water on earth was gone. Which might not be that long. At the moment, she found hard to work up any worry about that.

Everyone she cared about was either dead or gone, except Errol. He was the only reason she even bothered to put one foot in front of the other. Not just because she was fresh out of hope, but because she actually didn't care anymore if the world was ending. It was a terrible, *zhedyekas* world, and it deserved to end.

But . . . Errol. She had dragged him into this. He had always supported her, even though she hadn't always been very good to him. She had abandoned him once, and she wouldn't do it again. At least they could die together.

She finally turned off the shower, dried off, and got dressed in the clothes Errol's mom had given her—jeans and a t-shirt that fit her a little better than those they had stolen from the clothesline.

She found Errol still in the kitchen.

"Your turn," she said.

He nodded and went into the bathroom.

She got a glass of ice water and went outside, wandering around a little, trying not to think. A private plane buzzed overhead, a few crickets stridulated, a flock of swallows turned and reversed, as if they had all hit an invisible barrier and bounced off it. The sun was on the horizon, bright orange. She smiled a little, realizing how much she had missed it. But even that bit of joy didn't get very far. Why did the Reign still pretend everything was okay?

But then she looked closer, squinting; it was still too bright to be certain, but to her eyes, something was off.

She turned away, blinking at the spots in her eyes from looking directly at the solar light. She knew it was a no-no.

She whispered a Whimsy of Dimming and looked again.

The sky now appeared much darker, dark enough that she could see the planet Mercury and a few stars. The light of the sun too was much lower, as if she were wearing extra dark sunglasses.

The sun was . . . speckled. Sunspots? But some of them were *big*. She was fairly sure sunspots didn't get that big, or at least weren't supposed to.

So things *were* catching up here. She hadn't been wrong. Either the sun was going to go out and leave the earth a lifeless ball, or it was going to explode, or something equally bad. Probably explode. Here, the giant from which the world had been made were the elder stars that had gone nova, creating most of the elements from which planets formed. If the sun exploded and blew the solar system apart, *something* would emerge from the ruin.

In a way, it was a relief. Everyone in the High and Faraway would pay the price for her failure. But so would she. Veronica hadn't spared Errol and her anything.

She went back in to tell Errol, but he was asleep on the couch. Why wake him? They could both use some rest. She went into the guest room, closed her eyes, and was asleep in minutes.

THREE
BLIND SQUIRREL

W hen Errol woke up, it was morning. Birds were singing outside the window, and according to the digital clock, he'd slept eleven hours. So much for sneaking off during the night. But it was only six-thirty, and he knew there was no way his mother would be up yet. All he had to do was find Aster and get out of there.

Except his mother was in the kitchen, drinking coffee.

"Good morning," she said. "Do you drink coffee?"

"No," he said.

"Well, I've also got milk and orange juice," she said.

"Orange juice sounds good."

He sat down as she poured.

"Errol," she said. "I don't know where to start with you. Maybe after you father died."

"Mom, you don't have to do all this."

What he meant was, he didn't want to hear it, and he was now wondering why he hadn't said that.

"No," she said. "I do. Its part of the program. But even if it wasn't . . ."

"Program?"

She sighed. "I don't think it's a secret I had some trouble with alcohol," she said. "And some other things. It started when your dad was sick. After he died, I guess I kind of got out of control."

"You're not drinking anymore?" he said.

"It's been almost a year," she said.

"Congratulations," he said. "Is that it? Can I go now?"

"Errol, I know I wasn't there for you. I felt—Errol, I was thirty-five when Luther died. I felt like my life was over. I had a kid I had no idea how to deal with. I had expenses I didn't know how to pay. I was so reliant on your father. He and I, it wasn't ever easy, our relationship, me white, him black. You had to know that. But back then, it made us stronger. We depended on each other, stood back-to-back against the world. Together, we could handle it. Without him—without that back to lean against—I didn't know who I was, or what I wanted, or anything. I think I just wanted out. I told myself you were old enough to handle yourself. When you tried to commit suicide, it should have made me wake up, but instead I just ran harder from the whole thing. And when they said you would never come out of the coma, I was almost relieved. And I hated myself for that too. But then there was a miracle, and you *did* come out, and Errol—that's when I finally got it. I felt like God was giving me one last chance. I felt like I had to do something."

"You stuck me in Laurel Grove!" He said.

She reached for his hand, but he withdrew his. She patted the table, then withdrew her arm.

"Errol, I was in no shape to take care of you," she said. "The day you went into Laurel Grove, I checked into a rehab in Ithaca. It was the closest one that would take me without insurance. I thought we would get out about the same time, and we could try and make a clean start. But then I found out you broke out of there."

"But you stayed straight," he said.

"Mostly," she said. "First because I thought you would turn back up. I mean I backslid, some. But there was one morning I woke up and knew I'd had enough. And so I've been trying. I've got an okay job. I'm taking classes at the community college."

"That's . . . great," he said.

"And now you're back," she said. "And I don't know what's going to happen. I know you hate me. I don't blame you."

"I never hated you," he said. "I just . . .why didn't you tell me? About rehab?"

"Because I was afraid I would fail," she said. "I didn't want to disappoint you anymore."

"It's okay mom," he said. "I get it. I think . . . I . . ."

He was crying now, and he hated it. This couldn't be happening. He could *not* be letting her off the hook. There was no telling if any of this was even real. It could all be a lie. But she didn't seem hungover, and there were no empty bottles lying around . . .

No, he believed her, he realized. He just wasn't sure he believed this was forever. She could be back to her old self next week. Not that it would matter.

But that hadn't been her old self, had it? There had been another version of her, before his father died. One that loved him, watched over him, was always there. When he'd been born, she hadn't been much older than he was now.

"It felt like you didn't miss him," he said. "Like you didn't care he was gone."

She nodded. "I see that now," she said. "He left such a hole in me, Errol, I don't think I'll ever really fill it. It wasn't how things were supposed to happen. We were supposed to get old together, see your kids—our grandkids—grow up. Get wrinkled and creaky and . . . and all of that. I wanted it all. So I didn't end up with any of it. Not even you."

He reached over and took her hand. "It's ... just ... it's okay, Mom. I get it. I understand."

She closed her eyes and nodded. "When we lost your brother, I thought that was the worst thing I could feel. But— "

"Brother?" Errol said, startled. "What brother?"

"Oh," she said. "We never told you. We were waiting for the right time, but we kept putting it off, and then we started wondering if you ever needed to know."

"I had an older brother?"

"By a few minutes," she said. "He was your twin. He died right after he was born."

"A twin," he said, numbly. He looked up and saw Aster was standing outside of the kitchen, dressed.

"Mom," he said. "Aster and I have to do something."

She looked between them. "You two are in trouble, aren't you?"

"Whatever you're thinking," Errol said. "That's not it. Look. We have to go now. If I can, I'll come back, and we can talk some more."

"If you can?" her voice rose, and her eyes widened.

"Aster?" he said.

"Sure," she said. "*Svapdi.*"

Errol caught his mother as she fell asleep, easing her down and moving her coffee cup so she wouldn't face-plant into it.

"Did you hear all of that?" he asked.

"Yes," she said. "I've been sitting in the other room, waiting for you to get up. It's a small house."

"Great. So I won't have to explain. We've got to go."

***

A long with the clothes, Errol's mom had found an old pair of sneakers that were only a size off. They were not as comfortable as the moccasins Aster had been wearing, but they would attract less attention. Errol was wearing a blue-and-grey plaid shirt and jeans, an outfit she remembered seeing him wear to school, what was now years ago.

Errol was quieter than usual as they made their way along the back roads. She knew why, but after a while, she felt she needed to fill him in. She waited until the sun was high enough to present a full sphere above the tree line. Then she stopped him and did the Whimsy again, this time on both of them.

"Sunspots," he said.

"There were fewer last night," she said. "And they were smaller."

"So you don't think they're natural."

"No," she said. "And I bet if we had a radio or a television or something it would be in the news. I'm sure people are starting to freak out about this, at least a little."

"So you were right. This place is going down, too."

"It has too," she said. "It's all tied together."

"We'd better hurry, then." He started walking again.

She watched him go for a moment. He still thought there was something they could do, didn't he? In fact, he seemed possessed of even more confidence than he had the day before. As absurd as that was. Even if they got back into the Pale, crossed it into the Kingdoms—and if anything remained of the kingdoms that they could travel on—they would still have to make their way all the way back to where they had been, with nothing to guide them. Then they would have to go into what the Twins called the Under and find where the Sun was, and if there was anything left of her to revive, perform the sacrifice that made her Dawn. Except whom would they sacrifice? Even if the Twins had survived, which seemed unlikely, they would somehow have to meet up with them, too.

But then she understood what was lightning a fire under Errol.

It was rare that she actually felt stupid. But she did now. She'd heard Errol's conversation with his mother. She knew everything he did.

"Errol?" she said, as she ran to catch up with him.

"Yeah?" he said.

"You know I won't kill you. I can't."

"You figured that out too, huh?"

"Your mother said you were a twin," she said. "You think you can substitute yourself for Second."

"Yeah."

"Errol, it's just a coincidence."

He stopped and squared his shoulders to her.

"You once told me that there weren't many real coincidences in the High and Faraway, what with all the curses and spells and things coming down from above. So I really doubt this is a coincidence. It's what we have to work with."

"Right," she said. "I understand you. But I won't do it."

He stepped closer. "There was a time you would do anything to get the job done, finish your quest, fix things."

"That was before," she said.

"Before what?"

"Before Dad died, and Shandor, and Delia. Before Billy left. Before we *failed*, Errol. You're right, I put my goals ahead of everything and everyone. I did really terrible things. And for what? For nothing at all. I'm not that girl anymore, Errol."

"Well, I need that girl again," Errol said. "Everyone does. You can't possibly imagine my life is worth more than the whole universe. Especially since I'll die along with everyone else anyway. I feel like we've been handed one more chance to take a shot at this. We have to do it."

"I cannot seriously believe you think I could ever kill you," she said.

"I absolutely believe it," he said. "Because it has to be done. You'll see when we get there. You'll figure it out."

She started to retort, but then she thought better of it. Why argue? They were never going to get there, wherever *there* was; she would never have to make the choice of whether to sacrifice him or not. It was all moot.

Errol needed to feel like he was doing something, so she would play along with it.

They reached Attahacha Falls about midday. The last time they'd been here, the place had been abandoned. This time there were half a dozen teenagers present. Two were splashing around in the water, but the rest were on the banks, smoking cigarettes and drinking beer.

"I know those guys," Errol whispered.

"Yes," Aster replied. "I do too. We went to the same school, remember? We can't let them see us. Let's stay in the trees until we're farther downstream."

"Right," Errol said. But he didn't move. He was still watching the others. She realized one of them was Lisa, Errol's ex-girlfriend, and another was Bobby Strickland, who had been one of his best friends. She had never liked any of them, and they had been bad friends to Errol. She thought he had figured that out, so why was he hesitating? Was that yearning she saw in his expression? Was he going to go say goodbye, or something?

"Errol?" she whispered.

"Do you see her?" he asked.

"Who? Lisa?"

"Lisa?" he asked. "No. Veronica. See, standing on the falls?"

She turned back, concentrating. She whispered a Whimsy to see the unseen beneath her breath. But there was still nothing there.

"Oh, God," Errol murmured. His breath caught.

"What?"

"He killed her," he said. "Right there. He cut her throat . . ." he started forward, but she caught his arm.

"Errol, no. I don't see anything. And you know that happened thirty years ago."

"Yeah," he said. "I know. I just—" He wiped at the tears on his cheeks. "Wow, I'm so sick of crying."

"Come on," she said. "Let's get out of here."

They made their way through the denser growth below the falls, and after a hundred yards or so cut back down to the banks for the creek. They could still hear the kids back at the falls, but now they were out of sight of them.

"She looked so young," he said. "So happy. And then—she didn't know what was happening. She couldn't believe it. She trusted that guy."

"She told us all about this," Errol. "After she remembered."

"I know," he said. "But hearing about and seeing it are two different things. No wonder she became a *nov* and killed all of those men. And now, she's . . ." he trailed off. "There must be something I can do," he said. "Wherever she is, whatever she's become, there must still be a way to save her."

"I don't think she wants saving, Errol. I think she's way past that." She reached over and took his hand. He looked over at her startled. Like the first time, when they had been searching for Veronica.

"We need to be in contact, remember?" she said. "So when one of us sees the way through, we both go."

"Right," he said. "Sure."

They kept walking, another hundred feet, then another. Nothing felt different.

Errol bent and picked up an empty candy wrapper. "This isn't right," he said. "Last time we were through by now. I remember it started getting weird at that white oak back there."

"The in-between ebbs and flows, like a tide," Aster said. "The tide may be out right now. Just keep going."

They kept going, following the creek.

She had been avoiding thinking about Billy, because it was pointless to do so. But she wondered where he was, what he was seeing with those strange eyes. If any part of him remembered her, and if so, how a giant would remember such a small thing.

I could call him back, she thought. She had done it before, accidentally. She could do it again, if she wanted, especially if she were in one of the higher places they had traveled through. But as much as she longed for him, she was starting to understand how selfish she had been. The proper question wasn't whether she *could* bring him back but if she *should*.

Anyway, there was no point in Billy returning just so she could see him die. Let him perish on his own terms, where he belonged.

Errol stopped, and she realized she hadn't been paying attention. Ahead of them, the creek passed under a concrete bridge.

"Denkin's Road," Errol said. "We walked clear through."

"I don't think it's here anymore, Errol," Aster said.

Errol let go of her hand. "Well, we'll try someplace else," he said. "The Mall. Or —"

"I mean the Pale itself," she said. "It's either gone, or we're cut off from it. It could be the Reign is trying to break away from the rest of the universe in order to survive."

"Can it do that?"

"It can try. I don't think it will work."

"So we're screwed," he said.

She shrugged. "We can try someplace else, to be sure." It was something to do. Something to keep Errol busy.

Errol sighed and sat down on the moss-covered root of an oak tree.

"Maybe we should go back to the falls," he said. "I saw her, Aster. Maybe that means something."

"I think that's a bad idea," Aster said.

"Why? Because those guys are there? After all we've been through, you think I'm afraid of them?"

"No," she said. "But we're wanted by the police. If they report us . . ."

"There's not a phone for miles," he said. "How are they going to report us? Anyway, you can just do some of your juju on them."

"I suppose," she said, reluctantly.

A car went by on the bridge, the sound of its passage dwindling with distance until all was quiet again.

"Hang on," Errol said. "If the Pale is gone—if we're totally cut off from the Kingdoms, the High and Faraway—how are you able to do magic at all?"

She cocked her head. It was a good question.

"I guess I use the elumiris I carry with me," she said.

"But doesn't that come from over there?" Errol said. "Past the Pale? If the line has been cut—if you're unplugged—you shouldn't be able to do anything."

"That might be true," she conceded.

"Okay," he said. "Hear me out. There's another thing. That place, the Under. It's all the bad stuff that was in the original sacrifice, right? The Bad Soul. The part that resents being killed and torn up to make the world. But the Twins, they also said its where the souls of the dead go."

"Yes," she said. That had been bothering her too, like a little itch in the back of her head. Another thing she hadn't considered it worth thinking too hard about, given the circumstances.

But Errol had been thinking about it, hard, and he was visibly excited. He picked up a twig and started fiddling with it as he spoke.

"So the way I understood it," he went on, "What I was told — is that if you die in the Kingdoms, you get reincarnated someplace else depending on how much of this elumiris stuff you have when you die. If you shine brighter than when you were born, you end up higher and farther away. But if you shine less, you're born lower and lower down, until you end up *here*, which is the end of the line. If you die here, your soul just goes away."

"Essentially, yes," Aster said.

"So then who is in the Under?" he demanded. "All those dead souls. Where do they come from?"

"Rebirth has ended in the Kingdoms," she said. "The enemy is keeping those souls for itself, the way Mr. Watkins did. It eats them up, collects them."

"Yeah," he said, flicking the twig into the stream. "But in theory, that just started happening."

She watched the stick float downstream.

"You must have gathered by now how differently time works in the Highest Kingdoms than in the lower ones," she said. "The Twins talk of the events that started the curse as if they happened recently, as if creation didn't happen that long ago. But where I'm from, thousands and thousands of years has passed, and it took most of that time for the curse to trickle down to us. Here, it's been more like fourteen *billion* years."

"Exactly," he said. "So when we were with the Twins, it was also sort of like being back in time. So again, if souls just started going missing in the lower kingdoms like, last week, where did all of those ghosts in the Under come from? Who was Fire Thief harassing on the way to Hades in those stories of his? There's something screwy going on. Something no one is telling us."

Now she saw where he was going with this.

"Or something that no one knows," Aster said. "Errol, you're brilliant."

"Even a blind squirrel finds a nut once in a while," he said.

FOUR

UNDER

The First assault on the Moon took place almost immediately. Delia slept through it, learning of it only later from Dusk, who described several chimeric creatures trying to come over the edge. As she told it, the attackers hadn't been that hard to beat back; the living presence of the Moon attenuated their connection to the enemy and made them easier to kill. That didn't stop them from trying again, and again, but each time Dusk, First, and Fire Thief sent them packing.

Delia measured the days by the rising and subsiding of the pool in the Moon, but she didn't bother to count them; her body was her timepiece now, measuring at a slower tempo. The life in her swelled; the baby began to kick in earnest. At times she was quietly overjoyed, but then she would look over the edge of her refuge at the world below, and despair. A new life was coming, but what did she have to offer it? They had failed. The Universe was ending, and there could be no place for an infant in what was going to replace it.

Since her arrival here, the land below had been slowly breaking up, rising, swirling, forming into clouds. In those clouds she saw the stuff of nightmares, and eventually could no longer bear to look.

One day she watched Dusk, First, and Fire Thief leap beyond the rim. Flashes of lightning lit the sky, and the thunder was almost deafening. The Twins had said Dusk was becoming a thunder, but to Delia it seemed she was no longer in process. She could fly, draw lightning from the sky, kill monsters with a single blow of her weapon. Fire Thief had taken to calling her "Striker."

She watched the colors in the sky but did not go to the rim to witness whatever horrors the three of them were slaying. In time, the sounds of battle receded, the bright flashes of light became fewer and finally stopped, and all was quiet once again. Dusk and the others appeared on the rim. Fire Thief and First went to their watch-places at either end of the Moon, But Dusk made her way down the slope and sat across from Delia. Electricity still flickered in her eyes and ran in sparks along her arms.

"Are you okay?" Dusk asked.

"Yes," Delia said. "Thanks to the three of you."

"It's really more them," Dusk said, nodding at the landscape. "And the one you carry in you. Without that, we would be long dead."

"Moon is dying," Delia said. "He draws strength from my child, but it isn't enough. I can feel him slipping away, and when he is gone . . ." she sighed.

"It all ends," Dusk finished. She frowned. "I want to tell you about a dream I had."

"Go on," Delia said.

"I was someone else. A man. A thunder. I was angry and full of wrath, because the Moon betrayed my sister, the Sun. And because of what he did with his own daughter. And because he killed her. He was a bad person, the Moon."

"I've gathered that," Delia said.

"So I hit him. Many times. I cut him to pieces, and although he kept putting himself back together, I eventually did so much damage that he could never fully heal. And that's when it happened. The curse." She dropped her head down. "I did this."

"Not you," Delia said. "Surely. You're taking that thunder's place, but you aren't him. You're just somehow coming into contact with his memories."

"No," she said. "I'm *remembering*. I'm part of him, a shadow of him, just as Aster is a shadow of the Dawn. Anger, wrath, revenge—that *is* me. That is what I'm made of. Errol, Aster, Billy, Veronica—those are the only friends I have ever truly had, and I hurt all of them. And in the cave, my fury doomed us all. And *that* cannot be laid at the feet of that what you call the 'other' thunder. That was me. I am responsible."

"I don't accept that," Delia said. "You couldn't have known. You saw a monster, a threat, and you dealt with it. Besides, assigning blame at this point . . . what's the use of that?"

"None, I suppose," Dusk said. "But I thought you should know." She put her head down and was quiet for a moment.

"You have changed since I've known you," Delia said. "I don't mean the lightning and all of that. At the Island of the Othersun you did the right thing, defended your friends, even though you had to go against your family and it nearly cost you your life. And I can see that you care for Errol."

"I love him," Dusk said. "I never thought I would be able to say that about anyone. To know I will never see him again is awful. If I could see him again, if only to die with him . . ." She shook her head. "I've spent most of my life fighting, and for nothing. In the end, I have made no difference, gained nothing of lasting value."

"But you still fight," Delia said.

"Because it's my nature," Dusk returned.

"No," Delia said. "It's because you're like me. Despite it all, despite all of our failures, you still have hope."

***

Much had changed since Delia arrived on the Moon. Distant mountains had fallen, vast gaps had opened in the Earth, and the Moon himself had grown weaker, the in-and-out of his tides smaller. But the stars, strange as they were to her, had remained constant, one source of the hope that she had spoken to Dusk of.

But that, too, was changing.

They had begun vanishing, starting with the lowest ones she could see, just over the rim of the Moon. At first, she thought that was due to the dissipation of the Earth, the clouds that formed, coalesced, and broke apart. And she continued to hope that accounted for most of the stars she could no longer see. But she saw at least one of them just — go out. She was watching it, a red star in the constellation she had named the Mailbox, when it suddenly wasn't there anymore. The other points of light around it remained, so she was certain it had not just been obscured. It was simply gone.

It wasn't long after that that she had a visitor — the wooden puppet body the enemy had been using lately. It stood on a chunk of stone floating above the rim of the Moon. He was small with distance, but his voice was as loud as if he were standing next to her.

"Delia," he said.

She looked around, wondering where her protectors were.

"I'm not here to fight," he said. "That's why they aren't here. You're safe from me."

"You sound like David Watkins," she said. "That's not going to sway me. I know what he was. Looking back on it, I should have always known."

"David was just a body," the apparition said. "And that which animated him was just a fraction of what I am now."

"That 'fraction' was a rapist and a murderer," Delia said. "Whatever you are, you must be a thousand times worse."

"I haven't come here to argue about my nature," the puppet said.

"You told me two reasons why you aren't here," Delia said. "Why not stop wasting my time and tell me why you *are*?"

"Very well," The enemy said. "You must know by now that your cause is hopeless. Your continued resistance is brave but destined to fail. Still, I am impatient to finish what I began, and you are holding me up. So I offer you this; I can send you home."

"You mean back to Sowashee?" she said. "The Reign of the Departed? What good will that do? You're going to destroy that as well, aren't you?"

"The Reign of the Departed served as a prison for many of my fragments. I suspect it was created for that purpose. In a place lacking elumiris, there was no easy way to return to this, the true creation. But the consequence of that is that once I am whole, your home will not be a part of what is to come. It will remain a dull and lusterless place, but you will be able to survive there. As will your child. Here, you are both doomed."

Delia felt her breath grow a little short. Until now, she had never been able to imagine her child as something outside of her, and she realized with horror that she had never really expected it to happen. Back home she would have been seeing an obstetrician, going to birthing classes, buying cribs and car seats, and painting the baby room. All of the usual signals that the pregnancy was progressing and would have an endpoint. But here, with no real time, moving from one threatening situation to another, pregnancy had not felt like a process, but more like a condition. And when the condition ended, it would be not be in birth, but in oblivion, as she and her child perished together.

But now images crowded into her mind, of her pushing her daughter on the swing set in Threefoot Park, riding the carousel there, walking on the dirt road she'd grown up on, showing the girl how to make play animals out of maypops and twigs. The monster in front of her might not think much of her world, but there was beauty in it, and goodness. It wasn't a bad place to raise a child. Especially *this* child. Despite what Aster had opined, she knew she couldn't be sure that the baby wouldn't be some sort of monster. And if not a monster, nevertheless linked to some strange destiny involving this dying Moon. Back home, with no magic and no destiny, maybe they both could start with a clean slate.

It was an appealing thought.

"I'll give you this," Delia said. "You're saying what I want to hear. You *have* got me pegged. And if I believed you, I would agree in an instant. But I don't. I don't think you want me to leave here because I'm an inconvenience. I think you are afraid of me, or of my child, or both. I don't think you want us out of the way, I think you want us dead, or in your power. And I know you lied to me, just now. When this world is destroyed, mine will be too."

"You don't know that," the Enemy said.

"I do," she said. "I'm sure of it. I would bet anything on it. And I'm going to."

For a moment, the Enemy didn't answer.

"When your time comes," he finally said, "I won't make it easy. The child you carry within you will go first, and you will watch it happen. And then I will spend years murdering you."

"I know," she said. "Because you are vile and vicious and petty. That is the other reason I know I will never make it home alive if I take your deal. And I'm done talking to you now."

***

E rrol and Aster waited until it was almost dark to go back to the falls. By then the kids had all cleared out. He looked around, taking it all in, remembering times here both good and bad. Never knowing what had happened in this place, so many years ago. That he would be linked to it by the murder of someone he loved.

He looked for Veronica and her killer again, but no apparitions appeared. He was beginning to doubt that he had really seen anything at all. Maybe he just wanted to.

"What do we think?" he asked.

"Find the spot Veronica was standing on," Aster said. "Can you remember?"

He took a deep breath and let it out. "I think so."

They climbed up around the side of the hill until they were above the falls. Then he walked down to the little rocky shelf that protruded out above them. He remembered diving from this spot into the pool. In retrospect, it had not been the smartest thing to do. There had been a good bit of rain in the days before, so the creek was high. Even so, he'd hit the bottom with enough force to hurt his arms. If it had been a little shallower, he would have broken his neck. From then on, he had always jumped in feet first, which was only slightly less dumb. But he also remembered he hadn't really cared.

How long had he wanted to kill himself before he actually tried it? The way he remembered it had been an impulse brought on by alcohol and drugs, not something he deep down wanted to do. But now he was starting to remember things differently. It had been such a long, bleak year. He had spent a lot of it in his bed, ignoring the phone when his friends tried to call. He'd felt tired all of the time, partly because he couldn't sleep. And he had done stupid things. A lot of them.

He was tired now, too. Was he slipping into the same trap? Not understanding what was going on inside his head? Had his death wish come back? Had it ever really been gone? He thought it had, but now he wasn't sure what to think. Depression was so sneaky, it could disguise itself as almost anything, couldn't it?

He felt a slight tingle in his toes.

"I think this is it," he said.

Aster moved to stand by him. She took his hand.

"Are you ready for this?" she asked.

"I think so."

"Even if it works, I don't know what to expect," she said. "We might be wrong."

"We aren't," Errol said. "We can't be."

Aster nodded, tightened her grip on is hand.

"*Asmidi salyas*," she said.

Everything went still; Errol didn't hear anything but the rushing of the falls.

He felt something touch his foot. Looking down, he saw the creek was starting to overflow its banks. More and more water poured over the falls, but more was also building up around them, somehow. The stream covered his shoes and rose past his ankles to his calves.

And then the stone beneath his feet was gone, and he was falling. Water covered his head, and he sank like a stone. It was dark, very dark, but he could still feel Aster's hand in his. His lungs begun to ache, and then to burn. He tried to keep steady, to push down the panic that was starting. Had he just found another way to kill himself?

But then they came up out of the water, and air filled his lungs. And they were no longer at the falls.

He and Aster stood at the edge of a river. The water was visibly receding, as if here, too, there had been a flood.

"Are we here?" he asked.

"We're somewhere," Aster answered.

It was no longer dark. A faint radiance permeated everything, but was concentrated nowhere, as if the air itself gave off light. They were in a hollow space about a hundred feet in diameter, but they weren't enclosed in earth or stone, as they had been in Dawn's tomb. Instead they were surrounded by living vines, knitted together like a nest. Large, funnel-shaped flowers bloomed from the vines, some white, some purple, a few orange. The floor was of the same stuff. The river flowed out of one wall and though another. A few yards away the vines rose up in a roughly box-shaped mound. On the front of it was a very ordinary looking wooden door.

"What do we do now?" Errol asked.

"Knock, I suppose," Aster answered.

Errol took a breath, walked over, and did just that.

After a moment, the door cracked open. It was dark inside, and he couldn't see who or what was in there.

"Errol," a voice whispered. "You may come in. Aster, please wait outside."

Then the door opened wider. Errol glanced back at Aster, then went in.

The door closed behind him, and the darkness was suddenly replaced by warm yellow light. As his eyes adjusted, he saw the source was a little desk lamp. Standing next to it, hand coming off the switch, was Veronica. She wore a yellow dress with a little black belt buckled at the waist. She had curled her hair. She stood barefoot next to a twin bed, which she then sat upon.

"Have a seat," she said, gesturing toward a little chair on his side of the room.

He did, looking around. It was small room, with old-fashioned pink floral wallpaper. A desk with a mirror sat near the bed, surrounded by pictures pinned to the wall behind it. Some looked like snapshots, others like pages pulled from magazines. A cylindrical stool sat in front of it, and a brush and comb lay on its surface. A few items of clothing were scattered on the floor, including a beat-up pair of tennis shoes. Nearer to him was a dresser with three drawers. On top of that sat a little record player and a pink Silvertone transistor radio.

"If had known you were coming, I would have straightened up," Veronica said.

"That's okay," he said. "You know I don't care about that kind of thing."

"How things look, you mean?"

"Yeah," he said.

She nodded, then winked at him. "So you figured it out," she said.

"I guess I did," Errol said. "For a long time, it seemed to me like something was missing. I kept being told that when people die in the Reign of the Departed, they just . . . go away. But they don't, do they? They come here. The whole thing used to be like a circle, didn't it? You might sink way down—all the way to down to our dull little world—but when you died there, you just went on around and started over."

"Yes," Veronica said. "The place where you and I were born is sort of the foyer to the Under. But the Under wasn't always here, or at least not like this. It was more of a halfway house, a place where souls rested a bit before being reborn. It wasn't until things got broken way up high, until the Dawn was murdered, and the Sun hid out, that the Itch started trapping the souls, bottling them up here. Using them like batteries or fuel to pull the world back into pieces and reform himself. And he's almost done."

"And all of those souls?" Errol asked.

"They were his in the beginning," she said. "He's just taking them back."

"That's like saying it's okay for somebody to eat their own kids."

"No, it's more like somebody having a severed finger sewn back on." She sighed. "I wish you weren't here."

"Why is that?" Errol asked. "I'm happy to see you."

"Because I wanted you to be safe," she replied.

"I wasn't safe there," he said. "You know that."

"I do now," she said. "But at least I wouldn't have to be there."

"Be there for what?"

"To see you die," she said.

He shrugged. "When I go, I'd rather be with my friends."

"We aren't friends, Errol," she said. "Not anymore. After what I did—after trying to save your life—the Raggedy Man, he finally got me. I'm part of that whole mess now. We're on opposite sides of things. Enemies."

The look in her eyes, the set of her body, everything about her in that instant frightened him. But he couldn't stop now.

"I know that," he said. "I knew before I came here." He swallowed, then gestured at the room. "So—is this how your room was, back when?"

"Pretty close," she said. "Don't try and distract me."

"I'm not trying to distract you. I've got no tricks up my sleeves. I just want to talk to you," he said. "Can I come over there?"

"Why?" she said. "Do you want to make out with me?"

"That's not what I meant," he said.

"You can say what you need to say from over there," she said.

"Okay," he said. "It's just this. You may think he controls you now, or you may not. Either way, I don't believe it. You don't back down, Veronica, or give up, or take shit from anyone. I know you can fight back against all of this. I know you can help us. Please, you have to at least try. I believe in you. And I love you."

She cocked her head and made a little face.

"You're right about the Raggedy Man," she said, after a long pause. "It isn't him. It's me. It is what I've become since I saw you last. You may have loved who I was, Errol, but you don't love what I am now."

"I do," he said.

"Really," she said. "Come here." She stood up. "Put your arms around me, Errol. Hold me close."

He got up and walked over to her. She kept her gaze steady on his; he read the expression on her face as both skepticism and resignation. Then they were close, their eyes inches apart.

And he embraced her. Only then did he smell the stench of rotten meat. Her back felt wet, lumpy, and something was . . . squirming there.

"What?" he gasped, releasing her.

She pushed him back. He looked at his hands and arms, which were covered in some sort of goo.

"I still look pretty from the front," she said. "But guess what."

She turned around.

The dress scooped down in the back, so he could now see what he had felt — the yellow bones of her spine protruding through blackened, worm-infested flesh.

Dazed, he took a step back, trying not to vomit.

"Oh, my God," he said.

"You see?" Veronica said. "Now you see. How about a roll in the hay, lover boy? Are you still up for that?"

"Veronica, what . . ."

"Goodbye, Errol. I'll leave the way back open for a bit. Just step back into the river. But you shouldn't linger. And don't return here."

FIVE

VERONICA

And then Errol was standing outside, next to Aster. Aster jumped a little at his sudden appearance.

"Errol?" she said it as if she doubted it was him.

"Yes," he said. "It's still me."

"And is she still . . . Veronica?"

He nodded.

"What did she say?" Aster said.

He held his hands up, staring at the sheen of corruption on them.

"She's not going to help," he said.

***

Delia watched Dusk, First, and Fire Thief dance along the Moon's rim. The sound of thunder was nearly constant, but the dark shapes they were striking down seemed numberless.

Since her conversation with the Enemy, the attacks had been stepped up. A lot. And the protection the Moon was offering was diminishing; she could feel it, just as she could feel the child within her preparing for her own struggle.

This isn't it, she thought. *Not yet.*

Behind her, she heard a scrabbling sound. She knew instantly something had slipped through the defenses. Something had come for her. She grabbed the spear lying beside her and used it to push herself clumsily to her feet.

She saw it now, skittering toward her, something vaguely canine. It wasn't all that large, which was probably how it had snuck in.

Closer, it looked like a jackal or a large fox, mottled yellow and black, with rings on its tail. But when it opened its jaws, the teeth looked more like those of a shark, and the mouth gaped unnaturally wide.

"Stay back!" she shouted.

It didn't, of course. She tried to remember those few hours of training, back at the village. She set her stance, gripped the weapon. She remembered how the Twins had told her to draw her power from the earth.

She waited, trying to keep the spear tip aimed at the beast, but as it drew nearer, it stopped its charge and instead began a dance, circling her, changing direction. Dodging in and out.

Footwork. If she stood still, she remembered, she was an easier target. She had to move, too. She started shuffling, back and forth, jabbing when the animal was close, but careful not to overcommit. She was starting to feel a little more confident.

But then it was suddenly *faster*, dodging, coming in, and then leaping with blinding speed.

And then something leapt inside her, too, coming up through the soles of her feet, quickening everything in her. The jackal looked as if it was in slow motion, drifting toward her. She put the point if her spear in the hollow below its breast and braced the shaft against the ground.

Then everything snapped back the way it had been, and the beast screamed like no canine she had ever heard as the stone tip of the weapon sheared through its chest and exited through its spine. The spear directed the force of the blow into the stone.

The monster's eyes were a foot from hers, burning with fury for several more seconds before they went dull and lifeless.

She heard something else behind her and tried to pull the spear out of the corpse, but knew it was useless. She fumbled for her knife as she turned.

"It's me," Dusk said. She looked down at the carcass. "You did well. I'm sorry. There are so many of them now. It's becoming difficult."

"You're bleeding," Delia said.

Dusk acknowledge that with a nod. She had her fist thrust into her side, where blood was steadily leaking out.

"You need help," Delia said.

"I do not think it is a mortal injury," Dusk said. "I have become different. My wounds heal more quickly than they used to." She put her back against the stone and slid down to a sitting position.

"I need rest, though. I think we have beaten back this lot. They can only come when the Moon is darkest, and the water is lowest. But I worry another like this might have slipped through and is yet hiding. I will stay with you awhile, unless you object."

"No," Delia said. "I would feel safer."

She noticed First walking along the rim, moving slowly, as if stalking something. Water began trickling over the edges of the basin, into the pool.

Dusk gazed out over the water, her gaze a bit unfocused.

"Do you still have hope?" she asked.

"Yes," Delia answered.

"And that hope," Dusk said. "What is it?"

"To see my child born," Delia said. "To know she has some chance of survival. And you?"

"I hope only for a good death," Dusk said.

"What about Errol?" Delia said. "Don't you hope to see him again?"

"I wish to," Dusk said. "But a wish is not the same thing as hope. In the hope, there must be some element of the possible. I know I shall never see Errol again."

"He and Aster are still out there," Delia said. "Billy would have taken them somewhere safe. They might have already figured out what to do. They could be on their way back here."

"Yes, with an army of Billy's giant kindred," Dusk replied. "And we shall ride on their shoulders, and spill the blood of the sacrifice, wake the Sun from her prison in the underworld."

"Now you're making fun of me," Delia said.

"No, I'm not." Dusk said. "I'm tired, that's all."

"Stay there then," Delia said. "Keep me safe."

Dusk nodded and closed her eyes. They stayed closed.

For horrible moment, Delia thought she was dead. But then she perceived the slow rise and fall of her chest.

First came up so quietly Delia didn't notice him until he was there.

"She okay?" he asked.

"I don't know," she replied. "I hope so."

"Let's get this out of here," he said, nodding at the dead jackal. He wiggled the spear on through and held it up to examine it.

"The point made it through without breaking," he said. "That's good. Nice work."

"It's nothing compared to what you, Fire Thief, and Dusk do every day."

"Yeah, but that's why we're here," he said. He lifted up the dead beast.

"There, there, brother," he said. "You did what you had to do. No blame to you. Let's send you off now."

She watched him carry the body up the Moon's highest pinnacle. And he began to sing.

She liked it when he sang, even when it was sad, like this. It was a very human sound, but it also had hints of birdsong in it, of cicada's chirring, of frogs croaking in unison.

The water had risen enough for her to touch it, so she trailed her hand in it, then made a cup of her palm and drank. It tasted clean and minerally.

As she looked back up, she noticed something green. Something growing at the water's edge. She couldn't tell what it was yet—it was just a tendril, a sprout. But she almost cried at the sight of it. The pool had life in it: fish and mussels and snails. But since she had come here, this was the first green plant she had seen. That had to be a good sign, didn't it?

***

E rrol stopped at the river's edge, staring into the dark mirror.

"What is it?" Aster asked.

"You asked me if she's still Veronica," he said.

"You know what I meant. If she's part of the enemy now—"

"She is," he said. "She told me so. But I'm not sure that changes anything."

"Errol," Aster said, "It changes *everything*."

"No," he said. "We're not done here." He looked back at the door, hoping it would still be there. It was.

"Stay here," he said.

This time he did not knock; he just pushed the door open. Veronica was still standing by the bed. She wasn't facing the door directly, so he could see both sides of her.

"What is it, Errol?" she said.

"I need you to know something," he said. "You said I couldn't love what you are now. That's not true. I never knew you when you were a living girl. You've been dead or half-dead

the whole time I've known you. Now you're just a more perfect version of that. You aren't alive and you aren't dead. You're
both. You can drain the life out of a person, and you can heal
someone who is broken. Don't you think this where you've
been headed this whole time?"

"Don't lie," she said. "You're repelled by me."

"No," he said. "I was surprised, that's all. I wasn't expecting
it. But I'm not repelled, Veronica. It's just death. It's part of the
universe. Without death there isn't any life, and if there were,
there wouldn't be any meaning to it. And death, death can't
exist without life either."

"You're getting awfully philosophical, Errol."

"I'm not strong, Veronica," he said. "I've got no magical
powers. I'm not even very smart. The only thing I might be good
at is reminding people who they are. And *you* are Veronica Hale.
You are human, and a *nov*, cruel and kind, sweet and awful, all
of it. I've always known that, and I've always been okay with it.
Why wouldn't I be now?"

He had been walking closer to her as he talked.

"Errol, I don't need your approval," she said. "I don't need
anyone's approval."

"I know," he said. "I know you loved me, though. I think
you still do. But I was holding you back from your real potential, and eventually you had to move on. But *he's* holding you
back, too. Don't you see? The cycle of life and death is broken.
It's been broken for a long time. There's no balance. But you —
you *are* the balance. Shandor was right — you are a goddess. But
goddess of what? Not of whatever that guy has planned. You
know what you're meant to be. What you *want* to be. Why are
you letting *him* call the tune?"

He was close now, and slowly reached out his arms. She
let him, and he pulled her in for another embrace. He felt her

heartbeat, her breath on his chest. He felt the exposed bone on her back.

Veronica remained stiff for a few breaths, but then she relaxed, and put her cheek against his.

"You know what will happen to you, if we take this road?" Veronica whispered. "I have seen it."

"I know," he said. "And it's okay."

"It's not okay," she said. "I worked so hard to save you—"

"And that's over," he said gently. "I don't need saving any-more, any more than you do. You can't avoid this because of me, because of any one person. If you really love me just . . . let go." He smiled. "Hey, I'm friends with the goddess of death, and I think she'll treat me right."

"I'm not ready," Veronica said. "I might be everything you say, but I'm also really new at this. I'm new at everything. I was sixteen when I died, and part of me still is. What if I don't get it right?"

"Anything would be better than what's coming," Errol said. "But you'll get it right. And when you get out of line, I'll remind you of who you are."

He pulled back and saw she was crying.

"What do you want me to do?" she said.

"I'm not here to tell you that," he said. "I think you know what to do. I'm here to be with you. And Aster."

"Yes," she said. "Aster. She still has the cloak from the cave?"

"Yes."

"Okay," she said. "Then we'd better go. It won't take the Raggedy Man long to catch on."

***

A ster looked back at the door, feeling left out. Errol and Veronica had always been a train wreck. That was fine, so far as it went. Mostly not her business. But right now it sort of *was* her business. She had seen the stuff on Errol's arms, smelled the corruption. What was Veronica now? And how could he forget what she had done?

Because he was Errol.

The door opened, and she watched as they stepped out. Veronica looked — the same. Which meant nothing.

"Aster," Veronica said.

"Billy is gone," Aster said.

"I know," Veronica replied. "I'm sorry. I really am. But it was the only way I could think of to save the two of you."

"You did it to stop me from becoming Dawn," she snapped.

"It was already too late for that," Veronica said. "The Sun had already been swallowed up by the Under."

"I have no reason to believe you," Aster said.

"Aster —" Errol started.

"No, Errol," Veronica said. "She's right. There's no reason for either of you to trust me. But there is this: this is my place. I'm part of it now. If I wanted to kill you, if I wanted to make you part of the Itch like me — I could have done that the minute you set foot down here. I don't have any reason to lie, or trick you, or anything like that. When I tell you I'm going to help you, you might as well believe it. Because you are completely in my power."

When she said it, Aster felt the elumiris drain from her. She tried to speak, but she couldn't remember even the most minor Whimsy. But she could *see*. Veronica was glowing. Lines of force flowed around her, like a magnetic field, but vibrant on one side and weirdly colorless on the other.

"*Zhedye*," she whispered.

Then her vision faded, and she felt power rush back into her. She looked Veronica in the eye.

"Okay," she said. "I believe you. But I'm still not happy with you."

"I don't expect you to be," Veronica said.

She turned a little, and Aster realized Veronica was half cadaver. She tried to keep her face composed.

She remembered when they had first found Veronica, in the pool in the in-between. In appearance she had been a fifteen-year-old girl, but once the water of life stripped that illusion away, she had been revealed as a long-rotten corpse. Aster had watched as Veronica's organs appeared, flesh filled out on her bones, and skin finally grew around all of it. Like everything Aster thought she had accomplished, that also seemed to be becoming undone.

"So what is the plan?" Aster asked.

"We go to where the Sun is, you put on the feather cloak, and you sacrifice me," Errol said.

"I told you, Errol, I can't do that," she said.

"It has to be you, I think," Veronica said. "It's your job."

"Anyway," Errol said. "I might have an idea. We might be able to cheat this thing."

"How?" Aster asked.

"Yes," Veronica said. "I'm very intrigued by this too."

"The automaton," Errol said. "The Enemy has been wearing it, right?"

"I think it helps him focus his presence," Aster said. "Keeps the chaos he's creating from swallowing him up."

"Doesn't matter," Errol said. "The thing is this. What if you can put me in there? In the automaton? And then sacrifice *it*?"

"Oh, I see," Veronica said. "Then she could slip you back into your body."

"Exactly."

"Would that work?" Aster said.

"Who knows?" Errol replied. "If it doesn't, we can just move on to plan B."

"Where she actually kills you," Veronica said.

"Ah . . . yes."

They Veronica and Errol looked at Aster.

It could work, Aster thought. She could try. And if it came down to plan B . . . well, she would see if they got there.

"Okay," she said. "Let's go."

SIX

ERROL

"This way," Veronica said. Only she didn't move; or maybe they *all* moved, but without a sense of motion. The vines, the flowers, Veronica's 'house' all began to blur, the colors began slowly shifting, as if they were inside of a kaleidoscope.

When Aster's vision settled again, they were standing on a flat plain. There were no sun or stars or moon, no obvious sources of light, but although it was dark, it wasn't pitch black either, but instead was shades of grey, like something on a black-and-white television. She didn't see any trees or bushes, nothing living except the three of them.

As her eyes continued to adjust, she observed that the plain wasn't as featureless or flat as it appeared at first glance. In the far distance, something like a thunderhead was growing up from the horizon with alarming speed. She thought it looked something like a nuclear explosion.

In the other direction, the horizon was much closer, only a few yards away. She would think it was the edge of a cliff, except for the peculiar way it curved, as if she was on a very small planet.

"He's tearing everything up," Errol said.

She turned back to the more distant horizon. In a few seconds, the cloud or explosion or whatever it was had more than doubled in size. The earth was ripping itself apart to feed its rapidly increasing mass. It not only looked bigger, but closer.

"It's done," a voice said. He appeared in the same instant, standing directly in front of Aster, about twenty feet away. The automaton she had built, the prototype of the one that had housed Errol's soul.

"Back off, you," Veronica snapped.

"We had a deal," the Enemy told her.

"It was a crummy deal," Veronica replied. "I'm making a new one."

"You can be replaced," the automaton told her.

Veronica smiled. "So can you, Honey."

For a moment, all was still, except for the commotion on the horizon, which now filled a quarter of the sky.

"Do it, Aster," Veronica said, before she blurred, grew larger, became a copperhead longer than an anaconda and struck at the enemy. The automaton howled, and a swarm of hornets emerged from his gaping mouth. Most of them formed a cloud around serpent Veronica, but some of them came for Aster and Errol.

Aster pronounced a Recondite Utterance, intending to call a whirlwind to sweep the insects away. Instead, a smokey column of air struck down from the sky, smashed into both combatants, and yanked them up toward the otherwise featureless sky, taking the hornets along for the ride.

"Wow," Errol said.

Aster quickly bent and opened her backpack. She took out the feather cloak and pulled it over her shoulders. As before, she felt a sudden rush of blood through her body. The feathers took on a rosy hue, and Aster's skin began to shimmer with golden light.

Veronica, still in serpent form, tumbled back to Earth; the snake went hazy, flowed, shrank, and Veronica stood there once more. The enemy was nowhere to be seen.

"Where is it?" Errol said, turning about, boomerang in hand.

"Look out," Veronica shouted. "He's —"

Before she could finish, she shattered like glass.

"Veronica!" Errol cried, rushing toward her. But the fragments turned into smoke and blew away.

And then the Enemy was there, right in front of Aster, reaching for her throat with its wood-and-wire hand.

But Errol was there, too, banging it in the side of the head with his throwing club. The Enemy staggered back a couple of steps; Errol followed, whaling on it, shouting with each blow.

"You! Should! Not! Have! Done! That!"

He swung again, but then the automaton moved *fast*. It caught Errol's weapon arm with one hand and punched him in the gut with the other. For an eyeblink, Aster didn't know what she was seeing; something red coming out of Errol's back.

Then she realized it was the Enemy's fist.

She felt it as if the monster had hit *her*, like physical shock shuddering through her body. A scream stuck in her throat.

Errol attempted to punch the Enemy in the face with his free hand, but the blow fell short, and his arm dropped loosely to his side.

"Aster!" he gasped. "You know what you have to do. Do it!"

"Errol . . ?"

He twisted, so Aster could see his face. Blood foamed from his mouth.

"Please," he gasped.

Shock, horror, revulsion — everything Aster felt — suddenly collapsed into a bright core of fury.

She stood straight and pointed her finger.

"*Eishdi!*" she yelled.

***

I t was weird, Errol thought, how little it hurt. At first, he'd just believed he had simply been hit in the belly. He had to actually see the arm sticking all the way through him, the flood of blood, to understand what had happened, and even then it was hard to comprehend the reality. What he did know was that he was suddenly very weak, and the automaton was *strong*. He found himself looking into its face—not blank, as it had been carved, but transformed by the horror inside of it into a ghastly imitation of life.

What was Aster waiting for? His vison went grey at the edges.

And then he was standing, dizzy, in a body that wasn't his, staring into his own glassy, dead eyes. He gasped and let go, watched his bloody corpse collapse. Like the wound that had killed it, it did not seem real. Blood covered the murder weapon—his new arm.

What have you done? A voice shrieked in his head.

"I've got you, you asshole, that's what," Errol said.

He felt it in there with him, like the cold tight knot in your stomach before you vomit from food poisoning, the grief so strong you can't breathe, the anger so sharp it cuts you. And there wasn't a little of it, but continents of it, worlds of it, and he was just the tiniest tip of a mountain, a square inch of real estate surrounded by the enemy's territory.

That's right, the Enemy said. *You are nothing.*

"But it's *my* real estate," Errol said. "I'm the landlord. This body was made for me, not you. By my friend. To save my life. And you. Do not. Belong. Here."

But the Enemy knew that now. It was trying to get out, to withdraw, to disconnect from the automaton. Errol felt panic so acute he almost thought it was his.

"Yeah, you can't do that either, dumbass," he said.

I can heal your body. I can make you a god. I will do whatever you want.

"Don't worry," Errol said. "You're going to do exactly what I want. Aster?"

She was staring at him, tears running down her face.

"You've got no body to go back to," she said. "You're not just in a coma this time. You'll actually die."

He tried to take a breath, but the automaton had no lungs. His fear was rising, but he pressed it back down. He had to get through this.

"I know that," he said. "I knew all along it would come to this. I just said what I had to to get you here. It doesn't matter. I'm willing. Aster, he's too strong. In a few minutes he is going to win. And I'll be dead anyway. You put this body together. Take it apart."

The earth shook constantly now. A glance back showed that half of the world was coming at them in a towering mass. And it was *fast*. Even if he managed to hold on for another few seconds, they were both going to be crushed.

"I can't let you go Errol," Aster said.

He reached out to her and placed the wood-and-wire hands on her shoulders.

"You're my friend, Aster," he said. "My best friend. For me, for everyone—please."

She closed her eyes, and his spirits sagged. But when she opened them, they were like flint. There she was, as he had seen her the first time he awoke in his own automaton. Aster Kostyena, who did not flinch, who did what needed doing, no matter what.

"If you see Dusk again," he said, "tell her I said goodbye."

"I will," she said.

The sky was falling on them.

"It has to be now," he said.

"I know," she replied. "Goodbye, Errol."

***

"This is the last battle," Dusk said, studying the sky.

"I know," Delia gasped.

"Are you okay?"

"I'm fine," Delia said. "I'm just giving birth, that's all."

"You're *what*?"

"That's why they're coming," Delia said. "This is what they've been trying to stop from happening."

"Why?"

"I've no idea," Delia said, then groaned as she had another contraction.

"I should stay with you, then?" Dusk asked.

"God, no," Delia said. "Keep them away from me. Until she is born. Please."

Dusk stood and gripped her spear.

"I will. I swear to you, your child will be born. But after that . . ."

"After that, we'll see," Delia said. "One thing at a time, right?"

Dusk nodded and then ran to join First in the fight.

The Moon had been fading fast in the last few cycles. He was staying dark longer, his internal tides had practically ground to a halt. Like a failing heartbeat, going slower and slower. And when it stopped, nothing would deter the demons out there from reaching her. And she had no doubt what would happen then.

She bit her lip as another contraction wracked her with pain. She didn't know anything about giving birth. She didn't know how far apart the contractions were supposed to be, or anything of the sort. Her only experience in the subject came from television and books, and she hadn't bothered to memorize the details. She had figured if she ever did get pregnant, she would have plenty of time and resources to get it all together before reaching this point.

But mothers and babies had been doing this for a long time, she told herself. How hard could it be?

Pretty damn hard, as it turned out. And mothers and babies had also been dying in labor for a long time, too.

"We're going to do this," she said. "We're going to."

Lightning flashed, filling the whole sky, and the thunder went on as if it would never end. She watched Dusk and First up on the rim; they looked like dancers, the way they moved, but with each motion they sent dark things flying. Fire Thief was on the other rim. He was a dragon, a tornado, an inferno, a giant raven. Dusk had told her earlier that the creatures couldn't come over just anywhere; there were certain points, like cracks, they could slip through. But as the Moon weakened, there were more cracks. That was how the jackal had gotten in. So besides giving birth, she had to keep an eye out for anything that might need spearing.

She was in the middle of another contraction when it happened; something burst over an unguarded section of the rim. It wasn't a jackal this time, but gargantuan cat of some sort. The fur on its head and shoulders was black, but the body grew lighter, and was spotted like a leopard or jaguar.

She gripped her spear, but she knew that it wasn't going to be any use. Not against this. And there was nowhere to hide.

Gripping the weapon so hard her knuckles were white, she scooted away from it, trying to get her back against the wall, but it was too far. As it began to full-on run at her, she pushed herself to her feet. Maybe if she could run up closer to Dusk and First.

"Help!" she yelped.

Her legs wobbled. She looked over her shoulder and saw it, right there. She tried to sidestep it but instead slipped and fell into the pool. She felt one paw hit her, and then she was underwater, and an instant later, the big cat hit the surface above her.

Even underwater she heard it scream. She kicked away from it, further into the pool, and surfaced. She didn't have a plan except to keep moving away from it . . .

But when then she saw it was floating on its side, steam rising from it, its baleful eye bereft of life.

The water killed it, she thought. Why?

Because it was where the last of Moon's strength was. And more things were slipping past her protectors now. The walls were crumbling. She had to stay in the water.

But could she give birth in the water? Would the baby drown? But people did that, didn't they? She had heard of that. It was surrounded by fluid already. All she had to do was get it into the air before it started breathing. What if she passed out?

But like everything else about this situation, she had no answers.

SEVEN

ASTER

The automaton broke apart at Aster's word, and the life went out of it in the same instant. She felt Errol go. For a heartbeat she knew boundless grief and remorse.

And then her heart beat once more; it rang like a gong, and she began to rise.

She was joy, she was lust, she was beauty, she was *time*. She was fire and sex, blood, birth, youth, old age, death. She was waking up from a long, lazy nap. Her cloak unfolded, expanded, raised up like wings, glowing, gold and coral and red, the red of blood, of sacrifice — of birth. She laughed, and broke from earth, broke from her body. She shimmered across the line of the world behind her. And then she advanced.

A wind blew before her. The monstrous thing of rock and smoke and darkness fell apart, crumbling into its own foundations, pierced and broken by rays of light. The plain collapsed, falling into the contours of hills, riverbeds, coasts. She grew longer, wider; the world continued to wake before her. Trees and grass pushed up from the bare earth; flocks of birds appeared in mid-flight. And now, behind her, she could feel another light rising. It was all wonder; it was all ecstasy.

And she felt the person who had been known as Aster Kostyena begin to die.

***

D elia watched as the edges of the Moon crumbled, cracked, and whirled into the maelstrom beyond. Overwhelmed, Dusk and First retreated into the pool with her, followed quickly by Fire Thief. Monsters poured over the broken rim but stopped at the water's edge.

That wouldn't last long, she could see. When the fractures reached the pool, it would empty, and them along with it.

"Oh, I see," said Fire Thief. "Keep at it."

She screamed and bore down. Dusk, bloodied from head to toe, took her hand. The water was only a few feet deep now.

"I'm sorry," Dusk said. "I wasn't able to keep my promise."

"It's . . . not over . . . yet," Delia gasped.

"Indeed," Fire Thief said.

And everything stopped. The monsters froze like statues. So did Dusk, the ripples on the water, the chaos in the sky.

Fire Thief swayed on his feet. He closed his eyes.

"I think you should push," he said. "Now."

Delia nodded, gathering her strength, bracing herself.

Fire Thief sat down in the shallows. As she watched, pieces of him began to drift away.

"What's happening to you?" she asked.

"I was hoping it wouldn't come to this," he said. "But this is all I have left in me." He laughed. "I did bring the fire," he said. "I did many things. I've loved, played tricks, talked monsters into killing themselves. I've lived beyond my age. What kept me here was you people, you mortals. Whatever I have done to you or for you, it was out of . . . well, vanity. But love, too."

"Stay with me," she pleaded. "Until she's born."

"I'll stay as long as I can," he said. "But it won't be long. Push. Push!"

And then she did. She didn't even try not to scream.

When her eyes cleared, only about half of Fire Thief was still there.

"One more, I think," he said. "Come on. It's time."

She bore down, panting, pushing with everything she had in her. Fire Thief smiled and pointed at the sky with his knuckle.

"There," he said.

She followed his gaze. A faint yellow glow lit the sky.

"What is it?" she said.

"They did it somehow," Fire Thief replied. "Somehow." He shook his head. "You people. Always surprising me."

Then Fire Thief slumped over and fell apart.

"No!" she said. "I'm not—"

Everything rushed back into motion. The water was draining away, quickly, and the dark things stalked nearer. First and Dusk climbed to their feet, lifting their shattered weapons.

"It was a good fight, First said. "And in good company."

"Yes," Dusk said, dim sparks flickering in her eyes. "It was an honor."

Then Delia pushed one more time, and as she screamed everything became light.

**

I t all became too big for Aster; she shrieked as Dawn pushed through her, out of her, leaving her a passenger inside of a goddess, no longer the bearer of her. A breeze came under her and bore her gently to the ground, where she collapsed, her body quivering, her skin hot, as if with fever. She turned east and watched, in awe, as the first sliver of the sun appeared, and Dawn flew on without her.

She sat on a stone, and she wept as the world kept rolling out, and life with it.

***

I n the darkness, a whippoorwill called, its plaintive, eerie voice near in the darkness. Errol kept still, listening to it. Further away, a screech owl sang, as if in answer. He remembered his father telling him the native Choctaw thought of both birds as sorcerers, harbingers of death or ill fortune, but he had always loved to hear them both as the sky faded and night came on. To him they had always seemed to be calling him to rest; they made the music that lulled him to sleep. Now they seemed more lovely than ever.

But soon, they stopped singing; it wasn't evening, but morning, and the darkness became grey. He now saw he was in a forest, surrounded by tree trunks rising up like the columns and buttresses of a cathedral. A thrush greeted the dawn with its high, sweet song. A mourning dove lilted its rising and falling cadence, robins began to twitter and trill. It was the dawn chorus, replacing the night one, and he had heard it many times. And he had been here before, too. In this very forest.

And as before, he saw a woman approaching, dressed all in white, with long locks of pale hair. He couldn't see her face yet, and as she approached him, she kept it averted, walking in a slow, gradually tightening circle.

"Son."

His father was there, standing a few feet away. He was as he remembered him, before he got sick.

"Is that really you?" Errol asked.

"I think I'm real," his father said. "I've been trapped in the dark so long, I guess I'm not sure."

"I saw you before," Errol said. "In a dream, I think."

"I know," his father said. "You weren't ready then. None of us were. But now things are moving again. Can't you feel it?"

"Am I dead, Dad?"

He shook his head. "Not quite. That's why we get to see each other. It won't be for long. I just wanted to tell you how proud I am of you. That I wish I could have been there for you."

"You were, Dad," he said. "You were always there. I always knew it. I knew you wouldn't just leave me."

"Never by choice," his father said. "We'll always belong to each other."

"I hope so," Errol said.

His father hugged him again, and it felt so real, so solid.

"I love you, son," he said.

"I love you, Dad."

And then he was gone, and the woman in white was there. He still could not see her face. But it was time.

"Okay," he said. "I'm ready."

She turned toward him then, and he saw her eyes.

"Hello, Errol," she said.

"Veronica," he said. "Was it always you?"

"No," she replied. "I'm the new, improved model. I think." She reached out her hand. "Thanks to you, probably. I could have gone another way. A really bad way."

He took her fingers in his.

"What now?" He asked.

"Well, Errol my darling, now you are officially dead. That's it for Errol Greyson."

"I figured," he said. "I was a little tired of that guy anyway."

"But *you* get to go again," Veronica said. "Like everyone else."

He nodded. "I know. But I'm still a little scared. If I don't remember you, or any of this—how is that different from dying?"

"That's the secret, Errol. Everything that ever was or will be is still here, right here in the center of things. You will always be you. And everyone else you are. "

"Okay, that makes my head hurt."

"Will it help if I take you myself?" she asked.

"Yes," he replied. "I'd like that."

"Okay," she said, squeezing his hand. "Then let's go."

***

When night fell, Aster hadn't moved from the rock. She was done with weeping, at least for the moment. She knew she ought to decide what to do next, but each time she approached the question, it felt as if there was no answer. They had won: Dawn had come, the Sun had risen. The universe was saved. And the quest that had driven her since she was ten years old was over.

But her quest and saving the universe had never been the same thing. *Her* quest—her real one—had been to restore her father to himself. But when she really examined it, Errol had been almost as important. She had watched him drift away, become self-destructive, growing up too fast. She had wanted to save him, too, and become his friend again. Her father was gone; Errol had died at her own hand. Billy, if he still existed, wasn't supposed to be with her. When it came to things that really mattered to her, she had failed utterly.

The Sun set, and the stars began to appear. She couldn't tell if they were the same as before, or if they, too, were new.

And then an orange sliver appeared in the east, and with silent majesty, the Moon rose. It was full, and round, and as it drew higher in the sky it shifted from copper to yellow to silver. It looked the same as she remembered, with its mares and plana. And for some reason, she felt the smallest of smiles on her face.

"You'll go up for a visit," a voice said, behind her.

"First," she said. "You survived."

"That I did," he said. "Nice work. I don't know how you pulled it off without Second to help out."

"I made a different sacrifice," she said.

"Oh," he said. "Errol."

"Yes."

He was silent for a moment. "Sorry about that. But it all went right, so he must have been willing."

"Errol always put others before himself," Aster said. "It was his nature." She pointed at the Moon. "What about him? Did he heal?"

"Her, you mean," First said. "No more Moon Man. Moon Woman, now."

She stared up at the orb as she absorbed that. "Delia's child," she said.

"Your sister," he said.

"And Delia?"

"She and Dusk are both up there. It's different now. Nice. The little girl is just a squirmer right now, but she will grow. I know they would like to see you."

No they wouldn't, she thought. Dusk didn't know about Errol yet, and Aster didn't want to be the one to tell her. She didn't have that much strength left. And her sister, her father's last legacy . . . no, she couldn't bear that either. Not right now, anyway.

"I don't think I will visit just now," she said. "Tell Delia I said congratulations. And tell Dusk Errol died well. Tell her he said that . . . he loved her, and to tell her goodbye."

"I'll do that," he said. "And what about you? What will you do now?"

And before she could open her mouth to say she didn't know, she realized she did.

"I want to go away," she said. "Away from people. Away from all of this. There's nothing here for me anymore."

First cocked his head. "You sure about that?" he asked. "You need a guide?"

"No," she said. "I was with Dawn. I saw everything. I can guide myself."

"Well, good travels then," First said. "And if you're ever back this way, come say hello."

"I don't think I will be," she said. "But thanks."

Aster watched First fly back up to the Moon. Then she began to walk.

EPILOGUE

The Brume sat cross-legged on the highest terrace of the Castle of the Winds, the one overlooking the apple orchard, watching the light of the rising sun slant long shadows from the trees. She puffed out a long breath of cold, damp air.

"The sun is back," she said.

"Don't pout," Mistral, her sister, said. "There will always be places moist and dark for you to enjoy."

"Of course," Brume said. "I'm not really sad. It means we aren't all going to die, like Haydevil said we would."

"To be fair to him," Mistral said, "that seemed inevitable yesterday."

"The longest yesterday ever," Brume said.

"Indeed," Mistral replied.

A wind blew, a wind with a familiar scent. It was warm, but oddly, that did not bother Brume. Until she noticed the apple trees. Their leaves all dropped and swirled in the wind, looking almost like a flight of starlings in murmuration.

"Oh, no," she said.

"What is it?" Mistral asked.

"The trees."

It hadn't stopped with the leaves; now the limbs shivered apart, and the trunks burst from within, and the shattered orchard lifted into the air.

"Mother!" Brume said. "What is happening to Mother?"

Mistral was silent, but she took her hand as Brume began to weep, her freezing tears blurring her vision. Then the warm wind was back, wrapping around her like a cloak.

"No need for that, my dearest," a voice said. "It's just that I've come out of things."

"Mother!" Mistral gasped.

Then the wind was solid, arms pulling her against someone.

Brume wiped her eyes, and saw her standing there, the most beautiful woman in the world. Just as she remembered her.

"Are you real, Mama?" she asked.

"Once again," her mother said. She wiped away her tears, and the three of them hugged.

"Where is Haydevil?" She asked.

"Downstairs, resting," Mistral said. "He was wounded in the fight."

"Come along then," Mother said. "Let us tend to him and wait for your father to return. His journey is longer than mine."

***

Four years after the Sun and Moon began turning again, Copper finally found her way through the baroque ways of the Kingdoms to the village of her birth. The castle lay in ruins, and much of the village had been razed. But people were there, building, trading, making. She hurried up the road that led into the country-side. It was spring, and the fields were fresh with green life—not like before, when it had been always autumn and always evening.

Her heart was beating hard in her chest. Not from exertion, for her travels had left her hard of sinew and ample in endurance. No, it was because she feared what she would or would not find.

The house had a newly thatched roof; the garden fence was in good repair, and a man with greying hair tended the garden. A dog she did not know barked, and the man glanced up at her.

For a moment their gazes looked.

"Who are you?" the man said.

"It's me, Da," she said. "Copper."

"Copper?"

He flung down the hoe and ran to her. She stood, rooted, still not believing it, even though she knew, even through she had seen with her own eyes the return of parents all across the kingdoms. But to see the man she only remembered as a stone statue running toward her, face wet with tears — she had never believed it would really happen.

Then he wrapped her up in a bear hug, and it was all real. He smelled like sweat and smoke and earth. He smelled great.

"You were gone so long," he said. "Your brothers thought you were dead."

"I wasn't gone as long as you were," she said.

He chuckled through his tears. "Sorry about that," he said. "In future, I'll try to do better. Come child, meet your mother."

***

After his swim in the creek, Brave pulled himself up onto the rocks and lay in the sunlight, enjoying the feel of it on his skin. He watched his father, a little downstream, spearing fish for the midday meal, and wished — as he often did — that he was old enough to help. He had a toy spear, but he had learned from experience it wouldn't do the job. When you have six winters, his father had told him. That was only a winter away.

A wind soughed through the willows. Vivid green dragonflies skimmed over the stream. Digger, the old white and yellow dog, made a strange sound in his sleep.

Brave saw someone was coming, walking along the stream. A woman, it looked like, but pale in color. She had white hair, like someone incredibly old. His father didn't seem to notice her at all, even though she walked within touching distance of him.

As she got closer, he saw that even though her hair was white, she was not old at all. In fact, she didn't look as old as his mother.

"Good Morning, Brave," she said, when she got close. Her mantle was pretty, half black and half white.

"Who are you?" he asked.

"I'm a traveler," she said. "I've come a long way to see you."

"Why?"

She shrugged. "Because I wanted to," she said.

"Are you a spirit?" he asked. "My father didn't see you. And you are so pale, like a cloud."

She nodded. "Yes, I'm a spirit. And I look over you, sometimes. Even before you were born, I looked over you."

Brave wasn't sure he believed her. But he liked the idea. She seemed nice.

"I can't stay long this time," she said. "But you may see me again from time to time. I just came to say hello, and to tell you about something I saw."

"What?" he asked.

"Giants," she said. "Far, far away, at the edge of the world, where the sea flows through caves bigger than you can imagine. Giants so tall their heads scrape the sky."

"Wow," Brave said, trying to imagine something like that. "What do they do?"

"They travel," she said. "They wade in the ocean and rest in the caves. They sing exceptionally long, slow songs only spirits can hear. And they are alone, always." She paused. "Except for one. I saw one that was not alone. He had a tiny person, perched on his shoulder. What do you think of that?"

Brave blinked, and in the brief darkness, he thought he could see it—the giant, and a small woman with a star on her forehead.

"That's a good story," Brave said.

The spirit brushed her hand across his head.

"I thought you would like it," she replied. "There is more to this world than you can ever imagine, Brave." Then she kissed his head and continued walking along the creek. He watched her until she vanished from sight. Then he lay back down and thought of stars and giants and the adventures waiting for him. And he was happy.